Sheri WhiteFeather is an award-winning bestselling author. She lives in Southern California and enjoys shopping in vintage stores and visiting art galleries and museums. She is known for incorporating Native American elements into her books and has two grown children who are tribally enrolled members of the Muscogee Creek Nation. Visit her website at www.sheriwhitefeather.com

USA TODAY bestselling author **Janice Maynard** loved books and writing even as a child. After multiple rejections, she finally sold her first manuscript! Since then, she has written fifty-plus books and novellas. Janice lives in Tennessee with her husband, Charles. They love hiking, travelling and family time.

You can connect with Janice at
janicemaynard.com
Twitter.com/janicemaynard
Facebook.com/janicemaynardreaderpage
Facebook.com/janicesmaynard
and Instagram.com/therealjanicemaynard

Also by Sheri WhiteFeather

Wrangling the Rich Rancher
Nashville Rebel
Nashville Secrets
Hot Nashville Nights

Also by Janice Maynard

Blame It On Christmas
A Contract Seduction
Bombshell for the Black Sheep
Too Texan to Tame
After Hours Seduction
Upstairs Downstairs Temptation

WILD NASHVILLE WAYS

SHERI WHITEFEATHER

SECRETS OF A PLAYBOY

JANICE MAYNARD

MILLS & BOON

First Published in Great Britain 2020
by Mills & Boon, an imprint of HarperCollinsPublishers,
1 London Bridge Street, London, SE1 9GF

ISBN: 978-0-263-27930-6

0720

MIX
Paper from responsible sources
FSC™ C007454

This book is produced from independently certified FSC™ paper to ensure responsible forest management.

For more information visit: www.harpercollins.co.uk/green

Printed and bound in Spain
by CPI, Barcelona

WILD NASHVILLE WAYS

SHERI WHITEFEATHER

One

Tracy

I answered the door, only to find Dash Smith, the hottest new country star on the planet, standing on my daddy's front porch.

"Hey, Tracy," he said, much too softly, as I just stood there and stared. He was as handsome as ever, with those expressive brown eyes, the rigid jaw, that slightly crooked, bend-a-woman-to-his-will mouth. I couldn't tell how his hair was styled beneath his baseball cap, but I was familiar with the inky black color.

He used to be my fiancé, back when both of us were struggling to make it. My damaged heart would argue that, somewhere inside the pain, I was still in love with Dash. That might be true. But that didn't mean I wanted anything to do with him.

"What are you doing here?" I hoped he hadn't tracked me down at my father's house to bug me about working with him. We broke up nearly six years ago, and I'd done my best to heal, focusing on my music and moving on to other lovers. Then just this year, during the height of his success, he'd started texting me from his world tour, prodding me to do a duet with him when he returned. Call me stubborn, but I wasn't going to make a record with my ex, no matter how badly my flagging career needed the boost. Besides, this was *not* the day to discuss it.

He frowned. "Didn't your dad tell you? I'm going with you to his surgery. I'm going to help afterward, too."

I clutched the doorknob, using it as an anchor. "No, he didn't say anything about you..." I shouldn't be surprised by Dash's involvement, though. He and Pop had remained friends throughout the years, texting and calling and seeing each other when they could. And now Pop was battling testicular cancer and would be having an orchiectomy this morning.

A faraway look came into Dash's eyes, and I suspected that he was thinking about his own father, who'd died from lung cancer a few years after our relationship ended. I'd attended the funeral, paying my respects and offering my condolences. I'd always loved his dad. Dash obviously adored mine, too.

With a lump forming in my throat, I glanced past him, taking inventory of the luxury SUV parked in the driveway. A broad-shouldered man sat behind the wheel. Considering how intently he watched us, he was probably a bodyguard doubling as a driver. Dash had grown up dirt-poor, and now he had millions of dollars and an army of people protecting him.

"Do you want to come in?" I asked. I couldn't go against my dad's wishes and block Dash from helping out. But damn, it hurt being this close to him again. His father's funeral was the last time we'd seen each other, apart from today. "Pop is still getting ready."

He followed me inside, leaving his driver in the car. "That's fine."

No, I thought, none of this was fine. Since Dash's recent rise to stardom, I'd become consumed with his fame, reading nearly every online article, concert review and gossip tidbit written about him. Sometimes I even checked to see if he had a girlfriend. He hadn't been linked to anyone, but he probably had enough groupies to keep him occupied.

During my short-lived brush with the limelight, groupies never chased me. A flutter of fans, yes. Hot men offering to fulfill my sexual whims… *I wish.*

For Dash, it was an entirely different story. His social media followers called themselves Dashers. Did his groupies have a cutesy little reference, too, for when they climbed into his bed to devour him? Maybe the Dine-and-Dashers?

He moved farther into the living room. "You did a nice job of fixing this place up."

"Thanks." I'd used some of the money I'd earned from my first album to help remodel the dusty old horse farm where I'd been raised. As for my own house, I was struggling to keep it afloat.

I wanted to revive my career, but not by riding Dash's coattails. A few gossip sites had named me as his long-ago fiancée, but no one seemed to care. Of course, if we did a duet, it might stir a deeper interest in our past. I had too many other issues to confront. Not just Pop's cancer and my financial problems, but things pertaining to my own health and the baby Dash and I should've had.

I put my hand against my stomach, remembering the ache associated with my miscarriage. The sadness. The loss.

"Are you okay?" he asked.

I blinked, realizing that I was spacing out in front of him. I lowered my hand. I couldn't tell him what I was thinking about. "It's just a lot to take in."

He roamed his gaze over me. "With your dad?"

"Yes." And everything else, too, I thought.

He shifted his stance, and I took a step back, not wanting to get too close. He stood tall and broodingly handsome. I was tall, too, and our bodies used to fit so perfectly together. But that wasn't something I should be remembering.

He said, "If you don't mind, I'd like for you and your dad to ride with me. I brought my best bodyguard along," he added, confirming who the man in the car was. "But some of my other security guys will be at the hospital, too. Mostly to keep the press at bay, in case they catch wind of me being there."

Good grief. I hadn't even considered the media. "What are you going to say if they do find out? Won't they wonder what you're doing at a cancer ward?"

"I'll just tell them the truth, that I accompanied a friend. But we're hoping to avoid that. The hospital is going to set aside a private waiting room for us. They already have a policy in place about celebrities and public figures. Their employees aren't allowed to ask for selfies or post anything on social media. If they do, they could lose their jobs. We can't do much about other patients or their friends or family, though. But my team has a plan in place that should eliminate me coming into contact with the public. We'll be doing everything we can to protect your dad's privacy, so you don't need to worry about that. I already discussed all of this with your pop."

Dash tucked the baseball cap lower on his head, and I assessed his ensemble. He wore indigo jeans and a pale-gray Western shirt, pricey sunglasses hooked in his front pocket. But even with the dark glasses and hat, he was still going to be recognizable. He'd become too famous not to notice. Every song on his debut album had been certified gold or higher, with some of them crossing over onto the pop charts.

"Are you sure my dad is okay with all of this?" I asked.

"He assured me that he was, but you can confirm it with him."

"I should probably check to see what's taking him so long, anyway." I also needed to get a grip on my emotions. How many years had I spent, wishing that Dash believed in love? He'd only asked me to marry him because of the baby, and that hurt as much now as it did back then.

I turned on my heel and walked down the narrow hallway, eager to get away from him. He'd admitted from the start that he thought love did more harm than good, and he wanted no part of it. I'd known that his feelings stemmed from his estranged mother and her abandonment of him and his dad, but I'd been foolish enough to think that I could fix what she'd broken.

I'd been motherless for a portion of my life, too. But mine hadn't run off. She died when I was in middle school, and Pop and I still missed her every day.

I knocked on his door, and he called out, "Come in!"

I inched my way inside and found him seated at his ancient rolltop desk. He was pulling on his boots.

With his graying hair and sun-weathered skin, he looked older than his fifty-nine years. He was a former rodeo cowboy, a bronc rider who'd never become as successful as he'd hoped. Of course, he was a horse breeder, too. But he'd also worked as a short-order cook when I was young, doing whatever was necessary to keep me in ribbons and bows, however tattered. As hard as he'd tried, we'd still been poor. But nothing like Dash. When he was a kid, they'd lived in a run-down trailer, going to food banks and collecting welfare in between his daddy's sporadic day jobs and music gigs.

"Is Dash here?" Pop asked.

"Yes." Only I needed to know what the deal was. "I don't understand why you asked him to do this."

"I didn't ask. He offered."

"To do what, exactly?"

"To keep you company at the hospital and to help with my recovery once I come back home, too. I thought it would be easier to have a man around, in case I get grossed out trying to change the bandages myself. It's not a good idea for you to do, either. That's just too personal for me."

As far as I knew, my father wasn't a squeamish guy. I'd seen him cut and bruised and climbing back in the saddle during his rodeo days. But maybe this was different. Or maybe he was making excuses.

I cautiously said, "I understand and accept that you

and Dash have done your best to remain friends and keep in touch. But we could've talked to one of your old bronc riding buddies about coming by to help you with the bandages. It didn't have to be Dash."

"I know, but I thought having him around might benefit you, too." He finished putting on his boots. "That it might sway you into doing that duet with him. Honestly, hon, why not let him help you get your career back on track?"

"I appreciate you trying to look after me, but I'd rather make a comeback on my own."

"Yeah, but I hate seeing how hard you work. You shouldn't have to bust your butt, balancing two jobs and trying to sell your songs yourself. Not when Dash is at your disposal. You need to take advantage of his fame."

I heaved a sigh. Pop didn't know that I was going through a personal crisis and that being around Dash was going to make it more difficult for me. And I didn't plan to tell him, either.

He said, "I'm sorry if I blindsided you by inviting Dash to come with us. But I think it would be nice for you to become friends again. I don't remember you ever fighting or trashing each other, not even when you broke up."

Yes, we'd parted amicably. After my miscarriage, I'd made the agonizing decision to end our engagement, and Dash hadn't tried to stop me. He'd just let me go, the desolation of our lost child drifting between us.

But I couldn't obsess about that now. "Let's just work on getting you well, Pop." My ailing father was my priority. And if that meant spending time with Dash to give my father peace of mind, then that was what I would do.

* * *

Dash's driver/bodyguard, a big stoic dude named Zeke, kept the motor running as we pulled up to a side entrance reserved for hospital personnel. Another of Dash's security guys was waiting for us there.

Zeke used a magnetic key card to unlock the door and usher us inside, while the other security guy parked the car. We made it into the building without incident.

We separated from there, with me taking Pop to get him checked in and prepped for surgery. Once I was alone, I would meet Dash in the private waiting room. I was glad that he wasn't going to be with me every step of the way. It had been tough enough riding in the car with him, while he and my dad talked horses and music and everything except the fact that Dash and I used to be a couple. I suspected Zeke could tell how uncomfortable I was. Analyzing people was probably a significant part of his job.

After I got Pop settled in, I wandered over to a vending machine. I wondered what Dash would do if I waited in one of the open areas instead of joining him in the private room. Would he send Zeke off to look for me?

I scanned the items in the machine and chose a candy bar. I cursed and got Dash one, too. It used to be a favorite of his. I had no idea if he even ate sweets now.

All these years later, he'd become a stranger to me. Then again, he'd always been an enigma: a man who used to hold me tenderly in his arms, without setting much store by love.

I cleared my mind and got a third candy bar for Zeke. I'd been taught to be polite. Maybe too polite? I reminded myself that I was doing this for my daddy. I didn't want to create any bad mojo today.

The private waiting room wasn't hard to find. Zeke stood outside the door, blocking anyone else from entering. He looked like a stone wall, dressed in a dark suit.

As I approached him, I gave him a chocolate bar. He tucked it into his jacket pocket, his lips curling into an itty-bitty smile. But his reaction didn't make him any less intimidating. If I ever got famous enough to have security, I was going to want someone like him on my side.

My success had been nothing compared to Dash's. But for me, it had still been pretty amazing. I understood why my father wanted that for me again. But being in this situation was torture. I was nervous about being alone with Dash.

Zeke opened the door, summoning me to his boss. Dash definitely had all the power. Men often did, in my estimation. It wasn't supposed to be that way in this day and age, but I'd just gotten trapped in a male-dominated situation. Unfortunately, my father was partially to blame. If he hadn't helped orchestrate this reunion, I wouldn't be in such close quarters with my ex.

The room was small, the decor beige and bland and generic. The door snapped shut behind me, courtesy of the bodyguard.

Dash glanced up, and I sucked in my breath. I wanted to leave a chair between us, but I forged ahead and sat beside him, hating how easily he commanded my attention.

I extended the candy bar I got for him. "I don't know if you eat these anymore."

He accepted it. "My trainer had me on a strict diet and workout routine when I was on tour, but I can cheat a little now."

He did look exceptionally fit, but he'd always taken care of himself. When I'd first met him, he was stacking bales of hay at the feedstore where we both worked, and had arms and abs to die for. Eventually, we'd bonded over our musical aspirations. But in the beginning, I just wanted to get my hands on that rock-hard body.

Did I look the same to him, with my long brown hair, medium blue eyes and natural curves? Either way, I'd matured, and so had he. He'd turned thirty while he was on the road, and I would be twenty-eight next month.

"Do you want to share this?" He unwrapped the candy bar and offered me a bite.

"I have my own." I showed him the one I'd tucked into a side pouch of my purse. I removed it and joined him in the chocolate-and-nougat fest. "Did anyone approach you while I was gone?" I asked. "Or take your picture?"

He shook his head. "The corridor I used was blocked off, so I was the only one who had access to it." He gestured to a door on the other side of the room. "I came in that way. But it's locked now."

And Zeke was protecting the entrance I'd used. "Your team really had it figured out."

"It helped that the hospital was so accommodating. They're used to dealing with celebrities in this town. I'm not the first, and I won't be the last."

True, but at the moment, he was the prince of Nashville. Everyone wanted a piece of him. Before he got famous, I'd had my piece, night after night, naked in his bed. The memory left me hungering for sex. I hadn't been with anyone for at least six months. I doubted that Dash could make the same claim.

"What did they say about the surgery?" he asked,

interrupting my wayward thoughts. "Are they going to come get us when it's over and talk to you about it?"

"Yes. They'll also decide if Pop should stay here overnight or come home today or if he'll need chemo or radiation afterward." It all felt so up in the air.

"I'm sorry he's going through this. And that you have to deal with it, too. I know how much he means to you."

Yes, he knew. I was aware that he'd shared the same kind of closeness with his father, too. He'd even inherited his dad's musical abilities. Kenny Smith should've been a star like his son. But he'd never progressed beyond coffee bars and shoddy nightclub gigs.

"It's a shame your dad didn't get to see your success," I said. "He would've been so proud of you."

He nodded. "It's been bittersweet, climbing the charts without him."

"I wonder where your mom is and what she thinks of your celebrity status."

He scowled. "I have no idea, but I don't want to talk about her."

Clearly, it remained a sensitive subject. I couldn't blame him for that. And since she'd left her family for a tremendously wealthy man, maybe she didn't give a hoot about Dash's illustrious career.

But I certainly did. We used to daydream about winning Grammys and CMAs and every other accolade out there. Except he'd done it without me. He'd already collected all sorts of Best New Artist awards.

Was I being an idiot, turning down the duet? No, I thought. I was being strong and independent, refusing to put myself at the mercy of the man I used to love.

Or still loved. Or whatever.

My feelings for Dash never failed to confuse me. I could kiss him right now and probably melt girlishly in his lap. I finished my damned candy bar instead, eating the last few gooey bites.

He reached over and ran his thumb over the left corner of my lips, and I flinched something fierce.

"What are you doing?" I pulled away, afraid of how instantly aroused I got.

"You had a piece of chocolate..."

I rubbed the spot he'd touched. "Is it gone?"

"Yes. I already got it." He pressed his hands against his jeans. "I didn't mean to startle you."

We gazed uncomfortably at each other. I glanced away, hoping that he would start a new conversation. I couldn't think of a single thing to say. The awkward silence was deafening. Problem was, I sensed that he was feeling the sexual tension, too.

A few minutes passed before he said, "Your dad told me that you're working at the feedstore again, running the front counter like you used to."

Well, shoot, I thought. Not exactly a topic I wanted to discuss. But better than the carnal quiet, I supposed.

I replied, "It's just a few days a week to make some extra money. I work as a virtual assistant, too, for a company that hires VAs to schedule social media content for their clients."

"My management uses a service like that."

"A lot of companies do." My income as a VA sucked, though. The pay at the feedstore wasn't any better. To steer the talk away from me, I said, "I heard that you bought a mansion, out in the country somewhere."

"It's a great place. But I haven't spent much time there yet. It's been a whirlwind year, being on the road."

He hesitated. "You should come by sometime and let me show you around."

Oh, sure, like I was going to pop over and say hello. "Have you invited my dad to see it?"

"Not yet. But I'd just gotten off tour when he told me that he was sick. I could tell how glad he was when I offered to help. I think he's worried that if something happens to him, you'll be all alone."

My heart clenched. "I have friends, people I see."

"Yes, but he's also hoping that his illness will inspire you to work with me. He wants your career to take off again."

"He already told me how he feels about that." And I didn't need to hear Dash repeat it.

"What about following through on our idea from the past? Remember how we used to say that someday we would do a special song together?"

"I haven't forgotten. But that was a different time, a different place, a different life." And I couldn't do it, not even for my cancer-stricken dad.

Dash sat back in his chair, broody as ever. "Let me know if you change your mind."

I didn't respond. He'd just removed his hat to run his fingers through his hair, and now I was analyzing how beautifully the strands fell into place. He wore it short on the sides and longer on top, in a stylish undercut.

"Are you dating anyone?" he asked suddenly.

I squinted at him. Was he seriously inquiring about my love life? Just the question alone served as a reminder of how lonely I'd become, intensifying my current hardships.

I steeled my heart and said, "Not at the moment. But there's been lots of men since you." I wasn't lying about that. I'd played the field, even if I hadn't done it lately.

A muscle pulsed in his jaw. He seemed jealous, but it served him right. If he'd loved me, we'd still be together.

He tossed his hat aside. "I've scored a lot, too."

"Of course, you have. Groupies galore."

He rolled his eyes. "As if that matters, with the way you used to chase me at the feedstore."

I could've smacked that smug look right off his face. "That's not the same as you having groupies now. You weren't even famous then."

"You still wanted me."

"You wanted me, too," I shot back.

"We both wanted each other." He leaned toward me, his dark gaze boring into mine. "Maybe we should kiss and see if it still feels the same."

Everything inside me erupted: the past, the present, my uncertain future. "Really? And what would that solve?"

"Nothing, except I think it would leave us both clamoring for more, like it did back then."

"I could kiss you without wanting more." Earlier I'd imagined melting in his lap, but I wasn't feeling weak or soppy now. My body had gone taut, my breathing shallow, and my anger was roiling. "I can control myself around you."

"Oh yeah?" he snapped. "Then prove it."

Screw him, I thought, while I stared him down. We'd barely ever fought before. Little tiffs here and there, but never anything major. I'd always suppressed my temper. But I refused to do that now.

I grabbed his shoulders and put my face next to his,

nearly bumping his forehead with mine. It felt good to be mad, to let the pain come rushing out.

"Here's your proof," I murmured hotly against his mouth. I was going to kiss him as if the world was about to end, then *never*, *ever* do it again.

Two

Dash

Maximum velocity.

Tracy thrust her tongue into my mouth, and my heart slammed against my rib cage. She wasn't wasting a bit of time, and I relished the full-speed feeling.

She tasted of lust and anger and chocolate. A strange sort of eroticism. She'd kissed me all sorts of ways in the past, but never like this. I returned the favor, devouring her with my pent-up passion. I pulled her onto my lap, and she rubbed against my fly.

Was she punishing me for everything that had gone wrong between us? The hurt? The loss?

She moaned, and I steadied her on my lap. I was hard beneath my jeans, ridiculously aroused. Being punished by her felt painfully good.

When she pulled back, we both caught our breaths.

"Did you get enough?" she asked, still straddling me and making me ache.

"No." I feared that I would never get enough, not when it came to her. She'd always been my sexual ideal. She used to be my dearest friend, too, and I didn't have many of those. "Kiss me some more."

She stared at me, stony, harsh, dead-on. "This is going to be the one and only time, so don't get used to it."

"Whatever you say." I wasn't going to argue, not while she was giving me a pulsating thrill.

She narrowed her pretty blue eyes. "Maybe I should just let you go find one of your groupies instead."

"I can't help that they chase me." Women wanted me because I was rich and famous. And yeah, I liked it. Fame was an aphrodisiac. Money, too. The bigger my financial portfolio, the stronger I felt. "You should sing with me, Tracy. We should make music together." I wanted to help revive her career. I needed to, I thought. After everything we'd been through, it was all I had to give her. A piece of my fame.

I touched her cheek, softly, slowly. She used to want a piece of my heart, but she looked as if she hated me now.

"Don't," she said.

"Don't what? Be nice?" I was still waiting for her to rekindle the fire. "You can bite me, if you want. You can draw blood."

"Maybe I will." She pushed my hand away from her cheek. "Just stop touching me like that."

She used to get sweet and dreamy when I was gentle with her. But she was different than before. Or maybe she was just different with me. "Did you let all of those other guys touch you in nice ways?" Were they allowed to take over where I'd left off?

Her voice sharpened. "That's none of your business."

I hated imagining her with other men. For some stupid reason, I'd assumed that she'd barely had any lovers since me.

She leaned forward, plundering my mouth once again. She didn't bite me, but her kiss was still brutal and filled with wrath.

I held her with an iron grip. I couldn't get those other men out of my mind. I suspected that was how Tracy felt about my groupies, too. We were both jealous, but that only made this hotter, somehow. Former lovers steeped in envy and locked in lust, I thought.

Unfortunately, it didn't last. This time, when she tore her mouth away from mine, she got up off my lap.

"I'm done with you," she said, standing to smooth her clothes, even though they weren't out of place.

I stood as well, and let out my breath. I needed to walk off my arousal. I paced the room, feeling like a caged animal.

Being punished didn't feel so good now.

And neither did my shame from the past. When she'd gotten pregnant, I didn't have the means to support a wife and child, and I'd been scared out of my wits.

But still, I'd tried. I'd offered to marry her, to give that poor kid a name. Of course, it was all gone now. The baby we'd conceived, our mixed-up engagement, even the adoring way Tracy used to look at me.

I quit pacing and spun around to look at her, this former fiancée of mine. I'd never even bought her a ring. I could barely make my rent back then, let alone purchase a piece of jewelry. I could afford to give her a gigantic rock now. But I wasn't going to marry her or have another baby. I was only trying to influence her career, if she would let me.

"That wasn't my intention," I said.

"What, the kiss?" She bit down on her bottom lip. "Then why did you bait me to do it?"

"It was an impulse." I noticed that her lipstick was gone. Not even a glimmer of it remained. I wiped the back of my hand across my mouth in case some of it had gotten on me. "I lost control."

"Well, my control was just fine."

"With the way you rubbed all over me?" I stared at her. "Yeah, right."

She glowered back. "I was teaching you a lesson."

I looked her up and down. She had a beddable body, packed with curves. She had wholesome features, though. When she wasn't made up, she looked innocent. I'd always found that fascinating. It made her seem like a chameleon, sultry one day and soft the next. I patted my knee, offering to let her climb back onto my lap. "Want to teach me another one?"

She jerked her chin. "Go to hell, Dash."

"I've already been there." The day my mother left had been the worst kind of hell. And so was the day Tracy had broken up with me. My aversion to love didn't make me any less human. Or any less hurt.

She resumed her seat. "You should be apologizing."

I slumped into my chair and crammed my hat back onto my head. "For what?"

"Making things more difficult."

I grimaced, feeling like a heel. "You're right. I'm sorry." I should be comforting her through her dad's illness, not causing turmoil.

She didn't reply, so I kept talking, hoping to make amends and lighten her mood. "Remember the Christmas when both of our dads went caroling with us? Mine brought his eggnog along, and yours couldn't carry a tune. What a pair they were."

She relaxed a little. "That's the same night I cooked for everybody."

"Best holiday meal I ever had." Not just the food, but watching her in the kitchen, following her dad's recipes. "It's nice that your old man taught you how to baste a turkey."

"And yours taught you to make his special eggnog."

"I can still whip up a batch when I have to." I'd spent this past Christmas on the road, and hosted a party for the crew. But I hadn't made the eggnog. The gathering had been catered.

She reached into her purse, retrieved her compact and reapplied her lipstick. After that, she checked the time on her phone. She seemed anxious for some news.

"Did they say how long the surgery will take?" I asked.

She put her phone away. "An hour, maybe two. I guess it depends on how it goes."

I studied her in the overhead light: the glossy pink lipstick, the way her long, thick hair cascaded down her back. Did she still flip her head over to blow-dry it? I used to like watching her get ready in the mornings.

We'd lived together in my apartment—a big, messy place above an old storage barn. Ratty as it was, I'd chosen it because I could make noise and practice my music there.

Only it was Tracy who'd gotten a record deal. Soon after our engagement ended, her career flourished. I was alone, night after night, feeling like a failure, while she'd moved on to bigger and better things. At the time, it had solidified my biggest fear. Her making it, and me being left behind. But I'd had other insecurities during our relationship, too, especially when she'd gotten pregnant. I'd downright panicked about becoming a father, worrying about how I was going to help support our child.

She checked the time again. "I wish we'd hear something."

"Do you need anything?" I asked, as a surge of emotion flashed through my veins. Our son or daughter would've been around five now and probably starting kindergarten this year.

"What do you mean, anything?"

"Something from the cafeteria. Or maybe a cup of coffee. I can have someone from my team make a food or drink run."

She shook her head. "I'm good. But they can get something for you."

"I'm all right." I didn't want coffee. I wasn't hungry, either. "The candy bar was enough for me."

"For me, too." She glanced at my mouth.

Was she thinking about the chocolate we'd tasted on each other's lips? The kiss that shouldn't have happened? I wouldn't be forgetting it anytime soon.

We waited in silence, and within the hour, a quick knock sounded, then the door opened and Zeke poked his head inside.

"The surgeon is here," he said.

Tracy leaped up from her seat, and the doctor entered, still attired in his scrubs.

I stood as well, and he acknowledged both of us

with a formal nod. He appeared to be in his midforties, with black-rimmed glasses, graying temples and an easy smile.

Did that mean it was good news? Lord, I hoped so. I moved closer to Tracy, to hear what he had to say.

Thankfully, the cancer hadn't spread beyond the testicle. But nonetheless, Tracy's beloved pop would be monitored over the next ten years, getting physicals and blood tests every three months for the first year, and less often as time went on. CT scans would also be done, and if all of those tests showed no sign of cancer, he wouldn't need further treatment. If the cancer returned, then he would require radiation or chemotherapy.

I'd taken care of my dad when he'd gotten sick, but his treatments didn't work. He'd been having some respiratory problems that he'd ignored, and by the time he discovered it was lung cancer, he was already in an advanced stage. He'd passed away within months of his diagnosis.

The doctor finished talking to Tracy, bade both of us goodbye and left the waiting room. Her dad would be coming home today.

She turned toward me, looking as if she might burst into tears. I assumed it was from relief. I wanted to hold her, to let her cry in my arms, but I doubted that she would welcome my touch.

She composed herself and said, "We're going to have to keep Pop from overexerting himself. You know how stubborn he can be."

I nodded. "How long are you going to stay with him?"

"For as long as he needs me."

"What about your work?"

"I'm taking some time off from the feedstore, but I can do my VA stuff from his house. I won't be losing that income." She furrowed her brow. "How often are you coming over to help?"

"I'm not driving back and forth. I'm staying there, too."

"Oh, my God." She gaped at me. "Seriously? There's not even an extra bedroom for you."

"I don't mind sleeping on the couch." I didn't have my own room when I was a kid, either. "Besides, your dad already invited me to stay for a couple of weeks. Or longer if necessary. It depends on how he feels."

She snapped her mouth shut. Clearly, she wasn't happy with the arrangements that had been made. But she was just going to have to grin and bear it.

She wasn't grinning now. And neither was I.

I couldn't seem to stop myself from stressing over the fact that I was still attracted to her. Or that, other than my runaway mother, she was the only woman who'd ever mattered to me.

While Tracy got her dad settled into bed back at his house, I stayed outside with Zeke to discuss a few things. He wasn't just my best bodyguard. Aside from the fact that he co-owned the personal protection company he worked for, he was also my security chief.

He lifted my suitcase from the back of the SUV and said, "I'll have someone bring your truck by later."

"Thanks. What about the security cameras?"

"It's done. I had them installed while we were at the hospital."

He removed his phone and showed me the app that would allow him and the rest of the team to monitor the perimeters of this property, keeping an eye out for the press or anyone else who might catch wind of me being here. The last thing I wanted was a persistent reporter or an overzealous fan hanging around and impeding Tracy's dad's recovery. There weren't any neighbors to speak of. The farm sat on enough acreage to separate it from other houses, but I was still concerned about strangers.

"I can download it on your phone, too," Zeke said.

"That would be great." Later I would teach Tracy's dad how to operate it. After all of this was over, the cameras would be moved into the barn. Tracy's dad was excited about that. Cameras could be especially helpful for monitoring a mare getting ready to foal.

I handed Zeke my phone, then stood back to study him. He had a naturally tanned complexion, hair as black as mine, and strong, broad features. He was an interesting mix of Samoan, Caucasian and Choctaw. I had a little Choctaw blood from my mom's side, but mostly I was Anglo. Some of my classmates used to call me white trash, their taunts cutting me to the quick.

Tracy had mentioned my mom earlier, but I'd lied when I'd said that I didn't know her whereabouts. A few months back, I'd asked Zeke to investigate her. And according to what he'd uncovered, she was no longer with the man she'd run off with. She'd had numerous lovers over the years. At last count, she'd taken up with a retired architect in Mexico and was living a reclusive life in a house he'd built that overlooked the sea.

I had no idea if she even knew that I was a celebrity. My music wasn't popular in Mexico. Of course, there was a part of me that wanted her to know, and another part that didn't give a shit. I'd only had Zeke investigate her to satisfy my curiosity about where she was.

"Here you go," he said, interrupting my thoughts. He'd finished downloading the app.

He showed me how to use it, and once he was gone, I went inside and placed my bag in the living room.

Tracy appeared from around the corner, then eyed my suitcase as if it might explode.

"Don't worry," I said. "I'll keep my stuff out of the way."

She made a weary sound. "It would be a lot easier if you went home."

I sat on the sofa, the same cozy spot where I would be sleeping. "Just give me a chance, okay?" I planned on making myself as useful as possible.

She sighed and plopped down beside me. "Should we go over the instructions from the hospital?"

"Sure." I'd won the first round, but I knew the battle wasn't over. Tracy was still unnerved by my presence. "We can divvy up your pop's care."

She removed the paperwork from her purse and read it to herself. I waited for her to give me the condensed version.

She said, "He needs to get enough sleep to recover. But he also needs to walk each day. Just a little at first, then increase it each time. He's supposed to avoid strenuous activities for the first few weeks, and he won't be able to drive until the doctor says it's okay."

"I can take care of the horses for him." I had plenty of time to devote to the animals. "I don't have anything going on except this. My tour is over, and I'm not going back into the studio for a while. My schedule is clear."

"All right, then I'll administer Pop's medications,"

she said. "There are pain pills and antibiotics for him to take."

"What kind of stitches does he have? Are they going to need to be removed or will they dissolve?"

She checked the instructions. "They'll dissolve. He needs to keep the incision clean and dry and change the bandage once a day. He can take showers, but no baths for the first few weeks. He can use ice packs for swelling." She glanced up at me. "I'll make a copy of this for you."

"Thanks. I think we're going to make a good pair."

She refolded the paperwork. "We aren't a pair."

I ignored her remark and said, "It's going to be interesting sharing a bathroom with you again." Her dad had his own bathroom, so we wouldn't be infringing on his privacy. "You always took forever getting ready."

She frowned. "You never seemed to mind before."

Was she thinking about how I used to watch her do her hair and makeup? "You never minded hanging around when I got ready, either." Sometimes she used to come up behind me in the mirror and loosen the towel that was wrapped around my waist, when I was fresh from the shower and attempting to shave. I'd never really been a morning person, but I'd enjoyed every naughty nuance of Tracy seducing me bright and early.

I blinked, and she stood and moved away from me. Had she tapped into what I was I thinking?

"Pop's got some laundry that's been piling up," she said, preparing to rush off. "I'll make sure there are clean linens for you to use tonight, too."

Tracy left the room, and I grabbed a rodeo magazine off the coffee table and paged through it, giving myself something to do.

About twenty minutes later, after I'd pretty much read it cover to cover, my phone chimed with an incoming text. I checked the message. It was Zeke, asking me to call him. He'd included a code we'd devised that pertained to my mom.

Why was he texting me about her? He'd only just left here a short while ago. Besides, he'd already told me everything he knew about her.

So maybe he wanted to discuss one of my "other" moms? Unfortunately, the public knew that my mother had split when I was a kid. Someone from our old trailer park had sold that information to a tabloid, and now, every so often, there were women on social media claiming to be her. My cybersecurity team contacted Zeke whenever things like that cropped up, and he always checked it out.

I went outside to the backyard and called him back.

"Hey," he said, answering straight away. "I'm sorry to bother you so soon, but I stopped by the management office and picked up today's fan mail. And there was a letter that caught my attention."

Sometimes he liked to go through my snail mail himself, screening it randomly. Otherwise, it was opened by my administrative staff.

"Go on," I replied, urging him to continue.

"It was from someone who said that her name is Lola, and that she used to sing and dance for you and your daddy."

His words hit me hard and quick. My mother's name was Darleen, but she used to sing "Whatever Lola Wants" and twirl around, pretending to be that character. I'd even memorized the song when I was little. "Mom never sang and danced in front of anyone like that except me and my dad, and I never told anyone about it but you." I paused. "What do you think this means?"

"It could be a message from her. Or it could be an imposter. She could've shared the Lola story with someone else, and they could've written the letter."

"What else was in it, besides Lola dancing for me and my daddy?"

"She complimented your music and said that she was proud of you. She also said that she didn't want you to be mad at her."

"For what? Walking out on me?"

"She didn't specify. But I suspect that you'll be hearing from her again. Whoever it is."

"More cryptic notes?" I was already frazzled by this one. I didn't know which scenario was worse: an imposter or the real deal.

My stomach clenched. "Is there a return address?"

"No, but it's postmarked Los Angeles, with a red lipstick mark on the back of the envelope."

As if it had been sealed with a kiss? My stomach tightened again. That actually seemed like something my mom would do, but why would she be reaching out to me after all this time? She couldn't have known that I'd had Zeke search for her. He'd been highly discreet about that.

"Can DNA be extracted from lipstick?" I asked.

"I don't think so," he replied. "But I'm going to have it examined, anyway."

"What about the flap on the envelope itself?"

"Most are self-adhesive now, but if there was saliva involved and if it's a viable sample, the lab can compare it to your DNA for a familial match. I'll also have it tested for fingerprints, just in case the person who sent it is in the system. Your mother doesn't have a criminal record, but an imposter might."

"What a thing to have to think about."

"I know. I'm sorry. Do you want to see the letter before I have it tested?"

"No." I trusted Zeke to do his job.

He said, "I have an old friend who works for US Customs and Border Protection, so I can check with him to see if your mom returned to the States and what port of entry she might've used. Anyone in the Los Angeles area could've mailed that letter or even sent it at her request, but at least we'll know if she traveled recently or was in California herself. I'll inquire about her boyfriend, too."

"Do whatever you need to do."

He cleared his throat. "I'll have all of the snail mail forwarded to me from now on. I don't know how long it will take for my friend at Customs to get back to me, but I can try to put a rush on the lab tests."

"Thanks. I should go." Of all days for this to happen. I could barely breathe. If this was my mother, was she trying to cast one of her mind-bending charms over me, like she used to do when I was a kid? Fawning over me one minute and ignoring me the next?

I ended the call and returned to the house. Tracy sat at the kitchen table, sorting through her dad's medications and putting them in a case with the days of the week stamped on it. Apparently, she was on a break from the laundry.

She glanced up and asked, "Where were you?"

"I was in the backyard. Did you think that I'd gone

home already?" I joked, making light of my actions and trying to keep her from suspecting anything was wrong.

She rolled her eyes. "I knew you had to be around somewhere."

Yes, I was around, standing right in front of her, faking a casual air. As overwhelming as it was, I would never tell her what was going on. She didn't need to know that my mom or someone associated with her had sent me a letter. Nor was I going to admit that I'd already been poking around in my mom's life, before that note had even arrived.

I jammed my hands into my pockets, and Tracy continued sorting pills. I wished I could bait her to kiss me again, to rub and touch me and let me put my hands where they didn't belong. I needed a diversion, something to take my mind off my troubles.

And take refuge in a woman who was no longer mine.

Three

Tracy

As soon as I woke up, the first thing that entered my mind was Dash. As much as I dreaded seeing him this morning, I was oddly aroused, too, just knowing that he was nearby.

Damn, but I hated feeling this way. I even rubbed my arms, trying to shed the tingly sensation.

I sat up and squinted at the light peeking through the blinds. This was the only room in the house that I hadn't redecorated. The girlish decor remained the same as when I used to live here. I'd removed the celebrity posters, though. The photos of the country stars I used to admire.

I couldn't begin to guess how many posters of Dash were out there, gracing people's walls. Maybe I should creep into the living room and take a picture of him crashed out on the sofa and make a poster out of it.

Wouldn't that give his loyal Dashers a thrill?

I cleared my cynical thoughts and climbed out of bed. I was fairly certain that Dash wasn't awake yet. He'd never really been a rise-and-shine guy. I'd always gotten up before him.

I headed to the bathroom, washed my face, brushed my teeth and put my hair in a ponytail. I would shower later, just in case Dash stumbled down the hall, needing to pee. I didn't want him banging at the door.

I finished quickly and rounded the corner, poking my head into the living room. I was wrong. Dash wasn't asleep. He was already up and about. I spotted him in the kitchen.

I strolled in there, even if I wanted to go back to bed and hide under the covers. He glanced up at me, and the tingling sensations came rushing back.

"Hi," he said, checking me out with a half smile, as if seeing me in my pajamas pleased him.

At least my ensemble was modest. He wasn't wearing a shirt, and I could've kicked him for it. He wasn't leaving much to the imagination, with that broad chest, those trained-to-perfection abs, the line of hair just below his navel that disappeared into his sweatpants.

"What are you concocting?" I asked, eyeing the mixing bowl and other things lined up on the counter.

"I'm going to make pancakes for your dad. For you, too, if you want some."

"Since when did pancakes become your specialty?" He'd never been much of a cook when we were together.

"Since right now." His smile turned a bit more crooked. "When I checked on your pop earlier, I asked him what he wanted for breakfast, and he said flap-jacks." He lifted his phone off the counter. "I googled how to make them from scratch, and this is as far as I got."

He was watching a recipe video? I almost smiled, too. But I was trying not to be too friendly. Or too dreamy. I didn't want him affecting me the way he was. "How long have you been up?"

"About an hour. I wanted to get a jump on everything and prove my worth around here." He set down his phone next to a carton of eggs. "I fed the horses and checked on the foals. There's some cute babies out there."

I sucked in my breath. I didn't want to hear him talk about babies, not even the equine kind. But it wasn't just the child we'd lost that made me hurt. I had some current fertility issues that I hadn't told anyone about. "You went outside dressed like that?"

Dash glanced down at himself. "I've got my boots on."

Yes, he was wearing a pair of rugged black cowboy boots, with his sweatpants tucked into them. "What about a shirt?"

"The horses don't care what I'm wearing. Besides, I'm going to hop in the shower after breakfast, and I'll put a shirt on then."

I sighed. "I haven't showered yet, either."

He waggled his eyebrows. "Well, aren't we the dirty ones?"

I ignored his double entendre. But disregarding him wasn't so easy. He looked deliciously messy, his hair falling in uncombed disarray, his jaw peppered with beard stubble.

I hastily said, "I'm going to check on Pop and see if he needs anything. If you want help with breakfast, I can do that as soon as I come back."

Dash removed a whisk from the utensil caddy. "Thanks. But I can handle it."

I left him to his task and made my way to Pop's room.

Since his door was partially open, I peeked in and got his attention. "Can I come in?"

"Sure," he replied, waving me forward.

I approached the side of his bed. He was propped against the headboard, using several pillows behind his back. I thought he looked tired, but I was glad that he was resting, like he was supposed to. I wanted nothing more than for him to get well.

"How are you feeling?" I asked.

"Still a little swollen, but other than that, I'm okay."

"Do you need an ice pack?"

"I'm using one as we speak." He gestured to his blanket-draped lap. "Dash got it for me."

"He's certainly been busy this morning." Tomorrow I would get up earlier than I did today, hopefully beating him to the punch. "He's trying to figure out how to make the pancakes."

"Really? He didn't tell me he didn't know how to make them."

"He's using a video as his guide."

Pop chuckled. "He's a good kid."

Dash had never seemed like a kid to me. But I wasn't an old cowboy like my dad. I was the lovestruck girl who should've been Dash's wife. "I offered to help him in the kitchen, but he said that he could handle it."

My father studied me for a silent second. "How's it

going otherwise?" he asked. "Are you two getting reacquainted?"

Yes? No? Sort of? "We're doing fine. But I'm still not making a record with him."

"I wasn't going to pester you about that." Pop grinned, his tired blue eyes twinkling. "Not today, anyhow."

"But you'll do it on another day, huh?"

"Probably." He laughed, then winced. "Ooh, I felt that."

I reacted with immediate concern. "I can get you a pain pill. You're going to need your antibiotics, too. But it might be better to take them with food, so you don't get queasy."

"I can wait until breakfast."

I tried for a smile. "I'll go make sure it's edible."

He returned my smile. "Thanks, sweetie. I love you."

"I love you, too." I'd gotten lucky having him as my daddy.

I made my way back to the kitchen, and everything seemed hunky-dory. No scorched skillet or lumpy pancakes.

I stood back and watched. Dash was in the process of flipping the next one and looked damned fine doing it. He even had a sexy dusting of flour on his sweatpants.

He shot me a sideways glance, and I wet my lips. I could've eaten him alive, devouring his mouth with mine. Lucky for me, I'd vowed never to kiss him again.

"Are you hungry?" he asked.

Was he kidding? He was making me famished, only with the wrong kind of appetite. "I could eat a small stack, I guess. But I'm going to get Pop his, first."

"Sure. Okay." He completed another perfect pancake.

I fixed my father a plate, along with a glass of orange juice and a cup of black coffee. I also removed his meds from the pillbox I'd prepared yesterday. He was supposed to take the antibiotics three times a day.

I put everything on a tray and brought it to him. Pop was impressed that my ex had nailed the pancakes on his first try.

When I returned to the kitchen, I noticed that Dash had put on a T-shirt.

"You got dressed," I said, stating the obvious. "I thought you weren't going to do that until after your shower."

"I didn't want to offend you while we were eating."

Offending me wasn't the problem. But I was glad that he'd covered up. I didn't need to drool over him any more than I already had.

I set the table, and he poured us both some coffee.

"Do you still take mounds of that French vanilla creamer in yours?" he asked.

I nodded and went to the fridge to get it. "Do you still like yours with just a bit of sugar and splash of milk?"

"Yes, ma'am." He waited for me to sit before he took his seat.

He was behaving like a proper Southern boy, I thought. Or as proper as a guy from the wrong side of the tracks could be.

"You look cute in your pj's," he said.

My pajamas weren't anything special, just plain blue cotton with a simple green trim. "You don't have to pay me compliments."

"I wasn't just saying it. I mean it. I always liked that you could be natural or glamorous. I could never decide which side of you was more appealing."

"There's no difference. I'm the same person, either way."

"Yeah, but it makes you seem different, like twins or something."

I foolishly asked, "Have you ever dated twins?" I shouldn't care who he played around with, but it was too late to take the question back.

"No. That would be weird, I think. I'd rather have one woman who seems like two."

Meaning what? That he would rather have me? Or someone who reminded him of me? I'd tried to replace him in bed. But none of my other lovers had ever satisfied me the way he did.

I reached for the syrup and poured it over my pancakes. I set down the bottle, and Dash picked it up and doused his, too. I noticed how slowly it dripped.

Thick and sweet and sticky…

I cut into mine and took a bite. How was I going to survive two whole weeks of this? Or however long it turned out to be?

I looked up and saw that he was staring at me. I had syrup on my lips, but now I was too self-conscious to lick it off.

Finally, he sipped his coffee, and I used my napkin to wipe my mouth.

"I'll do the dishes when we're done," I said, interrupting the silence. "I'll clean the kitchen, too."

He glanced toward the stove. He'd spilled batter all over it. "I'm not leaving that mess for you."

"You aren't the tidiest cook, that's for sure."

He shrugged. "Maybe I should've skipped the video and called my chef to talk me through it."

"You have a chef?" He hadn't mentioned it before now.

"Yes, but he doesn't make anything fancy for me. My tastes haven't changed. I still don't like the gourmet stuff."

"Me, neither." Pop had raised me on simple Southern fare, and that remained my preference, too.

"My chef used to work for the people I bought the house from, so I kept him on. I kept some of the ranch hands and caretakers, too. They've been at Pine Tower a long time."

His estate had a name? I should've expected as much. Big, rich places often did, and Pine Tower sounded strong and masculine, just like him. But it didn't matter how glorious his home was. I didn't aim to set foot in it.

We finished eating, and he cleared the plates, intent on cleaning up.

"I'm going to shower now," I said. I figured this would be a good time to get myself together and change out of my pajamas.

He nodded, and I left, still struggling with how anxious being in a domestic setting with him was making me feel.

I gathered my clothes from my room and took them into the bathroom.

As I stood beneath the spray of water, I tried to keep my mind off Dash. But it didn't work. He consumed my thoughts. I even imagined him using the shower after me, standing in the same stall, using the same liquid soap. I couldn't wait until he went back to his regular life. Having him here was killing me, and it was only the first day.

After I was clean and dry, I styled my hair and did my makeup. I didn't make my eyes too smoky, but instead lined them just enough to create a semblance of the glamorous "twin" Dash had accused me of being.

I dragged on a pair of skinny jeans and tied my blouse in front. Then I returned to my room and pulled on my boots, checking my reflection in the full-length mirror.

With a steadying breath, I went to find Dash to tell him the bathroom was free.

By now the kitchen was clean, and he was in the living room, studying a grouping of framed photos on the fireplace mantel. I moved closer, and he turned toward me.

He said, "I was just looking at your mom's pictures and thinking about how much you favor her."

"You used to say that before."

"I know. But it's been a while since I've seen these pictures, and you look even more like her now."

That was true. I did. As for Dash, he favored his father. But I'd never seen a picture of his mother, so I didn't really know what she looked like. Soon after she'd left, his dad had destroyed all of her photos. He'd kept the ones that Dash was in, but he'd scribbled over his ex-wife's face with a marker. He was sorry for his actions later, though, and cried about it, wishing that she would come back to him. Even after she'd betrayed him, he'd claimed that he'd never stopped loving her.

Dash, on the other hand, had rejected the idea of ever falling in love. He'd made up his mind, at twelve years old, that he would never let it happen to him.

I'd been fascinated with love since I'd walked my bridal Barbie down the aisle. But my parents had set a beautiful example. I'd grown up in a house brimming with love.

I'd lost my sweet mama without ever getting to say goodbye. On a Monday evening in late September, she'd died in a car crash on her way home from work. Sometimes Mondays still made me sad. The month of September, too. Just the leaves changing colors could trigger grief. But mostly I celebrated my mother's life. I'd learned to do that from Pop.

"This is my favorite," I said, pointing to a photograph of my parents together, a candid shot taken about a year before she was gone.

Dash traced the edge of the frame. "They look happy."

"They were." So very happy.

He paused, then lowered his hand. "Do you still have any pictures of us together?"

I hesitated, too, and shifted my gaze to his. "Yes, I still have them. They're in an old digital file." The most difficult ones were from when I was pregnant. I'd never really gotten a noticeable baby bump, but our child had still been there, growing inside me. I dared to ask, "Did you keep any of them?"

He nodded. "We look so young in them."

"We were young." But I didn't want to think about who we used to be. Or who we were now. I was already suffering from seeing him again.

He reached out as if he meant to touch me, but I stepped back, making sure that he didn't.

"You should go take your shower," I said, needing to be rid of him.

He frowned. "Yeah, I guess I should."

He walked away, but it didn't help. I was still affected by him—in my mind, in my body.

But mostly in my heart.

* * *

Two days later, I put a plan in motion. I needed to shatter my feelings for Dash. I needed to purge my fertility issues, too. I decided it was time to talk to Alice, my closest and dearest friend, about the secret I'd been keeping.

I called and asked if she was free this afternoon, and she invited me to her house for lunch. Now all I had to do was check in with Dash.

I went outside. It was a lovely summer day, and he was sitting on the patio, taking in the air. He'd spent time with Pop's prize stud this morning, working him in the round pen. Dash had always been a natural horseman.

He glanced up at me, then shielded his eyes from the sun.

I inched closer. "Can I ask you a favor?"

"Sure." He moved his chair to avoid the glare. "What is it?"

"I'm having lunch with a friend, and I wondered if you'd keep an eye on Pop while I'm gone." My father was sleeping for now, and I didn't want to disturb him.

"Of course, I can. That's what I'm here for."

"Thank you." A moment later, I said, "Actually, you have a business association with my friend's husband. Alice is married to Spencer Riggs." Spencer was a renowned songwriter that Dash was supposed to work with on his next album. Funny how people could be connected that way. But it only stood to reason that the hottest new songwriter and the hottest new country star would be planning on making hits together. "I've known Alice for a long time."

"Is she the one who helped jumpstart your career?"

"Yes." My debut album was a compilation of songs written by her late mother, and Alice had been involved in hiring me to record them.

"I heard that Spencer got married while I was on tour, but I didn't pay much attention to it. I don't know him that well yet. I've only met him a few times, but as soon as I'm ready to go back to work, I'm going to call him."

"He's a good guy. I think you'll enjoy collaborating with him. I was in their wedding party. I performed at the reception, too." It had been a beautiful experience, seeing Alice and Spencer so happy.

"Maybe we can get together with them sometime."

I blinked. "What?"

"To go to dinner or something."

"The four of us?" I shook my head, taking a moment to catch my breath.

He pulled a hand through his hair. "It might be a nice way for you and me to become friends again."

By hanging out with a married couple? I couldn't fathom it. "I think we should keep our relationships with them separate. We shouldn't fuss about trying to become friends, either." I didn't want to do anything with Dash, except get these next couple of weeks over with and hopefully never see him again.

He dusted dirt from his jeans, brushing his hands over his knees. "It was just an idea."

He sounded disappointed. But I couldn't cater to his whims. I'd done that when we were together, giving in to whatever he wanted, even if it hurt me. The first time I'd told him that I loved him, he'd freaked out and asked me to never say it again. Of course, I'd thought that I could cure him. That, eventually, he would accept being loved and would fall desperately in love with me, too.

I hurried up and said, “When Pop wakes up from his nap, he’s probably going to want to go for his walk.” He’d been getting a little exercise each day like he was supposed to.

“That’s not a problem. I can go with him. We can stroll down to the barn and back.”

Dash was definitely making my father’s recovery easier. But that didn’t mean I had to be friends with him. “I know that Pop appreciates your help. You’ve been wonderful with him.”

“I’m glad to do it. I’d be glad to help you in any way I can, too. I want to make a difference in your life, Tracy.”

I gripped the back of an empty chair. Did he have to be so accommodating? So willing? So irresistible? “I won’t be gone long. Maybe a few hours or so.”

“Okay.” He spoke softly. “See you then.”

I turned to leave. But unfortunately, I could feel Dash watching me. He was always roaming his gaze over every inch of my body, making me feel warm and dizzy and forbidden.

A short time later, I arrived at Alice’s house, and she greeted me at the door. She lived in a beautifully renovated home that Spencer had purchased when he was still a bachelor. In addition to his songwriting, he ran a dog rescue on the property, which was where he was this afternoon.

I went inside, and Alice reached out for our customary hug. She was a stunning blonde with short, spiky hair, and always wore the latest clothes. Although her primary ties were to the Nashville music scene, she worked as a fashion stylist.

After she prepared lunch, we took it outside and sat beside the pool, with its sparkling blue water.

We dined on salad, turkey-and-cheese sandwiches and a pitcher of sweet tea. For dessert, she provided an assortment of cookies her pastry-chef sister had made.

"I'm so glad your dad is doing well," she said. "I have a box of cookies to send home with you for him."

"Thank you." I'd told her over the phone that Dash was helping with Pop's care. She knew my entire history with Dash. Alice and I had been confiding in each other since we'd first met.

"I can't imagine what it's like for you to have to see Dash every day," she said.

"It's driving me batty." I attacked my salad, stabbing a cherry tomato. "You know how I was already struggling with his fame, and now I wake up every morning and there he is. I think about him when I shouldn't be, like when I'm in bed or in the shower."

Alice stirred her tea, making the ice in her glass swirl. "I know what that's like. I used to do that when I was trying to manage my feelings for Spencer."

And now they were married and planning a family. But it was different for me. I wasn't getting back together with Dash. But nonetheless, I needed to say what I'd come here to say. I braced myself and started with, "There's something important I need to tell you. Something I should have told you before now."

She leaned forward. "About what?"

I winced. "The likelihood that I'll never have kids." I went on to explain, as thoroughly as I could. "I started having irregular periods a while ago, but I thought it was stress, so I didn't see a doctor right away. I knew I wasn't pregnant because I hadn't slept with anyone in the last six months." I gathered my thoughts, troubled as they were. "My ob-gyn ran some tests and discovered what was wrong. I've got something called premature ovarian failure. It means that my ovaries aren't releasing eggs regularly and aren't generating normal estrogen levels."

"Oh, Trace. I'm so sorry. I didn't know that was possible for someone so young. You're not even thirty yet."

"It can happen to women and girls even younger than me."

Alice looked worried. "It's not life-threatening, is it? It's not related to ovarian cancer or anything like that?"

"No. But most women with POF are infertile." I felt the tears coming to my eyes. "And being around Dash is making it even harder. I keep thinking about the baby we lost and how I'll probably never have another one."

"That's so sad." She got teary-eyed, too. "Are you going to tell him about what's happening to you?"

"God, no. He's the last person I would ever tell. I'm not going to say anything to my dad, either."

"Are you taking estrogen?"

I nodded. "It's supposed to prevent some of the complications I might have later, like osteoporosis. People sometimes mix this up with early menopause, but it's not the same thing. The symptoms are similar, though. The doctor even said that it might lessen my sex drive. But that isn't happening. In fact, I'm actually feeling the opposite, getting hot and bothered over Dash."

"Well, that's good," she said, then quickly clarified. "Not that you have the hots for Dash, but that your sex drive is still going strong."

"I kissed him at the hospital when we were waiting for Pop's surgery. I did it to prove how much control I had and that I could kiss him just once and never do it again. But now he's all I think about."

"Remember when you encouraged me to be with Spencer to try to get him out of my system?" She shook her head. "But then I fell in love with him?"

"My problem is that I never really fell *out* of love with Dash." I glanced over at the pool. "I wish there was a remedy for that. Between Dash and my medical issues, I'm a mess."

Alice gave me a sympathetic look. "I know how much you wanted the baby you lost." She picked at her sandwich. "Is there anything that can be done to help you have kids in the future?"

"Some women with my condition are able to conceive on their own, but that's rare. Mostly they suggest in vitro or donor eggs. Only that's not foolproof, either."

"Do they think your miscarriage was associated with this?"

"No, but what if by some off chance, I did get pregnant and then lost it again? What if I'm prone to recurring miscarriages? There's no way to know for sure."

"I don't blame you for being scared, especially after everything you've already been through."

"My doctor suggested a support group. But I don't want to discuss my life with a bunch of strangers. I keep hoping that once Dash goes home, I'll be able to cope a little better."

"I'll always be here. You can talk to me anytime."

"Thank you." Without her, I would be lost.

When it came time for me to leave, she gave me an extra big hug, and I struggled not to cry on her shoulder.

I drove back to Pop's with his cookies on the seat next to me. Once I got there, I pulled into the driveway and stayed in my truck for a few minutes, preparing to see Dash again.

Finally, I opened the front door and spotted him and my dad sitting at the kitchen table, playing Scrabble.

They both glanced up and smiled. Then Pop said, "I was getting bored being in my room all the time."

"It's nice to see you up and about," I replied. Aside from his walks, he'd been holed up in bed.

"Come join us." He coaxed me over to them.

I set the cookies on the counter. Pop was thriving in Dash's care. It even seemed as if they were family. And they would have been if Dash and I had gotten married and had the baby. But all of that was gone, I reminded myself.

Long, long gone.

Four

Dash

I'd spent a week so far with Tracy and her dad, and it had almost come to feel like home. Today I was alone in the yard, watching the mares and their foals in pasture. A four-month-old filly, with a heart-shaped patch on her forehead, romped past me. She was a playful little thing, leaping and bouncing and crow-hopping, as if she was trying to make me smile.

I was restless, waiting to hear from Zeke. He hadn't gotten word from Customs yet, but he was supposed to receive a report from the lab today.

Would it reveal that the person who'd sent the letter was my mom, playing a cat and mouse game with me?

She'd always been a master at messing with people's emotions. Even when I was a kid, I knew she was different from my friends' moms. She needed more attention than theirs. Sometimes she even flirted with their fathers or older brothers or whatever guy was around.

My dad used to say that she'd been trouble from the start, but he'd still wanted her from the moment they'd met. She'd been fascinated with him in the beginning, too. She'd swooned over his good looks and noticeable talent. But when he didn't hit the big time, her feelings for him waned. She'd hated being poor. She'd loathed it more than anything.

Mom had grown up in foster care, with aspirations to be rich. Only she hadn't been interested in earning her wealth herself. She'd wanted a man to take care of her, to make her feel special.

If the letter writer was my mother, was that what she was after? To have her son make her feel special, for the kid she'd abandoned to share his success with her? Or was there another motive? I just wished that damned report would come in, with some sort of conclusive evidence.

Suddenly I heard approaching footsteps behind me. They were too light to be Zeke's. He wasn't here with the lab results. I sensed it was Tracy.

As she joined me at the fence, I turned to look at her. Her thick brown hair spilled over her shoulders and down her back. Her blouse was a delicate floral print that reminded me of the wildflowers I used to pick for her from a field near my old apartment. I used to nab flowers for my mom, too, from other people's yards. I'd gotten stung by a bee doing that once, which seemed rather fitting now.

Tracy said, "I just wanted to let you know that we're

getting a feed delivery today. They'll probably be here in about twenty minutes, so if you don't want to get recognized, you should probably go back inside soon."

"I will, thanks. How's your work going?" When I'd gotten up this morning, she'd been engrossed in one of her virtual assistant assignments.

"It's fine. I'm just taking a break." She tucked her hair behind her ear. "Pop is watching one of those goofy old Westerns in his room."

"He likes that early stuff. My dad did, too. Except his favorites were the singing cowboys. It doesn't get any goofier than that."

She laughed and nudged my arm. "You're a singing cowboy."

"Not in the movies." I laughed as well, and got a warm, fuzzy feeling from being silly with her.

I liked that she was joking around. But she sobered quickly, as if she'd done something wrong, and we both went quiet. The filly with the heart on its forehead came over to us, and I reached out to pet her nose. Tracy watched me with a sad expression. Was she thinking about the child we'd lost?

"I'm sorry," I said.

She touched the filly, too. "For what?"

"For everything, I guess."

"Everything?"

I hesitated, working up the courage to say what I meant. She watched me, waiting for my response. Finally, I said, "I'm sorry for not being ready for fatherhood when you got pregnant."

She drew her hand back. "It's over. All of that is over."

"I know, but I'm still sorry." As the filly wandered

over to her mother, I felt an even bigger sense of loss. "You deserved to have a partner who wasn't so damned scared."

She gripped the fence so hard I feared she might give herself a splinter. I was making her tense, bringing up a subject that pained her. But I couldn't seem to let it go. I'd spent years regretting how our relationship had ended, and now she was right in front of me. I would be a fool to pass up the opportunity to explain how deeply her miscarriage had affected me, too.

I gently said, "I've thought a lot about the baby, wondering if it was a boy or girl. Sometimes when I see kids around the age ours would've been, I try to imagine what he or she would've been like now. Would its eyes be blue, like yours, or dark like mine? Would it be calling your dad a funny name for grandpa?"

Her breath rushed out. "I've thought about things like that, too. But we can't change what happened."

"I know. I just wanted to say my piece." Was this conversation a mistake? Or was it good that I cleared the air? Tracy still seemed sad. I felt heavy inside, too. But that didn't stop me from asking, "Have you ever dated anyone with children?"

"No." She removed her hands from the rail. "Have you?"

I shook my head. "I wouldn't do it unless the kids were going to become a significant part of my life, and I haven't been serious enough about anyone to make that kind of commitment." A second later, I amended my statement by saying, "You're the only woman I've ever been in a relationship with, and look how I botched that up."

She glanced away. I'd made her uncomfortable again. That had become my forte, it seemed.

"You should go back to the house now," she said. "Before the delivery comes."

"Are you coming inside, too?"

She nodded, and we turned and fell into step together. A light breeze stirred the air and Tracy's hair blew away from her face, exposing a pair of tiny silver spur earrings.

"I haven't been to the feedstore since I got famous," I said. "But I should probably stop in sometime and say hello."

"They'd be thrilled, I'm sure. Maddie brags to everyone about how you used to work there."

"I can see her doing that." She was the brassy old lady who owned it, a bleached-and-teased blonde who smoked like a fiend and kept a flask of Johnnie Walker in her office drawer. "Maybe I'll drop by on a day that you're there."

"That's okay. You don't have to involve me."

Damn, I thought. Could she be any more difficult? "I'm just trying to find an excuse to see you when all of this is over."

She stared straight ahead. "That isn't necessary."

I refused to give up so easily. "I want to make it better, Tracy, to at least work toward healing some of those old wounds. I think we should try to be friends."

She tucked her shoulder away from mine, but I still could feel the heat between us. The emotional energy.

"I don't think us being friends will work," she said. "I just don't."

"So we're back to square one?" I countered. No

friendship. No future. No nothing. Just two people, mired in a heap of pain from the past.

Hours later, Zeke came by. I got into the passenger side of the car, and he remained behind the wheel. We didn't go anywhere; we stayed in the driveway at Tracy's dad's house. But the SUV gave us a private place to talk.

Zeke looked like his usual self, big and broad and professional, his suit expertly pressed, his tie knotted good and tight. I probably looked nervous; I was fraught with anticipation, eager to hear his news.

"The fingerprint tests were inconclusive," he said. "Too many people handled the letter and the envelope, and they couldn't get any clear prints. They couldn't extract DNA from anything, either."

Well, hell. "They didn't get anything useful?"

"The only thing they were able to do was to determine what brand of lipstick was used. It was from Chanel. Does that mean anything to you?"

"Actually, it does." I released the air in my lungs. "Chanel was my mother's favorite designer. She always wanted my dad to buy her one of their signature handbags, but he couldn't afford anything like that. He used to get her their cosmetics instead. For her birthdays, for Christmas." I glanced over at the report in his hand. "What's the likelihood that someone else, besides my mother, would have kissed that damned envelope with the same kind of lipstick she used?"

"I have some other information about your mother," he said, grabbing my full attention. "I did a little digging and discovered that all of her credit cards were canceled a few weeks ago. They were being provided by her boyfriend, but he took them away."

"They're not together anymore?"

"That's how it looks. She closed her bank account in Mexico, too. My assumption is that she's living on cash now. She didn't have a substantial balance, so it's not going to go far, especially if she's back in the States. But until I hear from my Customs contact, that remains to be seen."

Exhausted from it all, I ran my hands across my face. "She has to be the one who wrote the letter. Now that she and her current lover are on the outs, she's probably after my money. I figured she was, anyway. But this more or less seals it for me."

Zeke nodded. He looked sorry for the way it was turning out. But we both knew Lola the letter writer was trouble, no matter who she was. He said, "I'll text you as soon I get word on her possible whereabouts. Or if I come across anything else."

I glanced at the house. "I should get back inside." I didn't want to pique Tracy's curiosity, sitting in Zeke's car, having a long conversation.

She jumped to conclusions, anyway. When I entered the living room, she peered up from her laptop and asked, "Is there a breach somewhere?"

"A breach?" I parroted inanely.

"Did someone find out that you're here? Or is there a problem with the cameras that your team set up?"

"No. Everything's fine." My problem had nothing to do with her pop's house. "I was just having a routine meeting."

"Are you sure? Because I don't want the press swarming around here."

"Don't worry. That isn't going to happen." After she returned her attention to her laptop, I said, "I'm going to check on the horses." The feed delivery had already come and gone, and I was free to head outside again.

I needed to get some air, but I wanted to see the mares and their foals, too. I was fascinated by the little filly with the heart-shaped marking. I also appreciated how gentle her mother was with her, maybe because I'd never known what it was like to have a loving, caring mom of my own.

A week later, my stint as a caregiver ended. Tracy's dad was doing well and didn't need my help anymore. I didn't want to go. I liked being with Tracy and her pop, but I couldn't find an excuse to extend my stay.

Unfortunately, I still was waiting for more information about my mom, too. Nothing was happening, except for me going home.

I packed my bag, and Tracy's dad walked outside with me to my truck. He looked so much heathier, so much stronger. But his condition would still be monitored.

"Thanks for everything you've done," he said. "I'm going to miss you."

"You can come visit me anytime. Or I can come back and hang out and play Scrabble or whatever you want to do."

"That would be great. Valentine is going to miss you, too."

I smiled. Valentine was his nickname for the foal I'd grown close to. "I was thinking that I'd like to buy her from you." Of course, that was a waiting game, too. She couldn't be sold until she was weaned.

"I'd love for you to have her. We'll work out a deal later."

I wished I could work out a deal to take possession of his daughter. But I couldn't purchase her the way I would be doing with the foal. So far, Tracy hadn't even come out to say goodbye. She'd been in her room all morning. I assumed that she was avoiding me on purpose.

He said, "I guess you didn't have any luck convincing Tracy to record with you."

"No, no luck." Nothing had changed in that regard. "But I'm still open to it."

He nodded, and we talked for a bit more about inconsequential things. He didn't mention Tracy again.

When we said our final goodbye, he reached out to hug me, clapping me on the back in manly fashion.

After he went back inside, my phone signaled a text. I checked the message and saw the "Mom" code from Zeke.

I actually flinched a little. Had he heard from Customs? Or was it some other news that pertained to her? Whatever it was, I was going to find out soon.

I replied, telling him I was on my way home and to meet me there. Then I glanced up and saw Tracy on the porch.

She was here, after all.

She approached me, and we stared at each other. I wanted to pull her into my arms and hold tight. Hell, at this point I even imagined buying her a big-ass diamond and making her my wife, just so I didn't have to rattle around in my mansion by myself. Suddenly my fame didn't feel so great anymore, especially with my mother looming in the background.

"This is it," she said. "You're going home."

Back to Pine Tower, I thought. A big, beautiful, secluded place that I was still getting used to. "Have you made plans for your birthday?" I asked. It was a little over a week away.

"I haven't decided."

"It would be great if you'd spend it with me. We could go out on the town, and you can bring whatever friends you want."

"And get bombarded by the press? I'd never do that."

"Then you can bring everyone to my house. We can have a party there." I wanted to see her again, however I could.

"I don't think I'm going to be in the mood for a party. I'm sorry, Dash. I know you want to be friends, but I can't hang out with you. We've got too much history between us."

"Yeah, but there's fire between us, too." The sexual chemistry we'd been fighting, the heat that made our pulses pound. Even now, it was sizzling, moving through our bodies like a live wire. "You can't deny it's there."

"I don't want to talk about that." Her voice cracked, as though her throat was parched. "It makes no sense."

I disagreed. "I still want to be friends, but I want to get romantic with you again, too." I needed to soothe the ache deep in my body, deep in my bones. "If you give me a chance, we can start over and see where it leads."

She looked confused. "You want us to date?"

I nodded. "We could forget the past. We could let it go."

She searched my gaze. "And replace it with what?"

"Something new and fun. I can buy you pretty things and take you places I could never afford to take you before." I hoped that she understood how important it was for me to spoil her, to treat her like a queen. Even though it shouldn't matter anymore, I was still carrying around the shame of not being able to buy her an engagement ring back in the day. "I understand that you're concerned about the press, but I have access to private restaurants and clubs now." My world had changed, and I longed to bring her into it. "We could even jet off to a private island."

She went silent, and I waited for her to respond, hoping she would consider it.

Finally, she said, "It sounds complicated to me, being with my ex and letting him sweep me off my feet. You never loved me, Dash. So why should I bend to your will now?"

"Because love isn't the issue. I mean, come on, it's obvious that you don't love me anymore. But that's how it should be." I didn't want her pining over me the way she used to.

She stared unblinkingly at my face. Then she said, "No love, no muss, no fuss. Is that your theory?"

"It definitely makes things easier. And that's why I think it'll work now."

She shook her head. "None of it sounds easy to me. I don't need to go to fancy places or let you buy me pretty things. I just need to be my own person." She stepped back, wobbling a little in her boots. "You should go now."

My pride took an immediate beating.

That was it? That was her decision? To send me away? I couldn't stand the thought of us disappearing from each other's lives again, but what choice did I have? I couldn't beg her.

I slipped on my sunglasses, frowning beneath them. After an awkward pause, she walked toward the house.

I wanted to call her back over to me, to grab her, to shake her, to kiss her. But I climbed in my truck, hurt and frustrated that she'd rejected me, and drove off, leaving her behind.

I took the back roads to Pine Tower, thinking about her the entire time. There was a hole in the pit of my stomach. The emptiness of going home alone, I thought.

Once I got there, I stopped to chat with a group of fans gathered at the security gate, letting them stand beside my window and take some selfies with me. Even with as miserable as I was, I managed to smile.

Later, when I arrived at my big sprawling house, I spotted Zeke, sitting on the porch steps and waiting for me.

Instead of heading inside, I sat beside him and gazed out at my property, taking in the cool blue lake, the floating dock, the grassy knolls and thick green forest.

He removed his tie and tucked it into his pants pocket, waiting for me to speak. I turned toward him, and he squinted, probably seeing a reflection of himself in my mirrored lenses.

I asked, "What did you find out?"

He quit squinting and said, "Your mother took a bus across the border, from Tijuana, Mexico, to San Diego, California. She arrived three days before the letter was postmarked. My guess is that she's staying with someone, a friend or acquaintance, and that they picked her up in San Diego and took her to LA."

"I want you to search for her there."

"I will, but what do you want me to do if I find her?"

"I don't know." I couldn't focus that far ahead. "Do you still think I'm going to get another letter?"

He nodded. "Yes, I absolutely do."

"Then I wish she would hurry up and send it." But in spite of my impatience, it wasn't my mother who consumed me today. It was Tracy.

And how badly I missed her already.

Five

Tracy

I was back in my own house, sleeping in my own bed. Pop was doing much better and didn't need me to stay with him anymore. But when I was alone like this, all I did was think about Dash.

I was scheduled to work tomorrow at the feedstore, and here I was, tossing and turning. How was I going to get up in the morning refreshed and ready for work?

The feedstore itself seemed like a problem, too, since it was the place where I'd first met Dash. Everything in my life was intertwined with him, somehow.

The most disturbing part, of course, was that I still loved him. He assumed otherwise, but he was wrong. I was glad, actually, that he couldn't tell how I felt. Nonetheless, it wasn't healthy for me to care about him, and especially not after all this time. But my stupid heart didn't know the difference.

I sat up and tugged at my clothes. I was wearing a pajama tank top and skimpy little panties. It was hot in my room, the summer night humid and sticky. The swamp cooler in my house had gone out a few months ago, and I couldn't afford to fix it.

I had a fan blowing, but it wasn't helping. I turned on the light, rolled up the blinds, opened the window and stared out at the night sky. It was filled with stars.

Real stars, I thought. Not the celebrity kind.

I needed to figure out what to do about Dash. I certainly couldn't lose sleep over him every night.

Maybe my logic was skewed, but my gut instinct was to just have an affair with him and cleanse this crazy hunger from my blood. No dating. No friendship. No romance. Just down-and-dirty sex.

If I controlled the affair, if it happened on my terms, it might give me a sense of power and help me to stop loving him.

Dang, but how freeing would that be?

Besides, I needed a hot, wild romp. Otherwise I might end up feeling like an old maid—me and my failing ovaries.

Should I propose an affair? Should I actually go through with it? Or would it create even more problems? I couldn't be sure, but avoiding him wasn't working. He was still consuming me.

Of course, if I slept with him, I would have to lay some ground rules. And Dash would have to abide by them. I wasn't going to let him take over. I deserved to take a stand, to be a strong and independent woman, without the burden of love.

I reached for my phone and checked the time. It was 3:16. Whatever I did, I had to do it soon, because I couldn't go through this every night. Maybe I would run it by Alice after I got off work tomorrow. At least I could get her opinion.

I turned off the light and went back to bed, hoping that I was on the right track.

And that someday my feelings for Dash would be gone.

The next evening, Alice and I convened in her stylishly decorated living room, each with a Maltese dog on our lap. I ran my fingers through Cookie's fur. She was the one keeping me company. The other one's name was Candy, and they were the first dogs Spencer had ever rescued. Now they were part of his and Alice's family.

"What do you think?" I asked her. I'd just told her about my Dash idea.

She cautiously replied, "I understand that you don't want to have a conventional romance with him. But what if the affair backfires and leaves you longing for more? You could end up regretting it."

"What more am I going to be longing for? I was engaged to him and pregnant with his baby. I can't get those things back."

"I like that you're approaching this as a way to make yourself stronger. And that you'd be presenting him with a set of rules. But do you trust him to follow them?"

"He won't have a choice if he wants me back in his bed."

She angled her head, her platinum hair illuminated

by a multicolored chandelier. "It sounds like he wants more than that, though."

"Because he wants to take me out and buy me nice things?" I shifted in my seat. "How is that relevant?"

"What about his apology about the past? About not being ready for fatherhood when you got pregnant?"

"That doesn't change anything. Nor does it make him capable of love. He was clear about his stand on that."

She sighed. "It's not good that you still love him."

In the silence that followed, I petted Cookie again, and the dog snuggled deeper into my lap. Alice fussed over Candy, too, straightening her glittery pink bow. The dogs were orphaned sisters that had lost their original owner when she'd died. Spencer had found them, alone and afraid, hiding under his porch.

I glanced up and said, "You know the saying 'absence makes the heart grow fonder'? That's been true in my case. The years Dash and I have been separated have only made me miss him more. But if I fight it head-on, I might win."

Alice met my gaze. "If you want to have an affair, and he's willing to accept your terms, then go for it. It's got to be better than how things are for you now."

"Definitely." I sat a little straighter, gaining strength from her support. I needed as much girl power as I could get. "But I'm still not going to sing with him." I wasn't interested in a duet. That would give him too much control over me and my career. "It's just going to be sex. Then it'll be over, once and for all."

She smiled. "You look relieved."

"I am." But I was still nervous about following through and making it happen.

* * *

Later that night, I debated my options. Should I invite Dash over to discuss what was on my mind? Or should I do it over the phone?

I did neither. I tidied up instead, walking around my house, going from room to room, putting dishes away, dusting furniture, fluffing pillows and smoothing cushions.

Sometimes I cleaned when I was anxious. Other times I made a mess. Tonight, I was in cleaning mode. But it made sense, in a symbolic way, since I was trying to clean up my life.

Finally, I sat down and opened my laptop. Determined to keep things in perspective, I created a checklist, making my rules clear.

Was I traveling down a slippery slope, preparing to sleep with my ex? Maybe. But it was better than obsessing about him day and night.

After I finished the list, I decided to call. It seemed like the safest solution. Somehow, I just couldn't have this conversation face-to-face.

I dialed his number, but he didn't answer. It went to his voice mail. Now I was stuck, sitting here waiting to hear back from him. I considered cleaning some more.

But before I could pick up my dustrag, Dash returned my call. I answered on the fourth ring. I didn't want to seem too eager, which was weird. I was the one who'd contacted him to begin with.

"Is everything okay?" he asked. "Is your dad all right?"

"He's fine." I gazed at the embroidered Home Sweet Home pillow on my sofa. I'd purchased it as a gift for myself when I'd bought this house. "I wanted to talk about us."

"About me taking you out?"

"Yes." I forced myself to say it, as openly and honestly as I could. "I don't want to date or be friends. But I wouldn't mind sleeping with you again."

He went silent on the other end. Like when crickets chirped in a movie to show you how awkward it was. I had no idea what he was feeling.

Was he stunned? Aroused? Offended? Confused?

Or had the call been dropped, so he hadn't even heard my proposal? Wouldn't that just be my luck?

"Dash? Are you still there?"

"Yeah, I'm here. I just..." He hesitated. "Are you asking me to have a one-night stand?"

"I'm asking you to have an affair. I'm not sure for how long, exactly. A few weeks, a few months. It'll depend on how it goes and when we're both ready for it to end." I reached for my laptop and opened the list, doing my best to stay focused, to not get emotional. This was a huge step for me, and I couldn't let myself falter, even if my heart was beating a nervous cadence. "I have some rules that you'll have to agree to."

"Rules?" He sounded wary.

My heart was still pounding. I took a deep breath. "There's only five."

"Then let's hear them."

I went for it, rushing the words out. "First off, you can't sleep with anyone except me while we're together." His groupies were definitely off-limits. "I won't be with anyone, either." Not that I had other men waiting in the wings, but I figured it was only fair for both of us to be monogamous. "Secondly, we're not going out in public or letting the press know that we're seeing each other." I absolutely, positively needed to keep my trysts with him private. "Thirdly, you're not spreading the wealth and buying me things." I wasn't going to be controlled by his money. "The fourth one is that I'm not recording a duet with you, not before, during or after the affair." I didn't want him to keep bugging me about that. "And lastly, we walk away with a clean slate when it's over. No messy breakup, no emotional turmoil."

"Damn, Tracy. You're really being methodical about this."

"I just want to keep it focused on the affair." I wasn't about to admit how anxious I was about getting this right. Or that deep in my bones, I still loved him.

"But it sounds so…clinical."

I pressed the issue. "Are you interested or should I just hang up now?"

"Hold on, girl, give me a minute." He released an audible breath. "Can I impose some rules, too?"

"No," I said quickly. I couldn't let him take over. I needed to be the lover in charge.

"Can we start it on your birthday?" he asked.

I considered his suggestion. It had to start sometime, so why not on the day I was born? Or reborn, I thought, and reprograming myself to stop loving him. "We can get together that day, but you have to promise to abide by my rules."

"I will, but can we at least try to make it seem like a date?"

I challenged him. "It won't change anything. It'll still just be sex."

"Yeah, but it'll make me feel better for us to treat it

like a date." His voice turned raspy. "I want to be with you, Tracy. On your birthday, with you hot and naked in my bed. But I want to wine and dine you, too."

I fought a shiver. He was making me feel warm and sensual. But I still needed to hang tough. "You can wine and dine me at your house. But not anywhere else." I wasn't going to let him con me into going out in public with him. I wasn't going to date him for real.

"Okay," he conceded. "You can come over, and I'll have my chef prepare a meal. We can crack open a bottle of wine and soak in the hot tub, too. Will you stay the night? I'd really like it if you would."

Should I sleep at his house?

"Yes," I said. "I'll stay." It seemed less emotional than coming home late at night, disheveled, with the scent of his skin on mine. At least I could shower and change my clothes at his place in the morning. "I'll pack what I need."

"I'll have Zeke come get you."

"I can take my truck."

"If you're trying to keep this under wraps, then it would be better if your truck isn't spotted driving through my security gate. I've got some diehard Dashers who sometimes hang out there, and they might snap a picture of you or the license plate on your truck."

"Okay, I'll ride with Zeke." I definitely didn't want Dash's fans figuring out who I was and plastering my information all over the internet.

"I'm looking forward to seeing you."

"Me, too." I was also looking forward to shaking him from my blood, to living the rest of my life without my heart being entangled with his.

This affair had better cure me of my ills. If it didn't, I would just be sleeping with the man I reluctantly loved, with no relief in sight.

I fussed over what to wear on my birthday. I finally decided on a skintight dress and tall, sexy boots, making myself look like a sultry cowgirl. For the final touch, I curled my hair, tumbling it into massive waves.

Zeke picked me up, wearing his customary suit and driving the same luxury SUV I'd seen him in before.

I rode in the back seat, and I could feel him glancing at me from time to time in the rearview mirror. We didn't speak during the drive, other than for him to ask me if I wanted him to turn on the radio.

I agreed, and we listened to a country station. When one of Dash's hits came on, I wished I'd opted to leave the radio off. Hearing his twangy voice only made me more nervous.

As we traveled farther into the country, I gazed out the window. Plants and trees bloomed along the way, making everything look soft and summery.

We arrived at the gate, and sure enough, there were fans hanging around. Thank goodness they couldn't see me in the back seat, not through the darkly tinted windows.

Once we drove onto the property, and Dash's house came into view, I sat a little more upright. Now I understood why it was called Pine Tower. The blue-and-white country-style mansion was surrounded by a forest. There was also a private lake with ducks floating on the water. I assumed the equestrian facility was beyond the house somewhere.

"How many acres is this?" I asked Zeke. The sun was beginning to set, creating a hush over the land.

"Altogether, it's about three hundred." He gestured to his left. "I live in one of the guesthouses across the lake. So do Chef and some of the other staff."

"It's really impressive." Dash had gotten everything he'd always wanted.

And now he was going to have me, too. For a little while, anyway.

I glanced up and saw that he'd just come outside and was waiting for us on the wraparound porch. He looked like a mirage. The man I used to know. The man who'd become a star.

Zeke parked the SUV and opened my door for me. As he went around the back to remove my overnight bag, Dash started down the porch steps. When he smiled, I got warm all over.

I returned his smile, determined to enjoy the moment. And when he kissed me, I damned near melted. I slid my arms around his waist, relishing the feel of his whip-hard body against mine. I tucked my hands into the back pockets of his jeans, getting a nice tight grip on his butt, and we both sucked in our breaths.

Zeke cleared his throat, and we separated. By then, my bag had already been moved onto the porch.

After the bodyguard bade us goodbye and drove off, Dash kissed me again, and I rubbed against him. We hadn't even gone into the house yet, and we were already getting intimate.

Finally, he whispered, "Happy Birthday," in my ear.

Happy, indeed. I was tingling, my nipples hard beneath my low-cut bra, my panties silky against my skin.

He took my hand. "I'll give you a tour of the house

and let you get settled. Then we can have dinner in my bedroom, on the balcony."

"That sounds nice." I was eager for our evening to begin.

The house consisted of eight bedrooms and ten bathrooms. The main floor featured built-in bookcases, wood-burning fireplaces, a cozy den and a sunny kitchen equipped with an elevator used to serve meals to the master suite. I noticed a breakfast nook with bay windows, too. Also located on the bottom floor were a massive parlor, a formal dining area, a gym and a media room that opened into a music room, where Dash kept his equipment and awards and such.

Most of the bedrooms were upstairs. Dash's master suite offered a glamorous bathroom and two colossal-sized closets.

A staircase led from the balcony outside his room down to a garden with a lap pool and a hot tub.

He said, "There's a patio on the other side of the house with a full-size pool and entertainment area. But I use this one for myself."

"It's incredible, all of it." Every last detail.

"Thank you. You can unpack your bag if you want." He gestured to the closet on the left. "That one is empty. It's for…"

"Your lovers to use?" I tried not to frown. I didn't want to think of other women being here with him.

He nodded, then said, "There's a dressing room inside the closet, so you don't have to come out and change. The couple who lived here before had it designed that way. I can't take credit for how the place was built."

"It certainly seems to fit your needs."

"It's actually bigger than what I need. But I loved the layout. The lake is stocked with bass and catfish, and there's whitetail deer and rabbits and squirrels in the pines. But I don't allow anyone to hunt on the property."

"Zeke told me that he lives across the lake."

"It helps having my top security guy nearby."

"He said that your chef lives in one of the guesthouses, too. When can I meet him?" I'd only gotten a glimpse of him in the kitchen.

"I'll introduce you when he serves our meal."

"What's on the menu?" I'd gotten a whiff of all sorts of yummy aromas when we'd first entered the house.

"Buttermilk fried chicken, sweet potato fries, cheesy grits and collard greens with bacon." He smiled. "A lot of your old favorites."

"It sounds delicious." This was going to be a heck of a birthday. Me and my ex in his mansion, eating comfort food.

"I asked Chef to bake a cake, too."

"I can't wait." I'd always been a dessert kind of gal. The thicker and richer, the better. But mostly I was thinking about being with Dash.

Hot and naked. All night long.

Six

Tracy

The meal was amazing. Dash's chef had outdone himself. He was also a nice, friendly guy. I learned that he lived on the property with his wife and children. I hadn't expected that.

I gazed across the table at Dash, wondering about how many other people lived on the Pine Tower property. Was he surrounded by other families? Did it ever make him think of his own? Or did it remind him of the child we'd lost? My thoughts were shifting in all sorts of directions.

"Is Zeke married?" I asked, as I sank my fork into the dessert on my plate. By now, we were indulging in huge slices of the sinfully delicious chocolate-raspberry cake. "Or does he have any kids?"

Dash shook his head. "He's divorced. No kids."

"Do you know his ex? Or did they split up before he started working for you?" I shouldn't care, but I was sitting here with *my* ex, embarking on an affair. It was tough not to be curious about Dash's bodyguard and if his past influenced Dash in any way.

"It was before. He never says much about it, and I've never really been inclined to ask. His personal life is his business."

I returned to my cake. It didn't matter if Zeke was married or single or if Dash's chef had a zillion kids running around the property. I wasn't supposed to become emotionally invested in this place or its people. Besides, this wasn't the time to think about anything that would remind me of my broken engagement to Dash or the babies I would probably never have.

We both went silent as we continued to eat.

"Do you want to soak in the hot tub after we're done?" he asked a moment later.

I nodded, eager to relax and clear my mind. "Can we bring the wine with us?"

"Yes, but I'm more interested in taking your swimsuit off than playing drinking games." He cut into a sugared rose on his piece of cake and lifted the fork to his mouth.

"I never said anything about drinking games." My pulse pounded between my legs. He looked as if he was letting the flower melt on his tongue. My pulse pounded a little harder. "And just so you know, I'll be wearing a one piece." I watched him take another bite. "You'll have to peel it all the way down." It wasn't going to be as easy to remove as a bikini.

A slow smile spread across his lips. “That’s even better.”

My skin tingled from my head to my pink polished toes. My bathing suit was pink, too. A deep, dark magenta.

We finished dessert and put our dirty dishes in the bottom of a metal food cart his chef had brought into the room. At some point, Dash’s housekeeper would take the cart back to the kitchen and wash the dishes. All he had to do was text her to come by. Like the rest of his loyal staff, she lived in one of the guesthouses across the lake.

Once it was time to get ready for the hot tub, I changed in the walk-in closet/dressing room that Dash provided for his lovers or groupies or whoever he brought home. But for now, I was the woman attracting his attention.

I checked my appearance in the mirror, making sure that my suit wasn’t riding up in back. I also pinned my hair into a topknot to keep the ends from getting wet.

I emerged and saw Dash waiting for me. He was wearing beachy printed trunks.

I breathed as deeply as I could. He looked tall and tan and delicious. Clearly, he thought I looked scrumptious, too. His gaze lingered on me, far longer than was necessary, and the reality of what I was doing hit me like a ton of crumbling bricks. Soon I would be naked with the man I was trying not to love. But that was my choice, my way of tackling my feelings. I wasn’t about to end this affair before it had even begun.

He grabbed the wine and our glasses, and we took the balcony staircase to his private garden, where the hot tub awaited.

"I might take a quick lap in the pool first," he said, as we reached the bottom. "I like to swim before I soak."

"That's fine." I glanced around. The patio was beautiful, with all the plants and flowers and the artfully strung lights.

Dash turned on the jets. "You're all set."

"Thank you." I poured myself some wine and settled into the hot tub while he dived into the pool. He was a strong swimmer, and watching him made me hungry to touch him. But seeing him in this environment also made him seem larger than life. So different from the poor boy I used to know.

He swam two laps, then joined me, taking the seat next to mine. He slicked his hair back from his forehead and reached for the wine bottle that I'd left on the caddy attached to the side of the tub.

He filled his glass. "Remember how drunk you got on your twenty-first birthday? I had to tuck you into bed."

"I won't drink that much tonight." I topped off my glass. "Maybe I'll just get a little tipsy."

"To build up the courage to be with me?" He set his wine aside. "I'm not going to hurt you, Tracy."

"I'm not worried about that." He'd already hurt me years ago by not loving me. How much damage could he do now? "I'm drinking because I want to have fun." I wasn't about to admit that I was nervous.

He moved closer. "I've missed you."

I'd missed him, too, so danged much. But that didn't change what had gone wrong between us. "I'm only here for the sex."

"I know." He leaned into me. "It's just an affair."

He kissed me, warm and deep, with the water bubbling around us. Our tongues met and mated, and I wrapped my arms around him. I closed my eyes, as well as my heart. I couldn't let myself feel anything more than physical pleasure.

He ended the kiss, and I opened my eyes and looked into his. We stared at each other, unblinking, unmoving, steeped in the strangely tender moment.

"You need to stand up," he said.

"Why?" I managed to ask.

"Because I want to undress you now."

I climbed onto the bench seat, anxious to feel his hands on my body. "Is this a good spot?"

"It's perfect." He began removing my swimsuit. Down it went, from my shoulders to my feet, leaving me naked, water dripping softly from my skin.

He latched onto my hips, and I breathed in the night air. I knew exactly what he intended to do, and I welcomed it fully, aroused by the intimacy.

I widened my stance, and he put his face between my legs. I delved my hands into his wet hair, and he kissed me down there. He'd always been good at it. But he was even better now. Or maybe I was just desperate for it.

He deepened the pleasure, and I watched him, thinking how sexy he looked. He watched me, too, glancing up to catch my gaze. We stared at each other again, two people fighting the past. But for now, all that mattered was the way he was making me feel.

Slick. Hot. Wet.

I swayed on my feet, letting him take me to delectable heights. I rocked against his face. My old lover. My new lover. He paused to nuzzle my thigh, and I practically begged him to continue. I wanted more, as much as he would give me.

He resumed his ministrations, swirling his tongue, relentless in his pursuit to make me come.

As soon as the orgasm hit, I gasped out loud, my vision blurring, my muscles quivering. The wine I'd consumed went to my head. Or was it the thrill of the moment? I couldn't stop shaking. If Dash hadn't been keeping me steady, my knees might've buckled.

Once my climax ended, I sank back into the water, and he pulled me tight against him, holding me close.

"Am I going to have to carry you back upstairs?" he asked.

I clung to him. "I can walk. I just need a minute."

He nipped at my earlobe. "Maybe we should just stay here instead of going upstairs right away, and I can give you a repeat performance."

I shivered at the thought. "You'd do it again?"

"Damn right I would." He skimmed a hand down the center of my chest and over my stomach. "I'd do it a hundred times, if you'd let me." He paused for a moment as he stared into my eyes. "Just say yes, and I'll be happy to oblige."

I whispered a breathy "Yes," giving him permission to make it happen all over again.

We went back upstairs to Dash's room, and he removed his trunks and wrapped a towel around his waist. I was already naked beneath my towel, fresh from my second orgasm.

I sat on the edge of the bed and released the topknot in my hair, shaking it out to its full length. I was nervous again, but only because I wanted him so badly. But he wasn't making a move toward me. He was silent, still.

"Is something wrong?" I asked.

"What? No. It's just that we haven't talked about what to use, and I was wondering if you're on anything or if..."

I lifted my anxious gaze to his. I'd gotten pregnant last time because of a broken condom. But our story didn't end there. Once we'd realized what had happened, I'd gone to the pharmacy the next day for the morning-after pill. As it turned out, the emergency contraceptive hadn't been effective because I'd been taking some herbs that had stopped it from working. At that point I'd begun to believe that our baby was meant to be. But I'd been mistaken. Sadly, painfully mistaken.

"I'm not on anything," I said. Women with my condition could take birth control in case they spontaneously ovulated. But I wasn't going to tell him about my POF or how unlikely conception was. "Do you have condoms?"

"Yes, of course. I'm sorry, Tracy. I didn't mean to make this conversation awkward."

"It's okay. You're just being responsible."

"I'm certainly trying to be." He paused, then said, "Oh, before I forget, I have a gift for you."

I widened my eyes. "You're not supposed to be buying me things. That was one of my rules."

"This is different. It's your birthday."

He went to his closet to get the present. He came back with a medium-sized, shiny black box topped with a big silver bow.

He sat beside me, a little too confidently, and I got a suspicious feeling. "This better not be jewelry disguised in a regular box."

He shrugged, smiled and leaned toward me for a quick kiss. "Open it and see."

I didn't trust him, not one sexy little iota. I lifted the lid, keeping the bow intact. The gift was wrapped in sparkly sheets of tissue paper. It seemed too big to be jewelry, but too light to be something else. I was intrigued.

I removed the tissue and uncovered a gold body chain, decorated with rubies. Jewelry, for sure. An unconventional and erotic piece.

I held it up. Six chains draped in front, one of which would loop around my breasts. As for the rubies, they were everywhere.

"It's your birthstone," he said, pointing out the obvious.

My heart pounded. "It's gorgeous, but you still shouldn't have done it."

"It's too late. I already did. Besides, it's just a little enticement between lovers."

"Then I'll wear it for you." How could I not? I dropped my towel and stood to slip on the chain, hooking it around my neck. "Will you fasten the back?"

He nodded and rose to help me.

When I turned to face him, I caught a glimpse of myself in a nearby mirror. I looked wild and naughty, shiny and pretty.

He trailed his hand along the exposed parts of my skin. One of the rubies on the bottom chain dangled just below my navel. I covered his hand with mine and guided it lower, between my legs. He cupped my mound, and I moaned.

We kissed, and I pressed closer. I undid his towel, making it slip to the floor. I stroked him, and we kissed some more, hot and hungry for each other.

He removed a condom from the nightstand drawer,

and I pulled him down onto the bed. He sheathed himself, and I watched him, fascinated by how big and hard he was. I needed him inside me.

I waited for him to slide between my legs, but he said, "I think you should be on top."

To ride him? Like the cowgirl I sometimes was? That sounded sexy to me. "Should I keep this on the entire time?" I asked about the body chain.

He nodded, and I straddled him, eager to make his acquaintance. In the next breathtaking instant, I impaled myself, causing both of us to shiver. I moved up and down, rocking on his lap, creating a slow and sensual rhythm. He thumbed my nipples through the gold loops that encircled my breasts. He toyed with the ruby dangling below my navel, too.

"You look like a princess," he said.

I leaned forward, putting my face next to his. "Is that a fantasy of yours?"

"It is now," he whispered, then took my mouth in a heated kiss.

I met the thrust of his tongue, and things got wilder. He gripped my waist and thrust his hips, encouraging me to buck against him. I took him from shaft to tip, riding him hard and fast. I wanted us to come at the same time. We'd always been compatible in that way, so it wasn't much of a stretch. I knew it was possible. He seemed to know it, too.

Intent on touching me, he played with my hair, tangling it around his fingers. The chains on my body jangled, rubies winking in the light.

I dug my nails into his shoulders, branding him with sharp little marks, and he groaned his pleasure.

The room began to spin. Or maybe it was the climax

building in my loins. Dash was hard and heavy between my legs, and I was wet and slick.

I kept riding him, moving us toward completion. The sound he emitted was feral. He was close. So was I.

A fire burned in my belly, a sheen of perspiration misting my skin. Dash was sticky with sweat, too.

I felt him shudder, just as I shook. We came together, hot and fast and furious.

After it was over, he disposed of the condom, and I removed the chain and set it on the nightstand. He returned to bed and took me in his arms, holding me tight.

This affair was definitely off to a wild start, and I was desperate for every second of it.

We slept naked, and when I awakened the next morning, we were in a spooning position, the front of my body pressed against the back of his, my arm looped around his waist.

Was he still asleep? I could feel the warmth of his skin, the ripple of his stomach muscles. But that wasn't enough for me. I wanted to get sexual.

I kissed his shoulder in a loving way, then asked myself what I was doing. I didn't need to be sweet and affectionate to arouse him, did I?

No, I thought. I was drifting back to the old days, behaving like the foolish girl I used to be. Old habits and all of that. But it was too late. I sensed that Dash was awake.

He confirmed it by saying, "Morning," in a raspy voice.

I removed my lips from his shoulder and went right for his penis, reaching down to grab it.

"Morning, yourself," I said. He was already half hard.

He moaned and laughed at the same time. "I never could trust you in the daylight."

I stroked him, running my thumb across the tip. "I've always been frisky that way."

"Yeah." He turned around, bringing us face-to-face.

He crawled on top of me, pinning me to the bed. I stared up at him, feeling as if I'd just been kidnapped.

"Maybe we should have breakfast first," I said.

He raised his eyebrows. "And here I thought you wanted me for breakfast."

"I need real food." I was making excuses, though I was trying to keep my head on straight. I didn't like the kidnapped feeling. It gave him too much power, making me afraid that I would never stop loving him.

He kept looking down at me, as if he was trying to figure me out. I couldn't tell what he was thinking, but he didn't let me go.

"What do you want to eat?" he asked.

"Is your chef available?"

"No. It's just us."

"Then I'll have some cereal." Something simple and quick. Anything to get him to release me. His body was heavy against mine. But it felt good, so painfully, dangerously good.

"Hot or cold?" he asked.

I blinked. "What?"

"The cereal."

"Cold." I couldn't handle anything hot right now. He was hot enough. My former fiancé, in his big expensive mansion, holding me hostage.

"I'll go get breakfast," he said.

I just wanted him to hurry up. I was trembling beneath him, my limbs practically turning to mush.

He finally lifted his body from mine, giving me a chance to breathe a little easier.

He climbed out of bed and put on a pair of plaid boxers. Then he turned and said, "I want you to stay naked."

After he'd just gotten dressed? How was that fair? "You can't tell me what to do."

"Oops, sorry." He smiled his crooked smile. "Will you stay naked for me? Pretty please with sugary cereal on top?"

"Smart-ass." I considered throwing my pillow at him. But I was charmed by his playfulness, too. He always seemed to have conflicting effects on me. "I don't like the sugary stuff."

"Oh, that's right. You eat the grown-up cereal."

"Just go get it, and I'll decide what I'm going to wear. Or not wear," I added, impishly.

"All right." He hesitated for a second. "If you want coffee, there's one of those single-serve machines on the bar."

He left, and I decided to skip the coffee. Instead, I poured myself a glass of orange juice from the mini fridge. I debated if I should cover up or remain naked. I split the difference and rummaged through Dash's dresser, borrowing a pair of his boxers, the same plaid style he was wearing. I topped them off with the body chain. It took me several tries to reach back and hook it, but I finally got it done.

Dash returned with breakfast. He saw me and broke into a grin. "Damn. Could you be any hotter?"

"I thought it made an interesting fashion statement."

"For sure." He set down the tray. It contained the cereal, two plastic bowls, two spoons, a pitcher of milk and several cloth napkins.

We ate in bed, as cozy as could be. I sat crossed-legged with my napkin on my lap, and he sat upright against the headboard.

"Do you want to shower with me?" I asked. "Just as soon as we're done?"

He glanced at my scantily clad body. "Is that a trick question?"

"No. But my one condition is that you can't do anything to me while we're in there. Only I can do things to you." After the way he'd made me feel kidnapped earlier, I needed to get my groove back and be the one in charge.

He swallowed the cereal in his mouth. "You have an awful lot of rules."

"Don't worry. You're going to enjoy this one." I wet my lips, letting him know just how good it was going to be.

For both of us.

Seven

Dash

Tracy was immediately intrigued by the ceiling-mounted, rainfall-style showerhead equipped with LED lights that changed colors. As she made adjustments, I took a moment to gauge my mood. I wasn't sure how I felt about how things were unfolding between us. I wasn't used to having a lover call the shots, but Tracy seemed determined to have her way. If I didn't behave, I figured she would ditch me and go home, and I wasn't prepared to lose her so soon. I wanted our affair to last as long as possible.

"This is pretty," she said, as the water turned blue.

I was more interested in her, the curvy brunette driving me mad. She ducked under the spray and crooked her finger for me to join her.

I obeyed, anxious for her to touch me. But she soaped down instead, lathering her luscious body and washing her hair. I stood under the rainfall and watched her. She'd turned into quite the seductress, teasing me, making me wait.

I washed myself under the blue water, too. When it glowed green, Tracy was rinsing her hair. By the time it was purple, I wanted to do wicked things to her. Only I wasn't allowed.

She finally came toward me, and I thought I might die on the damned spot. She pumped liquid soap into her hands and reached out to lather me. I was already clean, but I wasn't going to complain about being extra sudsy.

She started at my chest and worked her way down, rolling her fingers over my abs. I sucked in my breath, and my muscles went taut. My erection was growing, and she hadn't even gotten there yet. She took her sweet time, making me suffer.

Finally, finally…she touched me there, stroking me to full arousal.

Tracy rinsed the soap from my body and dropped to her knees. Now I really was going to die.

She teased me with her tongue, and I put my hands in her shower-soaked hair. Water dripped down my face, but I didn't care. I lowered my head to watch.

She took me in her mouth and rocked back and forth, creating a slow and sleek rhythm. Yeah, I was dying for sure. My fingers were practically tangled in her hair.

She increased the tempo, using her hands and her mouth. I couldn't help it; I thrust my hips forward. She didn't seem to mind. If anything, she welcomed my participation. She even pulled me closer.

I groaned out loud. She looked beautiful as the light shifted from purple back to blue, creating an ocean-like shimmer and making her seem like a mermaid.

She glanced up at me, and our gazes locked. She was sultry. Sinful. The sexiest creature on earth.

She took me deeper, all the way to the back of her throat. Damn, it felt good, with all the ripples of heat coursing through me. I definitely wanted this affair to last. I even got the crazy urge that I'd gotten before, to buy her a diamond and marry her.

But I wasn't thinking straight, not with Tracy down on her knees. Still, I imagined her as my wife, living here with me, sleeping in my bed and sharing my love of music. Sharing my world.

She dug her nails into my ass, and my thoughts scattered. Was the water still blue? Or was it green?

All I knew was that my skin was hot, my blood sizzling through my veins. Tracy was taking me to the edge, as an orgasm continued building in my body.

Engulfed in pleasure, I started to shake and shiver, but she didn't finish me off with her hands. She let me spill into her mouth. I tried to watch it happen, but my vision blurred, leaving me in a fog.

Afterward, when Tracy came to her feet, she turned off the shower and rung out her wet hair. I merely stood there, staring at her.

"You okay?" she asked.

"Yeah." I was more than okay.

She got us some towels, and we dried off in the bathroom. I backed her against the sink, and she looked up at me.

"What are you doing?" she asked.

"I just want to thank you." I lowered my mouth to hers, kissing her, holding her gently in my arms.

She sighed, sweet and dreamy, but it didn't last. She wriggled away and darted off to my bedroom. When had she become so elusive? I didn't answer my own question. I didn't want to rehash all the reasons in my mind.

I followed her, and we both went into our closets to grab our clothes. Neither of us used the dressing rooms. We got dressed in front of each other, like we used to do.

"Will you stay for the rest of the day?" I asked.

"I can't." She buttoned her blouse. "I have work to do, a VA project I need to finish."

I zipped my jeans. "Maybe just for a few more hours? We could take a walk in the woods. Or go fishing or just sit on the dock."

"We can do those things next time I come over."

"And when will that be?" I was anxious to see her again, but why wouldn't I be, with how challenging it was to keep her in my grasp?

She sat down to put on her boots. "I don't know. We'll have to figure it out."

I persisted, trying to pin her down. "When do you work next at the feedstore?"

"Tuesday. But you better not come there, Dash." She shot me a warning look. "You can visit Maddie on a different day."

Screw that, I thought. I was going to do as I pleased and pop over on Tuesday. Only I pretended otherwise. "Whatever you say." I shot her a half-assed grin. "You're the boss."

"You're darned right I am."

She smiled, too, obviously thinking that I was being

compliant. But I couldn't give in to everything she said. I wasn't built that way.

I got curious and asked, "Do people ever recognize you at the feedstore?" It had been a while since she'd had a hit record, but she'd still made a bit of a name for herself.

"Sometimes an old fan will come in and wonder why I'm working there." She finished tugging her boots into place. "People think I should be rich. They don't understand that my success wasn't as big as it seemed. Not like yours," she added.

"I got lucky." But I'd also struck while the iron was hot, landing a number of lucrative endorsement deals. By the end of the year, I would be appearing in vitamin water ads that we'd filmed while I was on tour, racking up millions of extra dollars. "What do you tell your old fans?" I asked.

"About why I'm working at the feedstore?" She stood and smoothed her pants legs over her boots. "I just say that the owner is a friend, and mostly I'm doing it to help her out. Maddie vouches for me and tells people that, too. It's easier than admitting how tough things are for me now."

"It shouldn't be that way." She was just as talented as I was. She should've been a bigger star than she was, especially with her incredible vocal range, and I had the power to put her back in the spotlight if she would let me. But she was too stubborn to consider it.

She finished getting ready, but she didn't do her full makeup and hair routine. She kept it minimal: a long sleek ponytail, a light coat of mascara, beeswax lip balm.

"I need to text Zeke to come get you," I said.

"That's fine. I can wait on the porch for him." She went over to the nightstand, where the body chain was delicately coiled. "I'm not going to take this with me."

I frowned. "Why not?"

"Because this is the only place that I'm ever going to wear it. You can keep it here for me."

"It doesn't really seem like a gift if you don't take it with you." But that was her point, I supposed. Her way of reminding me that she'd restricted me from buying her anything to begin with. "You and your rules." She'd never told me what to do in the past. I cocked an eyebrow at her. "When did you become such a dominatrix?"

Her jaw dropped, her lovely little mouth falling open. "That's not what I am."

I shrugged. I even bit back a laugh. She was properly offended. Next time I should buy her a leather corset and a braided whip and really make her squirm.

I texted Zeke and walked Tracy onto the porch. While we waited for her ride, I reached for her hand and held it, wishing that she had agreed to stay with me for the rest of the day.

It was Tuesday, and Zeke was supposed to drive me to the feedstore. But we needed to deal with my mother first. Another letter had arrived this morning, and he was bringing it to me now.

I was anxious, of course. But I was glad, too, that the wait was over. According to what Zeke had said over the phone, my mom had revealed who she was. She'd even provided a phone number.

After Zeke arrived, we went into the den and stood

near a wood-burning stove, reserved for cooler days. He reached into his pocket and handed me the letter.

The envelope had another lipstick mark on it, another kiss, just like the first one. I removed the note and read it:

My dearest Dash,
Did you get my last letter? Did you know that Lola was me, your mama? I hope so. I really want to see you. Will you call me? I'm staying with a friend in LA, but I didn't tell her that you're my son, so you don't need to worry about her contacting the press or invading your privacy. We can keep this between us. I hope that you can forgive me for hurting you and your daddy. I love and miss you. Looking forward to hearing from you.
Sweet dreams,
Lola/Mom

Her number was below her signature. I refolded the note and returned it to the envelope, then glanced up and scowled. Zeke watched me with an unobtrusive expression, giving me time to voice my thoughts.

Battling the tension in my gut, I said, "I can't believe she told me that she loves me. That's such bullshit." The "sweet dreams" line bothered me, too. She used to say that whenever she got the maternal urge to tuck me in at night. But this wasn't a dream; it was a nightmare.

"How do you want to proceed?" Zeke asked.

I debated my options. I didn't want to call. I wasn't ready to talk to her. But I couldn't ignore her summons, either, not without the anxiety and guilt eating me alive. "I want you to verify that it's her."

He cocked his head. “You still have doubts?”

“No, but I don’t want to give her the satisfaction of giving in so easily. You can call and arrange a meeting with her in LA. Then you can ask her for a DNA sample. After it’s confirmed that’s she my mother, you can tell her that I’ll be willing to see her.” I could’ve suggested that he take a picture of her and send it to me, but I wanted Mom to know that I meant business, insisting on DNA proof.

“When do you want me to make the call?”

“Later today, after we get back from the feedstore.” I still intended to go there this afternoon. I was probably in for a fight with Tracy since she’d warned me to stay away. But I was even more determined to do whatever the hell I wanted, with Tracy and my mom. I wasn’t going to let either of them control me. Or define me. Or tie me up in knots.

My life was still my own.

D & M Feed was located on the outskirts of town. The D was for Maddie’s husband, Dave, only he’d passed on a long time ago, before Tracy and I ever worked there.

Zeke parked the SUV, and we both exited the car. I’d dressed for the part, donning nice Western duds and a straw Stetson. I expected to get recognized.

Sure enough, I did. As soon as we entered the store, a twenty-something redhead glanced in my direction and said, “Oh, my God.” She nudged her husband or boyfriend or whoever he was, and he did a double take. They put their heads together, as if they were deciding if it was okay to approach me.

I shot them a smile, and they came over, telling me

how much they loved my music and asking to take selfies with me. I posed with them and gazed across the entryway.

I spotted Tracy at the checkout counter with an annoyed look on her face. Clearly, she'd caught the commotion and realized that I'd disobeyed her.

More customers approached me. A couple asked if I would take a picture with their kid, a little cowgirl around five with soulful brown eyes. Her parents said that she liked to dance to my songs. My heart jumped for a moment, and I thought about the baby Tracy and I had lost.

The girl's name was Jilly, and she smiled shyly at me. I knelt to pose with her, and her mom said, "She's going to remember this forever."

I would, too, I thought, since Tracy was nearby. Jilly got brave and reached for me, so I went ahead and scooped her up for another set of pictures.

So yeah, there I was, holding a child in my arms. I'd done that before with other fans' kids, but this felt different. I was still looking across the store at Tracy.

Soon Maddie rushed out from her office. Skinny as a rail, with her teased-and-bleached hair and dusty old boots, she headed toward me. I finished the photos with Jilly and returned her to her mom.

Boom!

Then there was Maddie, throwing her bony arms around my neck. "As I live and breathe," she said in her raspy voice.

I hugged her, catching an overwhelming whiff of perfume, hairspray and cigarette smoke. She always smelled that way, sometimes with a nip of whisky thrown in.

"Who's that hunk of beef?" she asked.

I chuckled to myself. She must've caught sight of Zeke, standing like a sentry behind me. "He's my bodyguard."

"I wouldn't mind getting a piece of that."

"I'll just bet." I knew she was kidding. She'd always had a goofy sense of humor, as well as a decent heart. She stepped back, and we exchanged a smile.

The store wasn't overly crowded, but I still spent the next ten minutes taking more selfies with customers. Maddie got in the act and took some of her own, excited about posting them on her social media accounts.

As soon as there was a chance to escape, I asked Maddie if I could retreat to the break room for a while. She agreed, taking my arm and offering to escort me while Zeke stayed on the sales floor. I nodded to Tracy as we passed, but she barely acknowledged me. By now, she looked more sad than mad, making me emotional again, too.

I settled into the break room with its dingy interior and folding tables and chairs, and said to Maddie, "The place looks exactly the same."

"Yeah. But you don't. You're shiny and new." She put her hand on my cheek. "Our boy made good."

If only I'd had a mom like her. Maddie had never had kids, but she should've. "Do you think you could give Tracy a break so she can come back here and say hello?"

"Sure. I'll fill in for her. I can drool over that bodyguard of yours while I'm out there." She paused. "Are you and Tracy friends again?"

"More or less." I couldn't admit that we were having an affair. "I helped her when her dad was sick."

"Oh, that's nice." She stepped back. "I'll go get her." She gestured to an ancient white fridge. "You can have a soda if you want. I still keep them handy for you kids."

She referred to all her employees as her kids. "Thanks. But I'm good." I just wanted to see Tracy.

I waited, eager for her to show up.

When she entered the room, I tried for a smile but fell short. I hurt inside, and so did she. The old memories were reflected in each other's eyes.

"I told you not to come here today," she said, much too softly.

"I know." By now, I just needed to hold her. "But I want to a steal a kiss from you."

"You can't do that." She glanced nervously around. "What if one of my coworkers comes in? It'll give us away."

"How about the utility closet?" We used to go in there and mess around when we both worked here. I'd even knocked over a whole shelf of cleaning supplies during one of our more rambunctious sessions.

She shook her head. "That's even worse."

"You're right." It was toward the back of the building, and someone would probably spot us trying to sneak in there. "Why don't I just block this door with one of the tables? Then if someone tries to come in, we'll just say that the door is stuck. That'll give us some time to put the room back to normal."

She pulled her bottom lip between her teeth, already eating her lipstick off. "Do you really have to kiss me that badly?"

"Yeah, I do." As difficult as this day had been, I couldn't think of a better way to relieve my stress. "Come on, just say the word, and we'll do it."

Was she counting the erratic beats of her heart? Deciding what to do? I counted mine, punchy as they were.

One...two...three...

"I must be crazy to be going along with this," she said.

"Maybe we're both nuts." I hurried and barred the door. As soon as I was done, I backed her against the wall.

She lifted her face to mine, and we kissed. In the passion of the moment, I blocked everything out, except seducing her. She made naughty little sounds, and I moved against her in a carnal rhythm. I tunneled my hands through her hair, and she knocked my hat off my head. Apparently, it was in her way.

We stopped to suck in some air, then went right back to it. She kept making lusty noises, and I kept getting harder. I wanted to take this all the way, but I couldn't have sex with her here. But damn, I was tempted. Maybe I should just undo her jeans and work my hand inside, rubbing her in the sweetest of spots.

The doorknob rattled, and we jumped apart. Someone was trying to come in. Voices sounded on the other side.

"It's locked," a woman said, sounding confused.

"I didn't even know it had a lock," came the reply.

"Me, neither. But I think he's in there."

Shoot, I thought. Clearly, they were looking for me. Feedstore employees who wanted to meet Dash Smith.

I put a finger to my lips, warning Tracy to stay quiet. She nodded, and we waited for them to try the door a few more times and give up and go away.

Finally, after we heard their retreating footsteps, I plunked on my hat, and Tracy smoothed her hair.

"Am I flushed?" she asked. "Do I look guilty?"

I nodded, and we both burst out laughing.

"What about me?" I asked. "Am I still…obvious?"

She glanced at my fly. "Yeah, there's still a bulge."

"Like I have a sock stuffed down there? Rock stars used to do that when they went on stage. They called it sock 'n roll."

She scoffed at my ridiculous knowledge. "You're making that up."

"I'm not. I swear. They really did it, and people really called it that. But I don't need to enhance what I have, not when I'm around you." I flashed a macho smile and reached for her, but she ducked out of the way, stopping me from pulling her into my arms and kissing her again.

Spoilsport, I thought.

"I have to go," she said. "This was a longer break than it should've been."

I returned the table to its original spot, as if nothing had been amiss. "You should go by yourself, and I'll follow in a little while. There's probably a lot of fans on the sales floor by now. Word of Dash Smith sightings travels fast."

She didn't reply. She just headed for the door. But she did glance back, giving me one last breathless look.

I watched her leave, struggling with the way she made me feel. The emptiness every time she was gone.

Eight

Dash

The DNA test was a familial match to mine, proving who Lola was. I'd expected as much, but at least that part of the ordeal was done. The rest of it was just beginning, though.

I met with Zeke at my house, working out the details. This time we sat in the front parlor, a room decorated with reclaimed wood and rustic antiques.

"What does she want?" I asked.

"Aside from renewing her relationship with you? She wants to move back to Nashville. But she doesn't have any money to make the move or anywhere to live once she gets here."

"She wants me to relocate her?"

"Yes. She's hoping you'll do it soon because the friend she's staying with in LA is getting impatient for her to go. It was just a temporary arrangement between them."

I met his steady gaze. Zeke's eyes were darker than mine and hooded beneath his brows.

"What was your impression of her?" I asked.

"Your mom? She's a handful, I'll say that much. She cried a lot while I was there."

I wasn't surprised that she'd cried in front of him. My dad used to do anything for her when she cried. I'd been affected by it, too. Those dramatic tears. "Did she tell you that she was raised in foster care?"

"No. She didn't mention her childhood. But it's obvious that it shaped who she is."

Just as mine had shaped me. I got up from my seat and walked over to the window, standing next to the glass, making decisions in my head. Zeke sat patiently, letting me think it through.

Finally, I said, "I want you to arrange to bring my mom to Nashville and rent a place for her to live." What else was I going to do? Leave her to fend for herself and scurry around on the streets? "Make sure it's in a nice neighborhood, but that it's somewhat secluded, too. I'll work out a budget and tell my accountant to release the funds. It'll also include a car, some credit cards and a monthly allowance."

"I'll let her know. By the way, she told me that once she gets back to Nashville, she wants to change her name to Lola, as a way of starting over here. She plans to do it legally, through the county clerk's office. It's a simple process. Basically, it's just a form she'll have to fill out, with a filing fee."

"Lola Smith?"

"No. Lola Dorchester. She thinks her maiden name

suits her better than Smith. She's uncomfortable about keeping Smith as her last name because of how badly she treated you and your father."

"It's funny how all these years later, she's concerned about me and my dad." I cautiously asked, "If she was your mom, would you be helping her the way I am?"

Zeke frowned, giving me an indication of what his response was going to be. Normally he was difficult to read, rarely giving his feelings away.

He said, "If I was in your position, I would probably do exactly what you're doing. But I wouldn't be happy about it, either." We both fell silent, until he asked, "Do you need anything else from me? Or is that it for tonight?"

"That's it. I'm going to head over to Tracy's, if she has time to see me. But I can drive myself."

"If you're going to start spending time there, I should have cameras installed around her place."

"I'll talk to her about it." But for now, I just needed to touch her. Quickly, mindlessly, passionately. I hadn't seen her since the stolen kiss at the feedstore. I hope she'd agree to accommodate me. With the way she was calling the shots, I couldn't be sure.

Once Zeke was gone I called her, and she made it even more exciting. She told me that she had to finish up a job on her computer, but that I could come by *after* she was in bed.

"I'll leave a key for you under the mat," she said.

I got hard just thinking about it. "Will you be naked? Will you be ready for me?"

"Maybe," she replied, all soft and sexy. "I guess you'll just have to wait and see."

Even though she was offering herself to me, she was

still being elusive. “What time should I check under the mat?” I practically panted into the phone.

“Late. After midnight. Do I need to text you my address?”

“No.” I’d never been to her house, but I knew where she lived. I’d always kept her on my radar, even after we’d split up. And now, after everything was said and done, I still wanted her.

At the stroke of midnight, I got in my truck and prepared to drive to Tracy’s, immersed in anticipation.

I took the back roads. Though it wasn’t a ranch or farm, Tracy’s house was located in a patch of country, near her dad’s place.

There weren’t any headlights behind me; no one on my tail. I’d gotten lucky that the paparazzi weren’t overly interested in me right now. Lots of musicians laid low and rested after a big tour. Unless I did something to spark attention, like getting caught with my ex, they’d be chasing someone else.

I turned onto the road that led to Tracy’s house and saw the moon peeking through a copse of trees as I pulled into her graveled driveway and killed the engine. She’d forgotten to leave the porch light on. Or maybe she’d done it purposely. I couldn’t be sure.

I used my phone as a flashlight and knelt to lift the welcome mat. I didn’t see a key. But I keep looking, and finally in the back left corner, I hit pay dirt.

I unlocked the door and went inside. It was pitch-dark, so I continued using my phone for light. She hadn’t made this easy. But somehow, I only found it more thrilling.

More mysterious.

I crept down the hall. I didn’t know which bedroom

was hers, so I tried the first one, turning the knob slowly and pushing the door open a crack.

I turned off my phone to keep it from shining in her face if she was in there. I crossed the threshold and squinted in the dark. Was Tracy in the bed?

As my eyes adjusted to my surroundings, I caught a sudden glimpse of her. Her back was to me, and she was covered with a sheet. All I saw was the shape of her hair, spilling over her pillow. I couldn't tell if she was naked, but I was eager to find out.

I removed my boots and socks, then stripped off my T-shirt, pulling it over my head. I left my jeans on for now.

I got into bed with her. She appeared to be asleep, but I suspected that she was awake and playing a seductive game with me. I touched her hair, but she didn't stir.

"Tracy." I whispered her name and tugged the sheet from her body, one inch at a time.

She was bare, beautifully, sensuously bare. I traced my fingers down her spine, following the feminine curve of her body. She made a breathy sound and turned to face me. I leaned over her, and we kissed, opened-mouthed and carnal.

Heaven on earth.

I reclined next to her, and she unzipped my jeans and put her hand inside. I groaned and slipped my hand between her legs, giving her the same type of pleasure that she gave me.

We kissed and touched and rubbed. I was hard, and she was soft and wet. It was a damned fine combination. The best.

Together we shoved my jeans down my legs, and I took them all the way off. I wasn't wearing underwear.

This was a commando night. But before I discarded my denims, I secured a condom from the pocket. I'd brought several, making sure that I was well prepared.

I put on the protection and braced myself above her. She opened her thighs, and I slid between them, entering her in one fell swoop. I remained still for a second, savoring the feeling of my body locked with hers.

She wrapped her legs around me, and I pushed deeper in and out. But I was careful not to move too fast. For now, I wanted it to last.

I cupped her breasts, and she arched her back, her body feline in its grace. We kissed again, and she roamed her hands over me, lingering over the muscles in my back and shoulders as though they had been sculpted just for her.

It made me feel powerful, rough and strong and male. I could sneak into her room for the rest of my life and still want more. I envisioned her moving into Pine Tower with me. But I'd already had mixed-up thoughts about marrying her, so it was just par for the course.

I increased the tempo, needing to come, to clear my mind and lose myself in the friction.

She clawed my back, urging me on. Clearly, she was eager to come, too. I helped her along, lowering my hand between our bodies and rubbing her where it counted.

A gasp escaped from her throat as her nails sank deeper into my flesh. Would she leave lingering marks? Would I wake up tomorrow with evidence of her passion? I hoped so.

She came first, shuddering beneath me. I lost it seconds later, spilling everything I had into her.

In the silence that followed, I collapsed in her arms

and steadied my breathing. She nuzzled my neck. We didn't remain that way for long. I had to deal with the condom.

"There's a trash can by the desk," she said, and turned on a small nightlight.

"Thanks." I removed the condom and tied it off. I stepped over my clothes on the floor and tossed it away. In the light, her room was soft and warm, decorated in pale hues.

"Will you stay until I fall asleep?" she asked.

I turned to study her, our gazes meeting and melding. "Definitely." I returned to bed, searched for the sheet and covered both of us with it. "What about the key? Can I keep it, in case we ever do this again?"

"Yes." She extinguished the light. "It's an extra."

I was glad that more midnight rendezvous were possible. It excited me, making my body hum. But somehow that wasn't enough. I still had the notion to ask her to move in with me. But I remained quiet.

She cuddled in my arms, and I kept my eyes open, like a knight on the queen's watch, protecting what was mine.

She nodded off, drifting into a silent slumber. I buried my face against her hair, then got up to leave.

I didn't turn the light back on for fear of waking her. I searched for my phone in the dark and gathered my clothes. Luckily, I'd put my socks inside my boots or I probably would've never found them.

I got dressed in the living room, as quietly as I could. Would she consider moving in with me? Or would she insist on ending our affair? On letting it go?

I locked her front door and returned to my truck. I couldn't keep obsessing about this. I needed to go home and get some sleep. With my hands firmly planted on the wheel, I drove back to Pine Tower.

Alone, with the moon on my heels.

Zeke took care of my mother's relocation, and in a little over a week, she was back in Nashville. Her new residence sat on a hill, all by itself, surrounded by heavy foliage and iron fences. I was on my way to visit her for the first time now.

I rode in the back seat of the SUV, shielded by its tinted windows. When Zeke pulled into her driveway and hit the remote, closing the electronic gate behind us, I thought about how carelessly she'd abandoned me. How she'd said that she wanted to take me with her, but that her boyfriend—the guy she'd left my dad for—wasn't used to kids and couldn't handle having me around. She'd promised that she would send money and buy me gifts and come back to see me, but she'd never done any of those things.

And now I was paying her way. As twisted as it was, there was a strange satisfaction in knowing how much she needed my money. That the boy she'd left behind had grown into a successful man, beloved by millions. Yet I was still nervous, anxiety buzzing like mosquitoes in my gut.

I said to Zeke, "I'm not going to stay long."

He nodded, and I exited the car. I was sporting a pair of custom-made, hand-stitched boots. I'd paid top dollar for them. Ten grand, to be precise. After what "Lola" had done to me and my dad, I was perfectly fine with flaunting my wealth in her face. It seemed like poetic justice, somehow. But mostly I was still hurting inside, feeling the abandonment all over again.

I knocked on the door and took a deep breath, preparing myself for the moment I would first look into her eyes. Her lying eyes. I just hoped that they weren't edged with tears. She was good at crying, at making people feel bad for her, especially me and my daddy.

The door was flung open, and there she was, the woman who'd birthed me. She was older, but still tall and thin and strikingly attractive. She'd always gotten by on her appearance, using it to her best advantage.

She wore a silky white blouse and slim black pants. Her auburn hair was shorter than it used to be and styled in a sleek bob revealing a pair of glittery earrings. They didn't appear to be designer pieces. They actually reminded me of the costume stuff she used to buy at the Goodwill. Had she sold the pricey jewels she might've collected over the years? Was she being forced to wear cheap baubles again?

"Dash." Her voice quavered. "I'm so glad to see you." She moved forward as if she meant to hug me, but I stepped back, thwarting her effort.

Tears flooded her hazel-brown eyes. Just as I feared, she'd resorted to crying. I noticed her false eyelashes and how voluminous they were. She used to wear them before, too, on the nights Dad took her out. He'd always been so proud of how pretty she was.

"Come in," she said, dabbing at her eyes.

I'd yet to speak. I couldn't seem to find my damned voice. I entered the Tudor-style house. Zeke had already told me that it came elegantly furnished, and he was right. I spotted lots of glass and chrome, offset by carved woods and luxurious fabrics.

"Would you like a drink?" she asked, gaining her

composure. "I made a pitcher of lemonade. Or I could fix you a cocktail." She gestured to a fully stocked bar.

"I'll take the lemonade." Those were my first words to my mother after eighteen years.

She swept into the kitchen and returned with a tall crystal glass, garnished with lemon wedges. I took it from her. But suddenly I needed something stronger.

I headed over to the bar and spiked my drink with a double shot of vodka, making my own effing cocktail.

I felt her watching me. I turned and smiled like a snake, toasting her. "To my mother and her lies." I needed to get the venom out of my system, to say what I was feeling.

Her eyes watered again, her bottom lip quivering. "I'm sorry," she said. "What I did to you was despicable."

"Yeah, it was."

She toyed with a gold bangle on her wrist. It appeared to be a costume piece, too. I shifted my feet and noticed her eyeing my exorbitantly expensive boots.

She said, "Thank you for setting me up here. It's a beautiful place."

"I told Zeke to pick it out."

She angled her head. "You didn't see it before he rented it for me?"

"No." I felt a muscle tick in my jaw. "I left it up to him."

"The yard has a magnificent rose garden. We can sit in the gazebo, if you'd like. I already turned on the lanterns out there."

"I'd rather stay inside." I swigged my vodka-infused lemonade and asked, "What happened with the guy in Mexico? Why did your relationship with him end?"

"Hector?" With a dramatic sigh, she plopped down on a velvet settee and crossed her legs. "He treated me horribly. He was always ordering me around, correcting me, making me feel like I wasn't good enough for him. He comes from a distinguished family, and they looked down their noses at me, too. He didn't even let me keep my best clothes or jewelry. He took away the things he'd bought for me, and I'd already sold most of my other belongings before I met him. I was having a hard time then, too."

Apparently, I'd guessed right. She didn't have anything to show for being a mistress. Unless she was hiding her valuables, which was doubtful. She'd always been the type who liked to show things off.

"Does Hector know what I do for a living?" I asked.

"No. I didn't even know, not until he kicked me out, and I came back to the States."

"That's when you discovered I was famous? Right before you sent me the first letter?"

She nodded. "It's wild, isn't it? I was down and out and staying with an old friend in LA, wondering how I was going to survive. Then I flipped through the music stations on her TV, and there you were, in one of your videos." She folded her hands on her lap. "I tried to immerse myself in Hector's world. I shut myself off from America and everything that was happening here. And since you're not famous in Mexico, I never came across any news about you."

I took another swig of my drink. "I might make it there someday." I already had songs hitting the pop charts in Australia, Europe and Asia, but she'd probably figured that out by now. Or at least gotten wind of the world tour I'd been on. Knowing her, she'd researched my net worth already.

She brightly said, "As soon as I found out about you, I downloaded your album. I must have listened to it a hundred times by now."

I squinted. "Why didn't you just say who you were when you first wrote to me? Why all the cloak-and-dagger stuff?"

"I wasn't sure if you read your fan mail or if you'd get my letter. But I wanted to get your attention in a way that no one else could, just in case I was able to reach you."

"Zeke had it analyzed. He even had the lab test your lipstick."

"Really?" She seemed impressed by the lengths we'd gone to, trying to unmask her. "I'm so happy to be here with you."

I scoffed at her doe-eyed expression. "Yeah, I'll just bet."

She pouted. "Are you going to hate me forever?" When I shrugged, she touched a hand to her heart. "I'll do anything to make it up to you. In spite of how it seems, I always loved you."

I snapped at her. "Don't do that."

"Do what? Tell you that I love you?"

"Yes. I can't stand it when women say that to me." So far, she and Tracy were the only women who'd ever made that claim, and I didn't have to worry about Tracy saying it anymore.

"But don't your female fans say it all the time?"

"That's different. I'm just an illusion to them. A fantasy, not the real thing."

"Did I ruin you?" she asked, in a fussy-mom tone. "Leaving you all alone?"

"I wasn't alone. Dad was there." I finished my drink and slammed the empty glass on the bar. "And do I look ruined to you? I have everything I always wanted. You should see my mansion," I bragged, intent on impressing her, even if saying it out loud didn't make me feel any better.

She leaned forward. "Are you going to invite me over so I can see it?"

"No. And you better not tell anyone that I'm your son. If you do, I'll cut you off."

"Don't worry. I'm not going to do anything stupid." She gazed observantly at me. "Did Zeke tell you that I plan to change my name?"

"Yes, and I'm fine with it." At this point, I preferred that she become someone new. "I'm going to go now."

She stood. "Thank you for rescuing me."

Right, I thought. Because she was a damsel in distress. The thought almost made me laugh.

But after she rushed over and flung her arms around me, I wasn't anywhere near laughing. When I was a kid, I'd longed for her to come back, to hold me, to love me.

Only I couldn't face it now. I stood stiffly while she hugged me, unable to return her embrace.

She let go of me and asked, "When are you going to come back and visit me again?"

"I don't know." For now, all I could do was take one shaky day at a time. And try not to hurt as much as I used to.

Nine

Tracy

I'd been sleeping with Dash for a little over a month, but my plan wasn't working. I still loved him, aching every time I saw him, every time he touched me. Should I end the affair now and put myself out of my misery?

No, I thought. If I bailed out too soon, that might only make me want him more. My solution was to keep going, hoping and praying that I came to my senses.

Along with my struggles, I noticed how moody Dash had been lately. He could be up one minute and down the next. Nothing was clear, not when it came to his behavior. At least I was consistently frazzled. But I tried to be careful not to let it show. I didn't want Dash analyzing me or my actions.

He seemed happy today, but Pop was here with us

at Pine Tower, delivering Valentine, the foal Dash had purchased.

The three of us were gathered in the barn, getting the filly settled into her new home. She already had a people-friendly personality, and she was especially fond of Dash. He adored her, as well. They were a good match.

He would be putting a lot of time into her care and training. He intended to do quite a bit of it himself, but he'd also hired a trainer that my father had recommended.

Pop glanced over at me and smiled. He was happy today, too, just like Dash. But Pop's joy went beyond the horse. He was thrilled that Dash and I were seeing each other again.

We didn't tell him the truth, though. We allowed him to believe that we were a legitimate couple and not just two scattered people submerged in an affair.

"Do you want to go for a walk?" I asked my dad. I needed some time to clear my head, and since Dash was busy with the foal, I didn't think he would care if we slipped away.

Pop agreed to accompany me, and we let Dash know that we would be back in a little while.

My father took my arm, and we strolled along the lake, the sun bright and high in the sky, the weather warm.

"It sure is beautiful here," he said.

"Yes, it is." The land was green and lush, the water clear and blue. Even the forest seemed enchanted. I imagined fairies and gnomes and other mystical creatures inhabiting it.

As we stopped to watch the ducks, some swimming and others preening, a childhood memory flooded my mind. "Do you remember the report I wrote in third grade called 'How Ducks Stay Dry'?"

He nodded and smiled. "I think I still have it in the file cabinet in the garage, with some of your old report cards and drawings and whatnot. You were such a cute duckling yourself. Your mom and I were always so proud of you." He sweetly added, "I still am."

"Thank you." My heart warmed from his words. But would he still be proud of me if he knew what a mess my life really was?

He turned and gazed at me from beneath the brim of his hat. "Now that you and Dash are together, have you changed your mind about making a record with him?"

"No, I haven't. But you know how I feel about that. How I need to do things on my own." I wished that I could tell Pop the truth about my relationship with Dash. But my plan was beginning to seem odd, even to myself. Who sleeps with someone to try to stop loving them?

Was I going about this all wrong? Should I be encouraging Dash to love me instead? Was he more capable of it than he believed himself to be? Or was I being an idiot, just like I was before, longing for the impossible?

"Are you all right?" Pop asked.

I exhaled a jittery breath. "I'm fine."

"You seem anxious all of a sudden. Was it because I mentioned the duet? I'm sorry for pressuring you about that. If you need to handle your career on your own terms, then it's not my place to tell you otherwise."

At this point, I needed to handle everything on my own terms. But heaven help me, I longed for the kind of love that had bloomed between my parents. Something honest and true, something infinite.

"Are you sure you're okay?" Pop asked again.

"Yes, I'm sure. Let's go back to the barn and see how Dash and Valentine are doing." I didn't want to stay here under my father's scrutiny.

Unfortunately, when we returned to the barn, my emotions went from bad to worse, especially when Dash glanced up from the filly to smile at me. By now, I just wanted to pull him tight against me. To kiss him senseless. To close my eyes and block out those desperate yearnings of love.

Later, when we were alone, I acted on my urges, leading Dash to a vacant stall and devouring his mouth with mine. Judging by his fierce reaction, he was more than willing to be ravished.

When we came up for air, he said, "That outfit of yours has been driving me crazy all day."

I'd dressed for the hot weather in a T-shirt and cutoff shorts. "You've always had a thing for me in Daisy Dukes."

"And midcalf boots." He leaned back, giving me a slow, sexy gander.

I latched onto his belt loops, tugging him toward me again. "You better have a condom on you."

"I always keep one handy now that I'm with you." He dug a packet out of his wallet.

"Just hurry up."

He put his wallet away. "Damn, but you're on fire."

Yes, I was burning up, with passion, with a feeling of do-or-die. But I was the one who was trying to forget about love.

We kissed once more, then dived into a frenzy.

He peeled off my shorts and panties, leaving me

in my top and boots. I untucked his casual snap-front shirt and pulled it open in one swift motion, baring his beautifully tanned chest. He shoved his jeans and boxers down, and I watched his erection spring free.

He fumbled with the condom, cursing when he couldn't tear open the wrapper fast enough.

I keened out a moan when he finally thrust into me. He moved like a madman, hard and fast. My bare butt was going to be sore later, with how feverishly I was being jackhammered against the wall.

The stall was clean, but the scent of horses and hay still permeated the air, making us seem animalistic, too, as we panted and pushed and made primal sounds.

I bit down on my bottom lip so hard I nearly drew blood. I didn't even care if someone came into the barn and saw us. But I knew that wasn't likely. Dash had sent his ranch hands away earlier so he could have time alone with Valentine. And now he was getting time alone with me.

Dirty time, I thought. But this was what I wanted, what I needed to liberate my heart. Only it didn't work.

After our orgasms exploded and the sex was over, my problem wasn't solved. I was still consumed with love.

We got dressed and went into the house. And all the while, my thoughts were reeling. Was I being foolish? Or was it possible for Dash to love me? I wanted to believe the best, to cling to some sort of hope. But I was scared, too, of slipping back into my old ways and getting my soul crushed.

"Do you want to listen to some music?" he asked.

"Sure. Okay." I tried to sound more upbeat than I

felt, and it seemed as though I'd succeeded. He didn't appear to notice how conflicted I was.

I followed him into the music room, where he kept his guitars, his studio equipment, his gold records and awards.

While I headed for a black leather recliner, he searched for LPs to play on an old-school stereo he'd built. As much as he appreciated digital music, he'd been collecting vinyl for as long as I'd known him.

In regard to his own songs, most of his lyrics were filled with angst, influenced by his impoverished youth and his struggle to make his way in the world. His chart-topping album had a broodingly handsome image of him on the cover that made women want to save him. Me, included. And I was supposed to know better.

But apparently, I knew nothing. Because here I was, wishing all over again that he loved me.

He glanced up and caught my gaze, and my heart dropped straight to my stomach, where our baby had once nestled. He hadn't written any songs about that and neither had I.

No one except our dads had known that I was pregnant. We hadn't told our friends or coworkers. We'd planned to once I was farther along, but that never happened.

"I still need to call Spencer," he said, pulling me out of the past and back to the present.

"To work on your collaboration?"

"Yes, but then I thought it might be nice to invite him and Alice over first. Or is the four of us getting together still an issue for you?"

"We can hang out with them, if you want." At this point, I liked the idea of doing a couples thing. Spencer and Alice had overcome tons of obstacles to be together, and I admired them for what they'd accomplished. And maybe, *just maybe*, their happily-married, crazy-in-love vibe might rub off on Dash.

He studied me for a second. "Really, you're okay with it? I expected you to invoke one of your rules."

"Most of my rules have already fallen by the wayside." And by now, I had a new agenda. Mercy me. If he only knew.

"Then let's plan a barbecue, as soon as they're available. Maybe we can all go kayaking that day, too."

"I'll text Alice and see what she says." I suspected that she and Spencer would be happy to join us for food and a paddle around the lake.

Dash continued rifling through his record collection and held up two country blues albums that we'd both been reared on.

I nodded my approval, and he removed them from their sleeves and placed them on the stacking spindle. As the first one dropped onto the turntable and began to play, he came over to me. He crawled onto my chair, sending the recliner back.

I gripped the sides of the leather. "What are you doing?"

"Kissing you." He put his lips on mine, and I swooned like a schoolgirl. He was being warm and gentle, his touch slow and easy, as if he had all the time in the world. And he did, I thought. I would give him the rest of my life if it worked out that way.

My eyelids fluttered open and I gazed at his face, so close to mine. Was he capable of love? Was the shell he'd built around himself breakable?

There was no way I could end this affair without at

least trying to find out. But I had to stay strong, too. To keep my wits about me. I couldn't fall apart like before.

"What are you thinking about?" he asked.

A sigh escaped my throat. "You."

"What about me?"

I answered as honestly as I could, without giving myself away. "How amazing you make me feel, about how much I need you."

He kissed me again, and I floated into a romantic abyss, lost in the feeling of him.

The barbecue got off to a wonderful start. I set the table with picnic ware, and the four of us gathered on Dash's patio with his oasis-style pool as the backdrop. We didn't involve his chef. We did everything ourselves, like regular people.

Along with the burgers Dash had grilled, we dined on salads and sides and fresh-cut watermelon. For dessert, I'd made a big frothy bowl of strawberry trifle, and I put that out, too.

Dash nursed a beer while Spencer, a recovering alcoholic, drank ginger ale. Spencer didn't shy away from events where spirits were served. He even kept a bar at his house to accommodate his guests. But he attended meetings regularly, too. He didn't take his recovery lightly, and neither did Alice. He'd nearly relapsed during a difficult time in their relationship.

He and Alice made an attractive couple. Whereas she was blonde and fair, he was tall and dark. They'd both been wild in their youth. In some ways, they'd been cut from the same cloth.

Everyone chatted easily, and it felt good to be in the

company of friends. Yet even with as much fun as I was having, I was still worried about what the future held.

Were Dash and I cut from the same cloth? Did we have enough in common to make a relationship work? Or would we crash and burn like we did before?

Every so often Dash would look over at me and smile, but that wasn't helping my cause. He was giving me butterflies. So much so, I'd begun picking at the rest of my food, feeling too fluttery to eat.

After the meal, Dash took Spencer to the barn to meet Valentine, and Alice helped me clean up, carrying the half-eaten salads, sides and trifle inside.

"What's going on?" she asked. "I can tell that something is up with you."

Of course, she could. She knew me better than anyone. "I'm a bit of a mess, actually. I'm still in love with Dash. In fact, I've been resorting to my old ways and hoping that he's going to fall in love with me, too."

She furrowed her brow in obvious concern. "Do you think he's changed, though? Does he seem different to you?"

"He wasn't famous before, so that's changed him. But as far as the rest of it goes, I can't really tell. Sometimes he seems moodier than he used to be. But he's also been really attentive."

"That sounds confusing."

"I know. And if it doesn't progress the way I want it to, I can't let it wreck me like it did last time." I had to be a newer, stronger woman. Or so I kept telling myself.

I removed plastic containers from the cabinet and began scooping leftovers into them. Alice followed my lead and began transferring the potato salad from its bowl to the Tupperware. "You'll be all right. I know you will."

"I'm glad Dash suggested this barbecue. I even hoped that you and Spencer would be a good influence on him."

"Oh, wow. Now I'm feeling the pressure." She bumped my shoulder with hers. "But I'm flattered, too."

I wanted what she had. The love. The happiness. But for now, all I could do was enjoy the rest of the day and quit panicking about things I couldn't control.

After the men returned from the barn, we changed into our swimsuits for our kayaking adventure.

We used tandem kayaks and safety gear that Dash provided from his boathouse. He had everything we needed.

Spencer and Alice climbed into their kayak, Spencer in the rear and Alice up front, and launched off the dock. Both of them were experienced kayakers, so they managed it with ease.

Dash and I followed them into the lake. We had the same seating arrangement, with Dash behind me. Only in our case, our skills weren't equal. Dash was an expert, and I was a novice.

As we paddled through the water, I prayed that I wouldn't lose my stride and rock the boat. But I didn't need to fret. We glided along in perfect harmony, working as a team. Stable as could be, I thought. As if we belonged together for real.

Later that night, Dash and I went to his room to get ready for bed. He'd already stripped down to his underwear, but I hadn't gotten undressed yet.

"I need to talk to you," he said.

"What is it?" He seemed anxious, and I hoped that our relaxed mood from earlier in the day wasn't about to blow up in my face.

He sat on the edge of the bed and dragged a hand through his hair. "Now don't freak out, but I think that we should get engaged again."

I nearly pitched forward. Had I heard him correctly? Had he just proposed? Yes, by God, he had. Yet from the almost distant way he'd said it, I knew immediately that it had nothing to do with love.

I fought the air that had suddenly gotten trapped in my lungs and asked, "Why do you think we should get engaged?"

"Because I enjoy being with you, and I could see us having a good life together."

Desperate to squeeze in the L-word, I quickly said, "Most people think that marriage is supposed to be about love."

"Yeah, but it's different for us. We can still have a close relationship without the whole love thing. I mean, isn't that what we've been doing already? You can't deny that we've become friends again or that the time we spend together isn't fulfilling."

I wanted to cry, but I tempered the urge, forcing my tears back. I'd led him to believe that I didn't love him anymore, and now I was paying the ultimate price.

He proceeded with, "I'm lonely when I'm not with you."

He sounded more emotional now, more romantic, but loneliness wasn't love. Nor was it the bond I was looking for. My heart hurt from what he wasn't saying. The one thing I needed to hear.

He continued to express himself. "Marrying you has

been in the back of my mind since we started the affair. But I kept thinking I was crazy for having those thoughts. Then after being around Alice and Spencer today, I realized that it wasn't so crazy at all. That we could be as content as they are."

Apparently, they had influenced him, just not in the way I'd hoped. He'd completely overlooked how in love they were.

"I know our engagement faltered last time," he said. "But that's because I was scared that I didn't have the means to make things work. But I can give you a luxurious life now. You can sell your house and move in with me. I can buy your dad a bigger farm in this area or he can live at Pine Tower, too, depending on what he prefers." He made a grand gesture. "Just think of what an incredible wedding we'll have. I'll get you the dress and diamond of your dreams, and once we're married, you can spend as much time on your career as you want without having to work other jobs. Then, when you're ready, we can record together."

I shook my head. He had it all figured out. Every little detail of how he was going to manipulate my life. "Are you even listening to yourself, Dash? You're making this all about your success, and how grateful I'm supposed to be for it."

"Oh yeah?" he shot back. "Well, some support from you would be nice, some pride in how far I'm come. You know damn well that I grew up with nothing, and it made me feel like nothing."

"Yes, but that doesn't give you the right to try to buy me off now."

A muscle pulsed at his neck. "There's nothing wrong with a man wanting to take care of his wife."

I defended my position. “And there’s nothing wrong with a woman who prefers to take care of herself.”

He stood and came over to me. “Can’t you at least consider marrying me?”

“Not like this.” I couldn’t tell him the real reason I was turning him down. Or how painful it was to be this close to him, longing for more.

“Are you going to stop seeing me?” he asked. “Is this the end of our affair?”

I hesitated to answer, not knowing what to do.

“Tracy?” he persisted.

I wasn’t ready to let him go. I should be, but I couldn’t seem to walk away. People in love acted foolishly, and I was no exception. “We can keep it going for a while. Unless you want to end it.”

“I’m not going to be the one to call it quits. Not after I just offered to share my damned life with you.”

Okay, then. We were staying together for now, as awkward as you please, emotions still raw between us.

He went over to the bed and turned down the sheet. “It’s getting late. We should get some sleep.”

I began removing my clothes, but not all of them. Since he was in his boxers, I left my underwear on, too: a tan bra and low-rise panties. We climbed under the covers, but we didn’t touch.

He turned off the light, and I closed my eyes, lying fitfully next to him, tangled up in an affair that had gone horribly awry.

Ten

Dash

I spent the week after Tracy turned down my proposal shopping online, stewing in my own frustration and buying gifts for my mom.

At first, I didn't know if I was willing to see her again, and now I was making outrageous purchases. But at least Mom would appreciate whatever I gave her. I was only doing this to combat Tracy's rejection, but I needed to feel useful.

I was hurt and angry at the way Tracy had reacted to my proposal. Granted, I'd just sort of thrown it out there, but I was trying to share my home with her, to make music together, to be lifelong partners.

I'd assumed that comparing us to Alice and Spencer would've worked in my favor. But clearly, it hadn't.

Why did Tracy have to be so stubborn? Why couldn't

she rejoice in my success and give me the satisfaction of showering her with the riches I'd worked so hard to attain? She knew how painful my childhood was and how being poor had destroyed my self-worth. But it wasn't just about me. I'd always longed to share whatever I acquired with Tracy, giving her the things neither of us had when we were growing up. I'd panicked when she'd gotten pregnant because I was afraid of how I was going to give our child the life it deserved. My insecurities had gotten the best of me, damaging my relationship with Tracy, too.

And now…it was a mess all over again.

I glanced over at Zeke. He was helping me load the SUV with the stuff I'd bought for Mom. I hadn't told him that I'd asked Tracy to marry me or that she'd turned me down. I didn't have to explain myself to him. His job was to protect me, not discuss how fractured I was. Every time I thought about Tracy's rejection, I felt broken inside, as if someone had taken me apart and put me back together wrong.

"Is that all of it?" Zeke asked.

I nodded, and he closed the hatch.

Mom was expecting me, but she didn't know that I would be bearing gifts. I wanted to surprise her. In some ways what I was doing seemed twisted and sick. In other ways, it pacified me, especially since I was still hurting over Tracy.

After Zeke and I arrived at Mom's new place, I stayed in the back seat for a minute, gazing out at the night and wondering what my dad would think if he knew that I'd renewed my relationship with Mom. He'd loved her right up to his dying day. But he'd hated her for what she'd done to us, too. She'd had a toxic effect on him. On me, too, but here I was, feeding the fire. Of course there was a lonely part of me that needed my mother, regardless of how twisted it seemed.

I got out of the car, gathered some of the packages and walked to the door. I shuffled the items in my hands and rang the bell. Mom answered it, her eyes going wide.

"What's all this?" she asked, as Zeke approached us, with his arms full, too.

"Just some things I wanted you to have," I said.

"Oh, my." She looked like a cat on Christmas Eve, eager to play with the ornaments on the tree.

We entered the house, and she practically danced around the living room. We piled the first batch on the dining room table and went back for more. Once we brought the rest of it in, bags and boxes overflowed onto the floor. The table wasn't big enough to hold everything.

Zeke backed away, letting me know he would be waiting in the car. As soon as he left, Mom dived right in.

I sat on the sofa and watched her. The first thing she opened was a large black Chanel handbag. She gasped in sheer delight. I'd gotten her the most expensive one in their current collection. She went on to the next gifts, which were two pairs of shoes: Christian Louboutin slides and Manolo Blahnik pumps. She squealed and clapped.

I said, "You can exchange anything you don't want. Or if things don't fit or whatever. I gauged the size based on what you used to wear." Those old thrift store fashions she used to whine about.

She wasn't complaining now.

"This is so amazing." She had tissue paper flying

out of her hands. "Oh, look at this." She removed a gold Givenchy gown from its box. She held the garment lovingly against her, twirling, making the fabric spin.

I was rewarding her for hurting me, for tearing me apart when I was kid. Yet her excitement made me feel needed. Why couldn't Tracy need me in this way? The only valuable thing I'd given her was a birthstone body chain that she'd left at my house.

After Mom opened each and every gift, she ran over to me. I stood, and she hugged me. I returned her affection, allowing myself to embrace her, and she cried on my shoulder.

Tears of spoiled joy.

We separated, and she said, "No one has ever given me so many extraordinary things."

I gazed into her makeup-smudged eyes. "Not even any of your old boyfriends?"

"No, not even them. But now I have you, and you matter more than any of them ever could."

Rather than dispute her claim, I grabbed a silk blouse from the pile of new clothes and dried her tears with it.

"Dash!" She scolded me for soiling it. "That's a Versace!"

"Don't worry about it. I'll buy you another one." I didn't care if she blew her nose on it. There were more where that came from. I was only doing this to ease my pain over the woman who refused to marry me.

Tracy visited me the following day. I asked her to come over and hang out, sending Zeke to her house to get her, as we'd been doing all along. But now that she was here with me, we barely seemed like friends—

let alone lovers who were supposed to be continuing their affair.

We took a walk in the woods. On this hot and glaring afternoon, the towering pine trees provided some much-needed shade. We could've cooled off inside, but I didn't want to be cooped up right now, not even in a sprawling mansion.

"How have you been?" I asked, trying to break the ice. I hadn't seen her since the weekend she'd rejected my proposal.

"Fine. Just busy with work." She looked wholesome this afternoon, maybe even a bit messy. She had a loose hairdo that was half up and half down, a twisty bun of sorts, with long strands falling around it. Her clothes were simple: a plain beige T-shirt and skinny jeans tucked into natural brown boots. It was the same pair she'd worn with the Daisy Dukes when we'd messed around in the barn. I wished that she was in that kind of mood today. I would let her ravish me in a Tennessee minute, if she was so inclined.

"What have you been doing?" she asked.

"Nothing much." Just buying my mom a bunch of crap, I thought, and trying to survive the ache of Tracy not wanting to be my wife. After we walked a while longer, deeper into the woods, I asked, "Do you want to sit a spell?"

"Okay." She chose a tree and plopped down next to it.

As I joined her in the dirt, I heard a scratching sound. I looked up and caught sight of a squirrel racing up the trunk and heading for the branches. On closer inspection, I realized it was a mama squirrel scurrying around with her young. I tried to count how many there were. Five. Six. I couldn't be sure.

Tracy glanced up and saw them, too. "Oh, how cute. The one on the lower branch is watching us."

I smiled. "It's probably thinking about hiding some seeds in that sexy hair of yours."

She met my gaze. "You think it's sexy like this?"

"Yeah, I do." I thought everything about her was enticing. The thickness of her hair. The blueness of her eyes.

We stared at each other, and I considered kissing her. But somehow, I couldn't bring myself to do it. I wanted her to initiate the first touch. But she only drew her knees up to her chest, as if she was protecting herself from me.

A moment later, she asked, "Are you going to propose to me again? Is that why we're out here?"

"What? No." Even with as badly as I wanted to marry her, I wasn't going to subject myself to another rejection.

"You don't have a fancy ring in your pocket?"

I shook my head. I even turned my jeans' pockets inside out to show her they were empty.

"I just thought maybe..."

I leaned forward with an inkling of hope. "Would that have worked? Would you have accepted?"

Her breath hitched. "I'm sorry, no. You buying me a ring is the last thing I need."

I shrugged, refusing to let her see how flustered I was. Flustered, annoyed, hurt, offended. If I could get away with it, I would shove the biggest diamond in the world on her finger and make her wear it.

"Do you want to go inside for lunch?" I asked, feigning normalcy. I came to my feet. "We can make sandwiches or something."

She stood and dusted herself off. Was she trying to act casual now, too? "I am getting a little hungry."

Falling into step together, we trekked to the house, the sun beating down on us, making a trail of sweat creep down the back of my shirt.

We entered the kitchen through a sliding glass door, drank some water and rummaged through the fridge. After a quick debate, we decided on roast beef sandwiches on sourdough rolls with white American cheese. She put pickles and pretzels on our plates, and we entered the dining room.

Before we sat down to eat, I spotted something on the floor, in the corner, next to the weathered-wood buffet. A small jewelry-size box with a glittery bow. One of the gifts I'd gotten for my mom. Except that it must've fallen off the buffet when I'd piled all of the boxes and bags there last night, before Zeke and I had taken them out to the car.

Tracy turned and saw it, too, and my heart nearly stopped.

I went over to where it was and picked it up. I couldn't pretend that she hadn't noticed it.

"What is that?" she asked.

I couldn't think fast enough, so I stalled, panicking about what to say. Did she think it was a ring?

She moved in my direction, closing in on me.

"It's not what it looks like," I said.

She gazed suspiciously at me. "Are you sure?"

"Of course, I am." I couldn't remember what was in that particular box, but I knew it wasn't a ring. I hadn't bought Mom any rings.

"Then what is it?" she asked again.

There was no way I was going to tell her that it was

for my mom. After what my mother had done to me, I didn't think Tracy would understand why I'd let her back into my life or why I was buying her expensive clothes and jewelry. My feelings about my mom were complicated. But they always had been, even when I was a kid. And now that I was an adult, I needed to deal with it on my own. Pulling Tracy into it would only make it harder.

Struggling to keep my cool, I concocted a story. "It's for a friend. It's his anniversary this week, and he asked me to hold on to his wife's gift, so she doesn't scrounge around their place trying to find out what he got her."

She tilted her head. "Why was it on the floor?"

"I put it on the buffet last night, but it must have fallen off." At least that part was true. But I wished that I hadn't been so careless. Even Zeke had missed it.

She squinted at me. "Who is this friend?"

I wasn't about to implicate a real person. But I didn't want to make someone up, either, not at the risk of her checking to see if the guy existed. "Why does it matter who he is?"

"Why are you being so evasive? If you got me an engagement ring, then just tell me. It's not like I didn't suspect that you—"

"Fine. You want proof that it isn't for you? Then I'll open it." I grabbed a butter knife off the table and sliced the tape on the sides. I lifted the lid off the box. "There, see. Gucci earrings." I recognized them right away. Eighteen-karat gold, jade and diamond drops.

She peered into the box, studying them for a few contemplative seconds. "How do you know they're Gucci?"

Shit. The logo wasn't visible. I knew because I'd

bought the damned things, but that didn't jibe with the story I was telling her. "I can tell by the style."

"You certainly have a good eye for women's jewelry."

"Yeah, I guess I do. But I told you it wasn't a ring."

She studied the earrings again. "When is your friend going to pick those up?"

"He isn't. I'm supposed to bring them to their party on Friday night." In actuality, I planned to see my mom that evening. She'd invited me for dinner. "They live in a suburb just south of the city." I added that detail because I was trying to make it seem more believable. The real day. The true location. The designated time. "It starts at seven, but it's not a surprise or anything. It's a cocktail thing they planned together."

"You better tape the sides of the box up again and try to make it look like you didn't open it."

"I'll do that later." I fidgeted with the lid.

She watched me, a bit too closely. "I'm sorry if I put you on the spot about it being a ring. But you're still acting strange."

"It's been a strange day." I set the box down, needing to be rid of it. "Can we just eat now?"

She nodded, and I decided that if I bought Mom anything else, I would have the packages sent directly to her, keeping Tracy from stumbling upon them. I couldn't cope with another mishap.

We took our seats, the silence between us as thick as the lie I'd just told. But there was no way I was going to come clean about who the earrings were for.

My mom was my secret to keep.

Eleven

Tracy

Zeke gave me a ride home from Pine Tower. But as soon as I got in the door, I called Alice, fretting over Dash and his odd behavior. And now I was at Alice's house, in her room, telling her about my concerns.

She worked while we talked, sorting through a box of feather boas for a client and placing them in two distinct piles on the bed. Spencer was out of town on business and wouldn't be back until next week. The two Maltese dogs were nearby, though, curled up in a corner.

Alice frowned. "Are you sure you're not overreacting?"

I sat on a corner of the bed near the *maybe* pile. "I don't think the earrings belonged to a friend. I think Dash bought them. There was just something about how quickly he knew what brand they were." Something that gnawed at me.

"Then he must have bought them for you. But he changed his mind about giving them to you."

"Why would he buy me a gift like that? They're not anywhere near my style." My heart thudded in my chest. "What if they're for another woman? What if he got hurt and mad that I'd rejected his proposal and went back to one of his groupies?"

"Oh, Trace." She dropped a red boa into the *reject* pile. "He wouldn't do something like that, would he?"

"I have no idea. But I can't rule it out, either."

"Come on, let's think this through. If Dash bought the earrings for someone else, then why didn't he just hide them from you? Even if the box had accidently fallen on the floor, he still left it out in the open where you could see it." She cocked her head. "Where's the logic in that?"

"There isn't any, I guess. But if the earrings were for a friend's wife, then why wouldn't he just tell me his friend's name? Why was he being so secretive?"

"I understand your fear, honestly I do. But before you jump to any more conclusions, is there any way that we can investigate his story and see if it checks out?"

"Short of following him on Friday, I don't see how." I breathed in my pain. "That part of what he said sounded true. That he really does have plans that night. Maybe he'll be seeing the woman he bought the earrings for." I searched her gaze, my pulse skittering. "If I took the chance and followed him, would you come with me?"

"Yes, of course. I wouldn't want you doing something like that alone."

"Thank you." I'd rejected Dash's proposal, but we'd

agreed to keep seeing each other. It wasn't as if we've ended our affair or voided our agreement to remain monogamous to each other. But now I couldn't ignore the gut-clenching possibility that he could be sneaking around with someone else. "I appreciate you being here for me."

"Always." She closed the boa box. "I've never followed anyone before. Have you?"

"No. But I think we can do this. Dash said that his friend lives in a suburb just south of the city, and if that's where he's going, he won't be able to take the back roads to get there. He'll have to take the highway, which will work in our favor. I'll rent a car that he won't recognize, and we'll park on a turnout on the highway and wait until his truck or Zeke's SUV passes." I continued outlining the plan as it came together in my mind. "The party is supposed to be at seven. We should start our watch early to give ourselves plenty of time to look for him."

Alice appeared to be contemplating it all. "If Zeke is driving, he'll notice if we get too close. He's trained to spot that sort of thing."

"We'll just have to be as careful as we can. We should probably disguise our appearances, too."

"It sounds so covert." She furrowed her brow. "But if Dash really is going out that night, and we manage to follow him to someone's house, what are you going to do once we get there?"

"I just want to drive by and see if there's a party going on. I think that kind of activity will be obvious." I glanced at the fancy feathers on the bed. "There would be other cars parked on the street and other people going in and out. Dash wouldn't be the only guest."

"You're right. I just hope that we can pull this off and get to the bottom of things."

"Me, too." I needed to know what was going on, and I wasn't going to rest until I found out.

"You look pretty as a blonde," Alice said, as we sat in the economy car I'd rented, waiting on the turnout on the highway near Dash's house and keeping our eye out for him.

"Thanks, but I don't feel very pretty." I was too anxious to think about anything except the cars going by. We'd been here for about thirty minutes so far.

I glanced over at Alice, and she fingered the ends of her short, spiky brown wig. We'd chosen styles that mimicked our own hair, except in different colors.

I fidgeted in my seat. "It's all so crazy. Me chasing down a man who doesn't even love me."

She hesitated for a second. "What if he does love you?"

"What?" I gaped at her. Had she lost her mind?

"I know it's a weird thing for me to say, especially now. But as badly as he wants to marry you, it's starting to make me wonder if he might love you and not even know it. People can block out those types of feelings."

"Is he blocking out that he's lying to me, too?"

"We don't know that he's lying. And we don't really know what's going on inside of him, either. Spencer struggled with his feelings. He didn't realize that he loved me until we were in the midst of a crisis."

"That's not the same as what's happening between me and Dash." I leaned forward, watching the highway.

"I'm sorry. I just—"

"There they are!" I exclaimed, as Zeke's SUV

cruised past us. I recognized the car, but I knew the license plate number, too. "It's definitely them!"

"Then hurry up. Get out there."

"I can't just peel out onto the road." As jittery as I was, I felt as if I was learning to drive all over again. "Keep your eye on them, and I'll try to do this calmly."

"Okay." Alice stared out the windshield.

I merged onto the highway and stayed about three car lengths behind them, in the lane next to theirs. I'd prepared for this jaunt, reading tons of articles on how to tail someone and stay within surveillance range without being detected. Of course, none of those articles pertained to a situation like this, where the driver of the other vehicle was your celebrity lover's bodyguard.

"You're doing good," Alice said.

I maintained the speed limit, trying not to hyperventilate, my breathing coming in short, quick pants. I couldn't remember ever being this nervous, not even the first time I'd performed in public, and I'd gotten terrible stage fright that day.

What if I was wrong and Alice was right? What if Dash wasn't lying? Or cheating? And what if he really did love me?

No, no, no, I thought. I couldn't let my heart go there. I just needed to stay focused and follow him.

"Are you sure Dash is even in the car?" Alice asked. "I can't see him."

"He rides in back, where the windows are tinted really dark." I gripped the steering wheel, and we continued on our trek, my nerves in knots.

About twenty minutes later, Alice said, "You better change lanes. They're getting ready to turn onto the next highway."

"Which way?"

"Left. He's got his blinker on."

I merged into the lane where I needed to be. Luckily the Honda in front of me was turning, too, keeping a space between us. But once we made another turn farther on, I had to be more careful. By now, we were in a posh suburban neighborhood with less traffic and fewer places to hide.

I tried to stay as far back as I could, without losing sight of them. Finally, they turned onto another street that led to a small hill, and I drove straight past it.

Alice bobbed in her seat. "What are you doing?"

"I'm going to circle back. I don't want Zeke to see us turning right behind him."

"I hope we don't lose them."

"I don't think we will." I gestured toward the hill. "It looks like there aren't that many houses up there."

"Maybe you should have been a spy instead of a singer."

Yeah, I thought. Maybe I should've, considering the demise of my music career. Not that I'd had much time to focus on it lately. Between my dad's illness and my affair with Dash, I'd gotten sidetracked. But I still planned to keep pursuing it, putting more music out there on my own.

I waited a few minutes before I made a U-turn and came back around, creeping along the incline Zeke had driven up earlier.

Alice leaned forward, looking out her window. "I don't see the SUV. But you were right about it being less populated up here. There are only a few streets where they could've turned, and the one at the very top looks like a dead end."

I drove up and down the streets. The houses were few and far between, and the SUV wasn't parked in front of any of them.

"Maybe he pulled into a garage," Alice said.

Had I made a mistake by not following closer? "We still need to check the houses all the way at the top."

"Then let's go."

There was only one house at the top, and sure enough, we'd hit our mark. The SUV was parked in the driveway behind an iron fence.

"There's no party here," I said, my heart going numb. "Look how quiet it is."

"Watch out. The bodyguard's coming." Alice motioned with her chin. Zeke had just gotten out of the SUV and was striding toward the gate.

"I'll just act like I made a wrong turn." I looped the car around and retreated to the street directly below. I parked in front of a colonial-style house on the corner and caught my breath.

"Do you think he recognized us?" she asked.

"With these wigs? I don't know." I fought the urge to cry. "It doesn't matter to me if he did. It's over. I'm done. I don't ever want to see or speak to Dash again."

Alice put her hand on my knee. "Do you think we should wait a bit before you start despising Dash? It's only a little after seven. People are notoriously late to parties."

"Meaning what? That Dash was the first to arrive?"

"Don't you want to know for sure? I know it scared us when Zeke reacted the way he did, but maybe he thought we were party guests and was going to open the gate for us."

Should I let Alice be my voice of reason? From our

vantage point, we would be able to tell if any other cars drove up the hill. I caved in, and we waited.

Twenty minutes. Then thirty. We even pushed it to forty, and the only vehicle that passed us was a white BMW. But it pulled into a garage on the street we were on.

With my pain growing every minute we waited, I finally asked, "Can we give up this charade now and accept that Dash lied?"

"Yes." Alice's voice was deflated. "I'm so sorry. You deserve better than this."

"Yes, I do. And you know what? I'm not going to curl up in a ball like one of those little pill bugs. I'm going to confront Dash. Now. Tonight." Preparing to do battle, I removed my wig, pulled off the nylon cap beneath it and tugged at the pins. Once my hair was free, I fluffed it around my shoulders. "How do I look?"

"Like a force to be reckoned with." Alice got rid of her wig, too.

I zoomed back up the hill, adrenaline pumping through my veins. As bold as could be, I barreled straight ahead, blocking the gate in front of the house.

"Here we go," Alice said, as she watched the bodyguard stomp toward us. "Damn, but he's big."

"Not as big as I am right now." I shut off the engine and swung open my door.

I heard Zeke cuss before he asked, "Tracy, what are you doing here?"

"You didn't suspect that the blonde who made the wrong turn was me?" I grabbed the wig from the console and threw it at the gate. When it landed on the ground, the poor thing looked like roadkill. "Who lives here? Who is Dash with?"

"Just calm down and go home."

I glared at him. "I'm not going anywhere."

Zeke removed his phone from his pocket. Was he calling the police to report me for harassment? No way, I thought. He couldn't do that, not without creating a PR nightmare for Dash.

"Are you warning him that I'm here?" I asked.

"Yes, I am." He fired off a text.

I looked over my shoulder at Alice, and she opened her door.

"Is everything all right?" she asked me.

"It's fine," I assured her. I gazed pointedly at Zeke. "I'm not leaving until Dash comes outside."

Zeke's phone beeped, and my pulse jumped.

He glanced at the screen. "Dash says that he'll talk to you later, after you go home."

"I want to talk to him now," I countered.

Zeke shook his head. "Just go, Tracy."

"And let him finish his rendezvous with another woman? Screw you and screw him, too."

Zeke shook his head. "You're mixing everything up."

"Oh yeah? Then tell Dash to unmix it for me." I glanced at Alice again. She shielded herself with the passenger door, as if she was expecting a shootout. I stood out in the open, wearing my rage on my sleeve and welcoming whatever bullets came my way.

Zeke exchanged a few more texts with Dash, and my lying, cheating lover came outside. He looked angry. But I was fuming mad, too. What was that old saying, something about hell having no fury like a woman scorned?

Zeke unlocked the gate, and Dash approached me. Alice watched us for a second then slipped back inside the car and closed her door—giving me the privacy I needed to lay into Dash. Zeke backed off, too, and headed over to his SUV.

Dash grabbed my hand and pulled me toward the edge of the road. I yanked my hand away and met his gaze head on.

"I'm not with another woman," he all but growled.

"Then what's the deal with those earrings?" I snapped back. "And whose house is this?"

"I rented it for my mom, and I bought the earrings for her."

I flinched, shocked into silence.

"I got her a bunch of other gifts, too," he said. "I'm giving her all the stuff you won't let me buy for you."

I found my voice, hard and quick. "Don't use me as your excuse to buy things for her." I wasn't to blame for that. "How long has she even been back in your life?"

He told me the entire Lola story, and my heart hurt for him. He was letting his mother take advantage of his success and use him for his money. I glanced at the house and spotted a willowy figure peering out the window. She was watching us.

"Come with me," I said. "Leave her behind and come home with me."

"Seriously? After you accused me of cheating on you? I would have never done something like that."

"I was confused and hurt, Dash. I suspected that you were lying to me about the earrings, and I overreacted. But I've been struggling the whole time we've been together. I wanted to have an affair with you because I thought that if I slept with you, I could get some of my power back."

"What are you talking about?"

I forged ahead, forcing myself to say the words I knew he wouldn't want to hear. "I've never stopped loving you. Even after all the years we've been apart, my feelings never really changed."

He stepped back, away from the streetlight and into a haze of darkness. "You love me? But you've been lying to me and pretending that you don't?"

"I was trying not to love you, but it didn't work. Then I started hoping and praying that you'd love me, too. But you didn't, even though you asked me to marry you. Everything we've been doing has been a mess."

"You're right. It's a total mess. At least with my mom, I know where I stand."

I ached for him. And for myself, too. "She's just going to hurt you again."

"Not if I keep giving her the things she wants."

His reasoning made me even sadder than I already was. "I'm sorry that I accused you of being with someone else. I should've had more faith in you. But it's hard, loving someone who doesn't love me back."

"You know I'm not capable of that."

"Alice thinks you could be." My voice cracked. "Earlier, before we followed you here, she said that you could be blocking your feelings."

His voice was shaky, too. "I'm not blocking anything. I've always known that love was difficult for me, and I never denied that it started when I was a kid."

"With an emptiness your mother created." And now she was back, pulling his strings, treating him like a puppet. "I wanted to fix you the first time we were together. But my heart got crushed instead."

"And now I crushed it again." He moved closer to me. "We have to end it. We have to stop the cycle."

I lifted my hand to skim his jaw. "Maybe if we…"

"No." His expression went blank. "I can't be what you need, Tracy. I don't have it in me."

I lowered my hand. Touching him would only make the pain worse. "I'm going to go." I couldn't stay another minute, immersed in this kind of torture. "I won't ever bother you again."

He didn't say anything. He just stood in the shadows while I walked to the car, my footsteps echoing in the night.

I got behind the wheel, and Alice turned to face me. We didn't speak. I waited until I turned off his mother's street before I pulled over and burst into tears.

Crying over the man I still loved.

Twelve

Dash

I strode past Zeke, and he closed the gate, leaving me to my misery. He didn't expect me to confide in him. I wouldn't have, anyway. Losing Tracy was my pain to bear.

I returned to the house, and Mom rushed over to me with a dramatic flair. "Who was that girl?"

"No one." I made a beeline for the bar and poured myself a vodka on the rocks. I swigged it, letting it burn its way down my throat.

"She must've been someone to have upset you this way."

I didn't respond. I was an emotional wreck, torn apart by everything Tracy had said. That she'd never stopped loving me. That her heart was still yearning for mine. On top of that, I had to contend with Alice's disturbing opinion of me. The bit about me blocking my feelings and being in love, too, as if I was too scared or stupid to know the difference.

I wasn't stupid. But I'd always been afraid of getting too close, of repeating the mistake my dad had made with my mom, of needing someone so badly that you destroyed yourself over it. I didn't want to lose my soul to love. I was supposed to be immune to that. I'd done everything in my power to protect myself from it.

I frowned at my mom. She sat on the sofa and fingered the new Gucci jewels at her ears. The earrings I'd lied to Tracy about. But she'd lied to me, too, deceiving me about the nature of our affair.

"I wish you'd tell me what's going on, Dash."

"There's nothing to tell." It seemed as if my whole world was crumbling, yet I still had my money, my career and my mansion. The things I'd wanted to share with Tracy.

Did I love her? The thought panicked me. I felt the sheer terror washing over my bones. I'd spent my entire adulthood dismissing love, and now I was drowning in the sudden fear of it.

But what did love feel like? How would I know for sure? This had already been one of the worst nights of my life, and it was getting more chaotic by the second.

The uncertainty. The agony. The pounding of my heart.

Mom studied me. "You look positively miserable. Do you want to finish eating? Will that help?"

I glanced at our leftover dinner on the table. Roasted chicken and all the fixings. We'd been in the middle of it when Zeke had texted, alerting me that Tracy was outside. And now she was gone. I'd sent her away for good.

"I'm not hungry anymore," I replied. My stomach would cramp if I took even one more bite.

"Should we stream some music?"

I shook my head. "There's nothing I want to hear."

She gestured to the TV. "A movie, then?"

"I don't want to watch anything, either."

"Is there anything I can do to help?"

"No." But I was surprised by what sounded like genuine concern on her part. Or as close to genuine as she knew how to be. I studied her, then asked, "Why didn't you ever love my dad the way he loved you?"

She flinched. "What does that have to do with anything?"

"I just want to know, that's all." Love was the issue of the night, the word spinning around in my head. The emotion I couldn't seem to face.

She frowned and replied, "Relationships have always been hard for me." She fidgeted in her seat. "Some bad things happened to me when I was young, and I've just never been able to..."

Her words trailed off, and I realized how messed up she really was. Not that I hadn't always known it. But something seemed different this time. Or maybe I was just getting a better understanding of her, based on how messed up I was, too.

She fingered her earrings again. "I appreciate everything you're doing for me, Dash. Renting me this house and buying me gifts."

"I know." She equated love with material things, and she'd taught me to have that mindset, too.

"You're a good son," she said. "The best."

"Thank you." It was easy being the type of son she wanted, now that I had the means to please her. But I wasn't the best boyfriend or lover or whatever to Tracy. I couldn't give her anything that would validate me in her eyes.

No, that wasn't true. If I let myself, I could give Tracy the very thing she wanted most.

For me to love her.

The next few days were a living hell. Thoughts of Tracy consumed me, every moment of every hour. But I was still scared, panicked beyond belief.

I sat on my porch steps, waiting for Zeke. I'd asked him to come by and talk. I couldn't confide in my mom. She didn't have a normal understanding of love. My only option was Zeke. Plus, he was the only person I could spill my guts to who wasn't part of Tracy's camp. My dad was gone, and Pop was *her* dad. I couldn't tell him how I was feeling, not without involving Tracy. Spencer would be a problem, too. He was Alice's husband, and Alice was Tracy's best friend. Everyone was just too connected.

Zeke showed up with a troubled expression on his roughly chiseled face. He sat beside me and said, "Are you sure there isn't anyone else you want to have this conversation with?"

"Yeah, I'm sure."

He frowned. "I probably won't be very good at offering you advice."

I handed him a longneck beer. I'd barely touched mine. "You can't be any worse at this than I am."

He accepted the drink. "Don't bet on it."

I studied him. He wasn't wearing his customary suit. This was his day off, and he was in regular clothes: shorts, flip-flops and a Polynesian-print shirt. The other security guys filled in for him when he wasn't working, but I didn't need a bodyguard at the moment. I needed a friend. Either way, Zeke wouldn't be around forever. At some point, he would return to the corporate side of his business and assign another bodyguard to me.

I didn't know much about his personal life. But when I first hired him and his crew, he'd told me that he'd been raised in a house as big as mine. Zeke came from a successful Hollywood family, only he preferred to keep a low profile.

"Did you love your ex-wife?" I asked.

He winced a little. "What kind of question is that?"

"I just want to know if you've ever been in love. Like, really, deeply in love."

"Yeah, I have. And, yeah, it was with my ex."

I kept studying him, analyzing him. For now, it was easier than analyzing myself. "What happened? Why aren't you still together?"

"It was complicated." He swigged his beer. "Too complicated for me to get into. But it still affects me and how I live my life now."

I respected his right to be vague. But I still needed to hash out my problems. "What does it feel like?"

He gave me a disturbed look. "To get divorced?"

I shook my head. "To be in love."

"It feels like someone's sitting on your chest, smothering the crap out of you. But it feels amazing, too, when it's going right. All you want is to be with that person."

"I've always wanted to be with Tracy. Even the years we weren't together, I couldn't shake her from my blood. But I couldn't accept that she loved me, and I couldn't..."

"Love her back?"

I nodded. "In my family, love was a word associated with pain, a word that was used to manipulate and destroy. I watched my dad wither away because of it, and I vowed that I'd never let that happen to me."

"Love isn't supposed to destroy people. That's not how it's intended to work. Plenty of people have healthy, loving relationships."

I shot him a curious glance. "See, you are good at this."

He shrugged. "It's just common sense."

"Not to someone like me. Look what I'm doing with my mom. She abandoned me, and now I'm giving her everything she wants and trying to make her love me."

"Old wounds run deep."

"That's for sure. I've been going out of my way to buy my mom's affection, yet I've been denying Tracy what she wants."

"Those two women couldn't be more opposite."

I nodded and gazed out at the lake, knowing it was time to stop being afraid and admit the truth. That I'd always loved Tracy, even if I'd buried those feelings in the deepest, darkest part of me. I'd allowed my mother's rejection to ruin what I could've had with Tracy. What I still could have. Love wasn't the enemy. It could be my salvation, if I let it be.

Dear God, I thought. How easy was that? The burden I'd been carrying around had just been lifted from my shoulders.

But within seconds, my confidence fell, and a different kind of fear slammed through me. What if it was too late to win Tracy back? What if I'd hurt her too badly?

"I have to apologize for something," Zeke said suddenly.

I blinked at him. "I'm sorry. What?"

"I should have been more alert that night. I didn't have a clue that Tracy and Alice were following us. They outsmarted me, and I didn't catch on until it was too late." He shook his head. "I screwed up, and you paid the price."

"That isn't true. I got exactly what I deserved. Besides, if Tracy hadn't shown up, I probably never would've told her about my mom." But I didn't want to hide anything from Tracy anymore. No matter what mistakes I'd made, I needed to lay my heart on the line. And hope that she still loved me enough to take me back.

I stood on Tracy's front porch, in the dark, a black cowboy hat shielding my eyes. I'd driven myself here, all alone with my hopes and dreams and fears.

I pressed the buzzer, with my pulse thudding in my throat. I heard someone approach the door but it didn't open. Was that Tracy? Was she peering out the peep-hole? As far as I could tell, she was by herself. I didn't see any other cars in the driveway.

The door creaked open, and Tracy gazed at me through the crack. "What are you doing here?"

"I just want to talk." And ask her to marry me, I thought. I had a ring burning a hole in my pocket. A diamond I'd chosen with love and care. But would she accept my proposal? Would I be able to prove myself to her?

She invited me in, and I followed her into the house. Her living room was tidy, and there was a scented candle burning on the coffee table. Strawberry or cherry or something. She looked soft and pretty, and I longed to touch her, to skim my hand against hers, but I kept my distance.

"Can I get you anything?" she asked.

"No, thank you." She seemed leery of me. But I couldn't blame her. If I were her, I'd be cautious, too.

"Do you want to sit?" She gestured to the sofa.

I nodded and removed my hat, placing it on the coffee table. I glanced at the Home Sweet Home pillow propped up at one end of the couch and imagined her bringing it to Pine Tower if she moved in with me. But this wasn't going well so far. She sat in a chair on the other side of the room, as far away from me as possible, putting an even bigger gap between us.

I was so nervous that I barely knew where to start. I ran a hand through my hair. "I'm sorry about the way things ended. I never should have lied to you. I handled everything badly."

"You came to apologize?"

"Yes, but I have so much more to say, to tell you." I kept my gaze riveted to hers. "I love you, Tracy. I'm madly, achingly in love with you."

She gasped. "But you never were before. You—"

"I know the difference now." I tapped on my chest, in the vicinity of my heart. "I've always felt it, this heaviness inside of me. What Alice said was true. I've loved you all along without recognizing it. Even the years we've been apart, I couldn't get you out of my mind. I watched your career rise and fall, and then when I became successful, all I wanted was to see you again. To try to record with you, to do whatever it took to be around you." I stood and moved away from the couch.

"You were right to turn down my other proposal and not be interested in a ring from me. But I needed to get you one this time." I removed the case from my pocket and flipped it open.

She got up and walked over to where I was. She stared at the diamond, as if it was blinding her. Was it too big? Too showy? Had I chosen the wrong style?

"It's heart-shaped," she said.

My breath rushed out. "I wanted it to represent what I should've given you years ago. My heart. My love. My life."

Tears flooded her eyes. Was that a good sign?

I hurriedly said, "You don't have to sing with me or do anything that doesn't feel right to you. It's going to be hard to avoid the press, though, and I'm hoping that if you agree to marry me, you'll be okay with everyone knowing that we're together. I'd be happy to tell the world that we're engaged. I want nothing more than for you to become my wife."

"I've waited a lifetime for you to love me, to want me in this way." She searched my gaze, long and deep. "But are you sure you're not acting on impulse? Or that the decision isn't going to overwhelm you later?"

"I'm positive. But I can't sugarcoat it or promise that everything will be perfect, and especially now that my mom is back in the picture."

"That does present a troubling picture, but it's okay. It's not your fault."

I set the ring next to my hat on the coffee table, letting the diamond shine on its own. "At least our kids won't have to go through what I went through." I moved closer, desperate to touch her. "Marry me, Tracy, and be the mother of my children." I put my hand on her stomach, splaying my fingers across it. "We can't bring back the one we lost, but we can have lots of other babies."

"Oh, my God, no." She stepped out of reach. "I love you, Dash. But I can't do this." She gazed at me with pain in her eyes. "I can't marry you, not if..."

Dumbstruck, I merely stared at her. "You don't want to create a family with me?"

"Yes, I want to, more than you can possibly know." She clutched her middle. "But there's a secret I've been keeping, something that I should have told you long before now."

Thirteen

Tracy

I walked over to the sofa and sat down, inviting Dash to join me. This wasn't a conversation I wanted to have standing in the middle of the room. Truthfully, it wasn't something I wanted to discuss at all. But Dash had just asked me to have his babies.

The thought made me ache—in my heart, in my womb.

Once we were settled beside each other, I said, "It's extremely unlikely that I'll ever be able to get pregnant again. I have a condition that…"

Dash watched me with a concerned expression. "What is it, Tracy? What's wrong?"

"It's called premature ovarian failure. It's when the ovaries quit working before the age of forty. I'm taking hormones and vitamins, but there's no treatment that can restore it." I explained further, getting it all out there, even as personal as it was. "I still have occasional periods, but they're few and far between. At some point, they're going to stop altogether." I blinked back my tears. "I haven't told anyone about this except for Alice."

Dash frowned. "Your dad doesn't know?"

"I didn't want to worry him, especially when he had such a health scare of his own. I didn't see the point in telling you, either. You and I were just having an affair. There was no future between us. But now…" I rocked forward.

"It's okay," he said softly. "This doesn't change anything for me. I love you, and I want to spend the rest of my life with you."

I looked into his eyes. "But you just said before that you wanted me to be the mother of your children."

He reached for my hand. "There are other ways to have a family. We could adopt or use a surrogate or donor eggs or whatever else people do these days. But only if you'd be comfortable with any of that. If not, we don't have to have kids. It can be just us."

My heart clenched. "I want children, I absolutely do. But this condition just makes me feel so inadequate, as if I'm less of a woman, as if I failed somehow."

"That's not true. You're still the same person you always were, and I'd be lucky to have you."

"But I'm still hurting that our first baby was taken away."

"I know. I'm still hurting over that, too. I have so many regrets from the past. And now, seeing you like this… I'm so sorry for everything you're going through. I wish I could make it better."

"My doctor has been encouraging me to join a support group." I took a shaky breath. "Maybe I should do that. Maybe it would help."

"If partners are allowed to attend or sit in on some of the meetings, I'll go with you…if you want me there."

Suddenly, the tears I'd been fighting broke free and I burst out crying. Dash was doing and saying everything right, but by now, my emotions were spent.

He leaned toward me, and I latched on to him, bawling in his arms. He held me tight and close, comforting me the best he could. I glanced at the coffee table where he'd left the engagement ring he'd chosen for me.

The heart. The diamond.

He stroked my hair, and I put my head against his chest and listened to the beats of his heart.

So steady, so real.

I cuddled closer, drawing from his strength, from his love, from how much I loved him. Finally, I stopped crying and sat forward, catching the last of my shaky breaths.

"Are you okay?" he asked. "Is there anything I can do?"

"I'll be fine." I got up to get a box of tissues, drying my face and wiping my runny nose. "But there is something you can do that will make a difference."

"Anything, Tracy. Just tell me what it is."

"Ask me to marry you again."

He gazed longingly at me, then picked up the ring. When he got down on bended knee, my heart fluttered.

"Will you do me the honor of becoming my wife?" he asked. "Will you share my home with me? Will you be my partner in every way?"

"Yes," I eagerly replied. I couldn't wait for us to start

our life together, to make the best of whatever the universe had in store for us. He put the ring on my finger, and as the diamond caught the light, I saw hope in each and every facet. "Look at that. I'm wearing your heart."

He returned to his feet. "It's always going to belong to you. But I wish I'd given it to you a long time ago."

"I have it now, and that's all that matters." I wasn't going to dwell on the pain from the past, not anymore.

We kissed soft and slow, sealing our commitment, taking time to savor it.

After two or three more kisses, he said, "Thank you for loving me all these years. I never understood how important that was. Or how much I needed it."

I met his gaze. "You're welcome. But we still have a long road ahead of us, with announcing our engagement to the press, with me trying to rebuild my career, with our options for having a family. There's a lot to think about."

He nodded. "I still have to deal with my mom, too."

I reached out to hug him, comforting him in the way he'd done with me earlier. "Don't worry, Dash. I'll help you face that challenge." I nuzzled the side of his face, letting a bit of his beard stubble abrade me. "No matter what happens, we'll always be in this together."

After a bout of sweet silence, I led Dash to my room, wanting him in my bed. Right now, newly engaged, with his ring on my finger.

"It's been a while since we did this," I said, moving closer to him, inhaling the scent of his skin, of his clothes, of his cologne, of everything that was part of him. "We haven't made love since before the barbecue at your house."

He met my gaze. "I missed you, even when everything was falling apart."

"Me, too." I would never doubt or distrust him again.

He started undressing me, removing my blouse and putting his glorious hands on me. He divested me of my bra and peeled off my jeans, running his thumb along the elastic waistband of my plain white panties. I didn't want to turn the lights off in the room. I liked that he was looking at me, seeing all of me.

"We don't have to use protection. You know, since we don't really need it," I said. "Besides, I want to feel you inside me without anything between us." No barriers, I thought. Just him and me.

"I'll do whatever you want. But I think I should make you come first."

He dropped onto his knees, and I latched on to his shoulders. He'd already proposed to me in this position, and now he was sliding my panties down my legs…

Down and down…

All the way off…

He used his mouth, doing wicked things to me with his tongue, and I swayed on my feet. I felt as if I'd loved him for centuries. My fiancé. My future husband.

He worked his magic, my skin tingling, my sex going damp. As excitement pitched low in my belly, he used slow, deliberate strokes, making me sigh, making me moan.

I watched him with breathless anticipation.

He looked so strong and handsome and wild, bringing me closer and closer to a climax. He made a pleasured sound, and I got even more aroused. He was enjoying this as much as I was.

I wanted to tell him how good it felt, how he was doing everything right, but by now I was beyond words.

I merely shuddered and convulsed against his face.

He remained on his knees, teasing me, nuzzling me. It was sweet, sweet sin. Could I be any warmer? Any stickier?

Finally, he stood and kissed me on the mouth, intensifying the moment. I leaned against him, breathless once again.

Soon, he yanked off his boots, and I helped him get naked, tugging at his shirt and unzipping his jeans.

He backed me against the bed, and we tumbled onto it, falling down together.

I used my hands, making him fully erect. Then, wanting more, I slid down his body and swirled my tongue around the salty tip of him. His abs flexed, and I took him all the way into my mouth. He let me do as I pleased. For a while, anyway.

When he couldn't take it anymore, he made me stop.

He climbed on top of me, and we stared into each other's eyes. He entered me, and I lifted my hips, taking him deeper, relishing the feeling of having him inside me, of being this close. We moved in unison, thrusting in the same passionate rhythm. I wrapped my legs around him, holding him strong and tight. He rubbed his cheek against mine, making me warm and woozy.

He increased the tempo, and I arched my body, bending myself to his will.

In the next pivotal moment, I came in a burst of need, catching my breath with every hot, slick spasm.

With a look of sexy concentration on his brow, Dash

followed me, his muscles bunching, his arms straining above me.

I closed my eyes as he came, so glad that he was mine.

After the sex, we stayed in bed, indulging in cookie dough ice cream from the carton, passing it back and forth and licking the spoon clean. I'd been eating ice cream every night since we split up, drowning myself in sadness, and now I was celebrating.

Dash said, "I think you should move in with me before we announce our engagement. Otherwise, the press is going to bang down your door, trying to get pictures and interviews. At least at my place, you'll be behind a security gate."

"It's going to be crazy, having people take an interest in me like that." I'd never been at that level of fame before. "But I'm excited about moving in with you."

"Then will you pack some bags and move in with me tonight? I can arrange for the rest of your stuff to be trucked over later."

"That sounds good to me." I wanted to spend all my days and nights with him. The sooner, the better. "I'll call a Realtor and put my house on the market. I'll quit the feedstore, too." I couldn't work a public job and be married to him, not without his fans tracking me down there. "But I'll keep doing my VA stuff until my house sells and I have some extra money of my own."

"You can work in whatever capacity you want, but I think you should focus on your music. I won't keep bugging you about the duet, though. You can take everything at your own pace."

I looked into his dark, sexy eyes. "I'm going to do

whatever I can to rebuild my career, but I want to sign a prenup, Dash. I don't want any part of this marriage to be about your money."

He shook his head. "You really are stubborn about that, aren't you?"

"It'll make me feel better to know that I'm earning my own keep."

"I'm not going to fight you on your independence. I have faith in you and your career. But if you want my help, I'll always be ready and willing."

"Thank you." I watched him take a bite of the ice cream. "Speaking of money, what's the next step with your mom?"

He sighed. "I don't know. But honestly, I think she could benefit by getting some help."

"You mean therapy?"

He nodded. "The last time I saw her, I asked her about my dad, and she mentioned how hard it was for her to love him because of some bad stuff that happened to her when she was young."

"When she was in foster care?"

"She didn't specify, but that's my assumption."

"Do you want to continue having a relationship with her?" I needed to know how he truly felt.

"Yes, I do. But I can't just keep buying her things to win her affection. I want her to learn to care for me in a deeper way."

"Do you think she's capable of that?"

He nodded. "She seemed genuinely concerned for me when I was upset over you."

"Then you should talk to her about getting counseling, so she can explore those feelings. Plus, she needs to try to heal from whatever happened to her when she was young. Maybe you could even do family therapy at some point."

"That's definitely something to consider." He smiled a little nervously as me. "It wouldn't hurt for me to face my childhood issues, all that crap I've been carrying around. But I'm not sure how receptive she's going to be about seeing someone."

"Can I go with you when you talk to her?" I asked.

"Yes, of course. But are you sure you're up for it?"

"Absolutely. We're in this together, remember?" I intended to stand by his side in every way I could.

As soon as Dash and I entered his mother's house, I could tell that she was threatened by me. But I'd expected as much. She wasn't the type to welcome another female into her lair.

Dash introduced her as Lola, and when she reached out to shake my hand, she tilted her head at a haughty angle. I'd never seen a picture of her when she was younger, so I didn't know what she looked like before, but she fit what I'd imagined her to be. Along with her false eyelashes and bloodred nails, she had a trim figure and short auburn hair, styled just so. She sported an elegant dress and stately heels, a designer outfit Dash had purchased for her, no doubt. She'd paired her ensemble with several pieces of fine jewelry. Again, things that must have come from Dash.

Within seconds, she caught sight of the ring on my finger, staring blatantly at it.

Dash spoke up and said, "Tracy is my fiancée, Mom. We just got engaged a few days ago."

"Is that so?" Lola raised her delicately arched brows

at me. "Aren't you the one who was here last week causing a scene?"

"Yes, that was me," I replied. "But it was just a misunderstanding, and we worked things out."

"A five-carat misunderstanding," she quipped, accurately assessing the size of my diamond.

I moved closer to Dash, standing near him, supporting him. We'd already told my dad we were engaged, and he was thrilled for us. Pop had even cried a little, telling me how happy and proud my mother would've been. But all Lola seemed to noticed was the value of my ring. Was it going to be possible for this woman to become a better person? Heavens, I hoped so.

She turned to Dash and asked, "Are you sure you aren't rushing into anything?"

"I'm positive." He reached for my hand. "I've loved Tracy for years. I just had a tough time accepting it."

She paused, as if she was deciding what to say next. Was she worried that if she didn't start reacting favorably to his news, he would stop buying her pretty things?

She chirpily said, "Let's celebrate your engagement with some champagne." She strutted over to the bar, her heels clicking on the hardwood floors. "I'll put a bottle of Dom on ice."

Dash glanced at me, and I shrugged. We had time for a drink. We were here to discuss an important issue, to hopefully change the course of all of our lives.

While the champagne chilled, we gathered in the living room. "This is a lovely house," I said.

"Yes, it is," Lola replied. She smiled a bit too adoringly at her son. A second later, she spoke directly to him. "Dash knows how much it means to me."

He returned her smile, and once the champagne was chilled, she popped the cork and poured it into three crystal flutes. She gave us ours and raised hers in the air. "To the happy couple," she said.

We all clinked glasses, toasting the moment. A moment that wouldn't last. I doubted that Lola was going to be happy when she learned what our agenda was.

"We need to talk, Mom," Dash said.

"About what?" she asked, gazing at her drink.

"About coping with the past."

She whipped her head up. "What?"

"I think it would be beneficial for you to see a psychologist and work through the stuff that happened to you when you were young. And then maybe later, we can get therapy together."

"Oh, my goodness." Her breath rushed out. "It's been too long, too much time for that kind of nonsense."

"There's nothing wrong with getting help," I said, inserting myself into the discussion.

She quickly argued, "But things are fine the way they are. Dash is happy now." She turned to him. "Look how good everything is for you. You have an outstanding career, and you're engaged to be married."

"Yes, but my relationship with you isn't normal, Mom. I want more out of it than just buying you fancy gifts."

"But the gifts are nice," she countered.

Was she afraid of facing her past and having to learn to be the kind of mother her son needed?

"Just give the therapy a try," he said.

"If I say no, are you going to cut me off?" she asked.

He set his champagne aside. "You mean quit paying your way? I'm not here to blackmail you. But if you're not willing to see things my way, then maybe you should get a job and support yourself."

"A job? See, you really are blackmailing me. This is awful." Lola's voice quavered. "Just awful."

By now, she was playing the drama queen and trying to make Dash feel sorry for her. But he wasn't having it.

He kept his cool, even when she heaved a big woeful sigh. Like the heroine of an old movie on the verge of a fainting spell.

Fourteen

Dash

"I can't work," my mother said, pleading with me to let her off the hook. I figured that between getting therapy and getting a job, she would've chosen the therapy, but she wasn't agreeing to either.

What an ordeal. I glanced over at Tracy, appreciating that she was here with me. That'd she'd agreed to be my wife. That she loved me in a way that people were meant to be loved. My mixed-up mom didn't have a clue what that meant.

"Why can't you work?" I asked her.

"Because..." She lowered herself onto the sofa, as if she was so distraught that she needed to sit and fan herself, using a piece of junk mail she'd left on the coffee table. "I don't have any job skills."

"I'm sure there's something you'd be good at," Tracy chimed in.

Mom shot her an annoyed look. "This isn't any of your business."

"Don't treat her that way," I snapped, coming to Tracy's defense. "She's only trying to help."

"But everything was fine before you got engaged. You weren't trying to get me into counseling then. You weren't saddling me with a job, either."

I sighed. "You can't just sit around here and do nothing." That wouldn't accomplish a danged thing.

"What's wrong with me being a lady of leisure?" she argued.

"A person has to do something of value," I responded. "Or at least have some goals."

"But I'm too old and ill equipped to work."

Who was she trying to kid? "You're smart as a whip and highly attractive, too. I'm sure you'd find something that you'd excel at."

Tracy said, "Maybe you could work at a jewelry store or at an upscale boutique."

Mom huffed out a breath. "I'm not working as a salesperson."

"I think you'd move onto a managerial position in no time," Tracy replied. "You could even take some online courses and get an education."

"I can't believe this." Mom quit slouching on the sofa. She stood and refilled her champagne, posing with the flute. "Look at me, Dash. I'm not the type who was meant to work. I'm not meant to be analyzed by some pesky psychologist, either."

"But you're the type who was meant to abandon your kid and then come back into his life when you found out that he's rich and successful?" I stared her down, hurt and frustrated that she was belittling our relationship and ignoring the way it should be.

She glared at me. "Is that what this is about? You're punishing me for the past?"

"It's not punishment. I'm a grown man who's finally learned how to give and receive and accept love." I squared my shoulders. "But I can't make things right with you until you're willing to try."

"So you're taking everything away from me instead?"

"I'm not taking anything away. I'm just asking you to make a change. I can't begin to fathom what you experienced when you were young, and I'm sorry for any pain it caused you. But I know what I endured, and how it affected me."

She glanced away, as if she was getting emotional. But a second later, she said, "You had a tough childhood, but look how charmed your life is now. You're a millionaire. You're probably even on your way to becoming a billionaire. I don't see the harm in you supporting me without any strings attached."

"I see plenty of harm in it. I spent my entire life feeling like trash and thinking that I had to be rich to matter." I glanced at Tracy. "She loved me when I was poor, and she loves me now. My success has nothing to do with it."

Mom scowled. "But she's going to marry you, while I'm being forced to change my ways."

She sipped her champagne, a look of damnation on her face. "I should go to the press and tell them how utterly horrible you're being to me."

She was threatening me? No way, I thought. No effing way. "Do you honestly think that the public is going to side with you? What are you going to say that makes me sound so awful? That I'm trying to help you recover from your past? That I want us to attend family counseling, but you're refusing to go?" I wasn't going to back down, not now, not like this. "And just so you know, I have an entire PR team who manages my publicity, so if you go to the press, I'm going to fire back." For now, Tracy and I hadn't even announced our engagement yet. The last thing I needed was my mom doing it for us.

She clicked her shiny red nails on the bar top. "Your fans already know that I left when you were young, so why should I keep quiet? I might as well make my identity known."

"You don't care what people are going to think of you?" Tracy asked.

Mom shrugged. "Everyone already thinks I'm rotten, anyway." She paused, still clicking her nails. "In fact, I think we should all do a reality show together. The public would eat it up. Me as the glamorous villain, Dash as the world-famous artist and you as his love-is-everything fiancée or wife or whatever you'll be by then."

Tracy gaped at her. I did, too. Both of our mouths hung open.

Mom kept chattering. "You should talk to your agent about it, Dash. And then they can present it to whatever network they think will be interested. Who knows? There might even be a bidding war."

Holy cow, I thought. "I'm not making a TV show with you."

"But it's a way for all of us to be a family. And on top of that, it'll boost your fame and income, too. You'll be an even bigger star than you already are."

"I don't want to be that kind of star. And that's not my idea of being a family." I wanted something nice and nurturing and normal.

"Fine." She tossed back the rest of her champagne, all drama, all glamorous-villain. "I'll just have to get my own show. Or I'll join the cast of another show that's already established. I can still become a celebrity."

"You know what? You're right. You can do whatever you want." I wasn't going to worry about the repercussions her self-serving deeds would have on me. I was already in the spotlight, and once Tracy and I announced our engagement, she would be knee-deep in it, too. Fame was a part of our lives, either way. "I'm sure you'll find an agent to represent you once you tell them that you're related to me. But don't do it until after Tracy and I go public."

Mom frowned. "How long is that going to take?"

"It'll be sometime this week." We didn't want to drag things out any longer than necessary. "You won't have to wait long. Then you can have your life to yourself, just as long as you keep your distance from me and mine."

Mom moved away from me, and suddenly she seemed overwhelmed, as if being in a reality show wasn't such a great idea, after all. She paced the room, her shoes echoing on the hardwood floors.

Tap…tap…tap…

Was she having second thoughts about being excluded from my life? Was she afraid of being alone? Of being scorned and cast out?

She stopped and turned to me. "I'm sorry," she said shakily. "And I'm sorry for being rude to Tracy. I was just being obstinate, saying stupid things I didn't mean.

I do care about what people think, and I especially don't want you to hate me."

"I don't hate you." I spoke quietly. "But you need help. You can't go around using people and treating them badly."

Her breath hitched. "I know."

"Does that mean you're willing to give the therapy a shot?"

"Yes, but it's going to be hard for me. I'm not comfortable talking about myself like that, rehashing everything from my past."

"I understand. But it's got to be done." One step at a time. I chanced a smile at her.

Tears gathered in her eyes. "Are you still going to support me? Or do you still want me to get a job?"

"I'll support you." But mostly I was going to support her in emotional ways. Someday, I hoped she would see the full benefit of that and would be there for me, too. For now, I wasn't expecting miracles. But at least this was a start.

My mother reached out to hug me, and I felt her tremble in my arms. I could sense Tracy watching us.

Afterward, I smiled at the woman I was going to marry, so damned grateful that I had her support. That she was my miracle. That she loved me, just as I loved her—with every beat of our hearts.

Tracy and I went home and made love, touching and kissing and breathing each other in. She sat naked on my lap, riding me, her body arched, her hair falling down her back. I watched the way she moved, thinking how perfect she was. I cupped her breasts in my hands, rubbing her nipples, making them hard.

As she stroked me with her wetness, with her sweet dampness, I imagined what our honeymoon night was going to be like. I had no idea if we would be in a glitzy hotel or a cabin in the mountains or a bungalow on a tropical island. I just knew that we would be together, giving each other pleasure.

I pictured her in a lace corset and thigh-high stockings, lovely little things she would've worn under her gown.

I envisioned flower petals, too, lots of them, in pretty colors, scattered on the bed.

"I'm thinking about our wedding night," I said, pulling her into my fantasy.

"You are?" Her gaze locked on to mine.

"Yeah." I lifted myself up to kiss her, hot and quick. "About how romantic the sex is going to be." I kissed her again. "Wild and romantic."

She sank deeper onto my lap, milking my body with hers. "Tell me more about it."

"You'd be riding me, like you are now, and there'd be flower petals everywhere."

"What kind?"

"Roses, and they'd smell really good and sweet." I circled her waist with my hands, helping her move up and down. "You'd be dressed in wedding-type lingerie, except with no panties."

She bit down on her bottom lip. "What would you be wearing?"

"A tuxedo shirt, that you ripped open. And my pants would be on the floor, with my jacket and tie and your gown."

She shivered on top of me, aroused by our conversation. "Would I be wearing a veil?"

"While we're in bed? Hell yeah." That added a new element to the fantasy. "One of those shorter ones that I could lift every time I kissed you."

"What about my gown on the floor? What does it look like?"

"It's long and silky with antique lace and those tiny buttons up the back."

"The old-fashioned kind that are covered in fabric?"

"Yes, ma'am. But I would get so impatient when I try to get you out of that dress, I'd destroy some of them."

She leaned over me, her hair falling across the sides of her face. "You'd be that anxious to be with me."

"I couldn't help it." I was getting anxious now, too.

We switched positions and soon I was on top, thrusting into her, losing myself in the feeling of being in love.

While she gazed up at me, I slid my hand between her legs, rubbing her, heightening her pleasure. I watched her, listening to the carnal sounds she made and getting a thrill from it.

I was buried deep inside her when she came. I came, too, spilling into her, in hot anticipation of the bride and groom we were destined to become.

Two days later, Tracy and I convened in the barn, hanging out with Valentine and preparing to make our relationship known. On this picturesque afternoon we would be announcing our engagement, by way of Instagram.

We'd dressed casually for the occasion; we were just being ourselves. Along with jeans and boots, I wore a plaid shirt and Tracy sported a Western blouse with an embroidered yoke and pearl snaps. Her hair was long and loose, her makeup soft and feminine.

"Are you ready?" I asked.

"Yes, absolutely." She smiled, her blue eyes twinkling.

I removed my phone from my pocket. I liked that we had control of the pictures. Of course, once we posted them, they would be picked up by news outlets and celebrity gossip sites. But Tracy and I weren't flying blind. Until we were ready to give interviews, my publicist would be making statements on our behalf. Zeke and his team were in place, too, gearing up for the fans and paparazzi who'd be waiting to catch glimpses of me and my fiancée together.

Valentine came up to the barn door, and Tracy turned to pet the filly's nose. The horse nuzzled her hand, basking in the affection.

She turned back to me, and we posed with the foal in the background. Raising Valentine was part of the life we were building, and we wanted to show her off, too.

We took a variety of shots, making sure that Tracy's ring was visible in all of them. Nothing said engaged like a big, bright diamond. I was also going to hashtag the pictures with special phrases, letting everyone know this was the woman I planned to marry. Tracy had social media accounts as well, and her following would probably skyrocket today. But we were ready for that, too. The same internet security company that monitored my accounts would also be monitoring hers from now on.

We took more pictures, enjoying the process, smiling and kissing.

Finally, we sat down to scroll through them, choosing our favorites. We narrowed it down to two: one with Valentine and one without.

"This is it," I said.

"Do it," she said.

I posted the first picture, and Tracy cuddled close to me, watching the reactions and comments pile up. With the millions of followers that I had, we would be trending at lighting speed.

"It feels good," she said.

"Totally good." Our public life together had just officially begun. There was no going back. We were a couple in every way.

Epilogue

Tracy

Three months had passed since I'd become Dash's fiancée, and on this lovely fall evening, we were hosting an engagement party.

Pine Tower was filled with friends and family. My dad was enjoying every moment. I glanced across the parlor and saw him with Spencer and Alice, the three of them chatting companionably.

Pop was strong and healthy, his recent checkup showing no signs of cancer. That gave me great peace.

Dash's mother was here, too, looking as glamorous as ever, draped in a fashionable outfit, her jewelry glittering against her skin. She'd been seeing a therapist Dash had found for her, and as far as we could tell, she was making progress. Sometimes she could still be haughty or abrasive, but she would always apologize afterward. I think she truly wanted to change. Of course, she was great in party settings. She'd helped me organize this event, making every detail shine.

She and Dash hadn't attended any family counseling sessions yet, although that was still part of the overall plan. For now, Lola was working separately on herself. As for me, I was getting stronger, too, and attending a POF support group.

I smiled in Dash's direction. He stood near the buffet, enjoying the party, socializing with our guests.

My life had changed dramatically since we'd gotten engaged. I hadn't dropped any new songs yet, but the albums I worked so hard on before—the ones that had previously bombed—were gaining momentum among Dash's fans. He was certainly proud of me. But he'd believed in me all along. I was still being cautious about the duet, though. Which I realized didn't make much sense. There was no reason for me not to sing with the wonderful man I was going to marry.

I headed toward him, and he turned and caught sight of me. He excused himself from the people he was talking to and met me halfway.

He swung me into his arms, and we kissed. He'd already told me how gorgeous I looked in my shiny gold minidress and tall black boots. He looked exceptionally handsome, too, in a finely tailored suit, his hair stylishly messy, his beard stubble wildly sexy. I could've devoured him whole.

We separated and I said, "I've been thinking… I want to write a song together and record it after we're married."

His lips tilted upward in a heart-stopping smile. “You do? For sure?”

“Yes, for sure.” I grazed his cheek, running my fingers along his skin. “Our song. A love song.”

He touched my face, too. “About two people who beat the odds?”

I nodded, and we kissed again, so grateful that we’d found our way back to each other.

For all time.

* * * * *

SECRETS OF A PLAYBOY

JANICE MAYNARD

For Allie—

You have brought such joy to our family.
I love watching you grow up,
and I can't wait to see where life takes you!

One

"This floor is off-limits to the public."

Zachary Stone felt a moment's irritation. Perhaps he needed to add key access in the elevator. Today wasn't the first time someone had wandered where they shouldn't. The retail space for Stone River Outdoors was at street level. There was no reason for any customer to make his or her way to the seventh floor. But humans were curious creatures.

The woman at the far end of the hallway stopped to peruse an oversize photograph of Thunder Hole in Acadia National Park. "Ma'am," Zachary said, heading in her direction. The company had been the victim of corporate espionage in recent years, so he was more cautious now. "Ma'am. You shouldn't be here."

At last, the woman turned to face him. She was slender and tall, five-ten at least. Her hair was black, jet-black. And wildly curly. Natural? Perhaps.

Long-lashed eyes regarded him with a steady gaze. Her face was narrow, the chin pointed. Glasses with thin black frames gave her a studious air. When he drew closer, he could see the unusual color of her irises. Almost lavender. He remembered reading somewhere that the famous actress Elizabeth Taylor had violet eyes. This woman's were more periwinkle. Or maybe the shade depended on lighting and the clothes she wore.

The stranger carried herself with confidence, though her posture was relaxed. His obvious displeasure had no apparent effect on her.

Despite the fact that Zachary was on his home turf, the field gave him little advantage that he could tell. Again, he issued a warning. “Visitors are not permitted on this level. Please go back downstairs.”

The woman examined him from head to toe. “I have an appointment.”

That voice. The low, husky tone grabbed something in his gut and reminded him how long it had been since he had indulged in recreational sex. Too long, apparently. If one encounter with a stranger had him itchy and unsettled, he needed to get laid.

Finally, he processed her words. Then he frowned. “Appointment?” Suddenly things began to make sense. “You’re—”

She interrupted him. “Frances Wickersham.”

Frances Wickersham? “All of your correspondence said *F.* Wickersham.” He frowned at her.

One feminine shoulder lifted and fell in a casual shrug. “In my line of work, it’s better if clients don’t have preconceptions.”

“Ah.” He felt off his game, and that annoyed him even more. “Let’s go to my office,” he said. He ushered her down the hall and into the suite he had inherited at his father’s death. When the senior Mr. Stone had been alive, *all* decisions flowed through here. The decor had leaned heavily on dark cherry woodwork and traditional furnishings.

Zachary had ripped everything down to the studs and rebuilt. Now, the lighter colors and Danish furniture pleased him, as did the pale hardwood floors. He waited for his guest to sit, then took his place behind the CFO’s desk.

“Thank you for coming,” he said, trying to regain control of the situation.

"Of course." Frances Wickersham laid her soft leather briefcase on the chair beside her and shrugged out of her rain jacket with graceful movements. The outer garment was a black trench coat. Classic. Expensive.

Underneath, she wore black wool pants and a thin gray cashmere turtleneck. Her hands were long-fingered and bare except for a single band on her right ring finger. The braided gold circlet looked Celtic in design.

Without the rain jacket, he could see her feminine curves.

"So," he said. "Have we agreed to all the terms?"

A smile twitched her lips. "I'm here, aren't I?" She reached into her briefcase and extracted a contract. "Everything we discussed via email is included. I'd like for you and your siblings to look it over with each other and your lawyer. Assuming everything is satisfactory, I'm prepared to start on Monday."

Zachary took the contract and glanced at it absentmindedly before laying it aside. He had studied all the whys and wherefores. For a rather large amount of money, Stone River Outdoors, his family's adventure gear business, was about to hire a professional hacker to comb through the company's computers and see if someone was stealing money and/or proprietary designs. In the light of day, the whole prospect seemed vaguely ridiculous. But then again, *something* was going on.

F. Wickersham sat quietly, her gaze cataloging his office. "This is nice," she said. "Modern, but not cold. Kudos for thinking outside the box."

He smiled, pleased by her praise, though he didn't know why. "What makes you assume it was my idea? My work?"

She finished perusing her surroundings and settled that blue-violet gaze on him again. "You always said the Scandinavians were geniuses. And your senior thesis paper was about the founder of IKEA. At one time, you wanted to create the same kind of business for the luxury market. But I guess your family commitments got in the way."

His eyes widened. His fingers clenched the arms of his chair. "Excuse me?"

Her lips twisted in a wry smile. "You don't remember me at all, do you, Zachary? I suppose I should be glad. I was a teenage mess back in those days."

He gaped at her. "Frannie? Is it you?"

Two hours later, Zachary pulled up in front of his brother Quinten's classically beautiful two-story house with the warm brick and the white columns and told himself he wasn't nervous. Of course he wasn't.

He had offered to pick up Frances at her hotel and transport her to this dinner meeting, but she had preferred to hire a ride. Zachary was glad. He needed to wrap his head around the fact that Frances Wickersham was actually *Frannie*. His teenage nemesis.

A quick glance at his watch told him he couldn't dither in the driveway like an idiot. Fortunately, there would be four other adults to help carry the conversation. Zachary didn't know what to say to Frannie now that she was all grown-up.

Come to think of it, he'd seldom been able to win a battle of wits with her when they were both fourteen, much less thirty, almost thirty-one in his case. They hadn't seen each other in over a decade…not since the day they each graduated from the prestigious Connecticut boarding school for gifted students where Zachary had been incarcerated for the longest four years of his life.

Frannie had lived there, too, but unlike Zachary, *she* hadn't spent the whole time trying to escape. Honestly, he had a hunch that Frannie had actually liked boarding school.

He opened the car door and made a dash for the porch. November in Portland, Maine, had started out wet and miserable. Katie, Quin's wife, opened the door before Zachary could ring the bell. "There you are," she said. "Come on in."

"Am I late?" He followed her down the hall toward the formal dining room.

"The caterer has a sick kid. I told her we didn't mind eating right away."

"Ah." They rounded the corner, and Zachary sucked in a breath. Frannie was already there. Chatting with his family as if she had known them for years.

She looked up and met his gaze across the room. Was he imagining the weird connection? He glanced around to see if anyone else had noticed. Apparently not. Maybe he was working too hard.

They all took their places, and the salad course was served. Zachary waved a hand. "I suppose you've each introduced yourself to Frances?"

Farrell nodded. "Indeed. But we were just getting started, so feel free to fill in any blanks. Like for instance, the fact that you're actually friends with a professional hacker."

"That's stretching a point," Zachary said. "Frannie and I knew each other in high school. I had no idea who she was when we hired her."

Frannie gave him a wry smile. "You called me Frances a moment ago."

"I'm sorry," he drawled. "Would you prefer *F.* Wickersham?"

She made a face. "Actually, I don't mind being Frannie with people I know," she said. "It feels comfortable."

Farrell's fiancée, Ivy, lifted an eyebrow. "There's nothing wrong with Frances using an initial. Women in male-dominated fields have to fight for recognition. I would have done the same in her shoes."

Quin reached for more salad dressing. "I'm impressed as hell, Frannie. You must be freakishly smart. How did Zachary find you, anyway?"

"I didn't find *her* specifically," Zachary protested. "I talked to my buddy in DC, and he said that F. Wickersham was the best in the business. Stealthy. Discreet. And always successful. Why wouldn't I hire such a paragon?"

Frances's smile was a tad smug. "I have to admit. It was fun surprising Zachary. I've seen the tabloid stories over the years. The middle Stone brother, with an unending supply of gorgeous women on his arm and in his bed. Even in our high school, where the geek quotient was high, Zachary Stone was king. All the girls loved him, and all the boys wanted to be him."

Zachary felt his neck get hot. "Not *all* the girls," he muttered.

"Wait a minute," Farrell said, an arrested look on his face. "Wasn't Frannie the one who beat you out for that scholarship to Oxford? You were pissed as hell."

Frannie winced. "I never understood why it bothered him so much." She pinned Zachary with a questioning gaze. "Did you even *want* to study abroad?"

"No," he said, trying not to sound sullen. "I wanted to go to a party school. But I did want to win that damn scholarship."

Everyone laughed but Zachary. He managed a smile, yet inside, he remembered what it felt like to be a seventeen-year-old boy who had been beaten by a girl…yet again. And the same girl, at that. The world might see him as a confident, macho, eligible bachelor, but with Frannie, he'd always doubted himself.

"Poor Zachary," Farrell said. "He never wanted to be part of that school. But our father was insistent. He was so impressed that he had fathered a kid with an IQ of one-seventy, he was determined to see that Zachary was *challenged*."

Quinten snorted. "And all our brother wanted to do

was play football and date his way through all the girls in Portland."

Zachary desperately hoped the conversation would veer in another direction when the caterer brought in the main course of baked chicken and sautéed squash, but he was doomed to disappointment.

Katie continued the embarrassing inquisition. "So how big was this high school, Frannie?"

"Not that big." Frannie shot Zachary a rueful glance. "We were lab partners, project buddies. You name it."

"Enough reminiscing," Zachary said firmly. "Frannie. Frances. Why don't you tell all of us how you'll go about your investigation at Stone River Outdoors?"

"Of course." She finished chewing a bite of chicken and dabbed her beautiful lips. "I'll start with the places least likely to harbor a problem. The sales department. The entry-level positions. I can whip through those fairly quickly."

Ivy leaned forward. "And no one will know you're poking around?"

"They won't," Frannie said. "Your offices shut down at five. I'll show up at seven each evening and work until midnight."

Zachary nodded. "The only employee who has to be brought in on the secret is our night watchman. But he's worked at SRO twenty-five years. And we ran a thorough background check on him. Stanley's cool."

Farrell leaned back in his chair. "What happens if we're wrong?"

Frannie frowned. "What do you mean?"

"Well, we have no actual proof that anybody has done anything, really. A couple of my designs showed up in the marketplace while I was still working on them. The products weren't very good. And it's possible for two people to come up with the same idea at the same time. But it made me worry. I've moved my lab to my place on the northern coast until we can know for sure."

Zachary shot Frannie a sideways glance. "Farrell is our research and development guru. Katie has run his department for years, but more recently, she married Quinten."

Frannie chuckled. "That's not confusing at all. So, I'm only looking for stolen ideas?"

Zachary shook his head. "No. It's worse than that. Our father was killed in a suspicious car crash. Quinten was with him."

Frannie's eyes widened. "Seriously?"

"Yep." Quinten shrugged. "The crash jacked up my leg pretty badly. But I'm doing great now, and Katie, my sweet wife, makes sure I don't backslide."

"So you think the car crash might have been deliberate?" Frannie seemed puzzled. "Why?"

Zachary spoke up. "I'll field that one. We don't know what to think. But the timing alongside the stuff with Farrell's stolen ideas has made us jumpy. We'll be perfectly happy if you don't find a single thing wrong. Honestly. Hiring you is an insurance policy. We're hedging our bets. Covering every eventuality."

"I'm not cheap," Frannie said bluntly. "I don't want to take your money under false pretenses. We haven't signed anything yet. Everything you've described to me could be nothing more than mere coincidence."

Ivy laughed softly. "I'm sure the Stone brothers appreciate your transparency, but it will be money well spent for our peace of mind. Farrell and I are planning a Christmas wedding. I'd feel a lot better about taking a honeymoon if everything here at home is going well."

Frannie nodded. "And the rest of you?"

Farrell gave her a thumbs-up. "I'm in."

Katie raised her wineglass. "Me, too."

"And me." Quinten grinned as he snatched another roll.

Frances Wickersham turned in her seat and gave Zachary a cool, steady glance. "And you, Zachary?"

Frannie stared at Zachary calmly, hiding the fact that his mere presence in the room turned her back into a hormonal, overly emotional teenage girl. Her pulse fluttered, and her mouth was dry. Zachary Stone was both the same and yet different from the boy she had known so long ago.

His stunning good looks had matured, but the perfect features and flashing smile were no less jaw-dropping now than they had been when he was sixteen. The fact that he'd earned a reputation over the years as a playboy didn't surprise her. He was a man who liked women. And they liked him.

Frannie, herself, would have to be on her guard. She couldn't get sucked into his orbit. The residual fondness she felt for Zach was dangerous.

There was a reason she was a loner. It was easier that way. Less chance of getting her soft heart stomped on or her feelings bruised.

Zachary's thick chestnut hair gleamed beneath the warm light of the chandelier. His skin was perpetually golden, either because of all his time spent outdoors or because he had a dollop of Mediterranean genes somewhere in his DNA. Like his brothers, he was tall and lean and athletic. In high school, he had wanted desperately to play sports with Farrell and Quinten back in Portland.

Unfortunately, the gifted school in Connecticut had budgeted for microscopes and computers rather than football equipment and soccer fields. Zachary had been forced to find an outlet for his energy in intramural athletics.

Frannie unwittingly zoned out for a moment, but she finally realized that Zachary had not answered her question. "Zachary?" she said. "Do you want to do this?"

He seemed conflicted, and that was bad. Spending this

kind of money when one of the business partners wasn't a hundred percent on board could spark conflict. His hesitation hurt.

Finally, he gave her a terse nod. "I don't think we have a choice. The past couple of years have been tough. Quinten's injuries. Our father's death. The three of us learning how to run the company. We can't afford to lose what we've worked so hard to preserve."

"Well, then," she said. "I'll turn over every tiny pebble until we know for sure. Either Stone River Outdoors is in danger, *or* you have nothing to worry about. I'll have answers for you one way or another."

The conversation shifted then, allowing Frannie to finish her meal and witness the byplay between the other adults in the room. Watching the family dynamics in person helped her, but she already knew a great deal about the parties involved. She never undertook a job unless she was confident that she understood what she'd be dealing with. And whom. One of the perks of her skill set was uncovering secrets. She made no apology for the digging she did.

So far, her research told her the Stones were much like any wealthy family. They'd had their good times and bad. She had read about Quinten's competitive skiing accolades and the subsequent injuries that forced him to give up the life he loved. His wife, Katie, was an extremely loyal longtime employee who had fallen for the youngest Stone brother and married him earlier this year.

Frannie also knew that Farrell had been widowed tragically in his midtwenties and spent the next eight years alone. Petite Ivy Danby had come into Farrell's life recently—with her baby—and by all accounts, had coaxed the gruff, withdrawn inventor into taking a second chance on love.

Oddly, Zachary was not quite so easy to profile, despite

the reams of material Frannie had found online and the fact that she had known him fairly well before.

Zachary was an enigma. In school, he had been brilliant though reluctant to *apply himself*, as the report cards used to say. His brain was razor sharp, but he preferred to be known for his hijinks and his sense of fun. Zachary was never happier than when he was in the midst of a crowd, usually serving as the ringleader.

Though he did go on to get an advanced degree at Harvard, he had stopped short of a doctorate, either in defiance of his father's wishes or because Zachary was simply done with academia.

It made perfect sense that he was now the chief financial officer for Stone River Outdoors. His brothers would trust him to handle the money coming in and going out. She suspected, though, that the job was not one he found particularly fulfilling.

Since leaving school, Zachary had traveled the world. Extensively. His exploits were well documented. Though he could most likely have excelled in an individual athletic pursuit as Quinten had with skiing, Zachary was more often than not found with a gaggle of companions. Exploring remote sections of the Amazonian rain forest. Racing camels for the hell of it across sections of the Sahara. Dabbling with the idea of commercial space exploration.

Zachary Stone was brilliant, and brilliance required stimulation.

Frannie knew that firsthand. It was why she did what she did.

And then there were the women. Legions of them. Zachary Stone's name had been linked with any number of high-profile females. But he'd never come close to the altar. Though his older brother and his younger brother had found love, the middle Stone sibling continued to sail through life, noticeably alone.

Frannie didn't know what to make of that.

Once the caterer had served coffee and hot apple cobbler for dessert, Katie insisted the young woman head home to her sick child. Ivy stood and began gathering plates. "I'll help with cleanup, Katie."

Frannie joined them. "Me, too."

Katie shook her head. "Oh no. You're our guest this evening."

"Please." Frannie cocked her head at the three brothers, who had gathered at one end of the table and were arguing football statistics. "Save me."

The other two women laughed and agreed to let Frannie participate in what seemed to be a female ritual for this family. But Frannie had no quarrel with the status quo. She was eager to learn more from these women about the man who had once been her teenage crush.

When the kitchen was spotless and the dishwasher running, Frannie leaned against the counter and grinned. "So, tell me. What's it like to tame one of the Stone brothers?"

Katie sighed. "Well, it's not for the faint of heart. I work for one, and I'm married to another. Together, the siblings are three men who were raised by a single father. That tells you all you need to know."

"Because their mother died young, right?"

Ivy nodded. "Yes. It's probably understating the case to say they lacked a female influence. They're arrogant and stubborn and completely unwilling to accept limitations, but they can be surprisingly sweet despite all that alpha-male testosterone."

"They're pussycats at times," Katie agreed. "But never make the mistake of thinking you can pull something over on them. They hate being *handled*."

Frannie nodded. "Even as a teenager, Zachary had this incredible self-confidence. I envied him, to be honest. It took me years to feel comfortable in my own skin."

Ivy smiled. "I don't think it's ever easy for a woman to be seen as 'too smart.' You must have had female friends, didn't you?"

"I did. Oddly, though, most of my friends were guys. But it was because I was a tomboy, I suppose. Not athletic, believe me, but more interested in science than makeup and fashion. I was hopelessly awkward."

The kitchen door swung open, and Zachary walked in. "Don't be so hard on yourself, Frannie. You were cute in a quirky kind of way." He grinned at Katie and Ivy. "She had these oversize corduroy overalls, one forest green pair and one navy, and she swapped them out with half a dozen T-shirts."

Frannie gaped. "I can't believe you remember that."

"We spent a lot of time together, Bug. I have a damned good memory."

Katie lifted an eyebrow. "Bug?"

Zachary reached in the fridge for a beer and popped the cap. "Everybody at the Glenderry School for Gifted Children had nicknames, me included."

"We didn't pick them," Frannie said hastily. "Other students, usually upperclassmen, handed them out like toxic candy, and they invariably stuck. Of course, if you were popular like Zachary, they weren't so bad. Right, Stoner… or Stone Man?"

He shrugged, a light in his eyes. "Bugs are cute. *Lady*-bugs. You know."

Katie and Ivy gave her identical sympathetic looks. Katie shook her head slowly. "I'll bet you hated that nickname, didn't you, Frannie?"

"Oh yes." Although hearing Zachary speak it casually made it not so bad. He had never said it with malice.

Ivy, bless her, went to bat for wallflowers everywhere. "But look how you turned out, Frannie. You're tall and gorgeous and brilliantly successful. No one would ever guess that some dumb kid in high school named you Bug. Living well is the best revenge. Isn't that what they say?"

Though Frannie didn't have a lot of close friends, mostly by choice, she liked Ivy and Katie. In other circumstances, she might have enjoyed getting to know them better. Her chosen career left little time for socializing, and because she bounced all over the world, she had learned to be self-sufficient. As soon as she started her task at SRO headquarters, she would be immersed in the job. That's how she worked best. Head down. All her focus on the puzzle.

Looking for one single thread that could lead her to answers.

If such a thread even existed.

"Thanks for the vote of confidence, Ivy," Frannie said. "I've come a long way since my Glenderry days. Most people harbor a few unpleasant memories from adolescence. Mine aren't really so bad. It was better than being stuck in a regular public school and not being allowed to study all the things I wanted to… At Glenderry, there were no limits."

Katie shook her head slowly. "I'm glad you and Zachary had that opportunity."

Ivy frowned. "But *Stoner*?"

"It was a joke." Frannie grinned. "Zachary never touched drugs. Everyone knew that. He was too determined to stay in good shape physically. That's why it was such an aggravating nickname."

Zachary sighed. "I was what you might call conflicted. Glenderry was a hell of a good place for me, but I fought that reality every day. I just wanted to be normal."

Frannie smiled, a smile that started small and grew to include Katie and Ivy and Zachary's two brothers, who had joined the party in the kitchen. "Oh, come on, Zachary. You were *never* normal."

Two

Zachary couldn't decide whether he was insulted or amused when everyone in the room laughed uproariously. At him.

"Very funny," he muttered. "You're all off my Christmas list."

Frannie bit her lip, clearly trying to stifle more giggles. "I'm sorry, Zach. I couldn't resist."

Farrell winced. "Yikes."

"What's wrong?" Frannie asked.

Quin patted her arm. "We'll protect you."

"From what?"

Katie whispered loudly. "Zachary *hates* having his name shortened."

"No, he doesn't." Frannie stared at him. "Are they serious?"

Zachary shrugged. "I decided in college that Zachary had more gravitas. Nobody has called me Zach in at least ten years."

"Oh." She blinked. "Sorry."

"You shouldn't be," he said quietly, pulling her into the hall for a moment of privacy. "I called you Frannie when you're obviously a Frances now. All grown-up. Serious. Mature. We've come a long way, Frances Wickersham. But I still want to believe that sweet girl is in there somewhere. I liked her."

Her eyes were huge, the color deeper, darker now. “And I liked Zach,” she said. “But shouldn’t we keep the past in the past if I’m going to be working for your company?”

“We’re old friends, Frannie. It’s true I didn’t know that when I hired you, but does it matter? We shared a lot back then. Glenderry helped make us who we are today.”

“Do you like who you are?” she asked, her expression wary.

The question was spot-on. He might be a genius, but Frannie was too smart to believe any of his usual lines. “Maybe.” He said it grudgingly. “I’ve had to step up the past couple of years. My brothers have needed me.” And being needed was easier than mapping out his own future.

“So, you abandoned the serial dating and the globe-trotting?”

“You could say that.”

“Do you miss it?”

“Which part?” He drawled the two words for the sheer pleasure of making Frannie blush. “I may be in the midst of a dry spell, if that’s what you’re asking.”

Frannie sputtered and backtracked. “Your romantic life is none of my concern. I should get back to the hotel.” She pulled out her phone and tapped the app for the car service.

Zachary took her phone and held it over his head, ignoring her scowl. “The Frannie I knew was very thrifty. Why pay for a ride when I can drop you at your hotel on my way home? Or better yet…”

“Better yet what?” she said, not even trying to retrieve her phone.

He gave her his best nonthreatening, charming, cajoling smile. “On the way, we could stop off for a drink. I’d love to hear what you’ve been doing since the last time we saw each other.”

Her expression was equal parts suspicious and interested. “That might be fun,” she admitted. “Hotel rooms get old. Yes, Zach. I’ll let you take me home.”

“Good.” He handed over her phone. “I love my family, but I wouldn’t mind heading out in the next few minutes after we say our goodbyes.”

When they returned to the kitchen, the other four adults pretended they hadn’t been trying to eavesdrop.

Frannie smiled at Katie and Quin. Quin had one arm curled around his wife’s waist. “Thanks for inviting me tonight,” Frannie said. “The meal was great, and I enjoyed getting to know you.”

Quin nodded. “It was our pleasure. You’ll have to come again. Especially since it sounds like you’ll be here in Portland for a while.”

“Thank you. I’d like that.” Frannie turned to Farrell and Ivy. “Congratulations on your upcoming wedding. I’ve always thought December ceremonies were beautiful.”

Ivy leaned her head on Farrell’s shoulder. “If you’re still here by then, I hope you’ll come.”

Frannie shook her head. “That’s sweet of you, but I can’t imagine my role will take much longer than four or five weeks. I hope to take some vacation time after I finish with SRO, and then I have a huge job that starts in January.”

“Well,” Ivy said. “The offer still stands.”

After that, everyone moved en masse toward the front of the house. Farrell and Ivy were leaving, as well. Ivy’s daughter, Dolly, was with a babysitter, and Ivy wanted to get home to her.

In the car, Zachary turned the radio on low and adjusted his lights. The rain had stopped, but the air was thick and heavy. Fog reduced visibility to only a few feet. Beside him, Frannie was quiet. He remembered that about her. She didn’t chatter. Not that he would have minded. Conversations with a woman like Frannie were never dull.

The bar he had in mind was cozy and warm. Sometimes

on the weekends a lone jazz musician played. It was actually not the kind of spot he took his dates. But he often met friends there. The distinction was one he had never considered.

After finding a convenient parking spot on the street, he slid into it and scooted around to open his passenger's door. Frannie stepped out and turned up her collar. "Brrr... Is it colder now?"

"Feels like it." He put a hand under her elbow and escorted her to the building.

Inside Dante's, the warm, convivial atmosphere wrapped them in welcome. The bartender cocked his head. "We're slow tonight," he said. "Take your pick. Someone will be with you in a minute."

There were only eight small booths in addition to the bar itself. Four at the front and four at the back. Zachary headed for the most private of them all. It was tucked in the far rear corner near the restrooms.

The wallpaper in the bar was antique, and the comfortable leather banquettes were scuffed and worn. Over the bar, an enormous mirror enlarged the room, its vintage glass mottled with age.

Frannie shrugged out of her coat and looked around with interest. "What a cool place. It feels like Hemingway might walk in any minute."

"I hoped you would like it." Zachary shed his overcoat, as well.

The young woman who came to take their order cut to the chase. "You want hot coffee or the hard stuff? Nasty out there tonight."

"Frannie?" He smiled at his guest, feeling unaccountably relaxed and mellow. As long as he didn't dwell on the shape of her breasts beneath that clingy sweater, he could forget F. Wickersham was a woman. Maybe.

Frannie glanced at a drink menu. "I'll have a virgin strawberry daiquiri, please."

"And I'm driving," Zachary said. "So, keep the hot coffee coming. A shot of Bailey's in the first one wouldn't hurt, though."

When they were alone again, he studied her face. "You're not a drinker?"

She shrugged, her long fingers shredding a napkin. "It dulls me. I don't like that. I tried the social drinking thing at university, but I was no good at it. I prefer to stay alert. Plus, my college roommate was almost raped at a party, so it sobered me, if you'll pardon the pun. I work with men a great deal. It pays to keep vigilant."

He fell silent, realizing that he had no idea what it was like for a woman to survive in the twenty-first century. Everything was supposed to be equal, but that was a joke. Pay scale aside, the female sex was always going to physically be at the mercy of a larger, stronger male.

His stomach turned at the thought of some idiot guy trying to take advantage of a woman like Frannie. Echoes from the past disturbed him. "If I'm honest, I don't like the idea of you working alone at night," he said. "It doesn't feel safe."

She gave him a wry smile, then thanked the waitress when her daiquiri arrived. Frannie took a sip. "I've been doing this work a very long time, Zach. I can handle myself."

It wasn't the moment to argue, nor was it his place. He wasn't her brother or her father or even a lover. The fact that his company was hiring her gave him no rights at all when it came to Frances Wickersham.

So, he changed the subject reluctantly. "Tell me about college," he said. "Was Oxford everything you thought it would be?"

Frannie beamed, her joy lighting up her face and turning her from attractive to flat-out beautiful. "It was, Zach. I wish you could have gone, too. The history and the sheer respect for learning. My God, you would have wallowed in it. I had to pinch myself every morning. I loved it so much, I seriously considered settling in England permanently."

"But..." He swallowed the hot coffee cautiously, inhaling the aroma and tasting the kick of the liqueur.

She grimaced. "My parents would have revolted. I was already a disappointment to them, so I gave up the idea."

Zachary gaped at her. "You're brilliant and academically overqualified in every way, but you were a disappointment to them? How the hell does that happen?"

She shrugged. "They're both doctors. I refused to go into medicine. They think what I do is little more than a childish hobby."

"Ouch."

"Yeah." She curled her straw through her drink.

The burst of animation she exhibited when he asked about Oxford had faded quickly, making him wish he'd never mentioned her parents. "Do you have siblings? I'm sorry to say I don't remember."

"Nope. Just me. That's a lot of pressure for an only child."

"I can only imagine. So, what *did* you study?"

"I did a double major in computer science and mathematics. But I also took a ton of literature electives, just because I loved it so much. Can you imagine studying *The Canterbury Tales* and then actually *visiting* Canterbury? I was drunk on learning. Those were the best four years of my life."

"And did you ever think about an advanced degree?"

"I considered it. But I was ready to make my mark in the world. Does that sound arrogant?" She didn't give him a chance to answer. "My first job was a government gig in London. The *US* government," she clarified. "All classified stuff. When it was over, my parents were nagging me to come home. I had already figured out that private sector pay would be much better. So, I went home to Massachusetts, spent time with my parents and soon snagged a job with an enormous security firm."

"I'm impressed."

"I enjoy what I do. It pays the bills."

"Don't be flip," he said. "I know you. I *am* you. Beating the system gives you a charge. You love hacking. It gives you a high, doesn't it?"

She leaned back in her seat, eyes wide. A flush of hot pink crept up her throat. "Wow. No one has ever said that to me before."

"Am I wrong?" He dared her to lie.

The silence stretched between them. "No," she said finally. "You're not wrong. But I'm tired of talking about me. Let's focus on Zachary Stone."

Frannie felt uncomfortably exposed. No one she knew could have nailed her personality so succinctly. The fact that Zachary *had* shouldn't have surprised her. He was right in one way. They shared a guilty secret. Their mental agility was both a gift and a curse. Only someone in their shoes could fully understand that.

Hacking for Frannie was like a gateway drug. She needed bigger and harder challenges all the time to satisfy her hunger. At the moment, the spurt of professional excitement she experienced was all because someone might be targeting Stone River Outdoors.

Zachary summoned the server. "Straight coffee this time for me," he said. "And whatever the lady wants." He lifted an eyebrow. "Frannie?"

She bit her lip. "Will you judge me if I ask for nachos?"

That beautiful, masculine smile made her breath catch. "Never. I like a woman with an appetite."

She blinked. Had Zachary Stone just made a suggestive comment? Surely not. He wouldn't bother to flirt with *her*.

Because she was flustered, she went on the attack. "I've bared my soul," she said. "Your turn."

For a moment, his expression was bleak. Or maybe she imagined the flash of *something* in his dark-eyed gaze. "My tale isn't as fun as yours," he said, stirring sugar into the steaming elixir the server had dispensed from a glass pot. "I went to Penn State. Drank too much. Partied too much. Pulled myself together for the last two years and graduated with the GPA everyone expected from a *genius*. Did an MBA. Took the money my grandparents left me and circumnavigated the globe. Then Dad died and Quinten was hurt, and I had to make something of myself."

"You've been there for your family. I respect that."

"I don't know that I've done a lot. Keeping the finances in order isn't exactly rocket science."

"What did you want to do with your life, Zach? In high school you spent a lot of time pretending you didn't care about anything at all. But I know that's not true."

"Do you?" The sardonic comment was at odds with that same flash of disquiet in his eyes.

"Tell me," she said. "It's just us. And I'm good at keeping secrets."

For a moment she thought she had reached him, the genuine, complicated man beneath the carefree facade. But maybe she'd pushed too hard, because he changed the subject. The tension in his frame was the equivalent of a Keep Off the Grass sign. Zachary Stone didn't want to be dissected or analyzed.

Fair enough.

"I'd help you if I could," he said. "With the forensic stuff, I mean. But computers were never my forte. I know how to turn them on, but that's about it."

"Oh, please," she said, frowning. "Don't expect me to fall for that."

"So you *want* my help?" He grinned.

"No. I work alone. You're welcome to look over my shoulder once in a while. After all, you're paying the tab."

"I trust you," he said. "Though to be honest, I'm really hoping you don't find anything. It disturbs me to think that some person or some entity wants us to fail. Or at least to struggle. If we lose market share or even go under completely, our employees are the ones who will suffer the most. My brothers and I would be okay. We have investments and savings. But SRO provides hundreds of good jobs."

"Maybe it's nothing," she said, trying to erase the worry from his eyes.

He shook his head slowly. "I wish I could believe that."

The nachos arrived, and the conversation turned to lighter topics. Frannie licked a dollop of melted cheese from the corner of her mouth. "You're lucky to be so close to your brothers and your sisters-in-law. I always wanted a sibling. My parents were too focused on their work to try for number two. Sometimes I've wondered if I was an accident, but I've always been afraid to ask."

"Did you ever consider doing what they wanted? Becoming a doctor?"

"Not really. It wasn't a rebellion thing. Medicine didn't speak to me. If I'd had any leanings in that direction, I might have pursued them. To be honest…" She gave him a rueful smile. "I'm better alone than I am with people."

"You could have done research. That's usually a solitary field."

She shrugged. "Boring. For me, anyway. I love what I do. A lot. My parents don't particularly like it, but they've given up on trying to change me at this point."

"Good. You *should* be able to do the thing that makes

you happy." He paused, an odd look on his face. "I have an idea."

"Oh?"

"You don't want to spend the next two days stuck in a hotel room."

"I don't?"

"No. Why don't you let me take you north? To my place on the ocean. I think you'd like it. Keep the hotel room while you're gone if it's simpler. We'll cover that. But come with me, Frannie. I'd like you to see my home away from home. Please..."

Her brain went muzzy, and her body heated from her toes all the way to her flushed cheeks. Surely she was misunderstanding him. "Are you hitting on me, Zach?"

He blinked. Paled beneath his tan. And unless she was kidding herself, a flash of hurt swept through his gaze. "Why would you say that?"

The question was low. Taut.

Frannie swallowed, suddenly lost in high weeds. "Well, you do have a reputation. It's not exactly a secret."

His lips firmed in a grim line, and the hand that rested on the table curled into a fist. "I don't take women there. My getaway is for family and friends."

She had offended him. And maybe even hurt him. Regret curled in her stomach. "I'm sorry, Zach. I—"

He held up a hand, halting her stumbling apology. "Never mind. Bad idea." He signaled the waitress to bring their check. "It's late. I'll walk you back to your hotel."

She felt small and confused. Without overthinking it, she reached across the table and laid her hand over his. His fingers were warm beneath hers. "I misread the situation. I really am very sorry. It makes me feel good to know you consider us friends. If we could start over, Zach, then yes. I would very much like to see your getaway house up on the coast."

For several long moments, he was as still as a granite statue, his body language holding her at bay. Suddenly, he exhaled, and his shoulders relaxed. His smile was wry. "I deserved that, I guess. But I promise to be on my best behavior, I swear."

Frannie wasn't known for taking chances on the opposite sex. Men had disappointed her time and again. But still she said, "I trust you, Zach. Or I wouldn't have said yes." She pulled back her hand, mildly disconcerted by how much she had enjoyed touching him.

"Did you bring outdoor gear?"

"A coat and some dressy boots."

"Then we're gonna raid the store," he said, grinning. "I'll text Stanley to let him know we'll be there, so he won't call the police."

Twenty minutes later, they were pulling up in front of Stone River Outdoors. The window displays were classy and appealing. The SRO building sat on a prime piece of corner real estate. When they got out of the car, Frannie shivered. An icy late-night wind had kicked up, whistling through the downtown streets.

Zachary had them inside in moments. "I'm not going to turn on the overheads," he said. "I think we can see well enough with the security lights. Why don't you look for pants and a top over there? Anything that would do to spend some time outdoors. I'll grab several boxes of boots. What size are you?"

"Nine and a half," she said, wincing inwardly. She had never been the kind of tiny, petite woman men seemed to want.

"Got it."

When Zachary disappeared to the other side of the store, she flipped through the racks of sweaters and T-shirts and joggers and leggings and everything in between. She scooped up a mulberry-colored Henley shirt and gray hiking pants in her size. When she turned around to look for a dressing room, Zachary was headed her way carrying a parka over his shoulder and three shoeboxes in his arms.

He waved her across the store. "Might as well try stuff on. Either that or take everything in a couple of sizes."

"I don't mind seeing what fits. If you don't mind waiting."

The dressing rooms weren't locked. Zachary set his load of things on the bench inside. "Take your time. I'm going to text my manager to let her know I've raided her stock."

"Okay." Frannie waited until he exited the small space. Then she twisted the lock. Not that she thought he would intrude. But she *was* about to strip down to her undies, so she didn't want to take chances.

Quickly, she tried on everything, including the pair of boots that she liked the best. The top and pants were good. The boots seemed a little big, but once she put thick socks with them, they'd probably be fine.

When she exited the changing room, she found Zachary loitering nearby, but at a discreet distance. "How did those work?" he asked.

The two of them were standing in a mostly dark store. Moments ago, she'd been nearly naked. No matter how you looked at it, this was definitely an odd experience. She cleared her throat. "I like the top and pants. The shoebox on top is the pair that fits well. But I'll need socks."

Zachary reached in his jacket pocket and waved a small, clear plastic package. "Already got you covered. Come on." She trailed after him as he returned the two pairs of boots she hadn't chosen.

"Do you know how to operate the register?" she asked. "I have my credit card."

He stopped so suddenly, she nearly ran into him. When he turned around, he frowned at her. "Don't be ridiculous. This is my treat."

"I don't usually accept gifts from a client."

"Is that a rule?"

She shook her head slowly. "No. More of a guideline."

Zachary grinned. "Good. 'Cause you know how I hate breaking rules."

Frannie couldn't help herself. She burst out laughing. "You've never *met* a rule you didn't want to break. I swear you had detention every day for a month when we were sophomores."

He shrugged, looking big and masculine and gorgeous. "That was in my rebellious phase. They used to give me pages and pages of calculus problems as punishment. No one seemed to realize that I loved it."

"Well," she said, deadpan, "it was a school for smart kids, not smart teachers."

Now Zachary was the one to laugh. "I'd forgotten how sarcastic you are. I used to love that. You were funny and snarky, and we both shared a similar sense of humor. I wonder if that's still the same?"

"I suppose we'll have to find out."

Even in the semidark, she saw the flash of heat in his gaze. "Are *you* hitting on *me*, Frances Wickersham?"

Her heart beat faster. "Not yet, Zach. But give me time."

Three

Zachary woke up Saturday morning with a smile on his face, though he hadn't slept much the night before. He was still incredulous that he had impulsively invited Frances Wickersham for a weekend getaway, and even more incredulous that she had accepted.

After their clandestine shopping spree at the store, he had dropped Frannie off at her hotel and handed over the three shopping bags with her new gear. She had offered him a subdued good-night and skedaddled, as his dad used to say.

F. Wickersham was a conundrum. She certainly wasn't the mousy, shy girl he remembered. She was a full-grown woman. Assertive. Independent. And to his immense surprise, sexy as hell.

He'd never been one to go for the studious academic type. He dated women with big breasts and large personalities. In his experience, those types of women knew the score. They dated rich guys for the perks, and when it was over, everyone parted company happily. Nothing wrong with that.

To his knowledge, Zachary had *never* broken any woman's heart. He was a generous boyfriend and an even more generous lover. No complaints. No dings on his record. Five-star ratings across the board.

The fact that none of his relationships lasted longer than

three or four weeks had not been a problem. He was open and honest about what he wanted. Some women appreciated that in a man.

But he was about to embark on a "friendship" that skated into unknown territory. The all-grown-up Frannie fascinated him. As much as he was attracted to her kick-ass body, he was equally looking forward to matching wits with her.

In high school, Bug had kept him on his toes. What would it be like now that she possessed considerably more confidence and what he assumed was considerably more sexual experience, as well?

When she met his initial invitation with outright skepticism, he had understood for the first time that the playboy reputation he'd willingly cultivated might actually be a stumbling block for some women.

He hadn't been hitting on her. At least he didn't think so. Everyone knew the subconscious could be a crafty bitch. Had his libido been making plans behind the scenes? He couldn't deny that the thought of spending two entire days with Frannie on the northern coast was damned appealing.

When he pulled up in front of the hotel, she was ready right on time, wearing her own clothes still, but this time casual. Faded jeans showcased her long, long legs and narrow waist. Yet another cashmere turtleneck, this one navy, hugged her curves.

Zachary popped the trunk and hopped out to open Frannie's door. She tossed her coat, the one she had worn the night before, into the back seat. The bellman put her suitcase and carry-on in the trunk. Then Zachary handed the guy a twenty, and they were off.

"Have you had breakfast?" he asked.

"No. I snoozed the alarm three times."

"Drive-through okay?"

"As long as they have good coffee and plenty of carbs, yes."

Thirty minutes later, they were on the road headed north.

Frannie sipped her hot drink with a smile on her face. "Did you bring the Porsche to impress me?"

He shot her a sideways glance. "Is it working?"

She sighed, snagging one of the cinnamon sugar doughnuts he had suggested. "Would it surprise you to know I could buy a couple of Porsches of my own?"

"No. I think I always knew you would do well in your chosen career. Whatever that turned out to be. Why do you ask?"

Her profile was pensive. "You'd be shocked how many men lose interest when they discover that my bank balance is bigger than theirs."

"Small dicks," he said, shrugging.

Frannie's giggles made him smile. Turned out, he liked making her laugh.

"You haven't changed much, have you?" she said. "Still the same outrageous boy who enjoyed entertaining the class."

"Maybe. But life's gotten pretty damn serious. I lost my father. Nearly lost my brother. And that's after my sister-in-law died when I was barely out of grad school. Being an adult is not for the fainthearted."

Frannie touched his arm lightly, just a brush of his shirtsleeve. "It wasn't a criticism, Zach. The world needs more laughter. It doesn't mean we ignore the bad stuff. You've been a huge support to your brothers."

"I hope so." He reached for another doughnut. "I didn't mean to get maudlin. Let's talk about you."

"Let's not," Frannie said lightly. "How about the weather?"

He chuckled. "Cold. Might snow. That about covers it."

"How much snow?" Now the lady definitely sounded wary.

"I don't know. Does it matter? We have a fully stocked freezer and plenty of firewood for the fireplace."

"Aren't you worried about getting stranded?"

"Not particularly. We have lots of catching up to do."

"Oh."

Zachary couldn't deduce from that single syllable whether or not Frannie was enthusiastic about his statement, or intimidated. He snorted inwardly. This new Frannie didn't seem like the kind of woman to be intimidated by anything.

The trip passed quickly. Occasionally they talked about one subject or another, but mostly, the car was silent. Good silent, not bad silent.

Zachary was perfectly comfortable. Weird.

Eventually, they passed the turn to Bar Harbor and Acadia National Park and joined the two-lane highway that led north and east to Stone family property. Traffic was light on this gray November day. "Not long now," he said.

Frannie straightened in her seat and surveyed the countryside with interest. "I can't imagine you so far from civilization."

"People change, Frannie."

"Do they?" She turned sideways in her seat and eyed him so intently her gaze felt like a physical touch.

"Don't make a big thing of this," he muttered. "Both of my brothers have houses up here, too."

"But it was your idea, wasn't it? In the beginning."

"Why would you say that?" Her probing was making him regret his invitation. He didn't need someone digging around in his psyche.

"When we were in high school, one rainy afternoon after we had finished all our projects and we were stuck in study hall, you swore that you were going to get out from under your father's thumb one day. That you were sick to death of other people running your life. That you wanted to live somewhere you could breathe the air and run naked through the woods if you wanted to..."

"I said that to shock you."

"I know. You liked being outrageous and making me say, *Zacchh...*"

With his eyes glued to the road, he grinned. "You were so sweet and naive and so easily rattled. It was fun to make you screech my name."

"I used to wonder why you didn't ask for another lab partner. I always got the feeling you were irritated with me half the time."

He pulled off onto the side of the road with a squeal of tires and a flurry of gravel. Shoving the car into Park, he turned to face her, resting his arm on the steering wheel. "It was more than irritation," he said, remembering all that teenage angst. "And it was *all* the time. I was so damned frustrated. Nothing I did was quite good enough. You were at the top of every class, every ranking. I was supposed to be a genius. Everybody told me so. But there you were. Edging me out."

Frannie chewed her bottom lip. "I'm sorry," she said.

"Don't be sorry, Bug. It made me work harder—harder than I wanted to, in fact. If it weren't for you, I might have flunked out of Glenderry. You were the carrot. The prod. The itch under my skin."

She stared at him, big eyed. "I never knew you felt that way."

"Of course not. What teenage boy is going to admit he's competing with a *girl*? And losing?"

"It sounds like you thought of me as more of an adversary than a friend."

He sensed he had hurt her feelings. "There was a lot of gray area in my life back then. I was a horny adolescent stuck in a school where I couldn't do what I wanted to do when I wanted to do it. I was angry with my father, and I missed my brothers. You were probably the only person who kept me sane."

"Doesn't sound like it," she muttered.

He ran a thumb down her cheek, barely a touch, less than a split second. "You should never have to apologize for being brilliant, Ms. F. Wickersham. I didn't know how to handle that when we were kids."

She raised an eyebrow. "And now?"

"We'll see." He studied her face. The high brow. The pointed chin. The eyes that were an intriguing mix of deep blue and rich purple. And those cute, sexy glasses. Frowning suddenly, he reached out and slid them off her nose.

"Hey," she said indignantly. "Give those back."

He held them up to the light. "Frannie," he said. "You're a fraud." She grabbed for the eyewear, but he kept them out of reach. "These lenses are clear glass."

She turned red, her expression equal parts aggravated and mortified. "People expect smart women to look a certain way. It's already an uphill battle to be taken seriously. The glasses help."

Without another word, he slid them back onto her ears and smoothed her hair. "I apologize. It's not my business. But for the record, you don't need to wear them around me. I take you very seriously. I always have."

Frannie sat back in her seat, resisting the urge to put her hands to her hot cheeks. That was the most amount of personal information Zachary Stone had shared with her. Ever. And they had known each other pretty well back then.

Apparently, he was a damned good actor. She had known he wanted the Oxford scholarship. He'd made no secret of the fact that he was bummed when she won it and not him. But all that other stuff he'd said? That was news to her.

Because she honestly didn't know what to say, she mulled over everything and kept mum for the rest of the trip. It wasn't too long. Another thirty minutes. They left the highway and passed through a security gate, where Zach punched in a code. Now they were on a paved road—narrow, but paved.

"You may not like it," Zachary said out of the blue.

"Like what?"

"The house."

"So tell me, is it a rustic cabin in the woods or a lavish hideaway?"

"Neither. And it's not so much *in* the woods as it is surrounded by woods. It's on a cliff overlooking the ocean. Not a huge cliff. You'll have to see for yourself. It's smaller than either of my brothers' places. They have room for wives and kids and visitors."

"And you don't?"

His profile was etched with what looked like introspection. "Not really. I didn't see the point. What woman would put up with me? Besides, I still have that pesky aversion to being told what to do. I'm a terrible relationship risk. So I don't bother."

"I see." And she did see. At least in part. Zachary was a chameleon. Though he wanted people to believe he was open and carefree, she suspected the exact opposite was true. Zachary Stone was a man with deep layers.

They rounded a bend in the road, and Frannie caught her breath. "Oh, Zach. It's beautiful." At first glance, it seemed as if his entire house was made of glass. That was impossible, of course, but the front elevation facing the ocean was nothing but windows. Was it two levels? Three? She couldn't tell, because the sunlight reflected blindingly.

Her companion, who had grown more taciturn by the minute, pulled into the circular driveway and cut the engine.

When they opened the car doors, the scent of evergreens wafted into the interior. The air smelled like Christmas.

Actually, it *felt* like Christmas, too. At this altitude and with the wind off the ocean, Frannie reached immediately for her coat and slipped it on, buttoning it all the way to the neck and down to her knees. Zachary donned a coat, too, but it was more of a jacket, and he didn't bother to zip the lightweight navy wool.

She walked over to the edge of the drop-off. Zach was right. It could definitely be described as a cliff, but it wasn't all that high. Even so, the rocks below looked slippery and treacherous. There might be a narrow beach at low tide, but not now. She shielded her eyes.

"How do you ever leave?" she asked quietly, feeling the breeze and the warmth of the sun caress her face, each fighting for supremacy.

Zachary stood at her side, shoulder to shoulder. "I wouldn't if it were only me," he said quietly. "This is all a man needs."

"Or a woman. You're so lucky," she said. "How did you find this place?"

"The land has been in our family for several generations. A lot of it was sold off over the years, but thank God, my relatives kept the coastline." He noticed when she shivered hard. "We should get you out of the cold before you turn into a block of ice. Don't worry about your bags. I'll come back out for them."

They ascended the steps, and Zach unlocked the front door. When she stepped inside, there was that whole breath-catching thing again. It might have been the house, or it might have been the way Zach smelled, like a man who had been outside in the cold. Either way, she found herself dizzy.

Zach stood off to one side as she walked around the living room. He had created an amazing oasis that was both strikingly modern and yet completely at home in the midst of a forest. The furniture had sleek lines and crimson upholstery. The rug looked like a masterpiece from some modern art museum.

And then there was the fireplace. Though it was empty at the moment, of course, Frannie had no trouble at all imagining Zach lounging in front of the flames. Who was with him in that scenario? He claimed he didn't bring *women* here. Translation—his disposable, flavor-of-the-week bimbos.

Why would a man as brilliant as Zachary Stone bother with women who had no depth? The answer was fairly obvious, but it made her uncomfortable. Sex. Meaningless sex. He didn't care about their IQs. What did it take to please a man like Zach in bed?

Behind her, the male in question cleared his throat. "Well," he said. "What do you think? Do you like it, or is the ambience too much?"

She whirled to face him. "Not too much at all. It's magnificent, Zach. Truly. I'm so impressed. Will you show me the rest?"

His broad grin said her words of praise pleased him. Surely, he knew his home was a stunning masterpiece. Didn't he?

"Whatever the lady wants."

He led her out of the main living area into the kitchen, which wasn't huge, but was a cook's dream. High-end appliances. Italian tile backsplashes. A refrigerator big enough to feed a football team. And best of all, the kitchen was open on one side...open to the dining room that overlooked the forest. From the dining room, a guest could wander back to the living room, making a comfortable circuit. Good traffic flow.

"It's perfect," she said, already imagining lazy mornings of French toast and coffee and scrambled eggs. "Do you cook?" she asked impulsively.

He made a face. "I *can* cook, but I don't advertise that particular talent."

She cocked her head and studied his odd expression. "Why not?"

Zachary moved restlessly, opening the fridge and offering her a cola. When she declined, he popped the tab on one for himself. "It's too much of a cliché, don't you think? Wealthy bachelor prepares fine cuisine for his lady friend? I don't like them to get too settled."

"But you said you don't bring dates here."

"It's the same principle in Portland. My condo there has a great kitchen, too. I cook for myself. That's all."

"And your brothers? Your family?"

"My brothers would razz me unmercifully if they knew I could prepare coq au vin or chocolate soufflé. So I keep that to myself. Farrell's fiancée, Ivy, is a great amateur chef. I've helped her out in the kitchen a time or two."

"Where did you learn to cook?"

"I taught myself. I like to eat. And I get tired of restaurants."

"But you don't share your expertise with anyone?"

"I've made homemade pizza a few times for my brothers. Or grilled a steak. That's as far as it goes."

She was quiet for a moment, trying to understand. Yet again, Zachary was hiding his light under a bushel. He was brilliant. Multitalented. Yet the face he showed to the world was that of a shallow thrill seeker with little discrimination when it came to the opposite sex. It didn't make sense.

Then again, she couldn't really say she knew the adult Zachary Stone.

With every second that passed, though, she wanted more and more to understand what made him tick. What motivated him. As a teenager she had been intimidated by his good looks and popularity. The only arena where she'd felt comfortable around him had been academia. She'd held her own there.

Now, as an adult, her self-concept was healthier. More grounded. The fact that Zachary was a beautiful, rough-hewn, sexy man didn't bother her. Much. When she dipped her toes in the pool of sexual attraction, she liked to stay in the shallow end. She had no illusions about her ability to deal with the likes of her onetime school chum.

She no longer thought of herself as a bookish wallflower. But that didn't mean she was going to be stupid. For the next month, give or take, she would be working for Zachary Stone and his brothers to ferret out possible espionage at Stone River Outdoors. It was possible she and Zach might spend a fair amount of time together.

Frannie was absolutely *not* going to resurrect her teenage crush. Period. If her heart beat a little faster and her mouth went dry and her knees got all wobbly around him, she would manage to deal with those alarming reactions. Somehow.

A woman as smart as she knew better than to swim with the sharks. She liked Zach. A lot. He was one of the few people who could discuss almost any subject under the sun with her and be both witty and insightful on an astounding level.

Still, a meeting of the minds was a long way from a casual fling or romance or *hooking up*—whatever people liked to call it nowadays. She would keep her hormones where they belonged. Besides, there was absolutely no possibility that Zach looked at her sexually.

She was the irritating classmate who had made him feel less than.

"Do you think you could teach me?" she asked impulsively.

His eyes widened. "Excuse me?"

"To cook. I'm hopeless in the kitchen, but I've always

wanted to learn. I know you're busy, but I'll be in Portland for several weeks."

His lips twitched. "I'm surprised, Frannie. I can't imagine you being *not* perfect at anything."

She shrugged. "I think I've always been scared of trying to cook, because everyone talks about culinary disasters. It would demoralize me to fail badly, so after a few mortifying attempts right out of college, I quit trying." She eyed him cajolingly. "So, will you? Teach me how to cook while I'm in Maine?"

Zachary shook his head slowly. "I think I'm being set up. But let's put it this way. I'll think about it."

"That's good enough for now," she said. "Can I see the rest of the house?"

"Sure."

He led her upstairs. A library and gallery ran the length of the house at the back. "Wow," she said, feeling envy curl in her chest. It must be wonderful to have this to come home to when responsibilities allowed. Comfy overstuffed armchairs invited visitors to kick back and relax. Frannie itched to examine the paintings and books and sculptures, but Zachary kept the tour moving.

"Here's where you'll sleep," he said, his voice matter-of-fact.

The single guest room was actually a luxurious suite with a living area separated from the bedroom and private bath. She went to the window and looked out at the ocean. The water was gray and foreboding today...with wind-tossed whitecaps. Even in this mood, it was starkly beautiful.

"Too bad I'm only here for one night," she said. "Maybe I could stay and access your computers remotely." She said it jokingly.

Zachary took it as such. "I feel the same way," he said.

"Sometimes the family business is a millstone around our necks."

"You haven't thought about selling out?"

"It's crossed our minds a time or two. But we can't escape that whole family heritage thing. Farrell and Quin and I aren't keen to put an end to generations of Stone family history. Plus, anytime you sell a business like ours, you run the risk of having the new owners clean house. Some of our employees have been with us since we three were babies."

"You feel responsible for them."

"Exactly. When you hold another person's livelihood in your hands, the decisions you make affect more than yourself. What if they all lost their jobs?"

"That's a lot of pressure. At least you have siblings to help bear the load. Have you ever considered bringing in a few high-level employees who could take over and allow you and your brothers to step back?" She winced. "Wow. I didn't mean to sound like I have all the answers. I work for myself. I can't even imagine juggling the pressures of a company as big as Stone River Outdoors."

"No worries," he said lightly. "You're only voicing questions we've asked ourselves time and again. Maybe if we can rule out the espionage thing, we'll reconsider. It hasn't been all that long since Dad died and Quin was injured. We've been in survival mode. When things settle down, I imagine we'll take a look at the big picture and plan for the future."

"Makes sense." She wanted to ask where he saw himself in five years. But she didn't. It was too personal a question at this stage in their relationship. They had been close once. In a way. But the years that had passed since their last meeting created a chasm too great to cross in one day.

Zachary leaned against the door frame, watching her as she examined her surroundings. "Would you like to see my bedroom?" he asked.

Four

Zachary took note as a pale pink blush washed over Frannie's throat and cheeks. Even now, he could fluster her. Perhaps he shouldn't have enjoyed it so much, but it was fun. She was usually so calm, so self-possessed. He liked bumping her off balance.

Frannie wrapped her arms around her waist, calling attention to the way her breasts filled out that soft, fuzzy sweater. She didn't quite meet his gaze. "Sure," she said.

They stepped back out into the hallway, and he led her a few steps to his own suite, trying to see it through her eyes. Other than Katie and Ivy—and a lady who came in to clean once a month—no woman had ever set foot in his private domain.

This was where he came to be alone, to relax, to center himself. The bedroom itself was almost stark. Only a huge king-size bed, two small nightstands, and a single armchair beside the fireplace, plus a state-of-the-art telescope over by the wall of windows. The crimson duvet was the only splash of color. Everything else was charcoal gray and white. All of his clothes and personal belongings were tucked away in the huge master closet.

"Wow," Frannie said. "I don't know what to say. It almost reminds me of a knight's chamber in a castle. If the knight had unlimited money and really good taste."

"Check out the rest," he said. "The bathroom floor is heated, and the walk-in shower has triple rain heads."

He followed her at a distance as she opened doors and explored. Her murmurs of appreciation were gratifying. He realized, suddenly, that he had always courted Frannie Wickersham's approval. Apparently, old habits were hard to break.

When they finally returned to the bedroom, he pointed to the wall of glass. "I can open that center section in nice weather. I add a screen in the summertime, so I can listen to the ocean while I sleep."

She had been looking out to sea. Now she shot him a glance over her shoulder, her expression dreamy. "It's perfect, Zach. Like something out of a movie."

"Come up on the bed with me," he said.

"Excuse me?"

When her jaw dropped, he rolled his eyes. "Give me some credit, Frannie. If I was going to make a move, you'd know it. Seriously, climb up here and let me show you something." He patted the pillow. "Stretch out on your back."

She actually did as he asked, but her whole body was stiff, as if she expected him to pounce any second. He supposed he deserved that. His reputation was at least fifty percent exaggerated. But the fact that he never bothered to set the record straight meant Frannie had probably heard a salacious tale or two.

He reached for the remote that was hidden in a drawer in the bedside table. "Watch." When he pressed the button, a five-foot section of the ceiling and roof slid sideways into a specially modified space. Cold air rushed into the bedroom, but it was a kick to be able to look up into the sky and then watch Frannie's reaction.

She put her hands to her cheeks, her gaze awed. "Oh my gosh. That's incredible. How did you design such a thing?"

"Not easily," he said ruefully. "It was ridiculously expensive. And I had to enlist the help of a buddy of mine who's an engineer. We made it work. Eventually." He hit the Close button to keep them both from freezing.

Frannie turned on her side to face him, leaning her head on her hand. "I'm impressed, Zach. Really impressed. Maybe I should get you to build *me* a house."

The way she looked at him made something inside his chest squeeze. "You don't have a house?"

"No." She chewed her bottom lip as if the subject worried her. "I travel almost all the time. So I rent an apartment in Boston. A very nice apartment," she said quickly. "I suppose I could live anywhere, really. I grew up in Boston. It's home."

"But you're rarely *home*..."

"Exactly."

He studied her lips. They were full but not too full. Curved in just the right way. Bare. Not even lip gloss. The pink color was natural. What would they taste like? He blinked, taken aback by his own imagination gone rogue. He definitely should not be worrying about Frannie's lips. Or how they tasted, or really anything at all.

Why had he brought her up here on his bed? Was it because he wanted to brag about his fancy skylight? Or maybe he was trying this arrangement on for size.

Having Frannie *on* his bed, if not *in* his bed was...disturbing.

He cleared his throat. "It's almost one. You must be starving."

She nodded slowly. "Getting there. One more question, though. You really use that telescope over there, don't you?"

"Of course," he said, mildly affronted that she thought it might be for show.

"Tell me the specs."

Was this a test? "It's an eleven-inch Schmidt-Cassegrain reflector. I bought it in California straight from the manufacturer."

Frannie laughed softly. "Size doesn't matter, Stoner. Haven't you heard? Too bad it's cloudy this weekend."

He needed to kiss her. Needed it beyond all reason.

"I suppose we'll have to find other ways to entertain ourselves," he said hoarsely.

She blinked. More of that luscious pinky-rose color tinted her cheeks. Her skin was smooth and unblemished. He wanted to touch her cheek, stroke the line of her throat all the way down to her—

"I'm hungry," she said.

Zachary was hungry, too. What would she do if he leaned over and pressed his mouth to hers? Smack him, probably. Quit the job before she started. Leave him to explain to his brothers why their highly recommended hacker had bailed on them.

He nodded, reluctant to give up on the movie reel playing in his head. "I've got tons of good stuff in the freezer. I'll feed you."

Frannie slid off the bed and straightened her hair self-consciously. "Then let's get to it. Those doughnuts ran out a long time ago."

Forty-five minutes later, Frannie took a seat at Zachary's dining room table and waited as he served two plates of steaming lemon piccata chicken along with wild rice and broccoli. There were even yeast rolls. Zachary had refused to let her help. While he played chef, she explored his kitchen with interest, noting the contents of his cabinets and marveling at his well-stocked refrigerator.

For a globe-trotting bachelor, he was surprisingly prepared for any eventuality.

Once they finally began eating, she teased him about

it. "So, you could hunker down here for at least a month if you had to…right?"

He nodded, not at all perturbed by her amazement. "Maybe two," he said laconically. "I have a huge generator. We have to be pretty self-sufficient when we come up here. But I don't mind."

"You *like* it, don't you?" she said.

He gave her a narrow stare. "I do. I don't claim to have pioneering genes, but I think a man ought to be able to survive in the woods."

"But not solely with a pack of matches and a bow and arrow."

His masculine shrug was a thing of beauty. "I like my creature comforts. I cut my own firewood, but at night, I want to sleep like a king."

"Duly noted."

She believed him about the firewood. As they drove up to the house earlier, she had noticed several neatly stacked piles of logs. Zachary's broad chest and muscular arms said he didn't spend all his time at the roulette table or cruising in his yacht, if he had one. Zachary Stone was a man in his prime.

He was tough and strong and alpha to the core. In fact, *thinking* about his physical prowess made her quiver with an entirely understandable wave of feminine appreciation. She lifted a forkful of chicken. "This is very good, Zach. Did you make it?"

"Yes. There isn't a restaurant for miles around. Did I mention that I like to eat? Whenever I'm here, I usually whip up a couple of things and freeze the leftovers."

"I like a man who plans." Was there a nuance of flirtation in her own voice? She was self-conscious about being alone with her teenage crush. The boy she remembered had matured into a fascinating man.

Did he feel it, too? This odd *awareness*?

The latter part of the meal dissolved into silence. Perhaps they had exhausted the limits of their impromptu high school reunion.

Or maybe they were both beginning to realize that it was a very long time until tomorrow night, when they would return to the city.

Eventually, the meal was over. Frannie offered to tidy the kitchen while Zachary brought in their luggage and carried it upstairs. She liked Zach's house. Despite its definite air of luxury, it felt like a home. And it bore the stamp of its owner.

When he rejoined her in the kitchen, his cheeks were ruddy with color and his hair was mussed. "I was hoping we could go for a hike," he said. "But it's pretty cold, and the wind is rising."

"It won't be so bad in the forest, will it?"

He smiled lazily. "Is that a yes?"

"I don't remember hearing a question," she said, giving him an impish grin. "But to be clear, I'm tough. I've hiked the Pyrenees in February. So, bring it on."

"Okay, then. Your bags are in your room. Let's meet back here in thirty minutes."

She tapped his chest with a finger. His hard, oh-so-yummy chest. "Twenty," she said, fluttering her eyelashes like the kind of woman he liked. "Don't make me wait on you."

In the privacy of her bedroom, she groaned aloud. What was she doing? She knew better than to flirt with a confirmed bachelor. There was nothing for her with Zachary Stone, not unless she was prepared to be disposable and sexually available.

She knew she shouldn't get involved with any man under those conditions. So why was she feeling conflicted? She had a job to do for the Stone brothers. A job at which she was exceedingly good. If she were really as smart as her IQ suggested, she wouldn't let herself be tempted by the delicious hunk of masculinity that was Zachary Stone.

Competition had been the cornerstone of their teenage years. Today, Frannie made it back to the kitchen in nineteen minutes and ten seconds. Zachary was already there, leaning against the counter, looking smug. "Did you have trouble taking the tags off the new clothes? Did that slow you down?"

She gave him the evil eye. "Not at all. I answered a few work emails while I was up there. And did part of the *New York Times* crossword puzzle."

He chuckled. "Touché, Bug." He hefted a lightweight backpack. "I've got water and a few snacks. Let's head for the woods. The clouds are getting heavier by the minute."

She followed him outside, shivering as the cold air smacked her in the face. After the warmth of Zachary's house, the weather seemed even more unfriendly. "Where are we going?" she asked. "Anywhere in particular? Or just stretching our legs?"

"There's a big hill about a mile away. On the far side is a pretty waterfall. Not huge, but photogenic. I thought you'd like to see it."

"Then lead on."

She'd been expecting Zachary to set a brisk pace, and he didn't disappoint. Back in high school, he had played every intramural sport available. Frannie had avoided physical activity whenever possible. She'd been self-conscious about her white legs and her gangly body. Not to mention her bent toward clumsiness. In recent years, though, she had found exercise she liked. Yoga. Spin class. Jogging. She could keep up with Zach. Maybe.

Half an hour later, they stopped at the foot of the hill. Frannie tried to catch her breath. "I'd call this a small mountain, not a big hill," she said, peering up at the top where clouds hid the summit.

"That's probably because you're a city girl." He smirked.

She started up the path. "Don't kid yourself." She tossed the words over her shoulder. "I can whip your butt any day of the week."

Zachary wasted no time chasing her. He had longer legs, but she'd taken him by surprise and had a head start.

Her lungs burned. The muscles in her thighs cramped. Sweat beaded her forehead, despite the air temperature. She was determined to beat him to the top. The trail was narrow, not much room for passing. But when she finally had to stop and bend at the waist, gasping for air, her hands on her knees, Zach strode past her with an annoying masculine grin. "Meet you up there," he said.

This was dumb. She didn't have anything to prove. But unfortunately, Zachary Stone pushed all her buttons. She was *not* going to let him win.

In the end, it was a tie. She wasn't sure if he slowed down at the last minute or if her spurt of energy in the homestretch made the difference, but they burst into the clearing shoulder to shoulder.

Huffing and panting, they each leaned on trees and caught their breath. Frannie shed her parka, feeling stifled.

The promised waterfall was delightful. It bubbled up from an underground spring and rippled over moss-covered rocks on the way back down the hill. When she could breathe again, she pulled out her phone and snapped a few pictures. The scene was idyllic. She could imagine fairies and woodland sprites congregating beneath the moon.

The peace and purity were almost tangible.

Zach still leaned against the tree, watching her. "You surprised me, Frannie. I had to work to stay ahead of you."

She grinned. "You're remembering the old me. At some point in my twenties, I realized I wanted to get in shape and stay in shape. My work is more cerebral than physical. So, I learned to like exercise."

"I see that. Your endeavors have definitely paid off." He stared unashamedly, taking a visual inventory.

Frannie stood her ground. She knew she looked good. The activewear pants and top were flattering. Zachary's compliments flustered her, though.

Was she working for him or flirting with him? Could she do both?

They each downed half a bottle of water and ate a granola bar, not speaking…just enjoying the moment. Now that she was still, and her heart rate had returned to normal, Frannie began to feel the cold. She reached for her coat. "I think we should go back, please. It gets dark early in the forest. I don't want to be dinner for bears or wolves."

Zachary returned the water bottles to his pack, chuckling. "No wolves in Maine. And black bears aren't typically aggressive. I'll protect you."

She flipped her hair from beneath the collar of her coat. "Maybe I'll protect *you*, Zach. Girls can do stuff, too."

When she turned around, he gave her a suspicious smile. "Game on, F. Wickersham." Then he bolted.

His sudden challenge startled her so much, it was a full ten seconds before she got her feet to cooperate.

Going downhill was easier on the lungs, but harder in other ways. The path was more treacherous in this direction. "Wait up," she cried, fully intending to pass him if he stopped. But Zachary was a man with a mission.

He was agile and fast. She pushed harder, determined to catch him. She hadn't realized on the way up how many twists and turns the trail took. As soon as she had him in her sights, he would disappear around the next bend.

They were almost at the bottom when she heard a yelp and then what sounded like an animal thrashing through underbrush. Alarmed, she sped up. "Zach? Are you okay?"

She rounded the curve and nearly plowed into him. He was on the ground, trying to sit up. His face was pale. One of his legs was stretched out in front of him.

"What happened?" She knelt at his side, reaching out to wipe away a trickle of blood on his face. Something—a stick maybe—had cut his cheek when he fell.

He grimaced. "Caught my toe on a root. Went down hard. I think I've jacked up my ankle."

The terse explanation came via clenched teeth and choppy breaths.

She crouched over his foot and gently pulled up his pant leg. Already, the ankle was swollen and turning purple. Looking back at him, she winced in sympathy. "Do you think it's broken?"

He shrugged. "Don't know. Maybe just a bad sprain."

Frannie knew immediately that they were in trouble. They were a mile from the house and exponentially more than that from any kind of substantive help. She couldn't leave him in the forest while she went for the car. He might be in shock, and either way, sitting still as the daylight disappeared and the temperatures dropped courted hypothermia.

"We don't have a choice," she said, keeping her voice even.

"I know." His expression was resigned.

"Once we get you up, you'll have to lean on me, and we'll walk back. It won't be fast, but we'll make it."

He slammed his fist on the ground. "It was damned stupid of me. Racing on rough ground. I know better."

"This wouldn't have happened if I hadn't joined in. Let's just admit that we're two adults who made a bad choice."

His smile was a ghost of its usual wattage. "I can think of other bad choices that would be a lot more fun."

"Go ahead," she said. "Try to embarrass me. If it keeps your mind off your foot, I'm all for it."

"I'm sorry, Frannie." He looked miserable.

"No time for pity parties," she said firmly. "The sooner we start, the sooner we'll get back to the house."

She rolled to her feet and searched for a stick or anything that might help the situation. The ground was damp. Any fallen vegetation was either too short or too flimsy to work.

There was only one way to do this, and it involved a lot of physical contact.

"Help me up," Zachary said grimly.

"Can you use that little tree there for leverage?" She couldn't let him put weight on his left foot. It would be excruciating.

"Yep." With his right hand, he reached out and gripped the tree. It was a sapling, really. Nice and bendy.

Frannie squatted. "Put your arm around my shoulders and hang on. I'll stand up slowly. But give me the backpack."

He scowled. "I'm over six feet tall and two hundred ten pounds. *I'll* carry the pack. It's going to take everything you've got to support part of my weight."

She wanted to argue, but she sensed it was useless. An injured Zachary was like a wounded bear. Dangerous. "Okay. You ready?"

"Yes."

The next sixty seconds were rough. It was inevitable that his foot was going to make contact with the ground. When it did, Zachary cursed. He bit his bottom lip so hard, the small wound bled. If he had been pale before, he was ashen now.

Frannie steadied him when they were upright, giving them both time to adjust. "You okay?" She knew better than to hover or offer too much sympathy.

"I've been better."

The attempt at humor lightened the mood. "C'mon, Stone Man. I've seen you face worse odds than this. Remember the time you took Professor Gilbert's sailboat without permission and got caught in a storm? Everyone on campus thought you had drowned. But somehow you made it back and showed up for dinner, ready to take your punishment."

They started walking slowly, every step a challenge.

"I'd forgotten all about that," he said. "I had to mop the lunchroom twice a day for a month."

"You deserved it," she said. "Scared me—scared *us* to death."

"Were you worried about me, Bug? That's sweet."

She hadn't been worried. She'd been terrified. When he sauntered into the building, wet and windblown but unrepentant, she had wanted to smack him. Even now that memory made her stomach go hollow.

Slowly, they developed a rhythm. For once, she was glad she was tall. Zachary leaned heavily on her, hopping on his one good foot. The pace was excruciatingly slow, but she knew they would make it out. Eventually.

It was hard work. She wanted to shed her coat again, but she knew it wasn't wise. The light was fading faster than she had anticipated, the cold deepening.

The trail here was flatter and smoother than the hill where they had raced, but even so, she was probably going to have to use the flashlight on her phone for the last bit.

They were forced to stop every fifteen minutes. After the first half hour, her legs were wobbly with fatigue.

Zachary barely spoke. She had the impression he was concentrating all his energy on bracing against the pain. The silence suited her, because she didn't know what to say, anyway. He wouldn't appreciate sympathy.

They were so close they breathed the same air. She felt every bit of him pressed up against her side. His muscular arm around her neck was heavy, but nice. He smelled of sweat and expensive aftershave.

Eventually, she quit looking at her watch. It was too depressing. She could almost swear the hands on the dial were moving backward.

As expected, darkness came. She turned on the flashlight app and shined the light at their feet. They couldn't afford another mishap.

Just when she was beginning to fear they had taken a wrong turn somewhere, Zachary sighed deeply. "Almost there."

"Thank God."

She had no idea how he knew. After sundown, everything in the woods looked the same to her. But he was right. At last, the house appeared. And when it did, the snow started, a light, beautiful fall of perfect flakes that caught in their hair and melted on their faces.

Any other day or night, Frannie would have stopped to appreciate the hushed moment of wonder, but now was not the time. She was down to her last reserves of energy. She had no idea how Zachary was making it when his ankle must be killing him.

Even though their ordeal was close to the end, the steps were another challenge. Zachary thrust out his chin and tackled them without complaint. When they stood at the front door, he blew out air in a heavy exhale. "The keys are in my right pocket."

She wanted to say *get them yourself*, but maybe he was right. If he tried to let go and fell again, they would be in worse shape.

With her cheeks hot and her breathing suspiciously jerky, she awkwardly slid her left hand into his right pocket. It was a deep pocket. She had to reach and reach some more. At last, she felt the keys. She also touched his taut, warm thigh through the fabric of his pants, and maybe something else, but that was another story.

"Got them," she said. Zachary rested his weight against

the house as Frannie struggled with the lock. “Easy now.” She got them over the threshold, into the living room, and closed the door without incident.

Zachary dropped his head and sagged against her. “Thank you, sweet Jesus,” he muttered, the words barely audible.

Tossing the keys on the table, she urged him forward one hop at a time. “Let’s get you settled on the sofa. I know I said I was a disaster in the kitchen, but we had a big lunch. I can whip up a grilled cheese and open a can of soup. Sound good to you?”

She was talking too fast, practically babbling.

When she eased him down onto the cushions, upright, he pulled her with him. Taking her face in both hands, he said, “Thank you, Frannie. From the bottom of my heart. You’re an amazing woman.”

Then he kissed her deeply.

Five

Zachary was so relieved to be out of the cold and off his feet he barely knew what he was doing. At least, that was the rationalization he would use later for why he kissed Frannie. Her lips were soft and sweet beneath his. He tasted a remnant of chocolate from the granola bars they had eaten earlier.

He was in a hell of a lot of pain. He couldn't feel his fingers. Exhaustion weighted his limbs like concrete. Even so, every cell inside him perked up when his lips touched hers. Pressed. Lingered. Deepened the contact.

He didn't know if Frannie would have returned the kiss or not. Because when his brain processed what he was doing, he jerked back, embarrassed. Contrite. "Sorry," he muttered. "I think I'm delirious."

Frannie didn't say a word. She touched her lips with two fingers, shook her head slowly and stood. "I'll turn up the heat and bring you a blanket before I start dinner. Should we try to take off your shoe?"

Zachary was tough. He'd had broken bones, stitches and concussions. And lived to tell the tale. But the thought of anyone tugging on his ankle right now made his stomach heave. "Not until we have to… I don't think the shoe is making it worse. But you could bring me a bag of peas from the freezer to ice down my foot."

She nodded. "Okay. I'll be back."

Not long after that, he heard the furnace click on. Frannie appeared moments later with a thick wool afghan and the requested veggies. She put the frozen package gently on his ankle and spread the coverlet over him like he was ninety-five and she was his nurse. It was either funny or insulting or both.

He grabbed her wrist when she was in reach. "I'm not near death, Bug. It's only my foot. I can smooth out a blanket."

"Fine." The word was barely audible. She spun on her heel, but not before he saw she had tears in her eyes.

"Oh hell, Frannie. Did I upset you? I'm sorry. Really. Come here."

When he tugged her wrist, she lost her balance and sat down hard beside him. His foot was jostled in the process, but he swallowed the groan of pain. With his arm around her, he stroked her hair, feeling the way the silky black curls wound around his fingers. "It was a hell of a journey this afternoon, but we made it. Everything's going to be okay."

Frannie pulled back and glared at him. "Your ankle may be broken. It's snowing. And you don't have any cheese." That last bit came out as a wail. He tucked her face against his shoulder and pulled her close, feeling his body react to the woman in his arms, despite his compromised physical condition.

His dear Bug was shaking. She had shed her coat already. In his arms, she felt soft and wonderful. He had an erection that was doomed to disappointment, but even so, he gave in to the hunger in his gut. No man ever died from unappeased lust, right? The bigger shock was that he had let himself be turned on by *this* woman. This voice from his past. This highly trained professional who was going to help Stone River Outdoors.

Never had there been a worse moment for a man to crave

a woman. As much as Zachary wanted to undress her and kiss her from head to toe, he knew he couldn't go there.

She sniffed and sat up, easing out of his embrace. "I'm sorry. Everything piled up on me. I'm okay. Really. Do you need anything before I work on dinner?"

Her lashes were damp. A smudge of mascara did little to mar her beauty. Those periwinkle irises beckoned him. "Why don't I help with the meal prep?" he said gruffly, stunned by the combination of desire and emotion clogging his throat. "I can lean against the counter." His stomach growled loudly as if to emphasize the point.

Frannie leaped to her feet. "Oh no," she said. "Don't you move. I can handle this, honestly. It was just a momentary meltdown, I swear."

She fled before he could convince her otherwise.

With Frannie safely in the kitchen, he pulled up his pant leg and examined his foot. He'd really done it this time. He used his pocketknife to carefully slit the sock from the top edge to where the sock disappeared into his shoe. His ankle was swollen and puffy and sported a dozen shades of blue and purple.

Was it broken? He honestly didn't know. But he'd always heard that a bad sprain could be worse than a simple break, because the sprain took longer to heal.

Frustration washed over him, exacerbated by pain and also worry about Frannie. He'd brought her up here to have fun, not wait on him hand and foot. The terrible pun hardly registered. He'd never been good at sitting on his ass. He wanted to be up, going and doing. What he *really* didn't want was to have Frannie playing nurse.

She was only trying to be kind and helpful. He knew that. But when she touched him, however innocently, his body went on high alert. It didn't make sense. He'd had plenty of time when they were both teenagers at Glenderry to make a move on Frannie. They'd spent hours together back then.

He'd had strong feelings about Frances Wickersham when they were in high school, but they hadn't included wanting to have sex with her. Unless he had some sort of weird amnesia going on. Yet yesterday, when she walked back into his life, suddenly all he could think about was how soon he could get her naked.

When she entered the living room half an hour later carrying food, his first impulse was to jump up and help her with the heavy tray. Damn it. He was stuck on his back like a turtle upside down on its shell.

The feeling made him grouchy and even more frustrated.

Frannie set the tray on the coffee table. "I didn't know what you like to drink. I made decaf coffee. I'm afraid with your foot in such bad shape, you'll have trouble sleeping as it is. No point in courting insomnia."

He had a sudden vision of Frannie in his bed, smiling and sexy, trying various ways to help him *sleep*.

"Good idea," he said, hoping she didn't notice the hoarseness in his voice. "You didn't have to do this, Frannie."

She gave him an odd look. "We both need to eat. That forced march expended a lot of calories. Since you didn't have cheese, I found peanut butter in the cabinet. It's hard to mess up a peanut butter sandwich."

The wry look she gave him made his heart twist. "Tell me really why you don't know how to cook, Frannie. It doesn't sound like you."

"You could let this go, Zach."

"Or you could tell me what happened."

"How do you know something happened?" Her expression was mutinous.

"The Frannie I know would have checked eleven cookbooks out of the library and had them all memorized in forty-eight hours."

"Not everything in life can be learned from a book, Zach."

He stared at her. Heard the echoes of *something* in her voice. "Tell me," he coaxed. "Please. I really want to know."

She shrugged. "Fine. It's no big secret." She sat down beside him and ate a potato chip. He thought she was trying to wait him out, but he was benched and had no place to go. "I had a boyfriend my senior year in college," she said. "Things got pretty serious. Over spring break, his parents came to visit. They offered to take us out to a fancy restaurant, but I said I would cook for them." She gave him a sideways glance. "I may have a slight problem being an overachiever."

He grinned. "I'm shocked."

"Smart-ass." She said it with a smile, so maybe it was more a compliment than a criticism. "Our apartment was dismal. Tiny, and three floors up with no elevator. I was determined to impress our guests. So I bought flowers, put classy music on the stereo. And I made a shepherd's pie from scratch."

He raised an eyebrow. "Impressive."

"Just wait," she said, the words glum. "When we sat down at the table to eat, my boyfriend cut into it—the shepherd's pie, I mean. The crust was still raw underneath, and the chunks of meat were hard as a rock. To this day, I don't know what I did wrong."

"Surely his parents were polite."

"Oh, they were," she said. "His dad made a sweet joke, and his mother said I was too pretty to spend my time in the kitchen. But my boyfriend…" She trailed off, her cheeks flushing with something that made Zach want to hit the college boyfriend.

"What, Frannie? What did the jerk do?"

"He yelled at me. In front of his parents. Said I always

had my head stuck in a book, but I was too dumb to live life."

For several long seconds silence reigned. Zachary stomped down hard on his first reaction, which was to offer a few pithy descriptions of the college boyfriend. Instead, he touched Frannie's hand. "I'm sorry that happened to you, Bug. And it's not true. Please tell me you ditched the guy."

Finally, her expression lightened. "Oh yes. In fact, his mother helped me pack my things, and his dad helped me carry boxes down to the car. They apologized for their son, but the damage was done. I never really tried to cook again. Lame, right?"

"Not lame at all. But I promise you this, Frannie, with any free time you have while you're in Portland working for SRO, I'll teach you the basics. It's probably like riding a bike. You wrecked badly, and because you never got back out there, this whole thing has assumed nightmare proportions. You won't fail in my kitchen. I won't let it happen."

"Thank you," she said, snitching another chip.

He didn't touch her, because he didn't trust himself. But her story brought out every one of his latent protective instincts.

Suddenly, he realized the tray held only one plate and one cup. "Where's *your* food?" he asked, frowning.

She hopped up, and he was helpless to stop her. "I'm going to eat while I clean the kitchen. Yell if you need anything."

Zachary ground his teeth. She had made two sandwiches and coffee. How dirty could the kitchen be? Frannie was skittish around him. Maybe she was picking up on his feelings and didn't want to deal with them, or him.

Well, that sucked. He ate his sandwich in silence. This house had always been an oasis for him. He had embraced the solitude and the quiet. So why was he now discontented with the situation?

When he invited Frannie to his coastal home, he had anticipated that the two of them would get reacquainted. Spend some time outdoors. Maybe hang out by the fire and watch a movie…or reminisce.

The level of disappointment he now felt told him that he hadn't been entirely honest with himself. Perhaps he'd been looking forward to more than a platonic weekend.

Perhaps he'd been counting on coaxing Frannie into his bed.

This stupid ankle thing could be a blessing in disguise. He had no business getting Frannie naked…or even contemplating it. Sex was something he used to keep women at a distance. No emotion. Just orgasms.

But Frannie had always been able to see through him. She would never let him get by with mindless fooling around. With Frannie, sex would be *real*.

That was too damn scary to contemplate.

He finished his meal, brooding about today's turn of events. "Frannie," he hollered, suddenly unable to let her hide out any longer.

She came running, hair flying, drying her hands on a dish towel. "What is it? Are you okay?"

Every time he saw her, he was struck anew by how this confident, adult Frannie had blossomed from the girl who had barely been able to speak aloud in class.

"Quinten spent a few days here after his accident. He had multiple walkers and crutches in the beginning. I think there's still a pair in my closet. Will you please check?"

"Of course."

After she disappeared up the staircase, he slumped back against the sofa cushions, wishing he could pummel something. He needed an exit strategy. From today's debacle. From this not-going-to-happen romantic weekend. But mostly from his conflicted feelings about Frances Wickersham.

She was about to do a great service for Stone River Outdoors. Ferreting out any possible corporate espionage had to be the first priority. Zachary had a contact list full of amenable women who would be happy to share his bed.

Frannie was not for him. She needed a one-woman man. Zachary couldn't give her what she needed. Even if he wanted to…

What did a rich man's closet look like? If Frannie had ever wondered, now she had her answer. First of all, the closet was enormous. She could fit a small country in the space and have room to spare.

And despite her prejudices about men and how messy they were, Zachary's closet was meticulously organized. One entire wall was sporting equipment. Skis. Helmets. Canoe paddles. There was a fortune in this room alone.

She assumed most of his business suits and formal wear lived in his condo in Portland, though she spotted one or two dressy items here, as well. Most of the clothes were übermasculine shirts and vests and jackets and pants that an outdoorsman would wear. And much of it, though not all, carried the SRO tag.

Should she resist the urge to sniff a T-shirt? Or maybe snitch one for sleeping? Zachary would never know.

Laughing silently at her own absurd thoughts, she set to work locating the crutches. You'd think such a task would be easy, but she had to dig through all sorts of stuff. Finally, she located what she wanted deep in a corner behind a collection of high-end wet suits and kiteboarding equipment. Did Zach wear anything underneath when he donned one of those skintight shells? The thought of his naked body dried her mouth.

Focus, Frannie.

She extricated the crutches and exited the closet, closing the door behind her. Now, even more temptation beckoned. Zachary was stuck on the sofa. He wasn't going to walk in and catch her snooping.

His bedroom was fascinating. She'd seen it during the tour, of course, but now she took her time exploring. His feather pillows were expensive and plump. The sheets, when she turned back the covers, were incredibly soft.

The only personal note in the entire room was a small five-by-seven framed photograph resting on his nightstand. The picture had captured the three Stone brothers at a perfect moment. They were standing together—arms around each other's waists—near a ski lift, lifting their poles skyward with huge grins on their faces. The joy in the image made her smile.

The picture was likely taken before Quin's accident. She didn't think he had been able to ski last winter. From what Frannie had ascertained online and from the Stone family in person, the past two years had been grim at times and very hard at others. The siblings had gone from pursuing their own interests to being plunged into the high-octane environment of running a multinational company.

It couldn't have been easy.

Frannie sat on the edge of the bed for a moment, testing the mattress.

Though she was no expert when it came to the male sex, she was now fairly certain that Zachary was interested in sleeping with her. Too bad for him that she wasn't fluent in the kind of physical transactions between men and women where the only parameters that mattered were whether both parties enjoyed the venture.

Other than her cooking-disaster boyfriend, she'd had only two other semiserious connections with men. One lasted six months, the most recent one only three.

It wasn't that she didn't enjoy having a man in her life, but those relationships had been a lot of work. Being around Zachary again reminded her how much fun it could be when you knew another person really well and actually *liked* them.

Was it going to be up to her to draw a line in the sand? To keep the boundaries crystal clear? And what if she wanted to do something wildly impractical? What if she decided that sleeping with Zach was on her bucket list?

What then?

Under other circumstances, this two-day getaway might have played out very differently. Now, because Zachary was injured, sex was off the table.

She should be relieved. Really, she should.

But instead, she found herself wistful. How wonderful would it be to have a man like Zachary make her the center of his world? She'd spent her entire life wanting to be accepted and loved for who she was. Was it possible to find that person?

There was not a single doubt in her mind that sex with Zachary Stone would be epic. She couldn't imagine the man being tepid about anything. He lived life on a grand scale.

But she doubted if anyone knew him well. He was closed off emotionally…coasting by on his looks and his charm. Keeping people at a distance.

Across the room, a large mirror captured her reflection as she sat on her host's bed. She made a face at herself.

Zachary had told her he didn't bring his romantic partners here. Only friends and family. She believed him. Why would he lie about something like that?

Yet he had brought Frannie. Should she be honored? Or was it depressing that he never considered Frances Wickersham as someone for the girlfriend category?

Back in high school she had crushed on him so hard, it was a wonder he never noticed. That long-ago crush had been safe. Because there was absolutely zero chance the teenage Zach would have dated her.

They had been close, very close. Close enough to share

hopes and dreams. Close enough to argue and squabble and eventually make up, but without the kissing part. To outsiders, they might have seemed like siblings. But even though Zach had zero interest in Frannie romantically, their relationship had *never* been brother-sister in nature.

Maybe she couldn't define exactly what it was, but it wasn't that.

A glance at her watch told her she had dawdled up here long enough. Poor Zach was as helpless as a baby at the moment. She needed to get back downstairs.

When she returned to the living room, he shot her a glance that encompassed every bit of his frustration, even if it wasn't technically aimed at her. And for some reason, he didn't look helpless at all. He looked downright dangerous.

She gave the sofa a wide berth. "Found them," she said.

"I thought maybe you had gotten lost. How long does it take to locate a damn pair of crutches? My house isn't all that big." His expression and his words were stormy.

"Don't you snap at me, Zach. I'm the only person standing between you and starvation. Not to mention the fact that you can't make it to the bathroom on your own."

As she eyed him warily, his hands fisted, then gradually relaxed. His smile was rueful. "I am in a piss-poor mood. I apologize."

Frannie shrugged. "You're entitled, I guess. I turned on the porch light when I was upstairs. It looks like we have a couple of inches of snow already. Shouldn't we be calling for help? Under the circumstances?"

"It's my left ankle. I'm sure I can drive us back tomorrow."

She gaped at him until she realized he was kidding. "Very funny. But now that you mention it, do you have an actual plan?"

"I'll call Quinten in a little while. Hopefully, he'll be

able to bring his four-wheel drive and rescue us. If he's got a conflict, Farrell is next on the list."

"It's not as easy as simply getting home. You need medical attention. Broken bones have to be set."

"We don't know that it's broken."

"And we don't know that it's not." She held out the crutches. "Here. Be careful, please. I'll refreeze those peas. How is the swelling?"

He shrugged. "See for yourself."

She got down on her knees beside the sofa and carefully shimmied his pant leg up his calf. "Oh, Zach." The ankle looked dreadful. Puffy. Discolored. She touched it with a single fingertip and looked up at him. "Do you have any prescription painkillers? I think you'll need them to sleep." The stupid man hadn't even asked for an aspirin yet, though she should probably have thought to offer.

"I'll be fine." His voice sounded funny. "I don't remember your hair being so curly," he said quietly. When he took one strand and let it twine around his finger, she froze.

"I used to straighten it," she croaked. "When we were in high school. This is the real me."

He played with the curl absently, as if he didn't actually realize what he was doing. "Your hair was pretty back then," he said. "But I'm a fan of this *real* Frannie. Your curls are like bouncy silk." His words were husky. Intimate.

She swallowed hard. A man could have sex with only one good ankle…right? "Um…thank you?"

He took several more strands in his hand, playing with them. "You're a beautiful woman, Frannie. I'm sorry I never noticed that before. I was a dumb kid, I guess. Too immature to look beyond the surface."

"You dated cheerleaders and majorettes and beauty queens. I never judged you for the choices you made. Any other adolescent boy would have done the same."

"Maybe. But I wonder about all the quieter, sweeter, less *flashy* girls I missed along the way."

Several responses sprang to mind immediately. To be honest, she didn't care about all the girls he *didn't* date. She was just sorry he had never gone out with her.

Her cheek rested against his knee. When had that happened? Her head was practically in his lap. The gentle motion of his hand in her hair was both soothing and arousing.

She made herself stand up. "I'll take those peas now. And don't you want to visit the facilities?"

His wry, self-mocking smile told her he knew she was escaping the unexpected intimacy of the moment. "I'm going."

When he used one crutch to pull himself up, she offered an arm to steady him and then handed over the second crutch. "Are you light-headed?"

"Nope. Don't fuss, Frannie. The ankle hurts, but I'll be fine."

She wasn't sure about that. Even the strain of rising from his comfy spot on the sofa had made him lose color again. He was a stubborn, thickheaded man. It would have been a lot easier if he had let her help him.

As she watched, wincing, he made his way down the hall toward the powder room. In some homes that kind of half bath was tiny. At least Zachary's guest bath was roomy. He'd be able to maneuver.

She picked up his empty plate and the thawed bag of peas and carried them back to the kitchen. Maybe dessert would sweeten his grumpy mood. She found candy bars in his pantry. After selecting three different varieties, she returned to the living room.

Still no Zachary.

Stealthily, she tiptoed down the hall. He might have a concussion. What if he had passed out while she was in the kitchen?

The minutes ticked by. She listened intently. Was that water running in the sink? If so, she needed to vacate the hallway ASAP, so he wouldn't know she had been spying on him. Before she could move, a crash from the bathroom shook the wall beside her.

Zach!

A string of creative, high-volume profanity assailed her ears.

"I'm coming, Zach. Hold on…"

Six

There were times in a man's life when he had to swallow his pride. Whether he wanted to or not. Zachary knew what he must look like sprawled on the floor. His dignity was nowhere to be found. Before he could yell for Frannie, the bathroom door burst open, nearly smashing his skull.

His nemesis fell to her knees and crouched over him. "Ohmigod, ohmigod, ohmigod. What did you *do*?"

He pointed balefully at the small gray area rug. "One of the crutches..." He wheezed, trying to catch his breath. "I caught the edge of the mat on one of my crutches, and it slid out from under me." He had hit his ankle on the way down and nearly passed out from the jolt of fiery pain. Every bone in his body vibrated.

She ran her hands over his extremities—like the cutest TV doctor ever—and lingered at the abrasion on his forearm. Then she leaned over him on hands and knees and pulled up one of his eyelids. "Your pupils look dilated."

"Frannie..." Now he was wheezing for a whole different reason.

"Be still," she said. "We need to make sure you haven't damaged anything else." She pulled up his other eyelid. "Does your head hurt? Tell me where."

"Frannie..." Despite his considerable physical distress, his libido was hanging in there. And rising to the occasion. "Frannie..." He said her name with more force.

She frowned. "What?"

"Your boo—" He stopped short. "Your *breast* is in my face. And to be clear, I did *not* hit my head."

"Oh." Her face flamed. She sat back on her heels so fast she nearly toppled over. "What *did* you hit?"

"I fell on my butt. My elbow caught the counter. All things considered, it could have been worse."

She bit her lip, not saying a word. And Frannie usually had plenty to say.

"What?" he asked, aggrieved that she was no longer smothering him with worry. "What are you thinking?"

Her lower lip trembled. "I'm not *thinking* anything. I'm trying not to laugh."

He stared at her, outraged. "I could be dead," he said. "And you're laughing?"

Frannie's eyes watered. Her shoulders shook. And then the giggles came. My God, she was adorable when she giggled.

He lay there watching her, partly because it was *fun* to watch her, but also because he was calculating whether or not he could get up without help.

She gasped, wiping her cheeks. "Oh, Zach, I'm sorry. I really am. But I wish I had a video of the whole thing."

"Your concern is touching," he said dryly.

"I'm honestly worried about you."

"Oh, I can tell. I feel better already."

She smiled at him. "You swear you didn't hit your head?"

"I swear. Do you want to see the bruise on my ass?"

"Um, no." She looked around the small bathroom as if searching for a way out. It was so easy to disconcert her.

He stroked her arm. "I know you've heard stories about me, Frannie. But they're not all true."

"Why are you saying that now?"

"Because you seem jumpy around me."

"Even if only half of the gossip is true, you're a…" She trailed off, her look of uneasiness probably warranted.

"Playboy? Womanizer? Hound dog?"

"You could at least pretend to be penitent," she muttered.

"I've lived my life the way I wanted to live it, Frannie. I've never been dishonest with a woman, and I've always treated my partners with dignity and respect. I'm generous with my companions, and to my knowledge, I'm on good terms with everyone who has ever shared my…life."

"*All* of them?"

He sighed. "How many do you think there are?"

She lifted a shoulder and let it fall. "I don't know. Fifty?"

"Good Lord, Frannie. No."

Their eyes met, her gaze hesitant. "It would be okay if the number *was* fifty," she said. "I'm not shocked. You're a sexy, desirable man of thirty, almost thirty-one years. I can do the math. It's not a crime. Having sex, I mean."

His heart turned over in his chest. He'd always heard the expression and assumed it was a euphemism. But swear to God, he felt that organ bounce around painfully inside his rib cage. She was so damned brilliant and yet she seemed like a fawn in a wolf-laden forest. Somebody had to look out for her.

He cleared his throat. "We can circle back to this conversation. If the time is ever appropriate. But for now, let's agree that our friendship has stood the test of time. I'm happy about that, Frannie. Are you?"

She nodded slowly. "You seem the same, only different. Good different," she said quickly. "Maybe it's serendipitous that Stone River Outdoors hired me. You and I can enjoy our own reunion for two."

"Indeed." He rolled to his hip. "I'm going to stand up now. You might want to give me a wide berth."

"Put your arm around me. I'll help lift you."

"No." He shook his head, having decided this was a solo

effort. "If we try that, there's a good chance we might *both* end up on the floor. Just hold my crutches, please. Until I'm ready for them."

With two hands on the counter and the bathroom sink, he balanced on his good knee and pulled himself upright. It was slow, and it wasn't pretty, but he made it without bumping his ankle. The effort winded him. His forehead was damp. He held out a hand. "I can take them now."

Frannie handed over the crutches one at a time. "You're very strong, aren't you? To pull yourself up like that. I don't have much upper-body strength."

"Many women don't. I could show you a few exercises."

It was a perfectly normal, nonsexual offer. But Frannie blushed again. Which made Zachary's thoughts land on sex again. Which made his— He stopped himself short. None of that. He'd promised himself.

In the living room, he glanced at his watch and saw that it was not even eight o'clock yet. Far too early for bed. "Are you interested in a movie, Frannie? An evening by the fire? There's microwave popcorn in the pantry."

Her face lightened. "That sounds fun. I'll go do the snacks."

He flipped through his streaming app and found something he thought she would like. The movie starred Colin Firth and was set in the English countryside. A double winner. It wasn't Zachary's type of flick. But making Frannie happy made *him* happy.

When Frannie came back with the popcorn and a newly frozen bag of medicinal peas, he patted the sofa beside him. "Join me."

She set the popcorn bowls on the coffee table. "No. You need to elevate your ankle. Lie down, and I'll ice it again. I'll be gentle."

"Promises, promises."

As she carefully draped the bag of frozen peas on his

abused ankle, she shook her head slowly. "Is flirting your default?"

He thought about it for a moment. "Was that flirting? Maybe so. I meant it as a joke." Hadn't he?

"Ah. So you *weren't* referencing a mythical moment in the future when I might be torturing you? For fun?"

Because he had already put a handful of warm popcorn in his mouth, he almost needed the Heimlich maneuver. Which meant he didn't have the oxygen to answer.

Frannie pushed a glass of cola in his direction and sat in the chair adjacent to the sofa, close enough to touch, but farther away than he wanted her to be.

She tilted her head to one side and examined him like an insect under a microscope. "Out of curiosity, Zach, is that the kind of woman you like?" she asked. "One who's a little wild in the bedroom?"

He was no longer in imminent danger of choking to death, but her question took his breath again. "We're not going to go there, Bug."

"Why not? You're welcome to ask me what I want in a man. I have no secrets. Well," she said slowly. "Not about that subject."

Her offer almost made him reconsider. But no. He wasn't going to discuss his sexual preferences with Frannie. End of story.

"Eat your popcorn, woman."

She was quiet while he cued up the movie. Soon, they were both into the story. It was a good film. Funny. Charming. Much like Frannie herself. When it was over, she yawned and stretched. "I think I'll head upstairs and get ready for bed. That love seat over there is big enough for me. I don't want to leave you down here alone."

"Absolutely not. You'll sleep in the guest room where your bags are."

Frannie stood. Folded her arms. Glared at him. "I won't be able to hear you if I sleep upstairs. It isn't safe."

"I'm a grown-ass man. I can take care of myself."

"You nearly killed yourself in the bathroom."

"I've learned my lesson. I'll shove any and all small rugs out of my way."

She changed tack. "You don't have a shred of color in your face. The ankle is hurting badly. Am I right?"

He wanted to say no, but he couldn't lie. Not to Frannie. "All the devils of hell are pounding on it with hammers. I have some hydrocodone upstairs in my medicine cabinet. If you'll grab it for me, I would be most grateful."

"Why do you have narcotics?"

"I had my appendix out last fall."

"Oh." She chewed her lip.

"What, Frannie?" He could almost see the wheels turning in her brain.

"If you're drugged, I should be close to you."

"How close?"

"There you go again." Her grin was wry.

"Sorry. It's a flaw in my character, I'm sure. Please, Bug. The medicine? And I'd like my overnight case, too, if you can manage."

Frannie returned to Zachary's bedroom for the third time that day and rummaged in his bathroom until she found the requested prescription. The instructions said *take with food*. He'd already eaten a ton of popcorn, so she put the meds in her pocket, picked up the overnight case and hurried down to the kitchen to pour him a glass of two percent. The milk wasn't past its due date. He must have been up here in northern Maine fairly recently.

When she offered both to him, the pill and the drink, he sat up and muttered his thanks. She bent and kissed his cheek. "Your bag is right here. Call my cell if you need me. Promise?" His jaw was scratchy with stubble, his skin warm.

"I've been on my own a long time. I don't *need* any woman."

The sharp comment came out of nowhere. His mood had deteriorated, perhaps because his discomfort had increased. His disgruntled expression told her he had reached his tolerance for being coddled.

"I'll see you in the morning," she said quietly. "Good night."

He called her name as she left the living room, but she kept on walking. Maybe his terse pronouncement was his way of keeping her at a distance, because he didn't like being the subject of her amateurish nursing skills. Or maybe he really didn't want to be told what to do…even for his own good.

Her feelings were bruised, but it was probably for the best. She'd been getting far too chummy with Zach. Maybe that was another clue. As a young adult, he'd made the choice to go from Zach to Zachary. He called the shots with his life. That was apparently what happened in his relationships, too. When it was time, it was time.

Zachary simply walked away.

And there was the kicker. She wanted him physically and emotionally, but the thought of being intimate with Zach and then having him walk away made her cringe inside. Better to keep the status quo, no matter how her poor heart wove daydreams.

She slept restlessly. At three, the alarm on her phone chimed. After shaking off the remnants of sleep, she stumbled down the stairs and hovered just outside the living room. A gentle snore from the vicinity of the sofa eased most of her concerns. Even so, she tiptoed in and stopped several feet away.

It was dark. Zachary had somehow turned out all the lights. She should have thought to do that for him.

A few steps closer, and she was able to see that he was naked from the waist up. Her toes curled into the carpet. Her legs grew shaky. Surely, he wasn't completely naked. She didn't think he could get his pants off without help.

He'd managed to add logs to the flames. The pile beside the hearth was smaller. Maybe during the night, he'd gotten too hot and had shed part of his clothing.

Even in the modest illumination from the fire, his chest was a thing of beauty. He looked far less civilized than the CFO of a huge company. This was a man who would not allow himself to be domesticated. A man who didn't like being *handled*. Even when he actually needed help, he hated having to ask for it.

She hoped his ankle would heal quickly.

Since he appeared to be resting comfortably, she sure as heck wasn't going to wake him. Morning would come soon enough.

She inched away, intent on returning to her warm, soft bed, but a hoarse, gravelly male voice stopped her in her tracks.

"Frannie. Come back. Please."

She winced, knowing he couldn't see her expression. When she turned around, his eyes were open. "How are you feeling?" she asked.

He lifted a hand and wobbled it back and forth. "So-so."

"Do you want more meds? It's been long enough."

"Not right now. They make me muzzy." He sat up and ran his hands through his hair. "Come sit with me."

Frannie was a smart woman. Very smart. She knew this was the witching hour, that time of night when defenses were down, the real world seemed far away and people sometimes made stupid choices. Bad things happened.

Even so, she couldn't resist his quiet plea.

Her night wear was perfectly respectable. Navy flannel pants with cavorting sheep and a white T-shirt that had been washed so many times it was soft as a whisper. The fact that she wasn't wearing a bra was perfectly normal, though her lack of one made her feel vulnerable and underdressed.

She perched on the edge of the sofa, keeping a good three feet between her hip and Zach's. "You should go back to sleep," she said.

"I will. Eventually. I've dozed mostly." He grimaced. "I'm sorry I snapped at you earlier."

"You were hurting."

"That's no excuse. I really am sorry."

"Apology accepted."

"After you went to bed, I called Quinten. He's leaving before dawn to come rescue us."

"That's good."

"I told him we had about six inches of snow. Portland only got flurries."

"Ah."

He stared at her…so intently that her nipples furled beneath her top. Could he see? His gaze was almost a tactile caress. At last, he sighed. "On a scale of one to ten, how bad would it be if I kissed you?"

She sucked in a startled breath. "You already kissed me," she pointed out.

"Doesn't count. That was a thank-you kiss. Unpremeditated."

Maybe he didn't think much of that moment after their trek through the woods, but it had affected Frannie deeply. It had opened her eyes to dangerous possibilities. "It was still your lips and mine. What's the difference?" She wanted to hear his answer. Desperately.

"The difference is intent. All that talk earlier about what you like in bed made me wonder how you like to be kissed."

Heat rolled from the pit of her stomach up to her breasts

and throat. Too bad *she* couldn't strip off her top. She picked at a loose thread on her knee. "I've always heard that spontaneity is a plus."

He shook his head slowly. "The problem is, sometimes a guy can't tell if the woman wants the kiss or not. You see my dilemma?"

"I can't imagine any woman not wanting to kiss you, Zach," she said, being entirely honest. Her bones were melting into a puddle of yearning. Even so, this seemed like a big step at a dicey moment.

"Is that a yes?" His lips tilted the tiniest bit. The smile was hungry and wary and bold all at the same time.

Her throat tightened to the point of pain. "Yes, please."

Everything in the room went still. Two seconds passed. Then five. Slowly, Zachary leaned toward her and slid his hands beneath her hair. His fingers brushed her neck, warm and breath-stealing. His thumbs caressed the line of her chin.

"You were a very appealing girl, Frannie," he said softly. "But you grew up to be a stunning woman. I've wanted to do this for hours."

Her lips parted. She was about to say something, but Zachary put his lips on hers, stealing the words. The kiss was soft at first. Seeking.

She might have moaned. Did he notice? Did it matter? Her arms came up around his neck. The hair at his nape was silky soft when she ruffled it with a single fingertip. If Zach had intended the kiss to be exploratory, it got out of hand fast. His tongue delved between her lips, seeking hers, mating.

Her heartbeat deafened her. He was big and strong, and it felt perfectly right to be in his arms, even though somewhere in the far reaches of her brain, she knew she would pay for these moments of bliss.

"Zach..." She whispered his name, caught up in a weird

time warp between then and now. How many times had she fantasized about a kiss like this? Her teenage dreams hadn't come close to the reality.

He slid a hand beneath her T-shirt, his palm warm on her back. Wordlessly, she urged him to go farther. Her breasts ached for his touch. Apparently, Zach had more control than she did. He kissed the side of her neck, the tender skin beneath her ear. His free hand landed on her thigh, innocently enough. But possibly ready to trespass.

When he bit her earlobe, she shuddered. The fact that he so clearly wanted her made her heart sing. Maybe it was any port in a storm for Zachary. She chose to believe that it wasn't *only* pheromones and opportunity.

Now, it was her turn to explore, and she took her assignment very seriously, stroking his shoulders and his back and kissing his collarbone. Despite the fact that he was half-naked, his skin was warm beneath her fingertips. Zachary Stone was a man. In comparison, the handful of other males she had allowed into her life seemed little more than boys.

That wasn't fair, really. In Frannie's eyes, Zach had always been the gold standard when it came to available mates. The trouble was, he had never been *available*. Nor was he now—not really.

His arm around her waist held her close, but they were in an awkward position. Standing was a better idea, though Zach couldn't put weight on his foot. What would happen if she lay back on the sofa? The erotic image in her head made her weak and shaky. Desire was a liquid fire burning away her inhibitions, her good sense.

He kissed her again, more urgently this time, nipping her bottom lip with his teeth. "Frannie, sweet Frannie."

Even as she returned the kiss, panting…hungry, she recognized they were reaching a point of no return. If she let this go much longer, they were going to be in too deep. As much as she wanted to be intimate with Zach, everything about this was wrong. He was hurt. They hadn't seen each other in years until Friday morning. She suspected that nostalgia was driving this encounter on both their parts.

Worst of all, she was scared. Scared to reach for what she wanted. Scared he would never let her into his heart and his life. Scared that she needed something from him he could never give.

She was a planner. A "weigher" of consequences. This was no time to throw caution to the wind.

Being a responsible adult sucked sometimes.

"Zach." She put her hands on his shoulders and pushed.

To his credit, he released her immediately. "What is it, Bug? What's wrong?"

"I'm going back to bed. Upstairs. Alone. I barely know you. We're about to make a big mistake."

His frown encompassed frustrated male desire and an unwillingness to end their late-night interlude. "I would argue that you know me better than almost anyone, other than my family."

"You're not a teenage boy anymore. He's the Zach I knew."

"Maybe that's true. But the core of who I am is the same. You and I had something special at Glenderry, Frannie. Four years. Hundreds of hours spent together. You can't call me a stranger."

It took a lot of mental fortitude in the wee hours of the morning to stand up and step back. Knowing that she could soon be making love to Zachary Stone if she gave in to temptation and let nature take its course was painful and bittersweet.

She *willed him* to understand. "I've never been a creature of impulse. I don't think it's wise to start now. My work and my reputation are important to me. Your family has a potentially damaging situation brewing. My first priority has to be my job at SRO."

He didn't say a word for an entire minute, maybe two, his posture rigid. The tension in the room was palpable. At last, he sighed. Leaning back into the sofa, he closed his eyes. "I wasn't really thinking about SRO just now."

"I don't know how to do casual sex. I'm sorry."

"Are you so sure it would be casual?"

"Nothing I know about you suggests otherwise."

His expression was inscrutable. "I suppose I deserved that."

"Don't be mad, Zach. I liked what we were doing. A lot."

"But not enough to see it through."

"We're rebuilding our relationship, and I'm happy about that. Let's not ruin what we have."

Seven

That was the problem with really smart women. They knew how to undo a guy without even trying. Of *course* she was right. That didn't make Zachary's erection any less insistent. He was horny, damn it. And he didn't want just any woman—he wanted Frannie. He couldn't explain his reaction to her. He didn't really want to analyze it. Sometimes life dropped fun surprises into your lap.

Only now, Frannie had drawn a line in the sand. Business on one side, pleasure on the other. Zachary knew which side he wanted her to choose.

Frustrated and exhausted, he pulled the afghan over his legs and settled back into his temporary bed. In hindsight, he should have asked Frannie to bring him a real pillow. But she'd done so much already. He wasn't going to ask her to fetch and carry again.

Punching the sofa cushion into a more pleasing contour, he settled in, balancing his ankle carefully. As soon as he closed his eyes, Frannie was right there with him. He could still catch a lingering trace of her subtle perfume. The feel of her smooth skin was imprinted on his fingertips.

Kissing her had been the best thing to happen to him in months, maybe years. Who knew little Frannie Wickersham would grow up to be an intensely feminine woman with loads of sex appeal?

The fact that she was clueless about her own charms

made her all the more exceptional. If he were honest, he'd brought her to northern Maine hoping to impress her with his house and the setting. Instead—because he'd challenged her to that stupid race—he had ended up looking clumsy and helpless.

Not the best way to win a round with Frannie.

Why did it always have to be win and lose? They were adults now. He and Frannie weren't in a competition.

Yet maybe he had kissed her so she would forget he was sidelined for the moment. Had he been hoping a romantic interlude would erase the memory of his ungainly splat on the bathroom floor? The second accident had been pretty damn humiliating.

He wanted to impress Frannie. That's what he'd always wanted. And because his best had never been quite good enough, he'd hidden his insecurities and had posed as a guy of unlimited confidence.

Playboy. Mischief maker. Man of the world who didn't need anybody. The persona was a comfortable armor he had worn for a long time. Frannie was one of the few people with the ability to puncture his facade. That made her dangerous.

In any case, it was a moot point. Frannie was upstairs in the guest room, and Zachary was stuck on the sofa.

He stared at the fire, seeing the flames dance and shiver, imagining what it would be like to pull Frannie down onto the rug and make love to her there.

Oh hell. He shifted restlessly and groaned. His fantasy about Frannie was only making things worse.

Sheep. He would try counting sheep. At 4:32, he gave up. Apparently, he had slept just enough during the first hours of the night to make it hard to go under again. The combination of physical pain and erotic imagination created a perfect storm of insomnia.

For the next three hours, he floated in and out. His ankle

hurt like a bitch. He should have taken more medicine. The sofa was about six inches too short to be comfortable for an entire night. Sunlight was streaming into the room through cracks in the drapes when a text from Quinten said he would arrive by midmorning. Thank God. As much as Zachary had wanted to bring Frannie up here to the coast, he now wanted to leave.

After a trip down the hall, he washed up and wet his hair to make it cooperate. Then he went to the kitchen to check out the options. The peanut butter sandwich Frannie had fixed him last night had run out a long time ago.

He was careful. Very careful. He wasn't keen to end up on his butt again.

Just as he had formulated a plan, Frannie appeared in the doorway. "Good morning," she said quietly. A familiar dusting of pink on her cheeks told him she was embarrassed about last night. He planned to ignore that memory. For the moment. Otherwise, he might skip breakfast entirely and do something that would get him in trouble.

She had her hair up in a riotous ponytail. Her eyes were clear, her gaze wary. Her soft, figure-hugging jeans and button-up yellow shirt made her look fresh and beautiful.

Zachary felt like yesterday's leftovers.

"If you'll crack the eggs, I can scramble them," he said. "And I'll pull some sliced cinnamon bread from the freezer to make toast. If you'll be my sous chef, we can eat in twenty minutes."

She sidled past him. "Of course." Then she frowned. "But what if you fall into the edge of the stove and burn yourself? On second thought, maybe this is a bad idea. I saw some cereal in the pantry. We can eat that."

He counted to ten. He was sleep deprived, sex deprived and food deprived. At the moment, he couldn't decide which was worse. He took a calming breath. "I am *not* going to fall," he said. "I'm getting the hang of these crutches. The mixing bowls are in that cabinet beside you. I'll want four eggs. You can add however many you normally eat." Maybe his tone was unnecessarily gruff, but he was operating on very little sleep.

Frannie didn't argue anymore. She pulled the eggs from the fridge, broke them into the bowl and whisked them with a fork. Zachary added salt and pepper and a dash of milk. As it turned out, scrambling them was trickier than he thought, but he had committed to this course, and he wasn't going to back out now.

Once he got the knack of balancing on the crutches under his arms while holding a cooking utensil, he made progress. When the eggs were almost done, he asked Frannie to check on the toast. "Looks good," she said.

They sat down to eat ten seconds under his twenty-minute prediction.

It was a quiet meal. Today, the silence *was* awkward.

Fortunately, they heard the front door open with a muted crash. A loud voice hailed them. "Anybody home?"

Zachary grabbed his crutches and stood up quickly. Or at least as quickly as a one-legged man could manage. When Quinten appeared in the kitchen, the brothers hugged. "Have you eaten?" Zachary asked. "I can scramble more eggs."

"Nah, I'm good," Quin drawled, his eyes on Frannie. "Good morning, Ms. Wickersham. Sorry to hear you were stranded."

The smile she gave Quin was open and uncomplicated. Which irritated Zachary.

"Call me Frannie," she said. "It's not a big deal."

Zachary shook his head. "No, no, no. I'm the only one who gets to call her Frannie. Just like she's the only one who can call me Zach."

Quin lifted an eyebrow, giving his brother an incredulous look.

Frannie intervened. “Frances is fine. Or Frannie. Seems I’m answering to either these days. We’re sorry to drag you out so early on a Sunday morning. I’m sure your wife wasn’t happy about that.”

Quin snitched the last piece of toast. “She’s cool. Today we’d marked off for helping her sister paint her apartment.” He gave them a deadpan look. “I hate painting.”

“Well, in that case,” Frannie said. “You’re welcome.”

Quin pointed at the table. “Sit down, bro. Let me see that ankle.”

When Zachary shimmied up his pant leg, Quin winced theatrically. “Damn. That looks awful.”

Frannie nodded. “And it must feel worse than it looks. But your stubborn brother hasn’t been taking any pain meds.”

“Sounds like him,” Quin said. “Is it broken?”

“I don’t think so.” Zachary looked down at his foot. “It’s no *worse* than yesterday. That has to be a good sign, right?”

“Maybe. I’ve got a call in to my orthopedist. He said he’ll meet us at his office at four thirty this afternoon.”

“On a Sunday?” Frannie was clearly shocked.

Quin looked at her with a sheepish grin. “I’ve been on a first-name basis with half a dozen doctors since my accident.”

“But you’re doing well?”

“I am.”

Frannie began stacking the plates. “Let me get these in the dishwasher, and I’ll run upstairs. Packing won’t take long. I didn’t bring much.”

“Quin can handle the dishes. You go,” Zachary said. “But take your time. We’re in no big rush.”

When Frannie left the room, Quinten shook his head slowly. “What was this cozy little party all about?”

“I wanted to show Frannie the beach house.”

“I’ve never known you to bring a woman here,” Quin said, his expression troubled.

"Frannie's not a woman. She's an old friend. It's different."

Quin took the dishes and loaded them. "I think you should be careful about this situation, big brother."

Zachary glared. "What does that mean? Are you worried because she's going to be working for us? That's a contract arrangement. She's not an employee. We're not breaking any rules."

"I'm not talking about rules," Quin said. He wiped his hands on a dish towel and leaned against the dishwasher as it clicked on with a distinctive sound. "I was only with Frances briefly on Friday, but even I can see that she's different."

"Different how?" Zachary was about to be pissed.

"Well..." Quin joined him at the table and leaned back in his chair, tipping it on two legs. "She's not like your usual girlfriends. She's a serious, extremely intelligent woman."

"She's not intelligent," Zachary snapped. "She's brilliant."

"I don't care about the adjective. I care about the fact that she may not understand your rules. You don't do permanent."

"You're making a big deal about nothing," Zachary said. "Frannie and I are having fun. Reminiscing. This isn't serious. I'm sure Frannie is on board with that."

Frannie stood in the hallway, crushed, her every fear about getting involved with Zachary carved into bold focus. How was she going to endure this trip back to Portland? Layered with the pain that was embarrassment. She hated the fact that Quinten thought she might be vulnerable, and that he had gone so far as to discuss the subject with his brother. Though the irony of it all was that she *was* vulnerable. The depth of her disappointment told her she had been weaving teenage daydreams. A ridiculous activity for a mature woman of thirty.

She wasn't in love with Zachary Stone. Her only feelings for him were…well… She chewed her knuckle. Lust, maybe. Faint echoes of adolescent infatuation.

And yes…friendship. Was that pathetic or sweet? Men and women could be friends. Right? She and Zachary went way back. But apparently, he wasn't interested in anything long-term.

Her feelings weren't hurt. Really, they weren't.

To prove it, she bumped open the kitchen door with her hip and sashayed in to greet the two Stone brothers. "Ready whenever you are," she said brightly. Too brightly, judging from the bemused looks on their faces.

Zachary nodded. "Okay then." He glanced at Quin. "Will you bring down my big suitcase? It's in my bedroom."

"How'd you get it up there?"

Frannie laughed. "Preaccident." The laugh must have been convincing, because it made Zachary grumpy, and it made Quin laugh along with her.

"I'll get your bags, too," Quin said.

When the youngest Stone brother disappeared, the atmosphere in the kitchen grew strained. At least on Frannie's part. After all, Zach had no reason to be out of sorts. Other than his hurt ankle.

He tapped his fingers on the table. "Nothing happened last night. You don't have to feel weird."

She lifted her chin. "I don't feel weird. I just want to get back to my hotel room so I can kick back and relax."

"What does that mean?" His scowl would have been hilarious if she hadn't been gutted by the recent conversation she had overheard.

She shrugged. "I should have said no when you invited me up here. My usual routine is to spend the weekend fashioning my plan of attack before I start a new job on Monday. I wouldn't want to shortchange Stone River Outdoors."

Zachary's scowl morphed into confusion. "Was that sarcasm? What's going on, Frannie? I've never known you to be snippy."

In a flash of realization, she understood that in order to put their relationship back on track, she had to act as if their middle-of-the-night madness hadn't affected her at all. She had to shake it off. Pretend Zachary Stone was just another old friend.

Even if, deep down, she yearned for Zach to be something he wasn't, she had to face the truth. This reunion meant nothing earthshaking to him.

She had to match his casual attitude or risk letting him hurt her.

Could she do it?

"Sorry," she said, clearing her throat. "I didn't get my full eight hours last night. I'm not at my best."

He smiled, a warm, intimate smile. "Neither am I. But let me get my ankle rehabbed, and maybe we can try again."

Her throat was tight. "Sure," she said. "It could happen."

Then Quin came back, and things moved quickly after that. The men exited first, after Quin tossed the bags in the back of his huge, fancy four-wheel-drive vehicle. He offered a shoulder to his brother for the trip down the steps and into the vehicle. Luckily for Zachary, Quinten was a heck of a lot stronger than Frannie.

She watched the men joking and laughing as Zachary hobbled his way down the steps in the snow. She was wearing her new boots, and still her feet were cold. It was hard to believe that she and Zach had hiked yesterday in the forest and indulged in that stupid race.

Quin loped back up the steps. "Your turn, Frances."

"What do you mean?"

He scooped her up into his arms, ignoring her squawk of protest. "The snow is too deep. It will come over the top of those boots. This is easier."

She was laughing when Quin deposited her in the back

on the driver's side. "And who says chivalry is dead?" she teased.

Zachary didn't say a word, but his expression was disgruntled. He looked straight ahead, as if something on the other side of the windshield demanded his attention. His jaw was tight, his profile carved in stone.

Quin hopped behind the wheel and started the engine. Soon, heat circulated back to Frannie, warming her toes. Before pulling out of the driveway, Quin reached over his shoulder and offered her a manila envelope.

"Our lawyer gave us the official go-ahead last night, although Farrell and Zachary and I already knew we wanted to hire you. The contract has been signed, except for Zachary here. It will be waiting on you at the hotel desk. In this envelope you'll find a security badge and a key card that will get you anywhere in the building. My admin handles personnel matters. Let me know if you need anything at all."

"Thank you," Frannie said. "I'm eager to get started."

Quin drove carefully, negotiating the curves in the snow-covered road. "How do you keep us updated…or do you?"

"Definitely, I do," Frannie said. "Normally, I give my clients a written report every Friday afternoon until the job is complete. However, if something big comes up in the meantime, I'll ask all three of you to sit down with me so I can go over the information."

Zachary made a noise, somewhere between a harrumph and a *pffft*.

His mood was beginning to aggravate Frannie. "What? You don't like how I do my job? You haven't signed the contract yet. Feel free to change your mind. I can be on a plane tomorrow. This is a big investment on your part. I don't want to do this unless you're all three on board."

Quin glanced at her in the rearview mirror. "He's on

board. I'm guessing his delightful mood is because of the ankle. Give him some acetaminophen, will you, Frannie?"

She rummaged in her purse and found what she wanted. Reaching into the front seat, she handed them to Zachary. "Here. It's dumb to suffer for no reason."

Their hands brushed in the exchange, making her skin tingle. "Thanks," Zachary muttered.

Frannie sat back, sighing wistfully. They needed Quin. Without him, they would have been stuck. But she wished the weekend hadn't ended so abruptly. Maybe it was for the best. After last night's kisses, treating Zachary as a platonic friend was going to tax her acting abilities.

The trip passed quickly. Frannie dozed. The two brothers conversed easily. Work stuff. Family stuff. Sports.

Frannie had always wanted a sibling. Her childhood had been far too quiet. She was certain that hadn't been true in the Stone household. Three rambunctious boys. It must have been a zoo.

When they were almost back in Portland, Zachary turned his head and gave her an unreadable look. "How do you dive into this forensic business?"

"That depends," she said. "Does Stone River Outdoors have a VPN? A virtual private network?"

Quin jumped into the conversation. "We do. Problem is, our IT guys aren't top-notch. They're basically competent. Don't get me wrong. But I don't think they go out of their way to spot irregularities. Because SRO started as a small, family-run company, and because back in the beginning, my father and his father before him knew all the employees, certain business practices were what you might call *lax*."

"So, all your nationwide and international companies aren't linked?"

"We're working on it."

"Oh."

Zachary shook his head. "I know you must think we're

hopelessly behind the times, but you have to understand… my father was running things until he died. My brothers and I didn't get any say in big decisions. We've spent the last two years grieving, dealing with Quin's messed-up leg and trying to keep the business afloat."

"No worries. I've worked in all kinds of situations."

Quin spoke up. "I thought about asking our tech guys to help you, but I would feel better if we put *everybody* under the microscope. You can have my CEO office, and I'll give you the access info for the network."

"I could do that if you want me to," she said. "But I've found I can learn a lot from an employee's work space. The pictures they have, the sticky notes, the way they organize their files. If you don't mind, I'd like to physically go from one to the next."

Zachary shrugged. "All our employees are required to change passwords once every six months. They give them to Quin's admin, and she compiles a hard copy that's kept in the safe. Primitive, I guess, particularly to someone like you, but it worked for my dad."

"I'll make you a copy of the list," Quin said. "At least that will save you some time. No one in upper management actually checks the list. So, if you find one that doesn't give you access, let us know. It would be grounds for dismissal if someone has given us a bogus password."

"Got it." She was astounded that a company like Stone River Outdoors, with dozens if not hundreds of brick-and-mortar stores, had managed to retain a family feel. That could make her job harder or easier. Time would tell. As they approached the downtown area, Frannie tapped Quin's shoulder. "My hotel is on the corner over there. Thanks for the lift."

Zachary turned again, this time looking determined. "What if I pick you up at seven? Take you to dinner? Don't worry. I won't drive myself."

"Thank you," she said, pretending to look for something in the floor of the car. "I think I'll kick back and order room service tonight. I loved seeing your beach house. I'm sorry about the accident." Though she had her head down, she could tell that Zachary still stared at her and that her answer displeased him.

Apparently, even Quin could tell. "She's not on the clock until tomorrow night, bro. Let's not monopolize her time."

Frannie hopped out of the car as soon as it rolled to a stop beneath the hotel's portico. The bellman helped Quin with the bags. Zachary rolled down his window. "If you change your mind, let me know." The way he looked at her, all sexy and hungry, brought back their interlude on the sofa last night.

"Okay." Now that she faced him, close enough to touch, she almost said yes. The thought of spending a romantic dinner with Zachary was *very* appealing. But she didn't want to get into a situation where she let him break her heart. She knew it could happen. With two steps back, in the safest direction, she gave him a little wave and a smile. "Let me know what they say about your ankle."

Eight

Zachary winced when the doc adjusted his foot on the ice-cold table. "Do you think it's broken?" he asked.

The doctor stepped behind a half wall and said, "Don't move."

"Don't worry. I won't." Zachary had thought the pain was better, but having his ankle touched and maneuvered made his gut cringe.

After a buzzing sound, the doc was back, rearranging the injured foot one more time. "Almost done."

The doc took the last image and stuck his head around the partition. "You can go back to my office. Down the hall, second door on the right."

Zachary reached for his crutches, stood and hobbled to the exit. Both of his brothers were waiting in the doctor's suite. Farrell had decided to come for moral support.

The two Stone siblings grinned when Zachary awkwardly opened the door and made his way inside. "I think that guy's a sadist," Zach said.

Quin moved his leg out of the way before Zachary could poke him with a crutch. "I remember him as very kind and helpful when he was treating me."

Farrell chuckled. "Maybe that's because you tended to come here during regular office hours."

"I could have waited until tomorrow," Zachary grumbled. "I didn't *ask* you to pull strings."

The fortysomething doctor came through the door. "I've uploaded the images," he said briskly. He turned on a large-screen TV mounted on the wall and went to the computer on his desk. "Take a look."

Even with a healthy IQ, Zachary didn't know what he was seeing. Quin had more experience than his brothers with this kind of thing.

The doc smiled. "Good news is, I don't think anything is broken." He pointed to one area on the film. "This might be a tiny stress fracture, but then again, it could be an old injury. In either case, I want you to stay off the foot for a solid week to allow the swelling to go down. Come back and see me a week from tomorrow. We'll make a new plan then."

"But I can still use the crutches, right?"

"No. You need to be horizontal. With the foot elevated."

Zachary shot his brothers a visual plea for intervention. "Frannie starts work tomorrow. I should be there to help her if she needs it." What he really wanted was to figure out things with Frannie…to follow up on their intriguing "almost" interlude at his house on the north coast.

Why had she turned down his dinner offer? Didn't she feel the attraction that sizzled between them? Or perhaps she saw through his self-deception better than he did. Maybe Frannie didn't want to be one of a crowd. The thought stung his pride and shamed him.

Frannie would expect everything from a man…from him. And she would give her all in return.

That was a kind of intimacy Zachary didn't want or understand.

Farrell cocked his head, frowning. "From what I understand, Frances works alone. Besides, Quin and I will be around. She doesn't need you looking over her shoulder. Do what the doctor says, little brother."

* * *

Forty-eight hours later, Zachary was ready to climb the walls. He'd never been one for watching a lot of television. He had a few favorite action films on DVD, but seeing those only made him aware of his current limitations.

Ivy and Katie took turns bringing him carryout dinners. They were far more sympathetic than his own brothers. When Zachary asked about Frannie, all he got was blithe assurances that she was *making great progress.*

He had sent Frannie a text Sunday night to let her know the ankle wasn't broken. Her reply had been short in the extreme. I'm glad.

And after that, nothing.

What did she do when she wasn't sleeping? The late morning? All afternoon?

Curiosity consumed him. He wanted to know everything there was to know about Frances Wickersham. The depth of that wanting gave him pause. Why? Why was he so focused on her?

Quinten stopped by unexpectedly, breaking the monotony of Zachary's day. "I brought a bottle of wine and filet mignon," he said, holding up a bag that smelled amazing. "I figured you needed to keep up your strength. Unless you're still taking pain meds. Damn, Zachary. I wasn't thinking."

"Only over-the-counter stuff. And right now, I'd settle for human contact. I think I hate this condo."

Quinten put the food in the kitchen, poured two glasses of the wine and came back, laughing. "You outbid three other buyers because you were determined to have one of the premier views in the city. Now you don't like it?"

"It has too many walls," Zachary said. "I need to be outside."

"It's November. The weather is crappy. This too shall pass."

"How are things at work?"

"Translation, how is Frances Wickersham?"

"That, too."

Quinten sprawled in a recliner covered in charcoal-gray velvet. "As far as I know, she's fine. Farrell spoke with her briefly this afternoon. Stanley has to be off tonight. Farrell wanted Frances to know she didn't have to come to the office, but she said she was used to working alone. I gather she's a very self-sufficient woman."

Zachary shook his head, frowning. "That's what she expects you to think. From where I'm sitting, Frannie is like a fluffy newborn duckling, all cute and clueless about how bad the world can be."

"Wow." Quin stared him down, finishing his wine. "Maybe that's what you *want* to believe."

"Farrell is the one with the Galahad complex, not me."

"But you wouldn't mind at all if the lovely Frances Wickersham thought you were her hero, right?"

Quinten wasn't wrong. Zachary wanted to be Frannie's hero, so he could feel like he had the upper hand for once. But he wasn't going to admit such a thing to his little brother. "You're full of crap."

"And on that note, I'm out of here. My dear wife is waiting on me."

"Rub it in, why don't you?"

"That's quite a pity party you've got going. As someone who very recently screwed up my life, almost beyond repair, I'd suggest you try patience. It's a lost art among the Stone men, but it works wonders."

Thursday evening around ten, Zachary finally reached his limit. After showering and shaving, he put on jeans and a soft cotton shirt with a pullover sweater. It was still a bitch to get pants on and off without hurting his damaged foot, but he was motivated.

When he was ready, he summoned a car service and told the driver where to drop him off, then sent a text to Stanley to let him know Zachary would be on the premises.

Stone River headquarters was shrouded in darkness when he arrived. Zachary let himself in and rode the elevator up and up until he saw lights shining in one office on the far side of the fifth floor. He walked quietly down the hall and paused in the open doorway.

Frannie had her back to him. Her fingers flew over the computer keys so fast it seemed impossible. Tonight, her hair was down. The rich fall of raven curls made his fingers tingle. He wanted to touch.

She wore one of her signature cashmere turtlenecks. This one was a creamy white, which made her hair all the more beautiful.

"Don't be startled," he said. "It's only me."

Frannie spun around so fast in her swivel office chair she nearly slid onto the floor. She put a hand to her chest. "Zachary Stone. You scared me to death. You can't just say *don't be startled* and expect a person *not* to be startled." She glanced down at his foot. "What are you doing here? Quin told me you're under strict doctor's orders to be on your back with the foot elevated."

"I have been," he groused. "Four whole days. I needed a break. And besides, I wanted to see how you're doing."

She motioned at the desk scattered with files and papers. "This particular employee is kind of a mess. But she's not a criminal."

"Good to know. How is the investigation going?"

"So far, so good. I'll be doing the first report when I finish tomorrow night."

"In other words, don't bother you."

She smiled at him. "I didn't say that." But it was true

she enjoyed her solitude. Could a fun-loving man like Zach understand that?

"I've missed you."

She parsed his quiet statement for hidden meanings. He looked handsome and weary at the same time. His navy V-necked sweater over a navy-and-green plaid shirt emphasized his broad shoulders. Every time she was around him, she felt this odd energy. As if there was some connection between them generating electricity.

"It's only been four days. You're probably bored."

His eyes flashed. "Yes. I'm bored. But I was talking about you, Frannie. I've missed you. I enjoyed our time this weekend."

Oh boy. Did he mean the hike or the kisses or something else?

She'd had a long time to think about what had happened. Plenty of time. Did she want to be platonic *buddies* for the long haul with Zachary Stone? Or did she want something deeper, more exciting? An affair that might—when it was over—mean the death of their recently resurrected friendship?

It was a tantalizing question with no clear answer.

"I've missed you, too," she said, trying not to let him see how very much she was affected by his mere presence in this tiny office cubicle.

After a long silence, he came two steps closer. "Can you show me what you do?" he asked.

She nodded. "You'll have to sit down." She dragged a small wooden chair to the desk and placed it to her left.

Zachary had become more proficient and graceful with the crutches since they had been together. He eased into the chair, laid the crutches aside and nodded. "My ankle is getting better every day."

"Let's hope this unauthorized field trip doesn't set you back."

"You won't rat me out, will you, Bug?"

He was so close his aftershave made her woozy. In a good way. A tiny, fresh nick on his sculpted jaw told her he had shaved very recently. For her?

"Not if you behave." She chewed her lip and sat very still, trying not to touch him. The work space was limited. Focusing on what she did best, she pulled up a screen with several clicks. "This is where I usually hit the mother lode. I can see every website a user has visited. Often, if there's anything suspicious, I follow a thread and can even get into an employee's personal accounts if they've accessed them from work. Of course, sometimes that means getting a warrant."

"Seriously?"

"It depends on a company's rules. Here at SRO, your employee handbook says absolutely no personal use of the computer. It's not a problem if an employee checks email on his or her phone during a break. But there should be nothing other than SRO-related activity on this desktop."

He leaned closer. "And?"

"This one's all clear. So far. But the guy in 207 has porn on his. Not only is that *personal* use, but anyone dumb enough to look at porn on a work computer is probably not someone you want working for you."

"I agree," he said, shaking his head.

"It will all be in my first week's report."

He touched her hand. Not holding it. Just to get her attention. "I am so impressed, Frannie. You are incredible."

His praise made her uneasy. "Other people do what I do."

"Maybe. But I doubt they do it as well. You always did enjoy solving puzzles."

Her heart thudded in her chest. The answer to her dilemma stared her in the face. Zach was interested. Definitely interested.

But if she dithered much longer, she wouldn't be able to enjoy Zachary's company for the length of her stay.

She'd had four days to think about it. Nothing impulsive about this decision. But what if she made the wrong choice?

"Zach?"

"Hmm?"

They were so close she could feel his breath on her cheek when he spoke. She flipped her hand so she could link her fingers with his. "Would you like to come to my hotel room when I'm finished here?"

He froze. She actually witnessed the fact that every muscle in his body went still. But his eyes flashed with heat.

His Adam's apple bobbed as he swallowed. "Um…isn't it kind of late?"

Her confidence faltered. Was she wrong? He had sought her out, not the other way around. Had she misread the situation? The man said he missed her. Wasn't that code for *let's get naked*?

She released his hand and rolled her chair a few inches to the right. "Never mind," she muttered, mortified. She wasn't comfortable initiating intimate relationships. Clearly this was why. She didn't *know* the code.

"You should go home and get that foot elevated," she said. "I'm not finished here, anyway. Probably another hour before I'm done…" She barely even knew what she was saying. *Please, God, make him leave.* She was so humiliated.

Zachary, who seemed to have been in a momentary coma, shot to his feet, stumbling as he reached for his crutches. Then he sat down again, abandoning the crutches at the last minute. He leaned forward and slid one hand under her hair, cupping her neck. "Frannie. You took me by surprise." His beautiful chocolate eyes glowed with fire. "The answer is yes. I'd like that very much."

She wrinkled her nose. "Are you sure you're an international playboy? No offense, but you're kind of bobbling this."

His smile was rueful as he rubbed his thumb along the line of her jaw. "Well aware, Frannie. Well aware. You throw me off my game. I don't know how to act around you. Part of me wants to be that teenage boy who spent hours every week with you, and another part wants to pursue this...*attraction*. You're a fascinating, beautiful woman."

Frannie had taken tons of science classes along the way during her education. But nothing could explain the way her body quivered and melted and yearned all at the same time. She wanted Zach. Desperately. Wanted to feel him skin to skin. Wanted to know what it was like to have him enter her, fill her, take her wildly.

Her heart pounded so hard she was breathless. "I'm as conflicted as you are, Zach. That doesn't mean we can't have some fun."

He frowned. "Fun?"

"You don't think we'll have fun?"

His hot, determined gaze incinerated her. "If we do this right, fun will be way down the list."

The bottom fell out of her stomach. "Maybe I should finish here while you go home and grab a toothbrush."

He leaned forward and kissed her. Hard. Hungrily. "Screw the toothbrush. No way I'm walking out of this room without you."

"But I—"

He kissed her again. This one longer, sweeter, more coaxing. "Don't back out now, Frannie. Things are just getting interesting. Besides, it's a quarter till midnight. Your work here is done."

They exited the building together. The evening was windy and cold but dry. She tucked her chin in her coat and wished she had remembered to wear gloves. Zachary had summoned a car as they walked to the elevator and made their way downstairs. The driver was in the area and showed up less than five minutes later.

They got in. Zach gave the man directions. Frannie was prepared to huddle in her corner of the back seat, but her companion had other ideas. He wrapped an arm around her and pulled her against his shoulder.

How was it possible to feel safe and warm and yet at the same time incredibly aroused? This was Zach. Gorgeous, complicated, macho Zach. Frannie was thirty years old. She had been in physical relationships before. But never had she felt such a turbulent mix of excitement and uncertainty.

Being alone was safe. Anytime she let people get close to her, she ended up hurt. She knew in her gut that Zach had the power to hurt her more than most. She wanted so badly to get close to him emotionally and let him see the real Frannie. But that meant tearing down her walls. Lowering her shields.

Was it worth the risk?

At the hotel, they were the only people in the lobby. The tiny gift shop was closed. Zach had a quiet conversation with the concierge. The man disappeared and returned with a small paper sack. Then Frannie was in the elevator with Zach, and things were happening both slowly and way too fast.

She tried to make a joke, even though her throat was as dry as the Sahara. "So, you got a toothbrush after all?"

He grinned, looking for a brief moment remarkably like the boy she'd crushed on in high school. "Condoms, Frannie. And yes, a toothbrush."

"Oh." She knew she was blushing. She could feel the hot color sweep from her neck to her hairline. Zachary must think she was the most unsophisticated, naive woman he'd ever been with in a romantic way. It wasn't true. Frannie had traveled the world. She could order a meal in four languages. Rarely did any situation intimidate her.

This was different. This was Zach.

When they reached her floor and got out, she fumbled in her purse for her key card, then opened the door. Her room had a king bed and all the usual amenities. "Make yourself at home," she said.

Before Zachary could do more than nod, she grabbed a few things out of her suitcase and locked herself in the bathroom. Flannel sleep pants weren't going to cut it tonight. Luckily, she had packed her favorite robe. It was black silk embroidered with tiny red dragons. She had picked it up in Chinatown during a job that took her to San Francisco.

Since she had showered before going to work, she only needed to freshen up and add a spritz of her favorite perfume. After undressing and brushing her hair, she folded her clothes neatly and made a pile on the counter. When she glanced in the mirror, she liked what she saw. The black robe was sensual and flattering. But the woman's eyes held a wealth of wariness. There was no going back from here.

She had no idea what to expect when she returned to the bedroom. Surely Zach would want a turn in the bathroom. But he surprised her once again.

The man in question was propped up in her bed against the headboard, and he appeared to be completely naked. She couldn't know for sure, because the sheet covered him from the waist down. All the lights were out, save for the lamp beside him.

His rakish smile was like a physical touch. Her nipples budded tightly, painfully. She toyed with the knot in her sash. "I guess you're ready."

Zach nodded slowly. "If you are. Come here, Frannie. Let me warm you up."

Zach knew there was something different about this woman. This night. The difference perturbed him, because it signified that the encounter was something more than giving in to sexual attraction. He shoved the knowledge away, refusing to spoil the moment.

His Frannie looked amazing. Stunning. In the black robe with her black hair and creamy pale skin, she was the most beautiful thing he had ever seen.

Without warning, guilt flooded him. Quin was right. Frannie was different. Zachary probably shouldn't be here. But he was a selfish bastard, and he wanted her too damn much to walk away.

She came to the bed and stood opposite him. There was a lot of real estate keeping them apart. He patted the mattress. "Join me, Frannie. I don't bite."

"I have a feeling that's not true."

Her sexy little joke made him smile. "I forget how well you know me." When it seemed as if she would stand beside the bed forever, he flipped back all the covers, revealing his naked body. He was aroused. In fact, he'd had a hard-on since they left her office. "See anything you like?"

"Maybe." She pursed her lips, her gaze fixed on his erection.

The way she looked at him made his sex jerk and swell a millimeter more. His hands fisted. For some reason, it was very important that Frannie come to him and not the other way around. He didn't want to seduce her. This was a full-participation sport.

At last, when he was ready to beg, she climbed onto the mattress and scooted over to his side. She was still wearing the robe, but he could deal with that. Besides, she appeared to be naked underneath.

He held out his hand. "I want to touch you, Frannie."

She came down beside him and rested her cheek on his shoulder. "Ditto." She ran her hand over his chest, testing his collarbone, brushing his nipples, tracing his ribs, playing with his navel. "You are a beautiful and sexy man,

Zachary Stone. I could feast my eyes on you for a very long time."

He swallowed hard, overcome with emotion. This was Bug, his sweet Bug. Suddenly contrite, he asked the question he should have asked long before now. "Does it bother you when I call you Bug?"

Frannie lifted her head and stared at him. "Actually," she said with a bashful smile, "I like it. It makes me feel closer to you. As if what we had back at Glenderry was something special."

"It was, wasn't it?" How could he have missed that truth so long ago? It was only having Frannie back in his life that made him realize how very special *she* was.

He reached for the sash of her robe and fumbled with the knot. It was tied so tightly he was tempted to cut it. Finally, he worked it loose.

With one hand, Frannie held the lapels of the robe together. Her eyes, almost indigo in this light, were wide. "I'm nervous," she said. "I read parts of the Kama Sutra once, but it made me laugh. I don't think that's the right reaction. I don't want to disappoint you."

Her bald honesty cut the sand from under his feet. Made him stumble. Lust roared through his veins. Something else kept the lust bridled. Zachary couldn't put a name to that other feeling. Didn't want to, in fact. So he concentrated on the lust.

"That's impossible, Frannie. Together, we'll make a night to remember." It was a big promise. Once he'd given it, he wondered if she thought him arrogant. He was confident. That wasn't the same thing at all. He couldn't wait anymore. With Frannie helping, he slipped her out of the silky robe and tossed it aside.

Her body was a miracle of divine engineering. High breasts. A narrow waist. Hips that curved like the best valentine in the world. And legs? Lord help him, those long, wonderful legs that could wrap around his back and squeeze…

He rose up on one elbow and leaned over to kiss her. His pulse rate was in the stratosphere. When Frannie curled her arms around his neck and whispered his name, he was a goner.

Frannie wasn't content to let him be in charge. Perhaps it was inevitable given their history. "I want you," she said. She kissed him back, raked his shoulder with her fingernails, tugged on his earlobe with sharp teeth.

That last one got to him. Had his earlobe always been an erogenous zone? It never had before. He shuddered hard, telling himself not to come. "We have to slow down," he groaned. The whole damn thing was going to be over in sixty seconds.

Frannie chuckled, the low, feminine sound filled with sensual intent. "Fast is fun," she said.

Suddenly, he was reaching for the paper sack, ripping open a condom and covering his sex. What would it be like to take her with nothing between them? The dazzling idea stopped him for a moment, made him fumble. Then reason returned.

"Come here, woman." Kama Sutra be damned. He wanted Frannie under him. Helpless. Yielding.

She tugged a pillow into place and scooted onto her back. "You're the one being slow," she taunted. "Are you sure you're a stud?"

He shoved her legs apart and mounted her roughly. His mind went blank. Need roared like a freight train, drowning out the sound of sanity, pushing him to take and take and take. But Frannie was taking, as well.

She matched him thrust for thrust, nearly strangling him with her arms around his neck, scratching, biting, demanding. He fucked her hard, so hard the bed shook. "Tell me you want me," he gasped, barely able to catch his breath.

"I want you. More than this. All night. Don't ever stop." Frannie's words stoked the flames, sent him unbearably higher.

He shouted her name, and then he was over the top. He shuddered, emptying himself, giving her everything he had to give. Just when he thought he might have failed her, Frannie arched against him, let out a keening cry and found her release, as well. He held her as aftershocks shivered through her body.

In the seconds that followed, the room was quiet, save for their labored breathing.

When Zachary could move, he reached for the sheet and comforter and covered their damp bodies. Frannie was on top of him somehow. When did that happen?

Her body was limp, her face buried in the curve of his neck.

He pinched her butt. Not hard. Just enough to get her attention. "You okay? I've never known you to be this quiet for this long."

She put a hand on his sternum and levered herself upward. "I was wrong," she said soberly. "You *are* a stud. I'm all tingly everywhere."

"I can live with that." He reached out and played with one of her pale pink nipples. "I bought a dozen condoms," he said. "In case you were wondering."

Nine

Frannie wallowed in bliss. A comfortable bed. An inventive lover. The promise of a long night to come. What more could a woman ask for?

Years ago, when she was ten, maybe eleven, her austere, academic parents had broken character and agreed to take their only daughter to the county fair.

Frannie could still remember the sights and sounds and smells. Most of all, she could recall riding a dozen rides, eating cotton candy and feeling as if she was part of the most wonderful place on earth. It was inconceivable to her that in a few days, the entire entourage would pack up and move on to the next town.

In the car on the way home, she had dozed in the back seat, understanding for perhaps the first time that some experiences were magical, in part because they were rare.

Now, almost two decades later, here she was in a generic hotel room, feeling as if she was atop the Ferris wheel again. Nothing could take away this feeling. But there was a very good chance this was as good as it got.

Zachary stirred, nuzzling her cheek with his stubbly jaw. “That was amazing, Bug. You destroyed me.”

“We should probably get some sleep,” she said. “And what about your ankle? We need to get it propped up. Farrell told me you’re going back to the doctor Monday. I don’t want to be the reason you get a bad report.”

Zachary yawned and pulled her closer. "My foot is fine. Quit worrying. Sleep, Frannie. Relax. It's all good."

Amazingly, she did sleep. Having a man in her bed was a novelty. If she had thought about it at all, she would have assumed she would lie sleepless while Zach snored, unconscious. Instead, the night was perfect.

She awoke feeling rejuvenated, though a bit sore in places. They had indulged twice more during the wee hours. The first time slow and sleepy and lazy. A second time near morning was as hungry and wild as the first.

Now it was dawn. Frannie slid out of bed quietly and grabbed clean undies from her bag. In the bathroom, she wrapped her hair in a towel to keep it dry and took a quick shower. When she dressed in the clothes she had worn last night and returned to the bedroom, Zach was sitting up, running his hands through his hair.

He eyed her, unsmiling. "You have too many clothes on," he grumbled.

She knew she had to stand her ground. Otherwise, he would persuade her to spend the day in bed. As good as that sounded, she was afraid to indulge. Her willpower was shaky, and that scared her. She could handle a little fun and games with Zach. But she had to keep it light.

"You need to go home," she said firmly. "And I have to work on my report."

"You said you would be at SRO headquarters Monday through Friday nights. So you're not ready to write the report yet, correct?"

"I add to it each day. While the info is fresh."

"You can work at my place. Move in with me, Frannie. While you're here in Portland. It will be fun."

While you're here in Portland.

Those five words were the difference between fantasy and reality. But she had gone into this with her eyes open.

Sucking up her courage and any latent acting skills, she

sat on the mattress at his hip and leaned over to kiss him lightly. "Last night was great, Zach. But I'm not on vacation. I'm here to work. What if I grab us coffee from the kiosk in the lobby? And a Danish, maybe? I'll be back in fifteen minutes."

"Translation, get your butt in gear and be ready to leave."

"Something like that."

"You're a cold woman."

"Not in the slightest. But I *am* very serious about my work. And I can't do what I need to do with you hanging around tempting me."

"So, you admit I'm a temptation?"

His cocky smile amused her. "Yes, Zach. You tempt me."

She grabbed her purse and headed downstairs. Last night had been an eye-opener. So much so that she was already rethinking her decision to get involved with Zachary Stone. Despite the fact that Quinten had married recently, and Farrell was engaged, the middle Stone brother was not like his siblings.

Zachary navigated life on his own terms. Though he was not a hermit by any stretch of the imagination, he kept a part of himself walled off from genuine involvement with the rest of the world.

Frannie knew that because it was a familiar behavior. The cost of being different. All her life, she had wanted to *belong*. Those years at Glenderry—and her friendship with Zach—were the closest she had ever come to having a tribe. Her people.

She isolated herself in her adult life, because so many times, friends and lovers had disappointed her. She was too different. Too weird. No one took the time to understand her world and her point of view. Frannie was always the one giving and getting little in return.

What would it be like to have a man who appreciated her intellectual capabilities, valued who she was and complemented her, as well? Two halves of a whole. Not even her parents knew their daughter's wants and needs.

For a brief moment, Frannie had thought Zachary might be the one. Reconnecting with him delighted her. Seeing remnants of the teenage boy he had been and learning nuances of the man he had become was fascinating. The chance to spend time with him was one she couldn't pass up. Sex was something else again.

Men knew how to do recreational sex. Lots of women, too. But not Frannie.

She grabbed coffee and pastries and rode the elevator upstairs, all the while debating how to handle *the morning after.*

Thankfully, Zachary was dressed and ready and sitting in an armchair. Somehow, despite his crutches, he had pulled a second chair and the small table into a cozy circle by the window.

"I'm back," she said, wincing inwardly at the perky note in her voice.

Zachary smiled. "Smells wonderful."

They ate breakfast in silence. The coffee was hot and strong, the pastries fresh and satisfying. This was as good a time as any to ask a question that had been nagging at her from the moment she knew SRO had hired her and that she would be seeing Zach again.

"May I be nosy?" she said.

He waved his coffee cup at her. "Knock yourself out."

"I know that your father's death meant you having to take an active role at Stone River Outdoors as CFO."

"Yep."

"But I get the impression your job is more of a responsibility than a challenge. What are you doing to exercise your brain, to use your abilities?"

He scowled. "Why do you always have to do that, Frannie?"

"Do what?"

"Even when we were kids, you were always ragging my butt about reaching my potential. I am who I am. Not everyone is as smart as Frances Wickersham."

His bullheadedness made her angry. "*You* are, Zach. You're every bit as smart as I am and then some. It's wrong on so many levels to have a brain like yours and to waste it. Some people would even say it's a sin. You're a brilliant man, but you skate by with your charm and your good looks, and you want everyone to believe that's all there is to Zachary Stone. I thought by now your creativity and your inventiveness would have taken you down an exciting road or two."

By the end of her impassioned speech, his jaw was granite. "It must be nice to live in a world where you have all the answers," he said, the words tight with fury. He stood abruptly, grabbing his crutches, his coffee and Danish unfinished. "I'll leave you to your report, Ms. Wickersham. Maybe you and I should agree to disagree. You stick to analyzing computers, and I'll handle my own damn life."

When the door slammed behind him, Frannie winced. She'd really done it now. None of what she'd said to him was false. But seeing Zach's reaction made her wonder if deep down she wanted to push him away. She didn't know how to handle an affair with the all-grown-up Zachary Stone. So after a wonderful night, she had sabotaged things.

Maybe she wasn't so smart after all.

Saturday afternoon, she emailed her first report to the Stone brothers. Two of them responded. One didn't.

Zachary's silence made her sad and conflicted, and yes—angry, too. She wanted him to be something he wasn't, apparently.

Next week was Thanksgiving. A short week. She hadn't

told anyone that she planned to work right through the holiday. That was her business.

Saturday evening, she went to a movie. Sunday, she enjoyed brunch at a fun restaurant near the hotel. Spending time alone had never bothered her before. Now, though, any time her thoughts were free, she replayed the night with Zachary in her bed over and over.

It was easy to confuse a physical connection with emotional intimacy. What had been cataclysmal for Frannie was she was just another notch in the bedpost for Zach. While she understood that truth on an intellectual level, she yearned to believe he'd been as involved as she had been in the magic.

Now she would never know for sure, because she had deliberately severed the newly formed tie between them.

Monday night, she was back at work. She and Stanley, the security guard, had struck up a cautious friendship. The older gentleman was not much of a talker, but they exchanged a few words here and there. She thought it was sweet that he looked out for her well-being. Truth be told, it was comforting to know someone else was in the building.

By Wednesday evening, she had picked up a disturbing trail. She wouldn't jump to conclusions too soon. Too little information had the potential to create a false narrative. She'd learned that painful lesson the hard way in one of her early jobs. Before she presented a theory or even an outright accusation to the Stone siblings, she would have her facts crystal clear. No doubts.

When she shut down the final employee computer at midnight on Thanksgiving Eve, she exited the building surreptitiously. She didn't want to run into Stanley and have him question her about her plans for the holiday.

When she stepped outside, the night was silent and damp. Just enough sprinkles to make the air wet on her cheeks. Instead of calling for a ride, she decided to walk.

It was five long blocks. Not terribly far, but far enough to get some exercise.

She pulled up the hood on her raincoat, buried her phone in an inside pocket and set out. The empty streets said everyone was home preparing for the holiday. Loneliness was relative in her opinion. She had long ago made peace with the fact that her family was different. Both of her parents were older and came from small families. Grandparents on either side had long since passed. Thanksgiving was never a big deal, particularly since her mother was an indifferent cook.

Even Christmas was low-key. And Frannie was okay with that.

She liked her own company. The world was full of entertainment. Books. Movies. Research on the internet. She'd never understood people who complained about being bored. How could a person be bored when there was more to learn?

Even so, she couldn't deny that sometimes on nights like this one, she felt a hollow space in her chest. That same yearning to belong.

By the time she made it back to the hotel, she was chilled to the bone. Either the temps were dropping, or she was underdressed for the cold.

With her head down, facing into the wind, she rounded the final corner to her destination. Suddenly, she ran smack-dab into something hard and unyielding. A tall, built-like-a-tree man. One particular man. When she looked up at him, his features were shuttered, his lips pressed into a tight line.

Despite his body language, her heart leaped with joy. She was so damned glad to see him. "Zach," she said breathlessly. "Why are you here?"

He took her by the wrist. "Come in out of the rain. I've been waiting for you. You should have called a car service. Walking in this weather is nuts."

Inside the hotel, he tugged her to a far corner, a cozy grouping of armchairs sheltered by a grove of large plants. “Sit, Frannie.”

She didn’t like the tone of his voice, but she was tired, so she sat. When she removed her raincoat, she had to smooth her hair with both hands. She couldn’t imagine what it looked like. Her hair and humidity didn’t mix.

“I don’t understand, Zach. Why were you waiting for me?”

He looked the slightest bit guilty as he sprawled in the seat beside hers. “Stanley said he saw you leave the building at midnight. I assumed you would have flown out this morning for the holiday weekend. What’s going on, Frannie?”

Her eyebrows went up. “You’ve been spying on me?”

“I asked Stanley to keep an eye on you. I won’t apologize for that. A single woman in a strange city. Things happen.”

She sighed. “As you can see, I’m fine.”

“Thanksgiving is tomorrow.”

“So?” He frowned at her as if she had personally slaughtered all the turkeys. She didn’t have to explain herself.

“I assumed you’d be spending the holiday with your extended family.”

“There aren’t any. Well, that’s not technically true, but we’re not close.” She shrugged. “My parents don’t like making a big fuss about the holidays. Tomorrow will be a normal day, one or both of them at the hospital. Our relationship is what you might call strained, so I’d rather stay here and keep working.”

“I don’t like that.” His mulish expression was comical.

“You don’t have to like it, Zach. I’m a grown woman. And although I appreciate the fact that you were worried about me, you don’t have to lose a moment’s sleep. I’ve taken multiple self-defense classes. I can take care of myself.”

He reached out and took her hand. “I’m sorry we argued. You have a right to your opinion.”

She wrinkled her nose, twining her fingers with his, feeling the inevitable heat. "But I should have kept it to myself. I'm sorry, too."

"Truce?" he asked, with that intimate smile that turned her inside out.

"Truce."

His thumb stroked the back of her wrist. "Go upstairs and pack a bag, Frannie. Stay with me tonight, please? I'll take you to Thanksgiving lunch tomorrow. Quin and Katie are hosting at their new house. It will be fun."

"You could pick me up in the morning." Here she was again. Trying to pretend she wasn't infatuated, in lust, in something.

His gaze was filled with determination and another emotion she couldn't name. "Don't make me beg, Bug. I want you in my bed tonight."

Her stomach took a long free fall to the bottom floor. But she wasn't a coward. "I'd like that, too. Do you want to come upstairs with me and wait?"

He flushed, his eyes glittering. "Better not. We might never leave. I've spent the last five nights alone in my bed, Frannie. Didn't much care for it. You're lucky I don't take you in this chair right here. You across my lap. Think about it."

She *was* thinking about it. The image he summoned made her knees tighten and her abdomen pool with heat. "Okay, then. Alone it is."

"Good choice."

Thirty minutes later, Zach helped her into his car. She shot him a sideways glance, noting how well he moved. "I take it the doctor cleared you for driving?"

"He did." Zachary glanced to the left and right before pulling out of the parking lot, but there was no traffic at one in the morning. "We don't have to do anything tonight if you're tired," he said, clearly trying to be a gentleman.

She put a hand on his thigh. “I’m not *that* tired.”

The car lurched forward. “Don’t be a brat, Bug. I’m steering two tons of metal. Hold that thought.”

She was curious to see his condo. After spending time at his home on the northern coast overlooking the Atlantic, she wondered what kind of nest he had built for himself in Portland. As she’d noted at SRO headquarters, studying an individual’s personal space told her a lot about who they were.

Zachary parked his car in a numbered spot inside a gated area. When they got out, she caught his eye over the roof of the car. “The rain has stopped. Could we walk for a bit? I seem to have a lot of energy at the moment. That’s the downside of working at night. I always need to unwind.”

“I can help you with that energy,” he drawled.

“We’ll get there, I promise. But I need some exercise.”

She had unwittingly given him another opening to make a suggestive comment, but he refrained. “Whatever you say.”

When he took her hand in his, Frannie lectured herself sternly. This wasn’t a fairy tale. Zachary was no Prince Charming.

But it was hard not to indulge in the fantasy, despite the reality of the circumstances. There was no moon. The man in question wanted to get laid, but he would not be tamed. Still, a girl could dream. Picturing herself in the midst of a happily-ever-after wasn’t a crime.

Frannie didn’t know how far they walked. She was tall, so Zach didn’t have to alter his stride much at all. She was happy, giddy almost. Was she falling in love with Zachary Stone? The groundwork was there. He had been her first crush, her first romantic touchstone. Over the years when she had spent time with other men, she knew she hadn’t judged them fairly. They just weren’t Zach.

She and Zach had a lot in common—shared history,

shared interests. But unlike her adolescent memories, Zachary was a man now. Strong, sexy, the yang to her yin. Or maybe the other way around. Her Chinese philosophy was rusty.

Without warning, the skies opened up. Rain poured down as if someone had unzipped a cloud. Frannie yelped and huddled closer to Zachary.

He pulled her into the shelter of a building and tucked his coat around both of them. "Perhaps we should have checked the radar, Bug."

The light from a nearby lamppost illuminated the sheets of rain blowing sideways. Frannie shook with laughter as they huddled under the modest overhang. The only thing saving them was the fact that the wind was coming from behind the building. "You're going to regret bringing me home with you," she said.

Zach hitched his coat over their heads, and with his free hand took her chin and tipped it up. "Never, Frannie," he said. He kissed her hard, his urgency impossible to miss. They had been apart five days, and it seemed an eternity. "I missed you," he said.

"Same here." She leaned into him, groaning aloud. It was good, so good. Like diving off a cliff and landing in a warm sea of wonder.

Desperation and laughter. Yearning and satisfaction. An end to her doubts and a beginning. Perhaps yin and yang after all. She went up on her tiptoes, trying to get closer, trying to feel all of him.

"Too many clothes," he muttered. He snaked a hand under several layers and found her bare back. "Ah, that's better."

His hand was freezing, but she chose not to point it out. His fingers on the skin at her spine created a special kind of warmth. "Should we make a dash for it?" she asked in between kisses.

A police car drove by, slowed, then presumably decided Zach and Frannie weren't a threat to society and moved off down the street.

Zachary chuckled. "You're the girl. I'm tough. Whatever you say."

"I'm weighing how much I hate getting soaked versus how comfy your bed is..."

"Oh, it's comfy," Zach said soberly, his eyes dancing. "Very comfy."

Mother Nature must have taken pity on them. The rain slowed to a steady drizzle. "I'm ready," Frannie said. "Let's do this."

They set out at a pace just under a jog. The distance back to the car had multiplied. Even though the rain lessened in intensity, both of them were drenched by the time Zachary retrieved her bag from the trunk and led her inside his building. They dripped their way through the lobby and into the elevator.

Frannie moaned inwardly when she saw her reflection in the mirrored interior. She looked like the proverbial drowned rat.

"Stop that," Zach said.

"Stop what?"

He stared at her with a gaze that was hot and sexy and determined. "I don't care if you're wet," he said. "You're beautiful, Frannie. Head to toe."

She didn't know what to say. Receiving compliments had never been her strong suit. She didn't doubt his sincerity, but it was a relief when the elevator dinged, signaling their destination. Zach's condo occupied half of the top floor of the building. In the daylight, the view would be phenomenal.

At the moment, neither of them was interested. The drapes were drawn, shutting out the cold, dreary November night. When Zach began flipping on lights, Frannie was enchanted. His home on the northern coast in the woods was modern, but here, he had chosen classic furnishings. Lots of jewel tones and rich wood and velvet.

In front of his fireplace a faux bearskin rug invited all sorts of hanky-panky. "I like it, Zach," she said. "It's beautiful and comfortable. Very appealing."

"Thank you."

He shrugged out of his wet coat and hung it on a hall tree. Frannie did the same. They were still wet. Too wet. Frannie's teeth started to chatter.

Zachary eyed her with a small smile. "Before you freeze to death, I have a question. As my guest, you have dibs on first shower, of course. Or to save time, we could get in together. Your call."

She hadn't expected this. When the clock struck midnight, she had been planning to go back to the hotel, change into warm jammies and watch Christmas movies on TV. Now, here she was. Her choice. She had packed a bag, after all.

The problem was, she felt bedraggled. Wasn't a woman supposed to prepare carefully for a romantic night? Perhaps that was another problem. She was a planner. A plotter of details. In order to do her best work, she made endless lists and laid out everything in advance. No surprises. No room for error.

Spontaneity was scary. Especially when it came to the man who was stealing her heart.

Zachary stood there looking like the most wonderful serendipitous surprise. She stomped on all her doubts and jumped without a net. "I wouldn't want you to sit in those wet clothes while you wait on me. Sure. A double shower is fine."

Ten

The look on his face made Frannie very glad she had agreed. Maybe he had been expecting her to decline. For a split second, surprise flashed across his features. The next expression was impossible to misunderstand.

A man. Wanting a woman.

Hungry. Intent.

"Come with me," he said gruffly. He took her by the wrist and dragged her down the hall to his bedroom. She barely had a glimpse of his huge king-size bed before he pulled her into the master bath. Here, the amenities were hedonistic and luxurious in the extreme.

"Wow." Her vocabulary escaped her.

"The marble floor is heated," he said, flipping a switch. "Go ahead and take off your shoes. You'll see."

Taking off her shoes seemed a reassuringly small step. But when she turned around, Zach was already naked from the waist up. "You're right about the tile," she said, trying to pretend the sight of him didn't take the starch out of her knees.

What happened next was like a very slow game of strip poker. She removed her watch. He did the same. She unfastened the simple silver necklace she wore. Zach emptied his pockets of change and a pen. When she unzipped her black pants and stepped out of them, he took off his slacks and tossed them in the hamper.

Now she was naked from the waist down, but for her undies.

Zach wore fitted boxer briefs in dark gray with a navy stripe. The fabric outlined the interesting parts of his body, leaving nothing to the imagination, including the fact that he was fully aroused.

Her sex went damp and needy as if it had been waiting for just this moment.

Zachary watched her like an airborne hawk eyeing a tiny mouse on the ground.

He moved closer. "Need any help with that sweater, Bug?"

"Well, I—" She lost her train of thought when he took the bottom edge of the soft cashmere and began tugging it upward over her head. When he was done, her hair was even more of a mess. Zachary didn't seem to notice.

He was flushed, and she could swear his hands were shaking.

Now, only the bra was left. She was glad she had worn a nice one today. It was not particularly fancy, but the sheer blush pink flattered her skin. He cupped her breasts, one in each hand. As he weighed them and plumped them gently, he sighed. "It's a damn good thing I didn't know what you looked like naked when we were teenagers."

She rested her cheek against his bare chest, right over his heart. The steady *ka-thump, ka-thump* made her feel as if she had come home at last. But the feel of him pressed up against her was far more erotic than comforting. It was safe to say she had never responded physically to any man the way she did with Zach. She wanted him so badly she was tempted to skip the shower and drag him down onto the floor.

For a woman who prided herself on careful thought and intellectual calculation, this wanton urge to throw caution to the wind was terrifying.

She traced a tiny white scar on his collarbone, the pale indentation barely visible at all. “What’s this?”

His chest moved as he chuckled. “When Farrell was seven and I was five, Dad bought him a BB gun for Christmas. Before they got to the part about safety rules, Farrell had already shot me right there in the living room. I howled like a banshee. Three-year-old Quinten was sobbing, because he was scared and didn’t know what was going on in all the hubbub.” He shook his head. “It was a Christmas to remember.”

Frannie kissed the small imperfection, tasting the salty tang of his skin. “Are there any other scars I should know about?”

Zachary shuddered hard, wondering if his knees might buckle. One minute his Frannie was a prim librarian, the next an impossible-to-resist femme fatale. Never knowing which kept him on his toes.

He clenched his hands in her hair, that wonderful mass of black silk. He couldn’t wait to see it spread across his pillow. In fact, he’d enjoyed that exact fantasy a lot during the past few nights.

“Hold that thought,” he muttered. Releasing her was an actual pain. He reached into the huge shower cubicle and turned on the water, adjusting the faucet carefully. Normally he liked it scalding, but with Frannie in there beside him, medium hot would work.

When he turned around, his throat tightened. Frannie was naked. While he had been fooling with the water temperature, she had shed her bra and panties. Holy hell, she was incredible. It was that combination of pale, pale skin and jet-black hair. She reminded him of a fairy-tale character in a book he’d seen at a friend’s house when he was a little kid. The girl who ate the poisoned apple.

He was losing brain cells at an alarming rate. Lust

burned from the inside out. It dawned on him suddenly that he was the only one of the two of them still wearing an item of clothing. Before he could remedy the situation, Frannie reached out and touched him through his underwear. Her fingers curved around his erection.

Her smile was equal parts shy and determined. "I love your body, Zach. It's so different from mine." She stroked him gently but firmly.

He was pretty sure he gasped aloud. "I like you touching my body," he said. "So I guess we're a perfect match."

Though her technique wasn't particularly practiced, she worked him up to the point he had to call a halt or find release in a way he didn't want.

"Time-out," he croaked. He backed away, shed the boxers and took her hand.

"Do you have a towel for my hair?" she asked.

"It's already wet. Why don't you let me wash it for you?"

Her eyes rounded. He might as well have said, *let's both of us dance naked on the porch*. "You?"

"Why not? I have good shampoo. It's not girly, but it smells nice."

Long silence.

"Okay…"

He could hear the doubt in her voice. "What's the problem, Bug?"

She shrugged, looking uneasy. "You washing my hair seems awfully intimate."

Zachary burst out laughing. He laughed so hard, his shoulders shook and his eyes were wet.

Frannie crossed her arms beneath her breasts. "Why is that so funny?"

"My God, Frannie. You're in my house, about to step into my shower buck naked, and you're worried about a little shampoo between friends?"

"Laugh now," she said, her scowl dark. "But when I return the favor, you'll see."

He shook his head in bemusement, never quite able to figure her out. "C'mon. We both need to warm up."

His shower had dual overhead faucets and plenty of room to maneuver. The shower gel he opened was some he had bought on a recent trip to France. It was made for men, but the bold, spicy fragrance with the hints of orange and ginger could swing either way.

Frannie's naked, wet body kept distracting him. "Let me wash you first, and then I'll do your hair."

"I can wash myself."

"Maybe so, but humor me."

After he dumped a dollop of gel into his hand, he warmed it between his palms and then touched her. He hardly knew where to begin. "Are you getting warmer?" he asked, running his hands over her breasts simultaneously.

Frannie's low moan made the hair on his arms stand up. Other things were already up. He washed her neck and down to her hips and everywhere in between, but he kept coming back to the curves of her breasts. They were spectacular.

She had her eyes closed now, her arms loose at her sides. It was as if she was silently telling him he could do anything he wanted. The unspoken invitation seriously revved his engine. With another dollop of gel in his palm, he turned his attention to the space between her legs. When he stroked her there, her eyes flew open.

"So soon?" she asked. "You haven't done my hair yet. I haven't touched you. This seems premature."

He kissed her lazily, still pressing his fingers into the soft folds of her body. "Who said this was the only time?"

When she shuddered and came moments later, he didn't bother to count the minutes. They had all night.

Frannie was limp with pleasure when he shampooed

her hair. "You'd better let me do it," she muttered. "It's too much trouble."

He wanted to be inside her. Badly. But he was enjoying himself by pampering her. "Relax." He worked the shampoo deep into her long, wavy tresses and massaged her scalp. "I'm having fun, Bug."

Rinsing took some time. He used the sprayer. When the water ran clear, he kissed her long and slow.

Frannie twined her arms around his neck, distracting him with her lush curves pressed against his chest. "You could open a shop," she teased. "A day spa. You'd have women lined up for miles. Now sit down on the bench, and I'll wash yours. You'll see how wonderful it is."

Zachary closed his eyes, telling himself he could hold out a little while longer. He felt her dribble the shampoo over his scalp. Then she began rubbing her fingers around his ears, down to his neck, back up to his forehead. It was erotic. It felt damned good. But every time he peeked, her breasts were on eye level.

Finally, he snapped. He leaned forward and caught one raspberry nipple between his teeth. His hands settled on her slippery waist. "You taste good, Frannie."

She retaliated by spraying him in the face. "You're supposed to relax," she complained. "I don't think you're getting this spa thing at all."

He stood, turned off the water and sluiced water from his face with one hand. "Men know only two ways to relax. Alcohol, and what I'm about to do to you."

Her jaw dropped the tiniest bit before she snapped it shut. "Ooh. Promises, promises." Then she frowned. "But you didn't let me wash the rest of you."

"I'm clean enough. Out, woman."

He handed her a fluffy towel and took one for himself. The warm floor beneath their feet felt pretty damn fantastic. If it wasn't so hard and unyielding, he might have considered a little foreplay before they headed to the bed.

Frannie eyed him warily. "It takes me a long while to comb out my hair and dry it," she said.

"Oh no." Zachary was adamant. "No time for that." He kissed her again, lingering, letting her feel how much he needed her.

"I'll get your bed wet."

"I can buy a new bed."

"Zaacchh." There it was again. That sweet feminine squeal that made him smile. The same drawn-out syllable he had heard so many times in high school.

Thankfully, his ankle had improved enough that he could scoop her up in his arms, laughing when her towel disappeared and Frannie tried to preserve her modesty. Trouble was, she only had two hands. He dumped her on the bed and raided the nightstand for condoms. He couldn't remember the name of the last woman he had taken to bed. Did that make him a jerk? Besides, he usually indulged at the woman's house, not his.

Sex with Frannie was different. He couldn't explain *how* if anyone had asked him. It just was.

She was still worrying about the damp spots on his expensive damask comforter while Zachary was ripping back the sheets. "I want you, Frannie. Please. Get under the covers." He saw gooseflesh on her arms and legs.

Finally, he got his wish. Frannie's hair—that glorious wavy cloud of black—fanned out across his pillow. He felt a punch to his chest. For the first time ever, he allowed himself to imagine what it might be like to come home to this every night.

Frannie was dizzy with fatigue and seduced by the softness of Zachary's bed. The solid walnut four-poster reminded her of something in a king's chamber. Perhaps she was a captive, part of the spoils of war. She chuckled inwardly at her own whimsy.

Zachary dimmed the lights but left them burning at a low glimmer. He wasn't laughing anymore. He looked deadly serious. A man intent on conquering a challenge.

He wasn't going to have to fight very hard. Her earlier orgasm had been like an erotic amuse-bouche. It had only whetted her appetite for the main course.

Even in the midst of her arousal, one part of her cataloged all the ways a man like Zachary Stone had accumulated his considerable expertise in the bedroom. She wasn't a prude. She made no judgment about what a young, virile man had enjoyed with willing females of the same mind. But the part of her who wanted somewhere to belong also wanted to believe she was different. She needed to believe that she, Frannie, might be able to give Zach something no other woman could. The only thing those faceless women were after was his body…and maybe his money.

If this relationship had any hope of moving forward, Frannie wanted to be his partner, his all in all.

He reared up on one elbow. When he bent and kissed her belly, the skin contracted. "That tickles," she said, half-breathless with longing.

"Sorry." He kept doing it, so his denial wasn't convincing.

She reached for him and found the straining, pulsing erection that was so very fascinating to her. Warm velvet skin over the firm shaft of a man, a man who wanted her desperately. Didn't every woman deserve a man who would crave her? Didn't Frannie?

She squeezed him carefully, feeling the drop of fluid at the head, swirling her fingertip in the wetness. When Zachary shuddered and groaned, she felt invincible.

"I want you," she whispered. "Take me, Zach. Please."

He reached for the nightstand, grabbed protection, rolled

it on. When he came back to her, he spread her thighs with two warm hands. Then he stared.

She felt exposed.

Even more so when he lifted one of her ankles onto his shoulder. "Don't be afraid, Frannie. I won't hurt you."

In this position, she had no defense. But her very vulnerability aroused her and told her how much she trusted him already.

He entered her slowly, letting her adjust to his size. For the moment, he had all the power, holding her legs open, teasing her clitoris with his thumb. The dual stimulation shot her back to the top in seconds. Waves of frenzied sensation rolled through her abdomen and coalesced at the spot where their bodies joined.

A jolt of pleasure so intense, so immeasurably compelling, bore down on her. *Wait*, she cried. *Wait.* But she didn't realize the words were in her head. She climaxed hard, losing herself in him.

Zachary moved quicker, more wildly. Never did he lack control. He was protecting her, measuring his entry. His thrusts flirted with the point of pain, but not once did he give her anything but unadulterated pleasure.

Her mind went blank. All she felt, all she saw, all she wanted was Zach.

At last, he reached his limits. Easing her leg down onto the mattress and separating their bodies, he bent and kissed the soft fluff of hair at her sex. Then he entered her again and pounded like a guy who had been denied for weeks, months, years.

Frannie lost track of time. The world narrowed to this bed, this man. He said her name like a prayer when he came. His body tensed, shook, then moved frantically inside her, over and over until a second orgasm, even longer than the first wave, drained him.

He slumped on top of her, his weight considerable.

She was fairly certain they both dozed. The night had taken on a surreal quality. Just as she was sliding deeper, she remembered that her phone battery had been almost dead when she left Stone River headquarters. It wouldn't matter except that it was the holiday and her parents might call. Not only that, but one of her friends was about to have a baby. Frannie didn't want to miss either contact, even if she didn't see the message until tomorrow.

"Zach?" She rolled him onto his back and smiled when he grumbled in his sleep. "Zach?" She shook his shoulder. "Do you have an extra phone charger? I left mine at the hotel."

It was three in the morning, maybe later. The man couldn't be blamed for burrowing into the covers. She tried once more.

This time he raised up, bleary-eyed, and wiped a hand over his face. "My office. Big drawer. On the left. Come back quick."

After grabbing an angora afghan from the bench at the foot of the bed and wrapping it around her body toga-style, she tiptoed out of the bedroom. The house was quiet and dark, but not cold. A tiny night-light in the corridor provided just enough illumination that she didn't run into walls.

She and Zach had passed his office on their earlier mad rush to the bedroom. The door was halfway open. Frannie pushed it wider. Maybe tomorrow she would explore. This was Zach's personal space, very different from his SRO office. She smelled leather and Zach's aftershave.

The desk was more of an elegant table, piled with stacks of paper. She saw catalogs and pizza flyers and a city tax bill. Zach traveled often. Maybe he was so busy he simply dumped all his mail here and triaged it later.

He'd said the *big drawer*, but all of the drawers looked big to her. And they were crammed with stuff. She found a stapler and an ancient BlackBerry, but no phone cord. Even though he had told her to look on the left, she tried the drawers on the other side, too. When she opened one on the bottom right, it was as neat as the others were messy.

Curious, she picked up a thick stack of paper. It appeared to be a manuscript. The top page had only six words—*The Falcon's Revenge by Zachary Stone.*

What? Without thinking, she flipped to page two and began to read. By the end of page four, she knew she was trespassing. Zach's opus, at first glance, appeared to be a police procedural or a thriller or a mystery. It was too soon in the story to tell for sure, and she didn't have permission to go farther. Carefully, she replaced the top sheets, straightened the pile and put the whole thing back in the drawer.

Zachary was writing a book? Why hadn't he said anything? Didn't he know she would be interested? It seemed a glaring omission in the course of their recent reunion.

She sat there at his desk for several minutes, her mind racing, her fingers worrying the fringe on the afghan. It was dumb to feel hurt, but she was. Why wouldn't he share an endeavor so exciting, so personal? Frannie had rattled on and on about her world over the last couple of weeks.

The answer was both clear and dismaying, and in some ways, not a surprise at all. Zach was an island, a man apart. No one told him what to do with his life.

He might have thought Frannie would intrude. That she would offer to edit or ask if he had an agent or any number of other excited suggestions.

Her heart sank. It was true. When it came to Zach, she always wanted the best for him. If he had told her about his writing, she would have been all over him with a million and one different comments and questions.

For Frannie, it would have been the natural and loving thing to do. She and Zach were friends, more than friends…

She knew Zach was asleep right now. He wasn't going to come looking for her. Suddenly, she was tired and dispirited and so very disappointed.

Seeing him after all these years had rejuvenated her. The joy of getting reacquainted. The sheer fun of reminiscing about the past. More than anyone on the planet, he understood the way her brain worked. He understood *her*. And she had believed such an understanding was a two-way street.

But she was wrong. Zachary Stone was not her soul mate. He was just another guy taking what a willing woman had to give and offering nothing in return. She had reached out and opened up, but he hadn't. Not only that, but she had made spontaneous choices about being with Zachary. She had broken most of her own personal rules. And now she was in too deep.

Fighting tears, she turned to the small table adjacent to the desk, opened a drawer and finally found what she was looking for in the first place. After that, she went back to Zach's room, plugged in her phone, shed the afghan and climbed into bed.

Zachary roused enough to kiss her and pull her close. Half an hour ago, she would have thought this was the best moment of her life.

That was before she understood the intimacy was a charade. He hadn't given himself to her. Zach was like the proverbial iceberg. He had allowed her to see the tiny percentage above the water, but most of the real Zach was hidden away.

It was a good thing she had been awake for almost twenty-four hours. Instead of brooding, she slid into a deep sleep, not rousing until her phone beeped the following morning. When she got up and checked, there was a new baby boy in the world. The picture made her smile.

Then she looked at the time. "Zach!" She stood beside the bed and shook his arm. "Wake up."

He opened one eye. "Sleep," he groaned. "We need more sleep."

"That's your fault. It's Thanksgiving. What time do we have to be at your brother's house?"

"Noon."

"I still have to change. Do you want me to call a ride to my hotel? You could pick me up there."

He dragged her down into the bed, taking advantage of her naked state to cop a feel. "What I want is for you to come back to bed, sweet Frannie." He kissed her lazily but thoroughly, making her heart turn over in her chest.

She was bent over the bed at an awkward angle, with most of her naked body exposed. Zachary was temptation personified, despite everything that had happened. If she had her way, she would slide back under the covers, make love to him and pretend all was right with her world.

Instead, she slapped his hand away. "Behave, Zach. Are we supposed to be bringing food?"

He yawned, stretching his arms over his head, looking like a cross between a lumberjack and a male model. "I paid for a huge ham. Had it delivered to Quin's house yesterday. He and Katie are doing the turkey and dressing and sweet potatoes. Farrell and Ivy are bringing side dishes and dessert."

She wrapped herself in the afghan again. "Did you tell them you invited me?"

"Not yet. They would have been asleep last night. But it's fine."

"It's *not* fine. At the holidays, people fix nice place settings. Text them, please, so Katie won't be flustered when we get there."

He laughed. "You obviously don't know Katie well

enough yet. She's the most organized person I've ever met. But I'll text her. Quit giving me the evil eye."

When Zachary was occupied with his phone, Frannie decided to just change here. She reached into the small bag she had packed and grabbed clean underwear, black wool crepe dress pants and a teal silk blouse. Then she ducked into the bathroom to get dressed. She probably needed another shower, but there wasn't time.

Her hair was a disaster. Going to bed with it wet had turned it into a fuzzy cloud. Ruthlessly, she tamed it with a brush as best she could and then twisted it up in a sophisticated knot on the back of her head. Crystal earrings that matched her blouse completed the look. A little makeup, and she was good to go.

She threw open the door to the bedroom. "I'm ready."

Eleven

When Frannie came out of the bathroom, Zachary was still in bed, enjoying the warm covers and replaying the night before in his head. When he jumped up guiltily, Frannie surely noticed his erection, but she didn't bat an eye.

In fact, he thought she was acting strangely. "Give me ten minutes," he said. "And FYI, Katie and Quin are delighted you're coming."

By the time he was shaved, dressed and in the car with Frannie, they really were pushing their noon deadline. But they made it to Quin and Katie's new house with three minutes to spare. Frannie had been quiet in the car, unusually so. Was she regretting last night?

Zachary was on top of the world. He was happy that Frannie was sharing Thanksgiving with his family. Truth be told, he had been dreading the day. Two sets of happy couples. A cute baby. Zach the odd man out.

Not that he wanted to get married. He didn't. But it was nice to have a date today.

In the midst of all the hubbub, Frannie jumped right in, helping get lunch on the table. Of course, most of it was already done by the time Zach and Frannie arrived.

Ivy handed Frannie the baby. "Play with Dolly, will you? I'm going to put her down for an early nap in a few minutes, so the adults can enjoy the meal in peace."

Zachary wanted to laugh at the look on Frannie's face,

but he didn't. She held little Dolly as if the kid were a bundle of dynamite. And the fuse was lit.

He took pity on the woman with the high IQ and the apparent fear of infants. "You want me to hold her?"

"Oh yes." Frannie passed off the little girl with a look of relief.

Zachary put the baby on his shoulder and rubbed her back, laughing when Dolly pulled his hair. "You don't like kids?"

"I don't dislike kids," Frannie said. "I've never spent much time with babies. I don't think I'd be very good at it."

He gave her a wry glance. "You're good at everything you do, Bug. Babies aren't all that complicated."

"Maybe." She shrugged. "It's a moot point. I doubt I'll get married. And if I did, it wouldn't matter, because my work takes me all over the world. I'm not mommy material. I've made my peace with that."

"Isn't marriage all about compromise?"

She gave him a look he couldn't decipher. "What would you know about compromise, Zachary Stone? The world pretty much rolls your way from what I can tell."

That odd, unsettling comment was the last private moment he had with Frannie for the next hour and a half. Something about the conversation disturbed him, so he filed it away to study later.

The meal was a huge success. The various cooks had outdone themselves. In addition to the turkey and dressing, Katie had made her granny's sweet potatoes and produced made-from-scratch rolls that would make a grown man weep. Ivy, a very good cook in her own right, had brought several Charleston-flavored dishes, since she had lived there for so many years.

Dessert was both pecan and pumpkin pies. Everyone around the table took small servings of each. Farrell lifted a glass during the final course. "To Stone River Outdoors. May we not screw it up."

"Hear, hear." Zachary nodded. "Ain't that the truth."

Quin raised a toast to their guest. "And to Frannie who we hope will put our fears to rest one way or the other."

When it was all over, Zachary would have given a thousand dollars for a nap. He had a clue his fellow diners felt the same. Dolly was always up early, so Ivy and Farrell were yawning. Quin and Katie had gone to great lengths to make preparations for the lunch, so they *had to be* exhausted.

And since Zach and Frannie had still been awake at three, maybe even later, they, too, were sleep deprived. But there were piles of dirty dishes to deal with as well as stowing all the leftovers.

When no one moved immediately, Frannie spoke up. "I hate to introduce business in the middle of such a lovely occasion, but I wanted to let you know that I may have found something important. If I work some more this weekend, and if my suspicions are correct, I could possibly have it nailed down by Monday."

It was Farrell who frowned. "I don't like that, Frannie. Holidays are for family and kicking back."

Zach felt suddenly protective of Frannie. "Her parents weren't available this weekend. That's why I invited her here. But I agree with my brother. You shouldn't be doing SRO work these next few days, Frannie."

She seemed taken aback. Perhaps she wasn't accustomed to having her schedule questioned. "Well, then," Frannie said, "is there any chance the three Stone brothers might be free Wednesday afternoon to sit down with me? I'd like to go over my preliminary findings with you. Let you know what's unfolding."

Quin leaned forward. "Can you at least tell us which employee has kicked up warning flags? Perhaps we can help."

"Um..." Frannie hesitated. "I don't like making accusations until I'm sure."

Quin nodded. "Understood. We'll keep this under wraps. No judgment."

"Okay. If you must know, it looks like Edward Cordell may be at the heart of your troubles."

Zachary shook his head. "Impossible," he said flatly. "Edward and my father were best friends. Edward has worked for SRO over thirty-five years. You've made a mistake."

The room went dead silent. Zachary realized that his rebuttal had perhaps been harsher than he intended.

Frannie was pale, her eyes downcast. The other four adults at the table showed varying degrees of concern and discomfort.

Zachary stood up. "It's impossible," he insisted. "Edward taught me how to paddle a canoe. He got Quin interested in skiing. At Farrell's first wedding, Edward gave one of the toasts. You're wrong, Frannie, you have to be."

Katie began stacking dishes, and the uncomfortable moment passed. Zachary assembled a pile, as well. "Let's get this done. Football awaits."

Frannie was embarrassed and angry. Clearly Zachary had no regard for her capabilities as a professional. He had dismissed her premise as if she were a stupid child. His careless arrogance hurt, not only because she thought they had been growing closer, but most of all, because it meant he didn't trust her.

When the men eventually drifted toward the den, Frannie quietly pulled Katie aside. "Thank you so much for including me today. I don't want to be rude, but I'm getting a migraine, and I've summoned a ride to take me back to the hotel."

"I'm so sorry," Katie said. "Can I box up some leftovers for your dinner?"

"Thanks, but no need. Room service is great. I don't want a fuss. Will you make my excuses when the time is right? My car will be here in a moment."

Katie nodded, but she seemed troubled, perhaps reading the real cause of Frannie's precipitous flight.

As Frannie stepped back into the kitchen, she ran into Zachary. He steadied her with two hands on her shoulders. "What car?" he asked, frowning.

"I have a headache. I'm going back to the hotel."

"I'll take you. Don't be stupid."

"Zachary!" Katie said, giving him a chiding look. "It's Frannie's decision. Quit being so rude."

Frannie summoned a smile, hiding her emotional distress. "You stay and spend time with your family, Zach. I'll be fine. It was a lovely meal."

"If that's what you want."

He said nothing about meeting her later. His expression was shuttered, in fact, shutting her out. Once again, Frannie found herself standing on the outside, looking in.

At the hotel, Frannie put her cell on Do Not Disturb and did the same with the hotel phone on the bedside table. Her pretend migraine had become the real thing.

She slept for five straight hours. When she awoke, it was dark outside. This wasn't the worst Thanksgiving she'd ever had, but it wasn't the best, either.

The noon meal had been so huge she wasn't even hungry. Besides, she didn't want to give Zachary any way to infiltrate her fortress of silence, and ordering room service would do just that.

She had twenty-two texts on her phone, each one more frustrated than the last.

Well, that was just too damn bad. She didn't want to *see*

Zachary Stone, she didn't want to *talk* to him and most of all, she didn't want to have sex with him.

The man was a master at getting his way. It was better not to give him a single opportunity to test her willpower.

Eventually, the texts stopped. She told herself she was glad.

One of the movie channels was airing a Christmas classic. Frannie took a couple of aspirin, curled up in the big bed and indulged in a bout of self-pity. Maybe she should never have accepted this job knowing she would see Zachary again.

She was weak where he was concerned. Thirteen or thirty, the age didn't matter. She'd always had a thing for him.

The worst blow of all was admitting to herself that she was maybe, probably, falling in love with him.

Hearts didn't really break. She'd made an A in college anatomy, so she knew that the organ in her chest was stronger than it seemed at the moment.

There were some things, though, that textbooks couldn't predict or explain. Frances Wickersham wanted Zachary Stone because he was the one person capable of understanding and loving her exactly as she was.

The only problem? He didn't care. To him, Frannie was a fun time in bed, a pleasant stroll down memory lane.

He wasn't in love with her, and after today, she realized that he never would be.

When she awoke the next morning, her headache was gone. Her heartache still pained her. She remembered Stanley saying that Quin had given him the weekend off. A random guard would be filling in. Though the man had probably been briefed, he surely wouldn't have agreed to report back to Zachary.

Frannie decided to take her chances. She wasn't a fan of hunting down Black Friday bargains, and she was tired of sitting in her hotel room. Because headquarters was closed for the long weekend, there was no real reason to wait until the evening.

The skies were sunny, and the temperature had climbed into the upper forties, so she decided to walk. The streets were filled with holiday shoppers. City employees were out in force decorating streetlamps and hanging wreaths.

It was a beautiful, festive day. Frannie's mood was glum. She had been perfectly happy with her life until she came to Portland. Well, maybe she had occasionally been lonely, but she knew how to chase the blues away. Her world had been filled with work and occasionally an outing with acquaintances. She had long ago decided that romance was overrated.

And then she reconnected with Zach.

Gorgeous, hardheaded, brilliant, contrary Zachary Stone. The man who wanted to know everything about her, and then didn't share anything of his personal dreams. Didn't even bother to tell her he had written a book.

The man who told her all the time how smart she was, and then when it really mattered, dismissed two weeks of her complicated work with a vehement denial of her conclusions.

He didn't believe her about Edward Cordell. His words still stung.

When she reached the SRO building, she used her key card to let herself in. The offices were quiet and empty. She hadn't finished analyzing every computer in the building, but since she had stumbled upon what appeared to be a significant lead in her investigation, she would start there again.

If the trail led nowhere, she would be more than happy to admit that Zach was right. Unfortunately, Frannie was afraid the Stone siblings were in for a big shock.

She settled into her chair and got to work. One thing she

loved about her chosen career was how much it engaged her brain. She was never bored, and she never tired of the thrill of making a significant discovery for her clients.

Eventually, an alarm on her phone reminded her to stop for a break. She had snitched an apple and a yogurt from the hotel breakfast buffet. That was all the lunch she needed. Afterward, she did some yoga stretches and a few laps around the hallways.

The afternoon sped by. The deeper she dived into Edward Cordell's digital life, the more she found. A disturbing narrative was unfolding, and much of it involved the Stone family. Somehow, she had to find a way to convince Zachary that his blind loyalty was misplaced. It wouldn't be easy.

By five o'clock, she was ready to call it quits. She shut down the computer and carefully restored Edward's work space to the way she had found it.

After the barrage of texts yesterday afternoon and evening, she hadn't heard a word all day from Zachary. It was silly to let his silence hurt her feelings. She *had* been avoiding him, but she wanted him to at least have made an effort for more than one day.

On the other hand, she hadn't been very amenable. Locking herself in her room and shutting off the outside world was no way to build a relationship. She and Zach were both stubborn in their own way. At Glenderry they had argued often. Eventually, their friendship always won out. Their bond back then was strong.

Did it still exist intact? And was it flexible enough to weather the storm that was about to come?

She picked up her coat and bag and shut off the lights. When she turned to leave, Zachary stood in the doorway. She put a hand to her chest. "Why do you have to do that? At least text me a heads-up when you're going to sneak into your own building."

His expression was grim. "I didn't think you answered texts from me."

Touché. "You hurt my feelings yesterday, Zach. I was feeling a little raw and not inclined to talk to you."

The planes and angles in his face softened. "I'm sorry. But I still think you're following a rabbit trail. Edward wouldn't hurt us."

She counted to ten and changed the subject. "Why are you here now?"

He shrugged. "I thought we could go out to dinner."

And there it was again. The temptation. How far could she go with this thing and still be able to walk away?

"The restaurants will be crowded tonight. I think I'll crash early."

"Boring, Bug. We can do better than that." He reached for her hand, lifting it to his lips. When he kissed each finger and nibbled her pinkie, she knew she was lost.

"Zach..."

He lifted his head. "What?"

"If I locate the source of SRO's problems, I'll be gone sooner than later. I don't know if I want to get more involved."

He cupped her cheek, his gaze intent. "We're already involved, Frannie."

"And what happens when it's time for me to go?" That was about as clear as she could get other than asking flat out if this thing between them was sex for the sake of sex and nothing more. It was difficult to be coherent with him teasing her nipple.

His chin was scruffy, and his gaze was sleepy eyed. He gave her a slow smile. "I'm a big believer in carpe diem and forging my own path. We don't have to worry about the future, do we? It usually takes care of itself."

Her heart sank. She was a planner. In every phase of

her life. To be reckless with Zach was a huge risk. But the alternative was no Zach at all.

"Fair enough," she said calmly, not wanting him to see her turmoil.

"What's your favorite kind of meal? Thai? French? Seafood?"

She could definitely eat her feelings right about now, healthy or not. "Italian?" she asked hopefully.

"Whatever the lady wants."

He had parked a fancy SUV at the curb in a loading zone. Frannie put her things in the back seat and climbed in.

"It's not far," Zachary said. "But it's not downtown."

The fifteen-minute drive was pleasant. That wasn't a word Frannie would normally have used to describe *anything* about Zach. It was too bland. But today it fit. The interior of the car was toasty warm. Zachary's big hands on the wheel were confident. If she ignored the future, this was an evening she could enjoy.

At the restaurant, several employees greeted Zachary by name. Which meant Frannie couldn't help wondering how many women he had wined and dined here. The table where the hostess seated them was one of the nicest...close to the fireplace and far from the noise of the kitchen.

After they ordered, an awkward silence fell. If they couldn't talk about her investigation, what else did they have? Zachary's body language wasn't encouraging.

"I like all of your family," she said finally. "Your sisters-in-law seem perfect for your two brothers."

Zach relaxed visibly. "They *are* perfect. Katie smooths out some of Quinten's intensity. Farrell and Ivy both lost spouses, so this marriage is a new start for each of them."

"Is the baby Farrell's?"

"No. But he's in the process of adopting her. They're hoping to have the papers finalized before the wedding."

"How lovely."

The waiter brought their wine and a basket of garlic knots. Zachary shoved the bread in Frannie's direction. "We'll both eat some," he said. "So it won't matter later."

His wicked smile made her choke on her wine. Zachary just laughed.

The food arrived, and for half an hour, an unspoken truce kept the conversation mellow and agreeable. Over pumpkin-filled ravioli for Frannie and lasagna for Zachary, they talked books and movies and politics.

They both loved *Star Wars*. That hadn't changed since high school. Zachary told her about a few of his more exotic adventures around the world. Frannie shared stories from her work that weren't classified.

By the time dessert came, Frannie was stuffed. Fortunately, Zachary had ordered one to share. He offered her a bite. "Apple cobbler with cinnamon pecans."

"Mmm. Decadent." The smell alone was enough to make her gain ten pounds. But she couldn't resist when Zach held out his spoon and offered her a bite.

When the bowl was empty, he leaned back in his chair. "I would like us to spend the night together."

She blinked, trying to behave as if this type of thing happened to her all the time. "I'd like that, too," she said softly, knowing she had made up her mind. As much as it hurt, she loved him. She would enjoy Zach, even if the time was short. It was what she wanted. Call it a last hurrah. Or maybe closure. It was the only choice she could make. "Your place or mine?" she asked.

"The hotel is closer."

She could swear a tiny flame burned in his beautiful eyes.

Zach paid the check, and they drove back into town. When Zach reached out and took her hand, she curled her fingers around his, feeling torn in a million directions.

When she was with him, everything seemed brighter, more interesting. She was a confident, independent woman. That didn't mean she couldn't appreciate the manner in which he took charge and made her comfortable in a dozen small ways.

Everyone on the hotel staff knew her now. And this time, it wasn't the middle of the night when she and Zach made their way across the lobby. He was undoubtedly a recognizable figure also. What did the desk clerks think? The concierge?

The truth was, no one cared what Frannie did. If she was Zach's temporary fling, the only person impacted was Frannie herself. That meant the consequences were hers and hers alone. She was making a choice to walk on the wild side. Playboys liked to play. Apparently, Frannie did, too—when it came to Zach.

They were the only people in the elevator. When the door closed, Zach turned to her and groaned, slamming his mouth down on hers, gripping her hips hard enough to leave a bruise. "You're driving me crazy, Frannie."

"Ditto," she gasped.

On her floor, they barely made it out of the elevator and inside her room before he was kissing her again, ripping at her clothes and muttering indecipherable words that echoed their mutual urgency.

She realized in an instant that he'd been on a slow burn the entire evening. While Frannie had been trying to decide the future, Zachary had been focused on the here and now. Perhaps his way was better after all.

He lifted her off her feet, forcing her to wrap her arms around his neck. She gasped when he struggled but succeeded in dragging her panties down her legs and tossing the scrap of nylon aside. Then he raked his arm across the low built-in desk and set her down gently on the edge. Only the flat-screen TV remained on the attached, taller dresser. Everything else was scattered on the floor.

Frannie wore black leather boots and a gray knit midi skirt. Her top was a black-and-gray cable-knit sweater that buttoned up the front. Zachary shimmied her skirt up to her hips and unzipped his fly. He paused only long enough to deal with a condom before grabbing her ass and pulling her toward him.

When he shoved inside her, Frannie moaned. He was wicked and inventive and totally focused on her. His body was hot to the touch. She wanted to unbutton his shirt, but Zach was a wild man.

His jaw was granite. He kissed her in between thrusts. "You drive me insane, Bug. What am I going to do about you?"

In his panted question she sensed a confusion that mirrored her own struggles. Maybe this really was different for Zach.

His urgency fed hers. She felt her orgasm hovering near. Leaning backward on her hands, she taunted him. "Is that all you've got? Don't stop. Don't you dare stop."

When she came, her head arched back and hit the wall. The minor discomfort never registered. Her body shuddered, reaching for the last bits of pleasure.

Zach shouted her name and came, too. "Frannie, Frannie, Frannie..." He gathered her close and buried his face in her neck.

When she could speak, she stroked his hair with one hand. "Well, that was nice."

"Mmm..."

Now that the main event was over, Frannie realized her butt was cold, and the rest of her was sweaty. "We could try the bed next," she said, trying to be helpful.

"I can't feel my legs."

His aggrieved complaint made her laugh. "That's *your*

problem, wild man. I'm not the one who went all Tarzan on the furniture."

Finally, he leaned back and broke the connection. Holding out two hands, he helped her down. "What can I say? I seem to be addicted to you."

Twelve

Frannie searched Zach's face and his words for any clue that such a thing displeased him, but as far as she could tell, he was plenty happy with the current situation.

Leaning into him, she yawned. "Do you have a bag in the car?"

A laugh rumbled through his chest. "Unfortunately, no. When I left the house, I hadn't thought this through."

"You want to go home and grab a few things while I shower?"

He tugged on her hair to tip back her head and kiss her lazily. "Or you could come to my place."

This was a nice hotel, but it didn't hold a candle to Zach's condo. "That works. Give me ten minutes to freshen up, and we'll go."

She was in denial, trying Zach's carpe diem attitude on for size. Living in the moment. A lazy Saturday morning tomorrow…in bed with Zachary? She didn't have the courage to do the smart thing and keep her distance.

Her mind shied away from thinking about the danger in his apartment. That stupid manuscript lay in wait, mocking her, reminding her that Zach wasn't the open, uncomplicated man he seemed.

After a quick trip to the bathroom, she used the smaller of her two bags and grabbed jeans and a soft cotton sweater and the few other items she would need for an overnight stay. Did he mean for her to be with him for longer than that?

She hated the uncertainty.

When she was ready, Zachary carried her bag out to the car. At his condo, Zach flipped on the fire and opened a bottle of wine. "I'll be back," he said.

When he returned, he had changed into soft, black athletic pants and an old navy-and-white Harvard T-shirt that strained across his chest. His feet were bare despite the fact that it was November.

Now Frannie wished she had thought to change into something more comfortable. The clothes she had packed were for tomorrow.

Zach dropped down beside her on the sofa and found the tender skin where her boot ended and her bare leg began. He traced his finger back and forth. "You're welcome to my robe, Bug. I rarely wear it. You'll find it on the hook behind the bathroom door."

The outfit she was wearing was comfortable. If she were naked beneath Zachary's robe, she'd be opening herself up to all sorts of mischief. Then again, she had been fully dressed in her hotel room, and that hadn't deterred Zach at all.

"Thanks," she said. "I think I will."

In the bathroom, she couldn't help remembering her shower in this very room with the man of the house. Despite her recent orgasm, little licks of flame settled between her legs and made her restless. Had he turned her into a woman with perpetual cravings?

She had always enjoyed sex, even solo sex. But everything that had come before Zach seemed tepid in retrospect. Now she understood what all the fuss was about.

When she returned to the den, Zach had dimmed the lights and fetched a large blanket from somewhere. He patted the sofa cushion. "Join me, Frannie. I found a *Star Wars* marathon. How does that sound?"

"Nice," she said cautiously. She was good at statistics, among other things. The chances of the two of them making it through even one movie without jumping each other's bones were minimal at best.

She curled into his embrace with her cheek pressed against the side of his rib cage, cushioned by his T-shirt-clad chest. They both propped their feet on the coffee table. Those four feet, two masculine, two feminine, spoke to the differences between them. Frannie was a tall woman, and her feet were longer than the average female's. Beside Zach's, though, hers looked absolutely petite.

Was it odd to be turned on by a man's feet? His were big and well-groomed. Her arches were high, and her toenails were painted red. Frannie liked the way those four feet looked together.

He ruffled the ends of her hair as the opening credits began to roll and the distinctive music played. "What are you thinking, Bug? I can hear the wheels turning."

She shrugged. "I was admiring your feet."

That surprised him. He busted out a laugh. "Seriously?"

"Seriously. They're sexy."

He wiggled his toes. "If you like any of my body parts, I'm happy."

They were quiet…content…for the first forty-five minutes of the movie. But sometimes even George Lucas and Harrison Ford were no match for pheromones.

Frannie had been lulled into a haze of pleasure simply by inhaling the scent of Zach's shower soap. In his embrace, she felt at home. Like she belonged here. But what was Zach thinking? A niggle of regret burrowed into her contentment.

She had given so much of herself. Made herself vulnerable in every way a woman can. Had it been a giant mistake to offer him so much power over her happiness?

He seemed relaxed, too. Eventually, he began stroking her collarbone where the neckline of the robe had gaped. His left hand still held the remote, but the arm and hand he had tucked around her shoulder were free.

As caresses went, it was innocent. He never even strayed lower toward her breast. But already, the robe seemed too hot.

Frannie tried not to move. She tried to be quiet. When he turned and kissed her temple, a tiny moan slipped out. "Zach..." She whispered his name, perhaps not loudly enough for him to hear.

Zach hit the mute button and dropped the remote. Gently, he eased her onto her back and moved over her. The kiss started slow and sweet but ignited quickly into something else. When he unknotted the sash of her robe and peeled back the two sides, he sucked in a breath. "You can tell me to stop," he croaked, his gaze fixed on her breasts.

She reached up and cupped his face, loving the way his eyes darkened and his cheekbones flushed when he wanted her. "Don't stop."

Everything went hazy and slow after that. Perhaps Zach was trying to make up for the warp-speed sex in her hotel room. She wouldn't have complained about a single thing, but this was nice, too. So very nice.

He took her wrists and lifted her arms over her head. "Keep them there," he said, his teasing smile softening the command. His hands on her breasts were warm and firm. He licked her nipples lazily, wetting them again and again until they puckered and ached.

Finally, when she thought she couldn't bear it a moment longer, he returned to her mouth. The kiss was firm, his lips on hers reckless and persuasive.

They were pressed together, shoulders to knees. She

could feel the hard thrust of his erection against her stomach. “Get undressed,” she begged. Their time together was limited. The world would intrude far sooner than Frannie wanted.

“I’m having too much fun.” He muttered the words as he kissed the side of her neck, sucking gently. When his tongue teased the whorls of her ear, she gasped.

She was so ready for him that her hips lifted off the sofa. Or they tried to. Zach’s weight pinned her pleasurably. She was helpless. At his mercy. And she loved it. Loved him.

How could she not? She wanted this to be real, but she was so very afraid he was playing around.

He knew her intimately, her brain and her body. No other man had ever been so perfect for her. Not perfect. That was too much to ask. But definitely perfect for her. She wanted to tell him. He’d been the keeper of many of her secrets over the years.

Now, when it mattered most, she was afraid.

To have her love rejected would be crushing. But she would never know, because the only chance she would let herself take was this one more interlude.

At last, he rolled to his feet and stripped rapidly. What would it be like to share this with him every night? To share every aspect of his life?

Before she could pursue that fantasy, he was on her and in her, breathing her name.

He took her slowly this time…in measured thrusts that gave them both maximum pleasure. His eyes were closed. Did he care that it was Frannie welcoming him into her body? Or was she simply an available woman?

As if he had read her mind, he groaned five simple words. “I care about you, Frannie,” he said.

Was it true? He hadn’t trusted her about the company and what she had found. How could she trust him now? The tepid phrase shouldn't have affected her so strongly. But the way he said it gave her a sliver of hope. They shared a past, a significant past. Could he see her as part of his life going forward?

And I love you, Zach.

Because she dared not say what she really wanted to say, she kept quiet. The oddest mix of emotional pain and physical exhilaration wrapped her in confusion. She lowered her arms and linked them around his waist, feeling the way his skin radiated heat. This was where women and men connected.

All the differences between them faded as he gave himself to her physically, loving her well with his body but never yielding the parts of him that were his and his alone.

When it was over, and they were both sated and sleepy, they abandoned the sofa and headed for the master suite. Their shared shower this time was more platonic and expedient than before. They climbed into bed and settled with unison sighs.

As Zach reached to turn out the light, Frannie put a hand on his chest. "Wait," she said. "I have a confession to make." Her trespass had been weighing on her, and she couldn't stand it any longer. Though she hadn't snooped intentionally, the outcome was the same. She had learned that Zach had secrets, that he was giving her only a part of himself. Maybe telling him was a mistake, but she had to know. She would apologize and then see if he was willing to let her into his head and his heart, not only his bed.

He rolled onto his side, propping his head on one hand. "Intriguing. Is this some naughty position you want to try?"

She grimaced, sitting up cross-legged. "When I was here before, you let me borrow a phone charger. As I was going through your desk, I stumbled across a manuscript. *Your* manuscript."

His expression went blank. He scooted up against the headboard and folded his arms across his chest. "Did you read it?"

"The first four pages. Then I realized I shouldn't have, so I stopped. Why have you never told me about this? A book, Zach? That's so exciting."

At first, he didn't respond. His gaze was hooded, his jawline carved in stone. "There's nothing to tell."

Her heart sank, despite the fact that she had predicted this very reaction. "Are you kidding me?" She frowned. "This is amazing. You were always a better writer than me in school. Your term papers were works of art. But a novel? I'm so impressed. I have an agent friend in New York who would be willing to take a look, I'm sure. Or maybe you already have an agent. Do you?"

The words tumbled out, though she knew they were futile. She was trying desperately to reach him and going about it all wrong.

"Enough, Frannie."

He was curt. Distant.

"I don't understand. This is huge. And what an accomplishment. It *is* finished, right? Have you started on a second one?" She was so caught up in trying to break through to him that she forgot how stubborn he could be.

He rubbed his forehead with the heel of his hand. "The book is something I've dabbled with on occasion. Since my father's accident, I've had no time for *dabbling*, believe me. Leave it alone, Frannie. I know what I am and what I'm not."

The words poured forth in a torrent, their meaning clear. *Stay the hell out of my business.* Did he really care about writing? Or was this book one more in a long line of pursuits he had tried?

The level of her disappointment was probably disproportionate. Even though she thought having a completed manuscript was a big deal, Zach wasn't prepared to share his passion for the project or his dreams. End of story.

Even worse, this whole thing pointed to Zach's propensity to start things he didn't finish. Was Frannie just another something or someone he would dabble with and then walk away?

"I thought we were headed somewhere special…that we were finally connecting. That you cared about what I feel for you. But you're still hiding, Zach, still ignoring your incredible gifts and talents."

"That's your opinion, Bug. Not mine." The words were choppy. Curt.

"Fine. New topic." She tucked aside her hurt feelings—again—and changed tack. If he couldn't handle anything personal, he could at least deal with the business at hand. "I want to spend more time at headquarters this weekend. If we're having a meeting with your brothers on Wednesday, I need to have everything ready. It would really be helpful if you would sit with me tomorrow. I can show you the things I've found so far. I think it would convince you that your old family friend isn't who you think he is."

Zach had been displeased and reluctant to talk about his book.

Now, she had made things worse. His gaze went from discomfort to glacial. "I have plans," he said curtly. "I'm flying out to go canoeing with a friend in the Boundary Waters Wilderness."

"In November? Isn't it freezing?"

"We do it every year."

"Zach, this is your family's livelihood. Someone has tried to hurt you professionally and physically. Can't you cancel or reschedule?"

He didn't answer her directly. "I'll be back for the meeting on Wednesday," he said. "That's the best I can do."

She hadn't expected the night to go this way. Instead of curling up with her lover and drifting off to sleep, she and Zach were now on opposite sides of a chasm. Maybe it was her fault…partly.

Because of her need to connect with him, she had torn something fragile. In wanting to know where he stood, she had poked and prodded and exposed the truth about their relationship. It wasn't nearly as significant or as strong as she had imagined.

Her stomach cramped with regret and despair. "I think it's best if I go back to the hotel," she said, the words barely audible.

"If that's what you want."

His stony silence while she gathered her things hurt more than she thought possible. When she was wearing her jeans and sweater and had shoved her work clothes into her small suitcase, she turned to walk away.

"Do you want me to drive you there?" Zach asked. "I will. It's late."

She didn't want his reluctant sense of honor to offer her anything, much less his presence during an uncomfortable car ride. "No." When she glanced over her shoulder, he hadn't moved. He was still propped up in bed like the arrogant alpha male he was.

"Goodbye, Zach."

All the way to the front door, she half expected him to come after her. But she had underestimated his stubbornness and his need to call the shots. The frustrating man had to hold himself aloof. The dabbling might be important to him, but by hiding from the world and from Frannie, no one, including him, would ever know his true potential.

She let herself out and let the lock click behind her. The sound echoed the death knell of her dreams.

Her high school crush, her intellectual equal, her lover extraordinaire was not interested in what Frances Wickersham had to offer.

She slept on and off, enough to rise when her alarm sounded at eight thirty. Though her heart was a chunk of ice in her chest, she refused to cry anymore over a worthless, intractable, infuriating man. It was fun while it lasted. The sooner she could leave Portland and get back to her normal life, the better.

To that end, she dressed and headed for SRO headquarters. She hadn't asked Zach what time he was flying out. Imagining him on a plane, putting distance between himself and Frannie, gave her a hollow feeling in her stomach.

Even if he made it back for Wednesday's meeting, the two of them were done.

Work helped. It always did. She returned to Edward Cordell's office and continued compiling the notes she had begun.

The hours flew by. She had forgotten to bring anything for lunch. It didn't matter. She wasn't hungry, anyway. By three o'clock, her head was pounding, but she had what she needed. To finish the job, she had to tick off the last employee computers on her list. That should take her up until the meeting and then maybe a day or two more.

If things went well, she could fly home in a week.

She had hoped against hope that Zachary would agree to look at the evidence and change his mind about her findings. Even if he didn't want to believe her, she had prayed he would have a change of heart about their personal life.

When she heard a noise in the hallway, her heart leaped. He wasn't on a plane after all.

As she turned to make sure it was him, something hard made brutal contact with the back of her head.

The world went black.

* * *

Zachary was in such a vile, dark mood, it was a good thing no one passed him in the parking lot. He might have scared his neighbors.

He tossed his bags in the back of his car and headed out. Last night's skirmish with Frannie still infuriated him. Even so, the memory of her face when she left him was a raw ache in his chest.

Negotiating Saturday traffic was a breeze. He actually passed SRO headquarters, though the building wasn't technically on his route. Was she there? Did he care? He had his own life to live. He had done just fine without Frannie for a dozen years. He didn't need her now. He didn't need any woman.

Maybe he did dabble. Maybe he did live his life on the surface. But the temptation to do more than that with Frannie scared him. That fear was what had made him shut her out. Fear of failure. Fear of disappointing her and himself.

Even his denial of her findings was based on fear. If Edward was the problem, then Zach had failed his family in a big way. If he were really so smart, shouldn't he have suspected something before now?

As he approached the on-ramp to the interstate, a huge shadow of foreboding washed over him. Something was wrong. The sensation was so compelling, he pulled off to the side of the road and put his head in his hands.

Was he going on this trip because he still wanted to hang out with his friend, or to prove a point?

The sensation of danger lingered. He hadn't slept. That was all. He was tired and out of sorts. Of course things seemed bleak.

And then he remembered the only other time he had experienced this same sickening premonition. He and Frannie had been in tenth grade. One night, while walking back to her dorm, two senior boys—drunk—tried to sexually assault her. Zachary had shown up at the last possible second, after looking everywhere for her.

He'd taken in the grim scene in an instant. Incoherent with rage, he had beaten both boys with his fists until they crumpled to the ground. Frannie had finally managed to pull him away, fearing for his safety and hers. Fighting on campus was strictly prohibited.

Frannie had been understandably distraught. They had locked themselves in an empty classroom and stayed together, talking, until dawn.

He hadn't thought of that night in years. Until now.

Again, the dark cloud pressed in on him. With a curse and a jerk of the wheel, he made a U-turn and headed back to headquarters, driving twenty miles over the speed limit.

The sun hung low in the sky. He skidded into his reserved parking space and made a dash for the front door. His key card gave him a red light the first time. He had it upside down. A second try was successful.

Frannie could be anywhere in the building. But his gut and the detailed work she had done before told him where to go—Edward Cordell's office. When he rounded the corner and jerked on the knob, the door was locked. That was odd. He fumbled for his master key and used it.

His heart stopped. Frannie lay in a crumpled heap on the floor. The desktop computer was missing. Crouching beside her, he said her name a dozen times.

She was unresponsive.

He ran his hands over her body carefully. Her skin was warm. She wasn't dead. But she was unconscious. And her pale, creamy cheeks were abnormally colorless.

It didn't take more than a few seconds to identify the cause. A huge knot on the back of her head was bleeding. In fact, her hair was matted with blood.

His stomach revolted. *Frannie. Dear God, Frannie.*

There was no time for second-guessing. He dialed 911

and told them he was bringing her in. He sketched out her symptoms in a few terse words. The medical center was close. Zach could get her there faster than waiting on an ambulance.

At the hospital, Zachary gave them her name, and they took Frannie away from him. He was consigned to the emergency room waiting area.

He called Farrell and then Quin. Both of them, with their wives, arrived in less than twenty minutes. Ivy had Dolly in her arms. All four adults were white-faced.

"What happened?" Farrell asked.

Zachary swallowed hard, feeling shaky. He sank into an uncomfortable vinyl-covered chair. "I don't know. I've called the guard. He didn't see anything. When I found her, she was in a heap on the floor of Edward Cordell's office."

Quin cursed. "So she did uncover something."

Zachary felt the coals of guilt piling up on his head. "Apparently so."

Farrell touched his shoulder. "How is she?"

"They won't let me back yet. The wound on her head was bleeding. A lot."

Katie had tears in her eyes. "If she's badly hurt, it's our fault. We hired her, and we didn't give her enough protection." She frowned. "How did you know to look for her, Zachary?"

His sister-in-law was only saying what they were all thinking. He slumped forward, resting his elbows on his knees. "I nearly got on a plane," he said. "But I got this bad gut feeling. I turned the car around and went to headquarters to find her, but it was too late."

A young female doctor in scrubs came through the set of double doors. "Are any of you related to Ms. Wickersham?"

Zachary stood, wishing the room would stop spinning. "No. But she was hurt on the job. We're employing her at Stone River Outdoors. This is my family."

The woman nodded, her expression sober. "She's stable. But there may be a skull fracture. I've stitched up the wound. We'll have to run some tests."

"When can I see her?" Zachary asked urgently.

"Shortly. Can you tell me how she was injured?"

"Not exactly." Zachary shared what he knew.

The doctor's gaze narrowed. "So it sounds like the police need to be involved."

Zachary had been so rattled he'd never even thought about that.

Farrell must have recognized his panic. "Not to worry, bro. Quin and I are on it. And Katie or Ivy will bring you something to eat."

Soon, only the doctor and Zachary remained. The woman gazed at him kindly, but with a warning. "She'll have to give a statement to the police eventually, but not until I'm sure she's stable. I'll let you sit with her. But you absolutely cannot question her. Frances needs to be calm and relaxed when she wakes up."

"How long will that be?"

"No way to tell. This isn't unusual in the case of a head wound like she sustained. It may be an hour or three or five."

"What do I say to her if she asks questions?"

"She probably won't. With an injury this bad, she'll likely be in pain, even though we've given her acetaminophen. We can't risk narcotics at this stage, and anything in the naproxen family will be a bleeding risk."

"I understand." With the doctor's directions, Zachary made his way through the halls to a cubicle that at least had walls, thank God. The room was tiny, barely enough space for a doctor to do an exam or roll a computer station into place.

The nurse who was checking Frannie's vitals finished her tasks and spoke with him briefly. Then he was alone with the woman in the bed. Frannie's face was turned toward the door. The people caring for her had probably positioned her that way to keep pressure off the back of her head.

There was a strand of wavy black hair falling across her forehead. Zach tucked it behind her ear with a light touch.

The only other piece of furniture in the room was a narrow metal chair. Quietly, he set it beside the bed so he could hold Frannie's hand. The one without all the tubes and tape. Her fingers were cold. He pulled the cotton blanket higher.

"Frannie," he whispered. "It's me, Zach."

Not even by the flicker of her lashes did she give any indication she had heard him. Tears stung his eyes. She could so easily be dead. Was that what the mystery attacker had intended?

In cartoons, Zach had seen characters get bopped on the noggin and have some kind of epiphany. Today, Frannie had received a blow to the head, and painfully, Zach had been the one with the sudden blinding burst of clarity.

He bitterly regretted his fight with Frannie and his reaction about her finding his manuscript. Even worse was his inability to risk giving his all to her and being thought of as less than. In his cowardice, he had failed Frannie, the woman who had always believed in him.

In that moment, he knew he was in love with her.

The subconscious knowledge had apparently terrified him to the point he had been ready to get on a plane and fly away far and fast.

What if he had left town? What if no one had found her in time? What if she had died? He was ill at the thought... and scared, and he found himself praying incoherently, although he and the deity hadn't been particularly chummy in recent years.

"Don't let her die," he whispered. He rested his forehead on the edge of the bed, clinging to that small hand as if it was his lifeline.

"Wake up, Bug. Please wake up."

Thirteen

Frannie was drifting in and out. She wrinkled her nose at the unfamiliar smells. When she moved restlessly, she groaned. If this was a migraine, it was the mother of all migraines.

It was easier to keep her eyes closed.

She didn't know where she was. Or why she was in so much pain.

Vague wisps of memories slid into her mental view, but then floated away before she could focus. Her mouth was cottony dry.

"May I…?" The words barely formed. Could anyone hear her?

Perhaps she should try again to open her eyes. This time was a bit more successful. She could see a clock on the wall, though she had no idea of the day's date. Or even if it was day or night. Gingerly, she turned her head, inhaling sharply when a knife stabbed the back of her skull. *Sweet Jesus.*

One of her arms was tethered to something. Was she in the hospital?

When she turned her head the rest of the way, she saw Zach. He appeared to be asleep. His dark lashes lay like shadows on his tanned cheeks. His chin was covered with several days of stubble. She had never seen him so unkempt.

His cheek rested on the edge of the mattress. One of his

hands held hers. He was bent in what must be a terribly uncomfortable position.

She wanted to lift her hand and stroke his hair, but her brain couldn't make her hand move. Not only that, but she didn't want to let go of his fingers.

Slowly, without moving her head again, she ran her gaze around the room. Yep. Definitely a hospital. When she tried to account for her presence here, the burst of brainpower convinced her to let it go. Thinking was too hard.

The need for water became intense. "Zach," she croaked. His name barely sounded like a word at all, but he heard her. He lifted his head and sat straight up in his chair. "Frannie? Are you awake?"

She nodded slowly. "Thirsty."

"Of course." He moved quickly, picking up a pink pitcher and pouring water into a glass. Then he added a bendy straw. When he held the straw to her lips, she could hear the ice chinking against the plastic sides of the small cup. She drank thirstily, almost groaning aloud. "Good," she whispered.

Finally, even that was too much. She shook her head and closed her eyes.

The next time she woke up, Katie sat in the chair. The fact that Zach was gone made Frannie sad, but she didn't let on. "What day is it?" she asked, the words hoarse.

Katie stroked her hand. "Tuesday," she said simply. "Your throat is sore because you had a tube for a while. But you're going to be fine."

"Okay."

The other woman offered her water without asking. Frannie managed more of it this time. She wasn't going to ask about Zach. She wasn't.

Katie's smile was kind. "Zach has been here day and night. Farrell finally made him go outside and walk around the block. He'll be back soon. They both will. Can I get you anything else? Some food?"

The thought of eating made Frannie grimace. "No, thank you." She moved restlessly. Her body hurt all over, but her head was the worst. "Can I go home now?"

"Not yet, sweetie. Relax, and let us take care of you."

Frannie drifted off again. It wasn't a conscious choice. Exhaustion pulled her under.

Eventually, she surfaced again. Zachary was back, but he wasn't sleeping. His gaze was locked on her face. "You shaved," she said.

His laugh sounded rusty. "I was scruffy. And I needed a shower."

"Will you take me back to the hotel?"

He froze. "You remember the hotel?"

She frowned. Did she? Trying to piece together the memory made her weepy. "I don't know." She felt a tear trickle down her cheek.

Zachary looked aghast. "Never mind," he said quickly. "It doesn't matter."

He kissed her cheek and smoothed her hair. "You scared me, Bug."

"What's wrong with my head?"

He frowned. "You hit it. On the back. You needed a few stitches, and they think you may have a hairline fracture, but everything is healing well. There's nothing to worry about."

"I'm glad you're here," she said. She was too vulnerable and too wiped out to be anything but honest.

Zachary's expression was hard to read. "Where else would I be?" he said lightly.

She curled her fingers around his. "I think I remember your condo. You could take me there, right?"

His throat worked as he swallowed. "I would if I could, Bug, but the doctor says at least one more day. You have to eat solid food, and all your tests need to come back clear. It's not so bad. I won't leave you."

An attractive woman entered the room wearing a white lab coat and black pants. "I'm Dr. Maroney," she said. "You and I are well acquainted, Ms. Wickersham, but you've been out cold for most of it. I'm glad to see you looking perky."

"I don't feel perky." Frannie made a face.

The doctor laughed. "I'm sure you don't, but you're doing well. I'm a professional. You can trust me." The doctor looked at Zachary. "It's time."

Zach shook his head vehemently. "This is the first day she's sounded like herself. I think we need to wait."

Frannie looked from one to the other. "Am I missing something?"

The doctor pulled up a chair, putting herself eye to eye with her patient. "Something bad happened to you, Frances. That's why you're here. The police need to question you."

Frannie's heart pounded. "The police?" She felt her pulse race. One of the monitors started beeping.

"See," Zachary shouted. "It's too soon."

"Don't yell at my doctor," Frannie said, embarrassed.

The doctor smiled. "He's worried about you. But you're strong, Frances. You took a hard lick to the head. Yet you're still with us. That's cause for celebration."

"And the police?"

The doctor hesitated. "Do you remember what you do for a living, Ms. Wickersham?"

"You can call me Frances. I'm a…" Frannie searched her brain. "I use computers. I'm a…" Her head ached. "I'm a hacker."

"Yes." The doc nodded approval. "And where were you working most recently?"

Frannie shot a glance at Zach. "For him, right?"

The doctor spoke softly. "I want you to try to remember

last Saturday. It was less than a week ago. You went to the offices of Stone River Outdoors, the company Mr. Stone and his brothers own jointly."

Anxiety rose in Frannie's chest. "Last Saturday was a bad day," Frannie whispered.

"Why?"

"Well, I…" Frannie closed her eyes and let herself remember. "Zach left," she said dully. "On a plane."

"But what about the office where you were. Do you remember that?"

"Yes. I went to work. I was making progress on the case."

"And what happened?"

Frannie felt cold all over. "I heard a noise behind me. I thought Zach might have changed his mind. Before I could turn around, something or someone hit me on the back of the head." She started shaking. "Is that enough? I don't want to talk anymore."

Zachary burst into the hall, furious. He stared at the detective who had been listening at the door. "I hope like hell you got what you needed. She knows nothing. And you just put her through hell."

The truth was, Zachary himself had put her through hell. He had walked away from her, intending to get on that damn plane. He would never forgive himself.

The doctor joined them. "Ms. Wickersham won't have to do that again. But the police needed her statement."

"Screw that," Zachary muttered. He slammed his fist into the wall, seeing Frannie's face when she said, *Zach left. I thought Zach might have changed his mind.*

He had abandoned her. Told her he didn't care about her investigation. Questioned her judgment.

Even worse, he'd brushed her off when she wanted to talk about his book, when she'd been trying to connect to all the things he kept hidden, the "him" he never showed anyone else.

He was an asshole, and he sure as hell didn't deserve to have Frances Wickersham in his life.

But he loved her, and he refused to give up. He would strip his emotions raw and stand naked if it would make things right.

Seventy-two hours later, Zachary took Frannie home to his condo. The doctor, worried about her patient, had kept a very stressed Frannie a few extra days because of the unfolding events involving Edward Cordell. Ivy had gone to the hotel several hours ago, picked up Frannie's things and checked her out. Now there was no reason for Frannie not to stay with Zach.

The family was gathering in a few hours to hear Frannie's report. The police had made some arrests. Frannie had insisted on helping with their investigation once she realized that no one knew the chain of events like she did.

Zachary settled her on the sofa with mounds of blankets and pillows and snacks close by. Frannie shook her head with a wry smile. "I think this is overkill, but thank you."

"How do you feel today?" he asked. "And don't try to fib to me, Bug. I can read you like a book."

She refused to lie down. But she curled her legs pretzel-style and snuggled under a red wool afghan that flattered her coloring. "A lot better. Seriously. The headache is manageable, and I have most of my energy back."

"You don't have to do this tonight. Everyone will understand."

"I want to. Besides, once all of this is wrapped up, my job will be finished and I can head home."

His stomach tightened. "Maybe."

She folded her arms across her chest, cocked her head

and stared at him. "You're acting weird. What's going on with you?"

He came to her and sat down on the coffee table so they were knee to knee. "I know my timing is off, but this can't wait. I'm in love with you, Frannie."

She blinked. Shook her head firmly. "No. You're not. You're feeling guilty because I got hurt on SRO property. Don't worry. I won't sue you."

Her flip response frustrated him, but he held his temper, because he probably deserved that. This moment was too important to let her sidetrack him. "Even before I saw you in that bed, unconscious, I understood."

"Understood what?"

"That I loved you."

She pursed her lips. "May I ask you a question?"

"Anything."

"They told me you were the one who found me and called 911. How is that possible if you were on a plane?"

Thinking about that day made him shudder. "I was almost at the airport," he said. "Suddenly, I had this overpowering feeling that you were in trouble. Like that night at Glenderry when those two boys had you cornered. I turned the car around and drove like hell to headquarters, but it was too late."

She patted his hand. "Maybe not. The police think my attacker was probably still in the building. When he heard you, it must have scared him off and saved my life."

"I thought you were dead," he croaked, remembering. "There was so much blood, and you were unconscious."

"I'm sorry you had to deal with that."

"Don't apologize to me," he shouted, jumping up and pacing.

Frannie sighed, seeming to deflate. "It's all over, Zach. It's all over. I'm fine. Everything is fine."

Except it wasn't. He had told Frannie he loved her, and

she had brushed his declaration aside as if it were inconsequential. And he'd pushed her away when she had reached out to him, wanting to know and accept the real Zachary Stone. She had little reason to believe him now, given the way he had acted, but still.

Despite her protests to the contrary, Frannie was weak. She fell asleep after he fed her lunch, and she napped for almost two hours. While she rested, he paced.

He had to make her believe him. He loved her, and as scary as it was, he didn't want to hide who he really was from her any longer. He sure as hell couldn't let her leave Portland. If that happened, he might never see her again.

At five, his brothers and sisters-in-law arrived. Dolly was with a sitter. Katie and Ivy had prepared finger foods for the evening meal, perhaps understanding that Frannie wasn't up to sitting at the dining room table for long periods of time.

While everyone ate, the conversation remained light and low-key. It was Frannie who finally broached the subject that had brought them all here.

She surveyed the group with a smile. "This wasn't quite how I imagined making my report, but here goes."

Farrell held up a hand. "Before you start, I think I speak for all of us when I say how glad we are that you have recovered so well. You had us scared, Frances."

"Well, I'm fine," she said briskly. "Unfortunately, your paranoia was well-founded, as I guess we all now know."

Quin frowned. "And it really was Edward Cordell?"

Frannie never looked at Zachary. "Yes, but he had help. His twenty-four-year-old grandson was involved. The policy at SRO is no personal email on company computers. Edward abided by that rule...mostly. But twice, in the time before you began noticing irregularities and before the car accident, Edward slipped up and emailed his grandson from work. After I found that, I was able to hack into his personal email account, and it was all there."

"But why?" Katie asked.

"From what I could tell," Frannie said, "Mr. Cordell had been nursing a decades-long grudge. Mr. Stone Sr. *was* his best friend. But Edward felt like he had been cheated in some business venture the two of them were involved in back in the early '70s. Edward began using his grandson as a sounding board. The grandson bought into the notion that Edward was owed something more than a pension, and between them, they hatched a plan to destroy Stone River Outdoors as revenge."

Farrell was pale. "And the car accident?"

"Once I had the pieces, I spoke with the investigator you hired. We think the grandson paid a junkie to *cause* the accident, but it went too far. Perhaps it was only supposed to shake things up."

"And my stolen designs?"

"I found digital photographs. Apparently, Edward was in your office at some point, saw a sketch pad and snapped a few pics with his phone. He gave them to the grandson, who floated them on half a dozen disreputable websites and found a buyer. As you probably know, the police have arrested both men. The grandson was defiant. He had been planning more mishaps for SRO. But in Edward's statement, he apologized to all of you for letting his bitterness get out of control."

Ivy shook her head slowly. "What a terrible sequence of events. You three brothers lost your father, and now two more men will likely spend their lives in prison. It's like a Greek tragedy, only worse, because it affects the people I love."

Zachary stood and paced, feeling jittery. In a Greek tragedy, there was never a happily-ever-after when it came to love and romance. He had to rewrite the ending of this damned play, but how?

Farrell stood. "I think it's time for all of us to go home and let the patient rest."

Frannie shook her head. "I'm fine. I love the company."

Zachary heard the subtext loud and clear. She didn't want to be alone with him. Thankfully for his agenda, the family went home anyway.

Frannie stretched. "I'm sleeping out here tonight, Zach. This sofa is super comfy, and I like being near the fireplace."

He stared at her, feeling helpless. She was still fragile. He couldn't push her too hard. He had to abide by her wishes. But how could he get through to her? How could he make her believe that his love was the real deal and that he realized his mistakes and was willing to change?

Maybe it was a moot point. Maybe she didn't care.

"Okay." He shrugged. "If that's what you want."

Frannie was miserable. If she'd had her way, she would be staying at the hotel. But she knew without asking that neither Zachary nor any of his family would have allowed that. They all, to a one, felt responsible for her.

Their concern was touching, but Frannie desperately wanted to be alone. It was painful to remember how much she had put on the line and that Zach had rejected her love, even though she hadn't technically spelled it out in words. His reciprocal confession was suspect. No matter how badly she wanted to believe him, she had to face the unpalatable truth that he was probably acting out of guilt and remorse.

Zachary lingered after his brothers and their wives left. "I'm going to my room now," he said, the words oddly formal. "If you need anything at all, please call my cell."

She stared at his expressionless face, her heart breaking. "Thank you," she whispered. Then he was gone.

The powder room down the hall had a full bath. Even so, Frannie didn't have the energy for a shower. The nurse had helped her take one before leaving the hospital. That would have to do for now.

After changing into her pajama pants and T-shirt, she brushed her teeth and swallowed a couple of headache tablets. She really was improving hour by hour, but late in the day, the back of her skull throbbed.

When she returned to the living room, all the lights were out, save for the one she could reach beside the sofa. Zachary had tidied the area and brought out a soft bedsheet to cover the couch cushions, and also an extra pillow. Her blanket was folded back neatly.

On the coffee table, where she couldn't miss it, lay a thick pile of manuscript pages. *His book.*

Her legs gave out. She sat down hard, picking up the first few bits of the chapter along with the small note on top. She set the note aside, unopened, and began the book.

Fifty pages in, she started crying. It was good. So good. Brilliant, in fact. He had laid the groundwork for a mystery so cleverly that she wanted to stay up all night reading.

But it was late, and her stores of energy were depleted.

Reluctantly, she picked up the folded scrap of paper that wasn't part of the manuscript. Zach's handwriting, the handwriting she remembered so well, was bold and dark and compelling. The words were few:

I do love you, Bug. You're my potential.

Her heart constricted. Her chest hurt. She wanted so very badly to believe him. Why had he left his book for her to read? Was it a peace offering, or something more?

He'd said he loved her. But they had all been under tremendous pressure and stress. The situation was unprecedented.

For years, even in high school, Zachary had refused to reveal his true self. Or maybe he had never understood what he had to offer…had never believed or recognized his true strengths.

The thought that he might be expressing remorse or guilt or even another emotion he confused with love tore her apart.

There was only one way to find out, and it was risky.

On trembling legs, she made her way down the hall to his bedroom and stood quietly in the doorway. His bedside lamp burned with a soft, warm light. The rest of the room was shadowy. He wasn't sleeping, or she didn't think so. Instead, he lay on his back with one arm slung over his eyes. He was naked above the sheet he had pulled to his waist.

"Zach." She clung to the door frame.

He sat straight up in bed, his hair askew, his expression wild. Maybe he had been sleeping after all.

She winced. "I'm sorry. Did I wake you?"

"I wasn't asleep. I was thinking."

Frannie took a few more steps toward the bed but stopped in the middle of the room. "Thinking about what?"

His face was grief stricken. There were no other words to describe the anguish she saw in him. "About failing you. In every way. As a friend, as a lover, as a human being."

"You are who you are, Zach. And I love you…all of you."

He tossed back the covers and stood, closing the distance between them with three long strides. "Thank God." The way he dragged her against his warm body and buried his face in her hair made her want to weep. "I love you, too, Frannie," he said, the gruff words stark. "I swear it on my mother's grave."

She stroked his back. "Love isn't always enough. How could it work, Zach? You have two amazing homes here in Maine, a thriving company and a decades-long heritage. A family you care about. My job takes me all over the world.

Besides, at the risk of sounding unbelievably selfish, I like what I do, and it gives me a great deal of fulfillment."

He picked her up and carried her to the overlarge armchair by the fire, sitting down carefully and cuddling her in his lap. "I've been thinking about that, too, Bug. I've already spoken to my brothers, and they've each given me their blessing. I'm going to hire a suitable candidate to take over my position as CFO. There are plenty of trustworthy men and women out there who respect our company and would be a good fit."

She searched his face. "But why?"

"Because being CFO is not my passion. I want to travel the world with my wife, if she'll have me." He kissed her softly. "What good is having a fortune if I can't spend it doing something grand? We can visit Maine anytime, but my home will be where you are, Frannie. I adore you, sweetheart. And if you ever decide you want to try the mommy thing, I could be a kick-ass stay-at-home dad."

"You're serious…" She still couldn't quite believe it.

"That's why I left the book for you to read. So you would know for sure that I am whatever is way beyond serious. No one else has seen a word of that, Frannie. It's deeply personal to me. From now on out, everything I have is yours. Body and soul. Heart and mind. Until death do us part." His smile was lopsided, his gaze wary. "Will you marry me, Bug? I never did get a chance to teach you how to cook. And all that travel will give me a million ideas for new books to write."

Frannie touched his chin, kissed his jaw. "I can't believe this is happening. What if I'm dreaming?"

Zachary stroked her hair, twining a thick strand of it around his fingers. His brown eyes gleamed with happiness and mischief. "Then maybe we'll never wake up, Frances Wickersham. It will be our own private fairy tale. Stone Man and the Bug. Together again."

Tears wet her face, but they were happy tears, and Zach kissed them all away.

She rested her cheek over his heart. “Will you make love to me?”

He shook his head, looking pained. “The doc said no exertion for another week.”

“The doc isn’t here.” She pressed closer to his impressive erection.

Zachary stood and carried her to the bed. “I’ll hold you while you sleep, my love. But I’ll never hurt you again. You’re mine, Frances. Your gorgeous body, your generous, forgiving heart and your incredibly fascinating brain.” He settled her beneath the covers and scooted in beside her. “Sleep, sweet girl. Tomorrow is another day.”

Epilogue

Christmas Eve

Frannie stood in Quin and Katie's beautifully decorated great room, wondering if she would ever stop smiling. The wound on the back of her head was completely healed but for the occasional little ache or pain. Katie had treated her this morning at a fancy salon, where the stylist carefully washed and dried Frannie's long, thick hair and caught it up on the back of her head so that curls cascaded down her shoulders.

She was surrounded by beribboned garlands and swags of evergreens whose fresh, crisp scent reminded her of that first trip with Zachary to the northern coast. In the corner, a fabulous Christmas tree added a festive note.

In front of the fireplace stood a minister wearing a white robe. Ivy and Farrell were about to say their vows, flanked by Katie and Quin as their only attendants.

Frannie's heart was so full, she thought it might burst.

She sneaked a quick glance at the man by her side. Zachary Stone in a tuxedo, holding a baby, was about the most beautiful thing she had ever seen. His job was to pacify Dolly during the brief service, and then hand her over after the *man and wife* pronouncement.

Zachary caught Frannie staring at him and grinned.

I love you, she mouthed.

His quick nod and the way he reached for her hand and squeezed it told her more than words that her fiancé felt the same.

On the third finger of her left hand she wore the huge, flawless emerald he had given her to mark their formal engagement. The stone, set in a platinum band, was surrounded by tiny diamonds.

She and Zachary had discussed having a Valentine's wedding after her big January assignment was finished, but really, she would be happy to show up at the courthouse one day. It didn't matter.

The ceremony wound to a close, everyone cheering the new couple. Zach handed off the baby to her mom and her newly adoptive father.

While everyone else was occupied, Zachary pulled Frannie under the mistletoe and kissed her long and deep. When he lifted his head, his eyes were damp. "You're my best friend, Frannie Wickersham. My lover. My forever wife. I adore you."

She kissed him back, dizzy with everything the future held, stretching out before them.

"You were worth the wait, my dearest Stone Man. You were worth the wait."

* * * * *